"Lustbader has honed to a fine edge the art of creating dread as to what dark force lies around the next corner."
Los Angeles Times Book Review

"Eric Van Lustbader is an author who gets better with every book he writes."
Associated Press

"[Lustbader] writes some of the most erotic scenes in contemporary fiction."
Newsday

"His development of power politics is gaining more depth with each novel."
Publishers Weekly

Also By Eric Van Lustbader

Novels of Asia:
*The Ninja**
*Black Heart**
*The Miko**

The China Maroc Trilogy:
*Jian**
*Shan**

A Novel of America:
*Sirens**

The Sunset Warrior Series:
The Sunset Warrior
Shallows of Night
Dai-San
Beneath an Opal Moon

* Published by Fawcett Books

ZERO

Eric Van Lustbader

FAWCETT CREST • NEW YORK

This is for all my friends on Maui,
who helped me discover another side.
Aloha and *mahalo*.

Most especially,
this is for V.,
who—as always—helped so much.
Zero could not have been born without her.

ACKNOWLEDGMENTS

Many people were of particular help in the various difficult phases of research for *Zero*. Thank you.

To Marsha and Bruce, and German John for opening up Kahakuloa to me.

To Bud Davison and his "flight crew" at Butler International for all their aviation lore.

To Frank Toomey, vice-president, Bear, Stearns & Co., Los Angeles, for his explanations of the macro-economics theories that are so vital to the novel.

To Henry for the practicalities of editorial assistance.

To Stu, for flight command control.

I drew from factual elements and quotes used in an article by Richard Reeves of the Universal Press Syndicate, titled "Asia's Dreaded Superpower," printed in the *Honolulu Advertiser*, for the newspaper article that Lillian Doss reads in Book Four.

Very special thanks to Ronn Ronck for his invaluable assistance in opening the files of the *Honolulu Advertiser* on the Yakuza.

And to Kate for brainstorming and counseling above and beyond.

It is in changing
That things find purpose.

—Heraclitus

Goke no kimi
tasogaregao no
uchiwa kana

Her beauty clasped by twilight
the widow
gently wields her fan

—Buson

CONTENTS

Not another night.

The man known as Civet opened his eyes. A gray-green gekko was staring at him. Immobile, the tiny lizard clung to a wallpaper anthurium blossom. Its head was twisted so that it could continue to stare at Civet.

Not another night.

Beyond the screened window-doors, coconut palms whispered as cooling winds coming off the West Maui Mountains brushed their long, sensuous fronds in a lover's caress. It was here, to this special spot in Hawaii, that Civet always came after an assignment. After an extraction. But this went beyond an extraction, beyond even death.

Civet wiped the sweat from his high forehead. He felt his fingers trembling as the animus of his nightmare stalked him. But the presence of a nightmare meant that at least he had slept.

Yes, another night.

He saw the pale gold light flooding the tips of the palms as the sun rose above the peaks to the east, and thought, I've gotten through another night.

It was always like this after he completed a directive. Yet this was different. So different that his very bones ached with the knowledge that he had carried out a directive of his own making. His mind boiled with the understanding that this was either the beginning of his life—or the end.

Civet sat up in the huge bed. The sheets drifted around his waist as, wrapping his arms about them, he hugged his knees against his chest.

He glanced at the bedside table. On it was a half-empty bottle of Irish whiskey and a water glass. Civet found himself reaching for the bottle and caught himself. Quite deliberately, he turned his head away.

And was confronted by the gekko's unblinking stare. The bastard looks so accusing, Civet thought. But it was his own conscience, he knew, that transformed the gekko's stare into something more than dull curiosity. It probably doesn't even know what I am, Civet thought. But Civet knew what he was. Only too well.

He was cold. Cold and sweating. With a groan, he swung his legs over the side of the king-size bed. The expanse of bed covers behind him seemed endless. The empty space depressed him so that his memory brought back to him Michiko's scent, a heady combination of perfume and the musk of her own skin.

He was dizzy. He put his head in his hands and thought, Ah God, but I miss her. Even after all these years, the wound is still fresh. It seems just yesterday that I lay with her.

Thinking of Michiko was like putting an ice pick in his heart. But, he thought bleakly, it was better than contemplating what he had done. Three days ago. So different. How could he have known how different it would be? An eternity of agony, because now there was no turning back. It did no good at all to know that it was different this time. It only served to remind him of what he had once been, to make him feel more like Sisyphus, putting his shoulder to the rock, rolling it up the hill yet again. It made no difference that he had been at it in the service of his country. There had been no glory in what he had been—only medals engraved with his name locked in a sealed room, and blood on his hands. (Was that why he had gotten into the habit of burning his clothes after the completion of each directive—because of the blood?)

That, more than anything else, Civet decided, was the consequence of killing another human being: a descent into purgatory. The dark closing in each night like the accusatory finger of God. The river of life turned to dust in your hand, ashes that once God had animated with His breath. How much more terrifying then, to contemplate the death of millions.

Civet thought a lot about God these days. He felt now that with each assignment, with each life he expunged from the world, he was taking a step closer to his maker. At night, he trembled in the solar wind of His presence; he breathed in an energy beyond his comprehension. Yet it was a power that terrified rather than energized him.

Tracing it back—logic and connections were among his

strong suits—he at length came to the realization that his terror stemmed not from the fact that he was repentant for his sins, but rather that he felt no remorse for the life he had chosen for himself. But not even he would have thought that his life would have led him down this particular path.

For the first time in decades, he was truly alone. Which, of course, was why thoughts of God blew persistently through his mind. Everything now had devolved onto him. And he was a fugitive, running for his life. Once, already, they had almost caught up with him. Everything gone up in smoke. Almost. But he had evaded them; he had come here.

How long? he wondered. How long did he have until they tracked him down here? Two days; three, at most. They were smart. And they had the organization. Christ, no one had to tell him that! He almost laughed at the bitter irony of it; he bit his lip instead.

And now, he thought, it all comes down to one hellish gamble. Hope may spring eternal, but it is such a fragile thing. I am gambling everything—more even than my own life, oh, much more!—on an instinct. I believe, truly, that I am right. But what if I am not?

All around him he felt the stirring of ordinary people for whom two kids, two cars and an hour's commute to work were the parameters of life. Civet shuddered at the thought of living his life in any mundane fashion.

Yet it puzzled him sometimes, this lack of contrition on his part. He felt like a monk who, having come so far in his ecclesiastical studies, nevertheless finds himself unable to take his final vows.

During his life, he had been in many places of worship. Once, twenty years ago, he had almost been killed in one and had, in turn, been forced to extract his assailant. Piety, he had come to learn, rarely coincided with purity of spirit. Civet knew many men in his profession who went to church every week. They seemed to be the ones who enjoyed killing the most.

Civet did not enjoy his work in the same visceral, oftentimes sexual manner these others did. But surely, he told himself time and again, one cannot be as good as I am at what I do without enjoying it.

It was the shadow world of secrets he inhabited that Civet really loved. It was like an Englishman's cup of tea, ever present and warming. It made him feel apart, utterly independent, free. He was a fiercely painted kite riding the feral winds most people could not even imagine. He was made special; exalted, even.

Yet each aftermath was remorseless in its grip on him, and again he would return to purgatory. But this was different, and only he could know why.

The gekko was staring. Civet grabbed the bottle, poured himself four fingers. He looked at it, put it aside. He slipped off the bed onto his knees and prayed to a God he could not imagine, let alone understand. Was it Buddha to whom he prayed? Jehovah? Jesus? Civet could not say. But now, at this moment of ultimate crisis in his life—in, he believed, the future of the world—he needed to speak with something greater than himself. Michiko would have said it was nature. Civet could only bow his head and let his mind flow like a river to its source.

He threw the liquor into the sink. The ice he had not used during the night had melted, and he scooped some of the still-cool water. Then, to escape the lizard's disturbing gaze, he padded to the screen doors and let himself out onto the lanai. The lizard's scrutiny seemed to have become almost human to his keyed-up senses.

He was on one of the top floors, a strict stipulation with him. He was personally comfortable with the vistas thus afforded him and professionally at ease with the view of his immediate environment a high floor provided. He had been taught to be a very careful man.

Beyond the clattering palms and, below, the tropical profusion of the orchid gardens, the cerulean waters of the Molokai Channel beckoned invitingly. The early wind had died, and with a practiced eye, Civet knew that it would be a calm day. A great day for fishing.

He could already see the shining strand arrowing down into the water, could feel the tension on the line, the shuddering, and then the great monster tug as the onaga, the deepwater snapper he loved to eat, took the bait. Oh yes, he thought, happier now. The tang of the salt on his face, the challenge in the pull and leap of the big fish. That was the kind of activity that would wash his emotions clean of the detritus of the extraction.

Extraction was part of the jargon—as odd as the argot of an African bushman—that men in Civet's profession used to indicate a sanctioned killing.

Below his lanai he saw a couple in their twenties cutting through the grass in their jogging outfits. Disturbed, the mynas rose, cawing. And as his eyes followed the arc of the birds' flight, Civet saw the figure standing beside the coconut palm.

The figure was partially in shadow and yet the power that emanated from it reached Civet seven stories above.

Civet forgot the hopping mynas, the jogging couple; he was oblivious of the soft air, the spectacular view across to the island of Molokai, which he loved so well. He was fully concentrated on the figure. Civet, who was as adept at tracking as he was at killing, was used to identifying people at a distance.

Civet was now at the far end of the lanai. Palm fronds waved, partially obscuring the figure. But the angle was better, and at last Civet could get a look at the face.

The glass Civet had been holding crashed to the cement floor, and he found himself gripping the railing to stop himself from falling to his knees. Vertigo overcame him. His mouth was open and he was gasping for breath. It cannot be, he thought. Not yet. I need to rest; I'm exhausted from all this running. It simply cannot be.

But he knew what it meant: They had already found him.

He turned and rushed back into the room, scraping his knee on the edge of the bed. He staggered into the bathroom, where he vomited in great racking convulsions. He wasn't emotionally ready. Dear God, he thought, protect me from what I have to do. Protect those I love if I don't make it.

His imagination, racing in panic, unraveled what was ahead of him. Stop it! he admonished himself. He got hold of himself at last, splashed cold water on his face, into his mouth, across the back of his neck. Then he hurriedly dressed, put wallet, car keys, passport and a small eelskin case into various pockets of his tropical-weight jacket. He reread the postcard he had written in the dead of night, then he went out the door.

He avoided the elevator, taking the stairs two at a time. In the lobby, he hurried past pale-skinned tourists in garish aloha shirts. Deposited the postcard with the concierge, who assured him it would go out with the morning's mail.

In the belowground car park, he took a quick scan, allowing his eyes to adjust to the gloom. When he was satisfied with his security, he crossed to his rented Mustang. Got down on his knees and, with his customary thoroughness, inspected the underside of the carriage.

He looked along the entire length of the tailpipe, as well as in it. Places where the deadly items he had seen in the war's aftermath could easily be secreted. Finishing his check, he began *prana*, the semimystical deep breathing that allowed him to think clearly in difficult situations.

Still on his knees, he went over the car trunk lock, looking for the minute scratches that would indicate an intruder's attempts to pop it. There was nothing. He rose and unlocked the trunk.

A couple with a small boy came into the car park, and he was obliged to wait until they got into their car and drove away.

Working quickly, he transferred the contents of the trunk to the front passenger seat. Then he climbed into the driver's seat, put the convertible's top up. In a moment the Mustang's engine coughed to life, and throwing it in gear, Civet got out of there.

He took the Napili Road because he disliked the new highway that had recently been built further up the ridge slope. This, as well as his driving, was purely instinctual.

The face—the shadowed face! Its features burned into his mind, glowing like coals thrust into his eyes. There was a heat upon him, so unnatural that it made him shiver as if he had the ague. For a moment his resolve wavered; death cracked its bare knuckles in his face. His fingers, white upon the wheel, hurt with the unconscious power of his grip.

He fled Napili as if chased by a ghost. At the Methodist church, he turned right onto Honoapiilani Highway, a three-lane road where he could pick up speed.

He had just begun to accelerate when he saw the black blur of the Ferrari Marcello coming up behind him. It had taken the Kapalua Highway and now shot into the mainstream of traffic not more than a hundred yards behind Civet's Mustang. In an instant, he got a clear look at the driver. His heart began to race once again.

Blinking sweat out of his eyes, Civet wrenched the steering wheel to the right. At the same time, he trod hard on the accelerator. The Mustang gave a shrill squeal, and with a thick cloud of red dirt and torn foliage, he shot off along the wide verge.

Horns blared as startled drivers protested this dangerous maneuver. Glancing in his rearview mirror, Civet could see the black Marcello weaving in and out of traffic as it kept pace with him.

Civet cursed his American car which, in horsepower and maneuverability, was no match for the Ferrari. Back on the macadam of the highway, he took a sweeping curve at eighty-five. On his right, the water of Napili Bay glistened, on his left, the mountains, still mist-shrouded, rose in plateaus. One was open, inviting, the other arcane, mysterious. But both were powerful—much more powerful, Civet thought now, than I am, a puny human being driving a ton of welded metal.

Past Kahana's ugly new high-rises he sped. He used the wide verge to pass when he could. In some spots it was paved, in others it was packed red dirt, the ruts jarring his spine through the Mustang's mushy suspension.

Another glance in the rearview mirror confirmed that the Ferrari was fast overtaking him. It was now barely fifty yards behind.

They were fast approaching Kaanapali, Maui's largest resort area. This strip of five hotels and numerous condominiums was the major cause of traffic and pedestrian congestion on this side of Maui. It was to Kaanapali that Civet now decided to head. Within its warren of walks, restaurants, shops and high-rises, he would have the best chance of losing his pursuer.

Jammed on the horn, tramped on the brakes as a car began to pull out from the right. Cursing, Civet poked his foot at the accelerator as he heard the squeal of the intruding car's brakes. He had a brief glimpse of a woman's face, white with fear, as he sped by, his horn still sounding.

But the incident had had its consequences. The Marcello, thundering, was only twenty yards behind.

Civet concentrated on the traffic piling up in front of him in anticipation of the first of Kaanapali's three access roads. A road crew was at work here; traffic was being squeezed right. He was going much too fast. One-handed, he was obliged to swerve at a precipitous angle onto the verge to avoid rear-ending a slow-moving Nissan.

Civet was compelled to decelerate drastically, and a glance in his rearview mirror showed the Marcello almost upon him. Unless he could find a break in the traffic, he knew he would be finished.

Already the road ahead of him seemed smeared with grease. Colors fluttered, blue to green, red to orange, and back again. Light dilated as if the sun were running in and out of dense cloud with appalling rapidity. Jammed on his brakes. He was almost on top of the car in front of him! In the next instant, he saw a minute opening as the line of cars siphoning through the work area was halted to allow traffic from the resort onto the highway. What the hell, he thought, tramping on the accelerator.

Took deep breaths, trying to slow his hammering pulse and, at the same time, ignoring the blare of horns, the shouts, the screech of hastily applied brakes as he shot through the gap.

He was running at eighty again, but now the Marcello was on his tail, and as Civet went through maneuver after maneuver, a growing conviction began to dictate his next moves. When he had exhausted his entire repertory of evasive measures, he abandoned the idea of ducking into Kaanapali. He had no lead on the Ferrari and, consequently, no chance to disappear inside the resort complex.

They were heading toward the major access to Kaanapali. Here, the highway gained a median island, planted with palms and giant ferns, around which the two-way traffic divided.

His mind making rapid calculations, Civet accelerated through the traffic, weaving this way and that. Horns blared; people shouted at him. The median was coming up on his left. Civet slowed, switched to the right-hand lane as if he were about to turn into Kaanapali. The Marcello followed.

At the last instant, Civet accelerated sharply, cut the wheel hard over. He slammed into the rear fender of a Chevy; the right front wheel of his Mustang ran up onto the verge, so that for one terrifying moment, he was canted over at an angle. Then with a bone-jarring slam he was down, the Mustang rocking on its springs as Civet faced oncoming traffic.

He swung left onto the far verge, accelerated.

The Marcello, still pacing him, was now at a safe distance, separated from Civet by a line of intervening traffic and the median island.

Glancing over, Civet grinned. The adrenaline was pumping through him like the ocean shining in sunlight beyond the now-impotent Marcello. Civet felt the ocean's power energizing him, glanced back to the paved verge ahead of him and cried out.

Where just an instant before it had been clear, he now was bearing down on a pair of teenage girls clad in Fila jogging suits. All pink and powder-blue, their blond hair wrapped in ponytails, flying along behind them. So young, bursting with life. Their browned faces were serene as they ran. They were talking, laughing at something.

Christ, Civet thought wildly, they don't see me! At eighty-five, he was bearing down on them with hellish speed. Even as he applied the brakes, Civet knew he was going too fast to stop in time. To the left there was a fifteen-foot-high ridge decorated by wild bougainvillea. Bright sprays of pink, orange, purple trailing down the ridge.

He was too close, his speed too great. He was going to hit the girls dead on unless . . .

Civet turned the only way he could: right, into the oncoming traffic. If he could catch a break in the traffic, make the grass-covered median, he would be—

Screeching of metal, hot and tortured beyond its breaking point. The Mustang clipped the front end of an oncoming truck, taking out a headlight and part of a fender. It was too much for the Mustang, which lifted upward like a rearing stallion. When it came down, he was broken free of the seat belt.

Instinctively, Civet looked toward where the teenagers stood, backed against the ridge on the far side of the verge, fists in their mouths, horrified. They were safe. Safe.

Then he was tumbling, tumbling. In his mind's eye, he saw that face again. That haunting face! And for the first time today, he put a name to it: Zero.

A moment later, the Mustang screamed as if it were a living thing. Flames blew through the passenger compartment, igniting the world.

Hiroshi Taki lay bare to the waist. The sliding screens out to the garden were open so that the cool night air could caress his flesh.

There was an old man, Hiroshi thought, with untold power. And now he is dead.

Three days ago, Hiroshi had watched the last several moments of his father's life. He had seen the knowledge that he desired most in all the world in his father's eyes. It was the knowledge of the decades. There were many men within Japan—powerful, wealthy, influential men—who would certainly divest themselves of the trappings of their exalted station in life to be the recipient of that knowledge.

Yet it was Hiroshi Taki, eldest son of Wataro Taki, who was to be the recipient of this invaluable treasure trove of information that had helped build one of the most powerful shadow empires in the world.

Or so Hiroshi believed. Then a stroke had paralyzed the left side of his father's body—and mind. The knowledge was still there, to be sure. Hiroshi could sense it, a dark and deadly fish in the sea of pain that filled Wataro Taki's eyes.

It was not fair, Hiroshi had thought, for a human being like his father to endure such pain and frustration. Just as it was unfair for a man such as himself to be denied his birthright. It was not fair. But it was their *karma*, father and eldest son.

Of his brothers, Joji and Masashi, Hiroshi Taki had no thoughts at all. They were irrelevant. The birthright, the heritage of information was to be his. And now, with every moment, it was sinking further and further away from him. Until he was consumed with the desire to reach down inside his father's mind and extract the precious knowledge.

Wataro Taki's death three days ago had robbed Hiroshi of everything. It had taken away the awful pain. And it had obliterated everything of value within the old man's head.

I have been cheated, Hiroshi thought now in the darkness and silence of the night.

Unconsciously, his fists clenched at his side, brushing the flesh, dusky as smoke, of the slim girl who lay naked beside him. She stirred, her sleep momentarily disturbed, and Hiroshi made a soothing sound until she quietened.

I am the new *oyabun* of the Taki-gumi. I must take over the mantle of godfather of the Yakuza clans that my father fought for thirty years to obtain and maintain. And he has left me defenseless. Enemies abound all around me. Now that he is gone, they will be like vultures, circling in for the kill. I must protect the family, the clan, the power. But how? I do not even know whom I can trust.

Hiroshi Taki lay atop his *futon* and watched the parade of shadows marching across the beamed ceiling.

Outside, a figure was using the trees, never for a moment putting feet to ground. On the roof, the figure crossed the house, swinging down into one of the darkened formal rooms.

The figure, dressed in matte black, was hooded. Where a band of flesh appeared at the level of the eyes, it had been smeared with charcoal. The backs of the hands were similarly coated. The feet were covered in thin, crepe-soled shoes.

Still, the house was far from deserted, and the figure had to be extremely careful. Well-trained Yakuza, as the *kobun*— or soldiers—of the Taki-gumi were, had to be considered a precious commodity.

As a shadow, the figure passed through the formal rooms, the semiformal, the informal ones. Until it had made its way into the intimate rooms. The figure was comfortable in them all, feeling their space, the differing aspects of quietude which, as much as the architecture, defined them. The shadow had seen several *kobun*, but they had not seen it. Aware of their approaching presence, the shadow clung to the dark places where the other shadows abided. By closing off its spirit, it simply ceased to be, and they passed it by.

Hiroshi Taki turned to the girl lying beside him. He watched the even breathing, the soft rise and fall of her firm breasts. He thought not of her name but, rather, of the pleasure she gave him. It seemed now the only constant in his uncertain world.

He sighed deep in his throat, pressed his lips against hers. Her warmth transferred itself into him and he felt himself relaxing. There was a way through the awful maze confronting him. There was always a way. Wasn't that something his father had taught him—instilled in all his sons—years ago? Yes. Even enemies could, under the proper conditions, be recruited. Hadn't his father told them of the very man who had come to kill him many years ago and had stayed to save his life? Hiroshi had actually met that man. Such a miracle could be repeated, Hiroshi decided. Perhaps he could recruit that same man. He had saved Wataro Taki's life; could he do any less for his eldest son?

Yes, Hiroshi decided. That was just what he was going to—

The crash, like a clap of thunder inside the room, jerked him up.

"What—?"

The roof beams, shattering, rained shards of wood, plaster, tiles, down upon him. Moonlight canting in like a spotlight. And something following it down, glinting and hard. Impaling itself in the center of the sleeping girl's breast.

The poor thing coughed, arched up. Her eyes opened wide, a rictus suffused her face even as she reached futilely for Hiroshi.

A shape seemed to have leaped down the ethereal shaft of moonlight.

Hiroshi, squinting into the looming shadows, said, "Who—?"

A little laugh, low and dark as obsidian.

"Zero."

Hiroshi felt his stomach heave. He was abruptly dizzy. Zero! The assassin who for years had been terrorizing the

Yakuza ranks. Why was he here? Who had sent him? And who was he? Someone who was intimate with the Yakuza, it was rumored. Yet none could identify him.

He could hear the girl's last gurglings, reminding him of his own mortality; they filled up the room with death.

Hiroshi Taki, his right hand buried beneath the *futon* on which he sat, whipped it free of the covering and brandished a *jitte*. It was the traditional dagger first used by policemen at the end of Japan's feudal era. Between the hilt and the blade was a guard with a pair of steel horns jutting forward on either side. Hiroshi Taki was a master of this weapon.

Now, as the blade of Zero's longsword swept down upon him, Hiroshi drove the *jitte* upward so that the sword was caught between the dagger's own blade and one of its side horns. He twisted, and the longsword blade buried itself in the *futon* beside him.

Immediately he disengaged, trying to slam the side of the *jitte* into the assailant's throat. Zero struck his wrist a numbing blow, jerked the *katana* free and, with the same motion, brought the blade singing in toward Hiroshi's face.

Hiroshi, prepared for the strategy, used the *jitte* in the same manner as he had before. He employed the anvil, in an attempt to break the *katana* in two with the *jitte*. But Zero maneuvered the longsword so that the dagger clanged harmlessly against the blade. Hiroshi sliced desperately upward, sure that he would cut into the man's throat and end this threat forever.

But in a countermove too swift for even Hiroshi to follow, Zero deflected the *jitte*, twisted the longsword so that it lifted Hiroshi's weapon out of his grip, flung it clattering across the room.

Now Hiroshi watched with fevered eyes as Zero's gleaming longsword crossed the plane of the moonlight. A cold fire leaped through the room. When it reached the longsword's tip, the weapon blurred and Hiroshi cried out.

The first of one hundred small but deep wounds opened beneath the expert, surgeon's blade. Blood spurted. Hiroshi screamed, staring into the shrouded face. He struggled to free himself, but Zero had pinioned his arm with a superhuman strength.

Hiroshi heaved with the power of desperation and bit his lip as the pain lashed through him. Through his tears, he could see the bone popped unnaturally from its socket and knew that he had dislocated his shoulder.

"Who are you? Who are you?" he gasped.

He reached upward with his free hand, bloodying it on the longsword. Got a grip on the shirtfront. Peering, trying to pierce the darkness. "Who are you?" At the point of death, needing to know the secret. Because he thought he recognized . . .

That laugh again, chilling him.

"Zero."

In other parts of the estate, Hiroshi's men were awake, grabbing for their weapons, running toward his quarters. But by the time they arrived, there were only two corpses staring sightlessly into the silver brightness pouring through the hole in the rooftop. And it seemed to the stupefied onlookers that this place had been visited by the judgment of Buddha.

BOOK 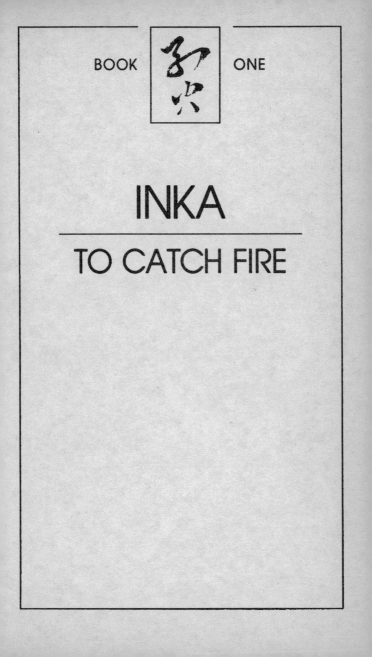 ONE

INKA

TO CATCH FIRE

Michael Doss began exhaling the *Shuji Shuriken* just at dawn.
The *Shuji Shuriken*, literally "cutting the nine ideographs,"
referred to the reciting of the nine magic words. Centuries
of Taoist tradition had been taken up by certain esoteric
Buddhist sects involved in swordsmanship, *ninjutsu* and the
like.

As always, Michael imagined the playing of the Japanese
bamboo flute, the instrument he had heard during much of
his training. Its hard-soft, yin-yang notes, reverberating only
in his mind, cut through the customs, dialects, mannerisms,
of whatever country he might be in to achieve some pristine,
essential truth required to give the *Shuji Shuriken* life. It was
not enough to speak the nine self-protecting words; they had
to be summoned and, once done, handled with the utmost
care and attention.

There was, after all, a kind of magic at work, ancient and
powerful.

Sitting cross-legged beneath the branches of a nodding plane
tree, Michael lifted his right hand, palm toward the earth.

"*U*," he said. Being.

He turned his palm upward.

"*Mu*." Nonbeing.

His hand descended to rest on his knee. Across the rooftops, Paris was coming awake. The pinks in the sky were
brightening along the ruffled tops of the clouds.

"*Suigetsu*." Moonlight on the water.

In the foreground, the almost mathematical structure of
the Eiffel Tower rose at his back. Still black from the remnants
of night, its gridlike starkness against the pastels of the rest
of the city made its proximity positively awesome.

"*Jo*." Inner sincerity.

"*Shin*." Master of the mind.

3

The first rays of sunlight sparked against the tower's up-swept tip so that it seemed for an instant to have been struck by lightning.

"*Sen.*" Thought precedes action.

"*Shinmyoken.*" Where the tip of the sword settles.

The sounds of stiff straw bristles swiping the dirt from the sidewalk below, a brief, exclamatory dialogue between Mme. Charvet and her daughter, the yelping of the dog with the maimed forepaw. The quotidian noises of the neighborhood.

"*Kara.*" Empty: the void. Virtue.

"*Zero.*" Where the Way has no power.

Michael rose. He had already been awake for two hours, practicing the swordsmanship he had been taught in the *Shin-kage* school. *Kage*, the basis for everything Michael had learned, meant response. That is, to react rather than to act; to be defensive rather than take the offensive.

Now he went through the high lead-glass doors from his terrace into the cool dim interior of his apartment. It was on the top floor of a gray stone building on the Avenue Élysée Reclus, a location that Michael had carefully chosen because of its proximity to the tower and the particular light afforded the Parc du Champ, at its foot.

Light was important to Michael Doss. One could even say essential. He threw off his *gi*, the traditional outfit of the Japanese swordsman, consisting of cotton trousers beneath a kind of divided skirt and a black cotton jacket tied at the waist with a belt of the same color. This last denoted rank.

He showered, changed into faded jeans, stiff with a mul-titude of smeared colors, and a white collarless shirt with the sleeves rolled up. He slipped Mexican huaraches on his feet and padded into the kitchen, where he poured himself a cup of green tea. Opening the refrigerator, he scooped up cold, sticky rice with two fingers, munching as he went through the long, littered living room.

Though he owned one of the finest printing firms in the world, Michael went into the office only a couple of times a week. Then it was only to supervise the manufacturing of the special color dyes that he had invented, patented, and that had earned his firm an excellent reputation. Museums, gal-leries and the most prestigious modern artists lined up to have his company print limited editions of their works for them, so true and brilliant were Michael's dyes and the complex coloring process he had refined.

At the far end of the enormous apartment he threw open

4

a set of inlaid double doors, and sunlight abruptly illuminated him. The deep-set olive-tinged eyes, the black, wavy hair that had a tendency to become unruly when, as now, it was left too long. His features—the prominent cheekbones, rather heavy jawline, narrow forehead—seemed almost biblical. People thought him stern, unforgiving, often difficult to move to laughter. But never judgmental. His saving grace.

The light flooded in from the skylight in the roof. Below was a huge space made up of bare walls and floor. In the center of the space—for, without furnishings of any kind, it could not in truth be called a room—stood a great paint-flecked wooden easel. Beside it, a paint box on a stool lay open, a palette and brushes sitting on its corner.

Michael crossed the space and stood in front of the canvas that the easel displayed. He sipped his green tea while his practiced eye roved over the painting. It was of two male figures, perhaps a generation apart. The figures were facing each other in a spare yet powerful landscape that managed to hint at a field by the edge of a forest. The overwhelming light of Provence underscored the tension between the men.

Michael was analyzing composition—what one did not paint was as important as what one did paint. And color, the harmoniousness of greens. As the Japanese said in summer, *"Yappari aoi kuni da!"* It is a green world!

After a time, Michael decided that here was too much forest-green, there too little apple-green. It gave the whole, he decided, too heavy a spirit. No wonder yesterday's work had left him unsettled.

He had just begun to squeeze out his paints when the telephone rang. He was not in the habit of answering the phone while he was working. He had only heard the ring because he had failed to close the heavy doors to his atelier. In a moment, his machine took the call. But not five minutes later, the phone rang again. The fourth time this happened, Michael put down his palette and answered the ringing himself.

"Allo?" He automatically spoke in French.

"Michael? It's Uncle Sammy."

"Oh hell, I'm sorry," Michael said down the overseas line, switching to English. "Is it you who's been calling?"

"It was imperative I get through to you, Michael," Jonas Sammartin said. "The real you."

"It's good to hear your voice, Uncle Sammy."

5

"It's been a long time, son. I've called to ask you to come home."

"Home?" Where was home? Michael wondered. Home is here on the Avenue Élysée Reclus, for now.

"Yes, home," Sammartin said. "To Washington." His uncle cleared his throat. "Michael, I'm afraid your father is dead."

Masashi Taki waited patiently while Ude cleared a path for him through the densely packed hall. It was cedar-lined, buttressed by rough-hewn cypress beams. It was windowless, being at the center of the Taki-gumi compound in the Deienchofu district of Tokyo, where huge houses and estates still existed. Great banners, covered in ancient calligraphy, hung from the ceiling in rows, giving the hall the aspect of some medieval gathering place.

He was in the traditional meeting gallery of the Taki clan, the largest and most powerful of all the Yakuza families.

Yakuza was a conglomerate term for the powerful gangster underground that, through the genius of Wataro Taki, had become in recent years international in scope, moving into legitimate businesses in New York, San Francisco and Los Angeles, and into real estate and resort ownership in the Hawaiian Islands.

A hushed silence spread through the crowd of lieutenants—bosses of their own subfamilies within the Taki-gumi—and *kobun*, the street soldiers who were, after all, the clan's lifeblood.

Masashi was the youngest of the Taki brothers. He was thin and dark, long-jawed like a wolf. In this he resembled his late father, Wataro Taki, godfather of the Japanese Yakuza society. His prominent cheekbones, unusual in a Japanese, lent his face a sculptured look that he had cultivated into a hardness that was intimidating.

Leading him toward the front of the room was Ude. He was a massive man, possessing those two most admired Japanese traits: bulk and strength. He was Masashi's feared right arm: the hammer of his lord's retribution.

As Masashi headed toward the raised dais at the far end of the hall, he could see his older brother, Joji, already at the place of honor before a stylized six-spoked wheel, the great family emblem of the Taki-gumi. This was yet another page that their father, Wataro Taki, had taken from the book of Japan's feudal past. In those days, each *samurai* warlord had an emblem that signified his presence in the land. Yakuza were not *samurai*—they were not of noble blood. Yet Wataro Taki had had the temerity to design his own family emblem—and thus, in an important psychological way, had elevated his clan above all other Yakuza clans.

Joji was a painfully thin man. He, too, had inherited his late father's lean, lupine look. But while in Masashi it manifested itself in the power of the wolf, Joji merely appeared unhealthy. True, he had been a sickly child, doted over by his mother. True, he had been a weak adolescent, lacking stamina. But the fact was that now he was never ill, rarely grew tired and was known as an indefatigable worker. His late father had employed him as the clan bookkeeper. It was said that Joji knew all the family's secrets; it was also said that nothing could ever cause him to betray those secrets.

Joji's black eyes, set deep in his skull, focused on Masashi as the younger man made his way like an emperor-general triumphantly returning home. It was a fact that though Masashi had openly disagreed with many of his father's policies, especially in recent years, he was nevertheless the brother with the charisma. It was logical to assume that the lieutenants—nervous about the present, concerned about the future—would gravitate toward him.

Joji waited until his brother reached the dais before raising his arms for silence. "Our *oyabun* is dead," Joji said simply. "And now Hiroshi, my beloved brother, the man designated to become the new *oyabun* of the Taki-gumi, has been taken in untimely fashion from the bosom of his family. Now I, as next in line, will do what I can to keep Wataro Taki's dream alive." He bowed his head for a moment before withdrawing.

He was surprised to see Masashi come forward to take up a stance to address the throng.

"When my father, the revered Wataro Taki, died, the entire nation grieved," Masashi began. "Thousands attended his funeral. Heads of state, presidents of corporations, bureaucratic leaders, paid their respects. An emissary from the Emperor himself was present." Masashi looked about the hall, catching the eye of a lieutenant here, a *kobun* there. "Why did this occur? Because my father was an extraordinary man. He was a tower of strength to whom all within the Taki-gumi could turn for support and protection. He was a fierce lion. All the Taki-gumi enemies feared him beyond even death.

"Now that he is gone, I ask you to think. What will become of us now? Who will you turn to in these increasingly troubled times? Who will ensure that our enemies will remain at their respectful distance?

"I am talking about not only the other clans. Historically, the Taki-gumi has been in the forefront of Japanese defense against Russian infiltration. We are less than one hundred miles from the Soviet Union. The Soviets look upon us with distrust and apprehension. They, like the Americans have done, would seek to subjugate us. This, my father fought against all his life. We must continue that tradition now."

Masashi's gaze continued to range around the hall. And, like all of the best and most charismatic leaders, his voice became intimate and pursuasive even as it increased in oratory strength. "Can the Taki-gumi keep its preeminent status among the Yakuza clans? Or will its many enemies circle closer and closer, biting off a piece here, a piece there, until nothing is left of this once-proud family?

"The answer, I submit, is already only too clear. Hiroshi, my beloved brother, would have provided fine, strong leadership in the tradition of Wataro Taki. But Hiroshi is dead. Murdered by an assassin known to us as Zero. Which one of our enemies hired Zero? Which one stands to gain the most from the Taki-gumi's sudden lack of a central presence?

"I say that our most pressing problem—our *only* problem— is in defining the future of the Taki-gumi. We can either weaken, be ripped apart by our enemies and eventually die. Or we can strengthen our hold, we can become more aggressive, we can seek to dominate those who would dominate us.

"The crisis is now. These are desperate times. Both for the Yakuza and for Japan. As proud Yakuza, we must seek our rightful place in the world of international business. As citizens of Japan, we must actively fight for the kind of equality we, as natives of these tiny islands, have always been denied. I ask you to join me in seeking a future, glorious and filled with prosperity!

"There can be only one *oyabun* of the Taki-gumi! It is I, Masashi Taki!"

Joji, stunned and gray-faced, heard the tumultuous roar of applause from the assembled clan members. He had listened to his brother's words with a sense of mounting disbelief mingled with dread. Now he watched with a kind of paralyzed awe as the men of the Taki-gumi rose to their feet like an

8

army of foot soldiers about to do battle. Then, humiliated and ashamed, Joji hurried from the hall.

Jonas Sammartin was not, strictly speaking, Michael Doss's uncle. At least, not by blood. But the lifelong friendship he had had with Michael's father made him seem more a member of the family than blood relatives from whom Michael's father had drifted away.

Philip Doss had loved Jonas Sammartin like a brother. He had trusted the older man with the safety of his family, with his own life. That was why it had been Uncle Sammy who had made the call to Michael, and not Michael's mother or sister. Or perhaps it was because Jonas was Philip Doss's boss.

In any case, the Doss family loved Uncle Sammy.

Philip Doss had rarely been home, and so it had been left to Jonas Sammartin to become a surrogate father to the family. Though Philip Doss, on his sporadic and unannounced homecomings, never failed to bring presents for his children from wherever he happened to have traveled, it was Jonas who had attended Michael's graduations. And since Michael always came home at least once a year when he was studying in Japan, it was Jonas who also had made it a point to be with Michael on his birthday. It was Jonas, too, who had played cowboys and Indians with Michael when Michael was a child. They spent hours tracking one another down, having shoot-outs, and powwows.

It had been that way as far back as Michael could remember. Often, Michael wondered what it was like to have a father who was really there. A father who played ball with you, whom you could talk to.

Now, Michael realized, he would never know.

Washington was gray when Michael arrived at Dulles International. From the air, the public monuments looked soot-encrusted and somehow smaller than he had remembered them. He had not been back here in ten years. It seemed like a lifetime.

He passed through Customs and Immigration, retrieved his luggage and picked up his rental car.

Driving again through Washington, he was amazed that its inner geography was still fresh in his mind. He had no trouble finding his way to his parents' house. Not home, he realized, as Uncle Sammy had said. Just his parents' house.

Dulles was a long way from town. Michael opted for the

9

airport-access highway rather than the more southerly—and direct—Little River Turnpike because that would have taken him directly through Fairfax. That was where his father had worked, where Uncle Sammy sat in his seat of power at the head of a government agency known as BITE, the Bureau of International Trade Exports.

Besides, he told himself, this way he was able to drive along the Potomac, to see the cherry trees in blossom, to think of the countryside of Japan, where he had trained in swordsmanship and in painting.

The Doss family's house was a white clapboard just outside Bellehaven, on the western shore of the Potomac, south of Alexandria. It was typical of Uncle Sammy that he had said, Yes, home. To Washington. Not Bellehaven, but Washington. To him, Washington was the power word.

The house had been far too big for the family, even when both children had been at home. Now its great wraparound porch, supported by Doric-style columns, seemed to echo with sounds from the past, mocking the silence of the present.

The house overlooked the Potomac past a long, sloping back lawn dotted with birch, alder and the enormous pair of weeping willows that Michael had loved to climb when he was young.

The massed azaleas in the front were coming up, but it was too early for the mock orange and honeysuckle to be in bloom.

As Michael walked down the red-brick path, the front door opened and he saw his mother. The wan light struck her face, and he could see how pale she was. She wore a three-piece black linen suit which was, as usual, in impeccable taste. A diamond brooch was at her throat.

Just behind her, Michael could make out the tall, powerful figure of Uncle Sammy, wreathed in shadows. Uncle Sammy stepped into the light, and Michael could see the shock of white hair catch the light. Uncle Sammy's hair had been white ever since Michael could remember.

"Michael," Lillian Doss said. When he bent over to kiss her, she embraced him with a fierceness that surprised him. Before they broke apart, he felt her tears on his face.

"Good of you to come, son," Uncle Sammy said, extending his hand. He had the firm, dry grip of a politician. His leathery, sunburned face had always reminded Michael of Gary Cooper's.

Inside, the vast house was as quiet, as somber, as a funeral parlor. That, too, had not changed since the days of Michael's youth. Even as he began to walk with them into the parlor, Michael felt himself shrink in size and age. This was an adult's abode; it always had been. He felt out of place, disconnected. Home, Michael thought. This is not home. It never has been.

Home was the rolling hills of Nara prefecture in Japan. Home was Nepal and Thailand. Home was Paris or Provence. Not Bellehaven.

"Drink?" Jonas Sammartin asked at the mahogany wet bar.

"Stolichnaya, if you have it." Michael saw that Jonas was already preparing two martinis. He gave one to Lillian, kept one for himself. He poured Michael's vodka, then held his glass aloft.

"Your father liked a good, stiff drink," Uncle Sammy observed. " 'Fortification,' he used to say, 'cleanses the system.' Here's to him. He was a helluva man."

Uncle Sammy still looked every inch the patriarch. But that was natural, of course. This was his family, even if by proxy, since he had none of his own. His personality was tailor-made for sailing through emotionally difficult situations. Uncle Sammy was the rock upon which weaker souls, drowning in emotion, could throw themselves with absolute assurance. Michael was glad he was here.

"Lunch will be ready momentarily," Lillian Doss said. She had never been a person of many words, and now, with the death of her husband, her thoughts seemed more recondite than ever. "We're having roast beef hash and eggs."

"Your father's favorite," Uncle Sammy said with a sigh. "A fitting meal, now that the family is back together again."

As if on cue, Audrey appeared through the gap in the french doors. Michael had not seen his sister in nearly six years. On that occasion, she had appeared at his doorstep, bruised and two months' pregnant. The German she had been living with for six months in Nice had not reacted well to the news that she was pregnant. He had had no interest in beginning a family and had shown the depth of his displeasure at what he termed Audrey's "stupidity." Against her sister's wishes, Michael had found her former boyfriend and had dispatched his own form of retribution. Oddly, Audrey had hated her brother for it. They had not spoken since the day he had brought her into the clinic to have the abortion. When he had returned to fetch her, she was gone.

Lillian went to her daughter, and Michael took the opportunity to speak to Uncle Sammy.

"You told me that my father died in an automobile accident," he said softly. "What exactly happened?"

"Not now, son," Uncle Sammy said gently. "This isn't the time or the place. Let's respect your mother's peace of mind, hm?" He extracted a small notepad, wrote on it with a slim gold pen. He pressed the slip of paper into Michael's hand. "Meet me at this address at nine tomorrow morning. I'll tell you everything I know." He gave Michael a sad smile. "This has been very difficult on your mother."

"It's a shock to all of us," Michael said tightly.

Uncle Sammy nodded. Then he turned toward the women, his voice warm and rich. "Audrey, my little darling, how are you?"

Lillian Doss was slender, almost willowy, and Audrey was cut from the same mold. Seeing the daughter, one could imagine how striking the mother had once been. However, there was more than a touch of Philip's solid determination in Audrey's face, and this gave her a proud bearing that contrasted sharply with the sadness that seemed to hold her in its spell. Her hair, now cut short for the first time in Michael's memory, was redder than Lillian's golden brown.

As Michael's younger sister—raised in a household where feminine traits were, by and large, shunned—she had done all in her power to compete with him on equal terms. Of course that had been impossible—it was Michael who had gone to Japan, not Audrey. As a consequence, she had become somewhat withdrawn.

Audrey's cool blue eyes regarded him now from across the sparely furnished room, a room that bore Philip Doss's indelible mark. In the study, Japanese screens, *futon* couches that Lillian complained were uncomfortable, contrasted with a futuristic Japanese black lacquer desk. Translucent rice-paper *shoji* across the windows brought intricate patterns of light and shadow into the room, making it appear larger than it was.

The walls were lined with bamboo-and-glass bookcases, which were filled with an extensive library of books concerned with military histories, analyses and strategies. Philip Doss's facility with foreign languages had been matched only by his endless enthusiasm for the intricacies of the military mind.

The gaps between the bookcases were filled with etchings, paintings or engravings of Philip Doss's heroes: Alexander the Great, Ieyasu Tokugawa and George Patton.

And there was the small glass case, empty now, that held

12

the small porcelain teacup when Philip was home. It was by far Philip Doss's most prized possession; it was why he often took it with him when he went abroad. It held a place of honor—clearly a reminder of Philip's time in Tokyo just after the war.

This room, Michael realized now, was filled with his father's presence. Each book, each pillow, each painting, was a part of Philip Doss that abided, impervious either to time or to mortal disease.

For a moment, Michael had an odd sensation. He felt as if he had stumbled upon the atelier of one of the great artists, Matisse or Monet. There was the same sensation of being in the presence of a great legacy—an immortal statement—that transcended human experience.

Stunned, Michael was impelled across the room. In an instant the exalted feeling that only comes with privilege had given way to a kind of stultification.

"I'm surprised you came." Audrey's eyes never left him.

"That's not fair," he said.

She regarded him much as a cat might, with the kind of impersonal curiosity that was hard to fathom.

"When I went back to the hospital in Paris to get you, they told me you had gone. Why didn't you wait for me? I didn't want you to be on your own."

"Then you shouldn't have gone after Hans. I begged you not to."

"After what that bastard did to you—"

"I don't think you have to remind me what he did to me," Audrey said coldly. "But there were other things. You had no idea how wonderful he could be."

"He beat you," Michael said. "Whatever else he was or did doesn't matter."

"It mattered to me."

"If you still believe that," Michael said, "then you're more of a fool than you were then."

"Michael Doss's morality, is that it?" Her tone had turned bleak. "The world doesn't conform to your rigid idea of morality, Michael. Whatever they taught you in Japan doesn't always work in the real world. We're not all soldiers of inner righteousness or whatever it is you worship. We're human beings. Good and bad. If you can't accept both sides, then you're left with nothing."

He could see her trembling with the effort to control her emotions. This was their father's sacred room, after all. "Like

I am now. Do you think it's easy to find a man who is un-attached? How many affairs I've had since Hans? And all with married men. Men who made promises it was impossible to keep. At least Hans was willing to stay. We would have worked something out. I know it. He would have missed me in a week or so. He would have come back; he always did. But not after what you did to him. Do you know where I went when I left the hospital? Back to Nice, to find him. But he was gone."

Tears standing in the corners of her eyes, but she would not raise a finger to wipe them away. That would be tanta-mount to admitting defeat in front of her father; to admitting that she was not Michael's equal. "So now I am alone. This is what your code of morality has done to me, Michael. Are you proud of it?" One tear sliding down her cheek.

Abruptly, she turned and, squeezing her mother's arm, half ran down the hallway. In a moment, they all heard a door slam.

"What was that about?" Lillian asked.

"I don't know exactly," Michael said sadly.

Lillian looked doubtful. "She's understandably over-wrought." She put her hands together. "I wonder if I should go after her." It wasn't much of a question and, in any case, the men were waiting. There was the meal to consider. She nodded her head, trying out a smile. "I expect we'd better go into the dining room. Lunch is ready, and Philip always did abhor cold roast beef hash."

"The shogun is dead! Long live the shogun!"

The old man with a face as weathered as a mountainside said, "He was not that. Wataro Taki was never the shogun."

Masashi Taki ceased his pacing momentarily. "I don't care what you call it. My father is dead."

The old man, bearded, with a rim of close-cropped snow-white hair surrounding a glossy freckled pate, said, "*Hai*. Your father is dead. But even more important for you is that your elder brother Hiroshi is also dead."

At that, a third man stirred. Ude had his suit jacket draped over his shoulder. His forearms, visible because of his short-sleeved shirt, were covered from the wrist up with *irezumi*, the intricate tattooing beloved of the Yakuza. On his left arm a fire-breathing dragon twined; on his right, a phoenix rose from the flames of a pyre.

Masashi Taki said, "Ude here did his work well. It was no

14

secret that this Zero uses the legendary hundred-cut method to kill his victims. Ude had no trouble mimicking that style."

Kozo Shiina, the old man, was sitting at a stone table in the center of his garden. It was a place of ten thousand species of moss and was thus filled with every shade of green imaginable. Moss was, by and large, a soft and delicate plant. But somehow this garden was neither. Rather, Masashi thought, it was austere, an altogether intimidating place. This was no doubt because its owner, Kozo Shiina, imbued it with elements of his own personality.

As Masashi watched, Shiina cut into a lemon with a pink pearl-handled folding knife. Swiftly, deftly, the old man turned the whole fruit into translucent slices. As they spoke, he took one slice at a time, dribbled honey on it and popped it into his mouth. He sucked all the juice out of it before chewing and swallowing.

"As I suggested," Shiina said. He had a disconcerting habit of scrutinizing your face as he spoke. "It does no harm to sow confusion. We would not want suspicion for Hiroshi's murder to fall on you."

Masashi shrugged. "That is the joke. I was not even next in line," he said. "Joji was. But Joji is weak. He is frightened of me. No one loyal to my father would follow him; they have too much sense for that. No. Our plan is perfect. When I denounced Joji at the clan meeting, all the Taki-gumi lieutenants agreed in one voice. One voice, one mind, *neh*? No one stood against me when I displaced him."

"And you are not concerned about the repercussions?"

"From whom?" Masashi sneered. "Joji? He'll be too busy fending off the *oyabun* from rival clans, who wish a piece of whatever remains, even to think of revenge."

Shiina popped another honeyed lemon slice into his mouth. When he was finished chewing, he said, "Joji is one matter. Your stepsister is quite another."

"Michiko." Masashi nodded. "Yes. I agree that she presents a problem. She is smart and she is strong. For many years she was my father's chief assistant. Before the rift that tore them apart."

"Do you know what happened between them?"

Masashi shook his head. "My father never spoke of it—to anyone. And my stepsister and I were never on close enough terms for me to ask her." There was a tiny rill that ran through the garden. Masashi was standing on the wooden bridge that spanned it. He put his hand on the railing. "I wouldn't worry about Michiko. I have already put into motion a plan that will effectively neutralize her."

"Then she has a weakness."

"*Everyone* has a weakness," Masashi said softly. "It is only a matter of finding it."

"And what is hers?" Kozo Shiina asked.

"Her daughter."

"Ah. I hope that you are right," the old man said. He was on the last of his lemon. "To this day I cannot understand why your father adopted Michiko. She was the daughter of Zen Godo, my most hated enemy. Though Zen Godo died in 1947, I have had to endure the machinations of his progeny. Michiko inherited much of her father's diabolical cleverness. Keep her to the shadows, Masashi-san. We have no room for error now."

"I know the stakes fully as well as you do," Masashi said, sounding irritable. "No. No. You were right. My father was no shogun; he had no desire to take control of all the clans. But I do. I will be the shogun that he refused to become. You have promised to make me so. I will be the first of a dynasty like the Tokugawa. This is not so different from the sixteenth century, is it? Today the *oyabun*"—he was speaking of the gangland bosses—"of the various Yakuza clans bicker and fight among themselves. Then, as now, the local warlords were continually feuding one against the other. Until Ieyasu Tokugawa, seeing a better way, was able to unite all the warlords under his banner. He became the first shogun—the supreme warlord—wielding power of a magnitude hitherto unknown. All of Japan lay at his feet. Now the same is true for me. It has begun. The Taki-gumi lieutenants have made me their *oyabun*. Within weeks, even days perhaps, all the Yakuza *oyabun* will swear allegiance to me, Masashi Taki, first Yakuza shogun!"

Shiina waited the requisite amount of time before he nodded, dismissing the subject. "There is still the question of what was stolen from you."

Masashi frowned. "It is still missing."

"Yet I have heard that Philip Doss is dead."

"That is true," Masashi admitted. "He died in Hawaii. There was a car crash. He went up in flames. This occurred two days before my brother Hiroshi's demise. For the second time we were close to getting Doss. My under-*oyabun* in Hawaii, Fat Boy Ichimada, reported Doss's arrival on Maui.

16

I instructed Ichimada to get him. Unfortunately, the car crash put an end to that."

"And the Katei document? Did that, too, go up in flames with him?"

"It is possible."

For the first time, the old man showed a flicker of anger. "And just as possible that it did not. We must find out, Masashi. If that document falls into the wrong hands, we are undone. Decades of planning will be for nothing. We are on the verge of victory. We need only another month or two. And then we will change the face of the world forever."

"Fat Boy Ichimada tells me nothing could have survived that crash," Masashi said.

"And . . . ?"

"And what?"

Shiina was finished with the lemon. He cleared the stone surface in front of him. A bird had lit on a branch above his head. He waited for it to finish singing, as if it were a participant in this discussion. At last Shiina said, "Where there is moonlight at night, it is easy to see the face of the water. It is a task anyone may perform satisfactorily. But at those times when the weather is overcast or when the moonlight is absent, it takes another kind of skill to discern the water's whereabouts." With the dregs of the citrus juice he drew one circle, then two, then a third, darkening the stone. "Has it not occurred to you, Masashi? Philip Doss stole the Katei document from you. You sent your men after him. For a week they searched for him. Three days ago they got a lead. You sent Ude. Ude came close to him. Just a whisper away. But at the last moment, Philip Doss managed to elude him. Doss disappeared. Only to surface in Hawaii to be killed in a car crash."

"So?"

"So." Shiina filled in the third circle with the juice so that in the light it became more prominent than the other two. "Has it not gotten through to you that *someone else* got to Philip Doss before we did? You sent Ude to *find* him, not to kill him. At least not until Doss revealed the whereabouts of the document. Now Doss is dead. He can no longer tell us.

"So, I ask you again: Where is the Katei document? Did it burn with Doss in the crash? Did he manage to hide it somewhere before his death? Did he, for instance, give it to someone? Send it to his son? Or has your man Ichimada got

17

his hands on it?" Shiina's black eyes bored into Masashi's. "I don't have to tell you the worth of that document. If Ichimada has it, he means to use it. He could have anything he wants from us for its return. Even an end to his banishment to Hawaii. Isn't that right?"

Masashi thought for a long time. At last he said, "Ude."

Kozo Shiina nodded. "Yes. Send Ude to Hawaii, to Fat Boy Ichimada. Ichimada knew Philip Doss from the old days. Who knows? Perhaps they were friends. Here." He handed over a small snapshot. It was black-and-white and grainy, as if it had been shot from a long lens. A surveillance photo.

Masashi recognized Michael Doss. Had Shiina had the son watched in Paris? It seemed so. He passed the photo to Ude. "Michael Doss," he said, and the big man nodded.

"Let us get to the bottom of this," Kozo Shiina said, "and terminate it, once and for all." His eyes bored into the two men. "We must retrieve the Katei document no matter the cost."

Lying in his old bedroom, Michael heard the scraping of the branches of the crabapple tree against the side of the house, just as he had when he was a child.

Sometime during the past several years his father had installed security lights outside. Now their glare, only partially filtered by the foliage, made patterns on the ceiling.

He tried to calm himself, but to no avail. Too many memories here. Too much unhappiness. Too much left unsaid. He thought of all the things he had wanted to say to his father but had not. Perhaps it was only a simple pleasure because it was so basic, but he had been denied it. It wasn't, Michael realized now, that he had had a bad relationship with his father. It was that they had had none at all.

He thought of delicate shadows, tendrils of the cryptomeria transfigured by the moonlight into a wild gypsy's dance. In his mind he heard the bamboo flute, the progression of its melody forever bitter.

In Tsuyo's home, where much of the *sensei*'s teaching had taken place, Michael, younger, more ignorant and utterly alone, had waited for the inevitable to take place.

Nothing, not even the inevitable, merely happens, Tsuyo, the master of many arts, had said to Michael upon Michael's arrival in Japan. *Everything, even the inevitable, arises from out of the great warrior's spirit. The great warrior's spirit fills*

18

everything; it is everything. It is the sole cause of all events, great and small.

But isn't there a place where the great warrior's spirit does not exist, where it isn't everything? Michael had asked.

Tsuyo's face turned grave. *In* Zero, he said. *In* Zero *there is nothing. Not even the hope of an honorable death.* For a Japanese warrior, Michael knew, nothing could be more terrible than *zero*.

There was a slender vase in the place where Michael slept while he was with Tsuyo. It was of fired clay that seemed to have no intrinsic color of its own. Each day at dawn, the one flower it contained was changed. And it was Tsuyo, not a disciple, who replaced the flower. One morning, curious, Michael awoke and went outside. There, in the garden, he found the *sensei* kneeling before his flowers. Carefully, Tsuyo chose one, then another—one flower for each student, each and every day.

It is the master's responsibility, Tsuyo once told Michael, *to attend to the minutiae of life. Only then will he appreciate the infinite palette that life offers. In small pleasures, one learns, there is profound satisfaction.*

Michael had wanted to put this unconfirmed wisdom to the test. He could think of no better place to start than with Seyoko.

Seyoko was a small, slender girl, the only female student in this exclusive school. She was also the best student. She wore her hair long (when she trained, it was pulled back from her face in a thick, braided ponytail) with straight-cut bangs that almost covered her eyes. When Michael dreamed of her— which was often—these dreams centered on her hair. Once he awoke believing he was still suspended high over a moonlit ocean, balanced on Seyoko's thick, gleaming braid.

She wore no makeup, although at sixteen she was not too young to use it. He remembered one evening when she arrived at a party Tsuyo gave for his students (a score in number), her lips painted a brilliant red. The effect was so startling that Michael spend the rest of the evening listening to the thudding of his heart.

As with all the students, there was a slender vase in Seyoko's room. It was Michael's plan to go out into the master's garden before dinner and pick a flower of his own choosing, which he would place in the vase in Seyoko's room so that after dinner, when she returned, it would be waiting for her.

Tsuyo lived in a tiny hill town three hours north of Tokyo.

From his garden one could see the Japanese alps. Often it seemed as if the sky were permanently ringed by these darkling slopes.

It was in the foothills of these glacial ridges that much of the students' training was carried out. The morning had begun bright and sunny, with only a few fluffy clouds scudding in the high winds. Just after lunchtime, the weather had changed abruptly. The winds had shifted, bringing heavy, moisture-laden air off the sea. Soon the sky lowered ominously, as zinc-colored clouds, streaked with dark, clotted undersides, stretched across the region. Thunder began to boom, made dull and echoic by distance.

Tsuyo, one eye on the weather, saw no reason to break off his lessons, but as a precaution, should a rain squall come up suddenly and cut students off from one another, he broke the class up into pairs. Michael and Seyoko were put together.

And they were together when the rain hit, slicing in almost horizontally, driven by a wind turned cold and howling. The world around them disappeared beneath sheets of gray-green water, so opaque they seemed lifted whole from the shoreline many miles to the south.

Michael and Seyoko clung to the layered shale, dark and running with rainwater. They were perhaps three hundred yards above the treetops of the valley within which Tsuyo's house was nestled. Pressed against the slick, slanting rock face, they were pummeled by wind, lashed by the downpour.

Seyoko was shouting at him, but it was impossible to hear what she said and he shifted to move closer to her. A slice of shale, loosened perhaps by the storm, gave way beneath his foot and he skidded off the narrow ledge. He stumbled and flailed, feeling himself tumbling off the ledge. His knees slammed into the rock face as he reached up to grab a handhold on the ledge. He was dangling off the side of the mountain, the squall beating mercilessly against him. Seyoko stretched herself along the ledge, reached down to help him up. The wind was howling, gusting against them in quick, angry bursts. Michael felt his strength giving out. He was supporting his weight while fighting the wind, which threatened to fling him outward into the dark void.

He strained upward, saw Seyoko fully extended, reaching down, her fingers grabbing at his shirt, digging in as she hauled upward. The gale, increasing in strength, caused her to lose her grip momentarily. Michael felt himself slipping downward, and he shouted involuntarily.

20

Then Seyoko renewed her grip. He saw the fierceness in her face, the determination. Nothing was going to make her lose her hold on him again. With agonizing slowness, Michael inched his way up the jagged rock face until he was able to get his hips back up onto the rock ledge. His right leg made it upward and he thought, I'm safe!

He heard the crack then, an eerie sound that seemed to rip through his entire body. He turned his head, as if part of him already knew the nature of that sound. He saw the section of the rock ledge on which Seyoko was stretched break apart in a great gout of mud and shattered shale. He cried out as he saw Seyoko's body begin to fall. "Hold on to me!" he screamed into the wind. "Don't let go of me!"

But it was too late. Seyoko, as if divining that only one of them could be saved, had opened her hands. Michael felt the palms of her hands, her fingers, sliding over his back as she loosed her grip.

Then the storm took her, flinging her into the abyss. Whirling like a pinwheel, she floated for an eternal moment within the dark heart of the maelstrom of wind, rain and shattered rock. Michael saw her face, calm, serene, staring out at him.

Then, with an obscene abruptness, she was gone, swallowed whole into the maw of the squall.

Michael heard himself breathing. He swung in a shallow arc, half on and half off the ruined shelf of rock. The wind tugged at him, as it must have done to Seyoko. And for a split instant he thought of letting go, of following her into that heart of howling darkness. A despair so profound that he lost all sense of his center overcame him. He beat at the unforgiving stone with all his might, hating it for what it had done to her. Only when he tasted his own blood, when the pain of the cuts, bruises and abrasions he had inflicted on himself broke through his semistupor, did he swing himself all the way up onto the gouged-out ledge.

Much later, in the silence of the night, the aftermath of the storm, did he creep out into Tsuyo's garden. He lifted his bandaged hands and clumsily cut a single blossom.

He went into Seyoko's room. Nothing had been disturbed. Search parties were still out, in what would be a vain attempt to retrieve her body. The police, already there when Michael made his way down the mountain slope, had taken statements from everyone involved. Tsuyo had left to deliver the tragic news to Seyoko's parents.

There was a peculiar quiet inside the house. Michael took

a wilted flower out of the vase, replaced it with the fresh one he had just picked. But he felt nothing. Now Seyoko would never see it, and he would never understand the profound satisfaction derived from this small pleasure.

He breathed in the air, pulling in the scent of her. He saw again her face as she spiraled away from him. What would have happened between them had not the storm caught them on the rock face? He felt a longing well up inside himself, a sadness he could not define. It was as if a thief had stolen his future from him. Like a warrior's death without honor, it made life's present hollow and devoid of meaning.

I am alive and she is not, he thought. Where is the justice in that?

It was the most wholly Western thought he had had in seven years.

When Tsuyo returned from his sad journey, he recognized this question in the face of his pupil. And thereafter, he sought to show the Way that would, if not provide the answer, at least allow Michael to ask other questions that would lead him to his own path.

Michael, in his own room in Bellehaven, threw the covers off, put his feet on the cool bare wood floor. He went to the window to get more air. Pulling aside the white crinoline that he had found old-fashioned even when he was young, he saw a shadow pass across one of the lights. He started slightly, seeing with eyes clouded by the past: Seyoko alive again. Then reality shifted into focus and he recognized Audrey's copper-colored hair. She wore jeans and an oversize cream-colored sweater with padded shoulders. She walked with her arms wrapped around her chest.

Dressing quickly, he went through the silent house. Downstairs, shadows lay everywhere, like drop cloths in a house seldom used, so that only basic shapes remained.

He opened the front door and peered out at Audrey's startled face. Her hand was on the knob.

"Christ," she breathed. "You scared the hell out of me."

"Sorry."

"But then you were always scaring the hell out of me." She hugged herself as if she was cold. "You love to move around in the dark. You were always pouncing on me. You said you loved to hear me scream."

"I said that?"

"Yes. You did."

22

"That was a long time ago," Michael said. "We're grown-up now."

"We may be grown-ups," she said, slipping past him into the house, "but neither of us has changed."

Michael closed the door and followed her. She had gone into the study. Soft light burnished her creamy skin. She sat on a *futon* sofa, crossed one knee over the other, hugged a pillow to her. "Having you as a brother was like living with the bogeyman. Did you know that? When Mother and Dad were out was the worst. When we were alone together."

Michael stood in front of her. "You came to me in Paris when you were in trouble."

"Because I knew you wouldn't tell them—about the abortion. Because of your strict code of honor."

"You mean sometimes it comes in handy."

Audrey said nothing. He saw the freckles sprayed across the tops of her cheeks and remembered her laughing in a swing as he pushed. Years ago.

"It is a useful thing," he said. "But it's not something that can be turned on and off. One has to live by it completely or not at all."

Perhaps she heard him at last. She put her head back and closed her eyes. Some of the tension seemed to ebb from her. "Oh God," she whispered, "I've made such a mess of my life." Then she was weeping, her shoulders shaking.

Michael knelt and put his arms around her. He felt her embrace, the quick, surprising strength of her that accompanied the burst of emotion. Her head was in the hollow of his shoulder. "I never even had a chance to say goodbye to Dad," she cried softly.

"None of us did," he said.

She pulled away enough so that her eyes locked on his. "But he always spent time with you." She sniffed heavily. "You were his pride and joy."

"What makes you say that?"

"Oh come on, Mikey." She tossed her head. "You were the one he sent off to Japan when you were nine, studying God only knows what kind of impossible philosophy. Training with Japanese swords—"

"*Katana.*"

"Yes. *Katana.* I remember." She wiped the tears from her face. "Dad made sure that you never needed anyone. You were as independent and confident as the steel blade you learned to use."

23

He looked at her. "You're describing someone who is inhuman, not independent."

"Maybe that's what I thought you were."

She had bristled, and he recognized a resurgence of their old sibling rivalry. He smiled a little to reassure her. "But I'm not, Aydee." He deliberately used the nickname their father had given her.

"There were things—intimate things, growing up things—that I longed to confide in him," she said. "But he was never there. Uncle Sammy always had him at the end of a very short leash."

"Now you're talking like Mom," Michael said. "Uncle Sammy was always here when Dad wasn't. He was like—well, Nana, the English sheepdog in *Peter Pan*. Uncle Sammy was there to protect us."

"That was because Dad was always away," she said. "Don't you see? Uncle Sammy monopolized Dad's time. He had his job, and he had you. He managed to be in Japan often enough to visit you. In the end, there was nothing left for me."

"But you had Mom," Michael said. "You were always her favorite. I remember lying awake in Japan and resenting being so far away from her. I never got to know her, Aydee, whereas you and she are far closer than Dad and I ever were. You two tell each other things you'd never tell anyone else. I don't think Dad was that close with anyone, even Mom. They just never had that much time together."

Audrey put her head down. "Maybe," she conceded. "But maybe—this is what's kept me up tonight—maybe I failed Dad in some way. I think I was so busy resenting him that when he did come home, he didn't want to spend much time with me."

"Is that what you really believe?"

"I don't know," Audrey said softly. She put her chin on her forearms, closed her eyes. "Remember that time when Dad took us up to Vermont to teach us how to ski? God, but the weather was foul. The biggest snowstorm I'd ever seen came up while we were away from the lodge. We couldn't see a thing. I had no idea where we were. I started crying. I called and called, Mike. I thought Dad would hear me all the way back at the lodge. Do you remember?"

Michael nodded, remembering the fear he had felt for them both.

"I got hysterical," Audrey said. "I was freezing even through my ski suit."

24

"With that wind, it must have been thirteen below," Michael recalled.

"I wanted to run, Mike," she said. "But you grabbed me, and together we built this shelter out of snow. You got us out of that terrible, bone-chilling wind. You put my head into your chest. I remember breathing into your heartbeat. God, I was so frightened. But I never got any colder. We huddled together for warmth until the storm was over. Until Dad came and found us." She lifted her head, stared at him. "You were my Nana, my protector, that day. Dad couldn't believe how smart you were. I remember how he kissed us both. I think it was the first and only time I remember him kissing us."

"He kept saying, 'I thought you were dead. I thought you were dead.' " Michaél got up, went behind the desk to the *shoji*-covered window. The rice-paper screens played up the illumination from the security lights. He was uncomfortable with her memories of how Philip had admired him; it was a subtle admission that their father had not had the same feeling about her. Did he realize that he was just as uncomfortable with her expression of her sisterly love for him?

"I guess Mom asked Dad to put these security lights in," he said.

Audrey turned, one arm along the back of the sofa. "Actually, no. I was here when Dad put them in. They were his idea."

Michael was looking at the pattern the shadows of the trees made along the side of the house. "Did Dad say why he wanted them?"

"He didn't have to," Audrey said, and when Michael turned to stare at her, she shrugged. "I assumed Mom had told you. There was a break-in attempt."

"She didn't tell me," Michael said. "What happened?"

Audrey shrugged again. "Not much. Apparently, a prowler tried to get into the house. Into this room. The thing was, I was here. It was about three in the morning. I couldn't sleep, as usual. I heard someone at the window, just about where you are now."

"Did you see who it was?"

"No. I just took out Dad's pistol and fired it through the window."

"Security lights," Michael said. "That's just not like Dad."

"No. Not at all."

He came back to where Audrey was sitting. He saw that her legs were curled beneath her. She seemed more relaxed.

25

"Michael," she began. He sat beside her. "Do you know how Dad died?"

"In a car crash, Uncle Sammy said."

"Yes, I know that."

There was silence for a time.

At last Michael said, "What are you getting at, Aydee?"

Her face was composed, serious. "You're the bogeyman. You tell me."

"Where is it?"

The thick brown finger pointed.

"I want it."

The thick brown finger wiggled.

"You promised that I would have it."

Having wiggled, the thick brown finger stirred the small pile jumbled on the center of the koa-wood desk top. The pile was charred. It was making the room smell smoky.

Fat Boy Ichimada sighed. And in so doing, his impressive stomach rubbed up against the edge of his desk. "I don't have it." His small, bowlike lips opened and closed. His double chins wobbled. "I want it and I don't have it."

His black eyes lifted to the two men standing uncomfortably before him. They were virtually identical. They wore matching aloha shirts, wildly colored surfer's swim trunks and thong sandals.

"What," Fat Boy Ichimada said, "is your explanation?"

Outside, the Dobermans began to bark, and both Hawaiians turned their heads to look out the windows. A pair of boys just in their teens, long blond hair flying, ran by. Each held a brace of dogs straining on choke chains. They headed off into the thick, tropical foliage.

"Someone's crossed the perimeter," one of the Hawaiians said.

"Maybe it's the police," said the other.

"It is nothing at all," Fat Boy Ichimada said with conviction. "Just a wild boar. The spoor gets their hackles up."

"The dogs' or the surfers'?" the first Hawaiian said. It was a joke of a sort and, in any case, rhetorical.

"This is Kahakuloa," Fat Boy Ichimada said. He spoke in finite statements, as if whatever he said was carved in stone and not to be contradicted, ever. "There are no police here unless I summon them." Kahakuloa was in the extreme northeast section of Maui. Only one small two-lane road linked it with the nearest real town, Wailuku, to the south. To the

26

north, a scarifying, unpaved track at the edge of sheer cliffs wound around to Kapalua. It was navigable—when it was passable at all—only with a four-wheel-drive vehicle of sufficient height. Many a car had been stranded after the deep ruts had stripped muffler, oil pan and drive train off the undercarriage.

"Then the dogs are superfluous," the first Hawaiian pointed out.

"There are always tourists," Fat Boy Ichimada said. "Hikers, hippies, curiosity seekers and the like who need to be dissuaded. This is private property, after all."

The first Hawaiian laughed. "Yah," he said. "The tons of grass moved in and outta here is real private, ya, bro."

Fat Boy Ichimada heaved himself up. He was a big man by any standards; for a Japanese, he was a giant. He stood over six feet tall, a veritable mountain of a man. His small facial features accentuated the fact.

He had fists the size of bear paws. There were stories—perhaps apocryphal, perhaps not—that he had killed men with one clout of his fist.

Fat Boy Ichimada had been on one Hawaiian island or another for seven years. He knew as much about them—or more—than many natives, who were too busy tending to the millions of tourists who yearly flocked to paradise to recall the history of their heartbreakingly beautiful land.

"You are new with me, so I have been patient with you up to now. But ask around. I am tolerant with my children. As far as my employees go, there are only two situations. The job well executed and the job not executed at all. For the one, I reward handsomely. For the other, I have no tolerance whatsoever. I do not wait for history to repeat itself. Those employees who do not deliver that which is asked of them do not work for me again. They do not work for anyone again."

Fat Boy Ichimada was aware that during this speech, the two Hawaiians had begun to fidget. He wondered whether or not that was a good sign. He had not liked the idea of hiring new people at such short notice. But after he had made his decision, this matter had become far too delicate and explosive to use anyone known to be in Ichimada's employ. Now the major drawback of hiring from the outside was making itself manifest.

"You answer me at once," he said, "or I will tell the boys to loose the Dobermans. I keep them hungry. All the time hungry. They work harder that way." Fat Boy Ichimada's smile was without an ounce of warmth. "They are like people in that regard, *neh*?"

"Is that meant to frighten us?" the first Hawaiian said.

"You have a mouth on you," Fat Boy Ichimada said neutrally.

"You got a attitude problem, bro," the first Hawaiian said. "You think you're better than those golden boys out there?" He jerked a thumb in the direction that the boys holding the Dobermans had gone. "No way. You an' them's just *haolies*— you're outsiders. Got as much right to be on our land as a piece of shit in the living room."

Without dropping his gaze, Fat Boy Ichimada thumbed the intercom. "Kimo," he said into the speaker, "unleash the dogs."

The first Hawaiian's hand snaked beneath his aloha shirt. There was a snub-nosed .38 in it.

Fat Boy Ichimada was already in motion. It was astounding to see a man of his size move with such speed. In a blur he had leaned across the desk, his right hand extended. The edge of his hand, the yellow callus as hard as steel, smashed into the Hawaiian's wrist with such force that the gun clattered to the floor.

The first Hawaiian howled, and Fat Boy Ichimada struck him with the tips of two fingers just above his heart. The second Hawaiian, standing transfixed with fear and awe, never saw a man hit the floor so hard or so fast as his brother did.

By that time, Fat Boy Ichimada was around on their side of the desk. His size-fifteen loafer came down on the .38, covering it completely. He hauled the semiconscious Hawaiian to his feet. Holding him so just the tips of his toes dragged on the wood floor, he brought him to the door, opened it and threw him down the rough, wooden steps.

"Watch it!" he called, his bulk filling the entire doorway. "Here they come!"

When Fat Boy Ichimada locked the door and turned back to the room, he saw the second Hawaiian's ashen face. "Hey," he said almost amiably, "you okay?"

"Are they really coming?" the second Hawaiian managed to get out.

"Who?"

"The Dobermans."

"The Dobermans are eating lunch," Fat Boy Ichimada said, sitting down behind his desk again. He opened up a jar of macadamia nuts, popped a handful in his mouth—and half the jar was gone.

While he chewed, Fat Boy Ichimada watched the Hawaiian's eyes. He was enjoying this as fully as he was enjoying the macadamias.

"My brother—"

"I am waiting for my explanation."

"But he—"

"If he doesn't shit his shorts, he will be fine. Let him be."

The second Hawaiian did not know whether Fat Boy Ichimada was making a joke.

The thick brown finger probed the charred remains. "This is all that is left of his personal effects, you tell me." The finger stirred the ashes, bits of papers, the edge of a wallet. "But there isn't enough here for me to believe that it went up in smoke. I want it and I don't have it." Making runic patterns. "Tell me why."

The white-faced Hawaiian swallowed. "We were there," he said, "just after it happened. We'd followed just as you—"

"At Kaanapali."

The Hawaiian nodded.

"You saw the body." It was not a question but, rather, a reminder of an earlier statement.

"We saw it. The fire was still burning, but they managed to get it out of the wreckage very quickly."

"The police."

"No," the Hawaiian said. "The paramedics." He was familiar with interrogations and knew he was the subject of one now. He wondered, if it came down to it, whether he should lie or tell the truth. He thought about his brother outside with the unleashed Dobermans and something lurched inside him. Hatred and fear commingled, vying for supremacy.

"You saw them take the body out of the car."

"Pry it out's more like it."

Fat Boy Ichimada nodded. "Go on."

"There was already quite a crowd. The police were spending a lot of time directing traffic around the crash site. We had our opportunity. You told us what to look for."

"And these things?" The thick brown finger buried itself anew in the ashes on the desk top. "How did you get them?"

The Hawaiian shrugged. "Like I say, the cops were busy with traffic along the highway. They needed volunteers right off to fight the fire—to help get the driver out."

"So you and your brother volunteered."

29

"We were at the car. Right there," the Hawaiian said. "We got everything there was. But as you can see, it was all burned. 'Cept this. We found it near the car, so it wasn't singed or nothing." He held out a short length of braided cord of a red so dark it was almost black.

Fat Boy Ichimada stared at it, expressionless. "What about the trunk?"

"Popped open on impact. Wasn't nothin' there that shouldn't've been."

Fat Boy Ichimada's mouth pursed. "But it is not here, is it?"

"Not what you described."

"I want it."

"I know."

"Find it."

The Ellipse Club was located on New Hampshire Avenue, almost midway between the John F. Kennedy Center for the Performing Arts and the Watergate Hotel. From its lofty, thick-curtained windows one had an unobstructed view of a slice of Rock Creek Park and, beyond, the Potomac River.

Michael had not heard of the Ellipse Club, but in a city that was home to a thousand clubs, organizations and associations, that was hardly surprising. Besides, he never had been a member of Washington society.

He went up the granite steps of a building with an imposing Federal-style facade. A uniformed steward met him in the vast entryway and, after hearing his name, nodded, gesturing. He was led up a wide mahogany-ballustraded staircase, through a second-story gallery. The steward knocked on a paneled oak door, then opened it for Michael.

The room, large and high-ceilinged, had about it that unmistakable air of a gentleman's club in the traditional sense. Over the years, a conglomerate of well-worn leather, dusty velvet, cigar and pipe smoke and men's cologne had seeped so thoroughly into the furniture, carpet, even the walls, that nothing short of complete demolition would eradicate it.

Three huge windows were spaced along one wall. In between, leather wing chairs dark with age and use were ranged against the cream-and-gilt walls. At each end of the room, glass-and-patinaed oak cabinets displayed an impressive array of vintage ports, sherries, brandies and Armagnacs dating back to the mid-1800s. Two large portraits filled walls otherwise studded with brass sconces. One was of George Washington, the other was of Teddy Roosevelt.

The center of the room was dominated by a massive, carved fruitwood conference table around which eighteen chairs were arrayed in perfect order. A dozen of these were occupied as Michael entered. The air was blue with smoke.

Jonas Sammartin, unwrapping steel-framed glasses from his head, rose, hurried to greet him. "Ah, Michael. Right on time," he said, extending his hand. "Let's sit down." He led Michael to an empty chair at the conference table.

Michael took a moment to glance at the people there. It was clear that they were involved in serious discussion. He was stunned to discover that he recognized almost all of them. Four of them were Japanese, a delegation, it seemed clear. The leader was Nobuo Yamamoto, president of Yamamoto Heavy Industries. His company was Japan's largest automobile manufacturer, as well as the designer of its new, experimental high-technology jet planes. If Michael remembered correctly, the Yamamoto family concern rose to prominence during the years just prior to World War II, when the firm was engaged in making the world's most advanced airplane engines. Time had indeed changed, but the Yamamotos' prosperity certainly did not.

The other distinguished Japanese was the head of his country's preeminent electronics firm. Michael recognized him because there had been a recent article about his computer-chip division in the *International Herald Tribune*. It focused on the company's increasingly adversarial position with the United States government regarding imports and escalating American import tariffs.

As for the Americans around the table, they read like a who's who of government. Michael read the slip of paper Jonas slid across to him, matching names with faces. There were two cabinet members, the undersecretary of defense, the head of the House Foreign Trade Subcommittee, the Senate Foreign Affairs Oversight Committee chairman, and two men whom Michael recognized immediately as being the president's top advisers on foreign policy.

The younger of these two men was speaking now. "—is clear evidence that certain Japanese electronics firms have been dumping semiconductors on the market like crazy. I am not accusing anyone at this table, but I urge you to take this under advisement. Unless this illegal practice is ended immediately, the Congress of the United States will end it for them."

"This is true," said the chairman of the Senate Foreign Affairs Oversight Committee. "In this matter, both Houses are unanimous in intent. We are preparing to pass serious import tariffs in order—as we see it—to protect American companies who cannot compete with their Japanese counterparts."

"Congress is responsive to the will of the American people," the House representative said. "Pressure on us is fierce, and it's mounting. Senators and representatives are listening to the panic talk. I come from the great state of Illinois. All my constituents can think of is, less imports means more jobs for Americans."

"Pardon me for saying so," Nobuo Yamamoto said, "but enacting this legislation will also mean a period of economic isolation. Forgive my forwardness, but that is something your country cannot endure at this juncture in its history. Your enormous national debt, already caused by a slackening in American exports, will become intolerable. Isolationist legislation will strangle *all* exports." Yamamoto had a square, open face, topped by steel-gray hair. His eyebrows were white and bushy; his neat moustache was the same color. He had a clipped, precise manner of speech and though, like all Japan-born Japanese, he had some difficulty pronouncing *r*'s and *l*'s, he was not at all self-conscious about it.

"It is no secret how weak the U.S. economy is these days," Yamamoto continued. "In the past, when our imports were making their initial impact overseas, the export deals your agricultural sector made could keep you afloat. The surplus wheat and grain you would sell to India, China, Russia, and the rest more than offset the business losses at home from the influx of high-quality Japanese cars and electronics.

"It used to be you could make a good living feeding the rest of the world. But no more. You have exported so much technology that you lost your best customers. Now you are doing less subsidizing of your own farmers, and their surpluses are going for ridiculously low prices on the world markets.

"But all of this is your own doing. You had ample opportunity to regear your own industry to create high-quality products. You had ample time to adjust your agriculture to a changing worldwide economic picture. The fact is that you did neither.

"It seems to me unjust that you will now punish us for something that is not of our doing."

"One moment," said the older of the president's advisers, an economist of some note. "You make no mention of your country's impenetrable import barriers, your obstinate refusal to abide by agreements your own government signed with ours regarding the proliferation of Japanese computer chips on an already glutted world market."

"And you," Yamamoto said steadfastly, "make no mention of the steadily rising yen which, combined with my company's self-imposed export limitations to your country, has severely limited profits and caused us to reevaluate our current business methodology."

"Is it not true, Mr. Yamamoto," the economist said in a rising voice, "that you had no intention of ever limiting exports to this country on your own? Is it not true that what you charitably define as 'self-imposed export limitations' were in fact forced by the American quotas? Is it not also true that your company has repeatedly and willfully farmed out the manufacturing of automotive parts to Korea and Taiwan so you can evade this government's automobile-import quotas?"

"Sir," Yamamoto said in an unruffled tone, "I am seventy-six years old. It has been my avowed wish to see Yamamoto gain a ten percent hold on the worldwide car market. I doubt, now, that I will see my dream fulfilled before I pass away."

"You are not answering my allegations," the economist said, red-faced with frustration.

"Such scurrilous questions do not warrant answers," Nobuo said. "The reputation of Yamamoto Heavy Industries is unassailable. By you or by anyone else."

Michael was studying the Japanese carefully. As Nobuo Yamamoto spoke, Michael noted several things. The first was that Yamamoto was the clear spokesman for the entire delegation. Though the head of the electronics concern was a man of great esteem in Japan, he was nevertheless deferring to Yamamoto here in this room. Since, to a Japanese, face—outward esteem—was everything, this fact was not to be taken lightly. It was Yamamoto who was scoring all the points; it was Yamamoto who was gaining great face.

The second was that Yamamoto was cleverly directing both the tone and the content of this meeting. He wanted this adversarial confrontation and had baited the Americans into making fools of themselves, to boot. His words, delivered so calmly, so neutrally, were nevertheless calculated to wound

33

the Western psyche as deeply as possible. The idea of a foreigner telling Americans how to run their own economy must seem intolerable to these men. But as with all Japanese negotiating, there was a hidden agenda here. Michael began to wonder just what it might be.

"You seem oblivious of the consequences of your actions," the younger of the president's advisers said. "Your seeming obstinacy to taking responsibility for the international ramifications of your actions is appalling. I would like to point out to you that unless we can come to some basic formula of compromise here, the future economic outlook for Japanese products in this country will be bleak indeed.

"If the Congress of the United States does in fact pass the protectionist legislation now pending, Japanese profitablity in cars, computers, consumer electronics and the like will plummet. I need not remind you, Mr. Yamamoto, that the United States is currently Japan's most lucrative overseas market by a wide margin. Can you imagine the chaos caused in your country by abrupt closing of such a market? This is precisely what we are suggesting will occur unless we get written assurances from you and the members of your delegation that some restraints will be imposed."

"I appreciate the gravity of the situation," Yamamoto said. His eyes regarded the American coolly. "But I must reiterate that we refuse to be unfairly penalized for a situation not of our making. But as a concession to our American friends, we have agreed to a compromise. You have the papers before you. And—"

"This!" cried the economist, brandishing several documents. "This proposal is ludicrous. It is less than a quarter of the minimum cuts we require!"

"What you *require*," Yamamoto said, making the word sound somehow unclean, "can hardly be construed as a compromise. Your proposal asks us to cut off both our hands."

"In order to save the body," the senator said, smiling. "Surely you can see the wisdom in such a proposal."

"What I see," Yamamoto said softly, "is an insistence that Japanese industry return to the state it was in twenty years ago. This is intolerable. Imagine your own reaction were I to make such a proposal to your government."

"You'd never be in that position," the economist said. He was obviously on the attack. "Let's cut all the fairy stories and get down to business. You're going to take our proposal and like it, and I'm going to tell you why. Because your alternative is such a drastic curtailment of Japanese exports into the United States that you'll think you're back in wartime."

The atmosphere in the room had become chilly. Michael had seen the president's older adviser wince. But it was too late to undo the damage. Yamamoto sat stiffly in his chair. His gaze, directed at the economist, was unwavering. "No one is forcing your consumers to buy our products," he said. "But the fact is that people recognize quality, and quality is what they seek out. Quality is the hallmark of Japanese products. As a nation, we have labored for three decades to overcome the American slogan 'Made in Japan' as meaning 'made cheaply.' Now that we have succeeded, you cannot expect us to relinquish what we have fought so hard to attain. I am afraid that you are asking the impossible. And frankly, I am surprised that you are even making the suggestion of coercion."

"There has been no talk of coercion, Mr. Yamamoto," the younger of the president's advisers said lamely. "If there is a confusion in terms, it is only because we are men of different cultures and languages."

There was silence for a time. Nobuo Yamamoto's stern face seemed to dominate them all, even the powerful visages of Washington and Roosevelt looking down upon the tense scene from their places of honor on the cream-and-gilt walls. "Apologies," Yamamoto said at last, "require the sincerity of contrition." He pushed his chair away from the table, and the others in the Japanese delegation followed suit. "There is, I am afraid, no sense of that purity here. In such an atmosphere, an honorable solution is quite out of the question." With that, he led his delegation from the room.

Jonas did not wait for the postmortem. He took Michael out into the gallery as quickly as protocol dictated. They saw Nobuo and the Japanese contingent heading down the wide staircase to the first floor. Was it his imagination, or did Michael see Yamamoto's dark eyes lock on his face for a moment before the Japanese disappeared down the staircase?

Jonas led them into an adjacent room, which was laid out like a library. Bookcases, Oriental carpets, more deep leather wing chairs filled the space. Between the chairs, small oval mahogany tables held silk-shaded reading lamps.

As soon as they sat down, a steward appeared. Jonas ordered coffee and brioches for them. They were near a tall, lead-glass window. Willows bent in the wind, sweeping down to the Potomac. Birds fluttered in their branches.

"What did you make of that?" Jonas asked as their breakfast was brought in.

"Quite a show."

"A spectacle, yes!" He sipped at his coffee, which he drank black. "Damn Japanese! They're as hardheaded now as they were during the war and immediately afterward."

"Someone should have vetted the American delegation more carefully," Michael said.

Jonas looked at him. "Really? Why do you say that?"

"Because of the economist."

"Oh, him!" Jonas grunted, waved his hand. "He's a genius, really. Brilliant man. I don't know what the president would do without him."

"He may be a genius at economics," Michael said, "but he's a patsy when it comes to diplomacy."

"You mean that remark about the war. That was unfortunate."

"I wonder," Michael said.

Now Jonas was interested. "Meaning?"

"Yamamoto maneuvered the entire proceedings." And when he saw the look on Jonas's face, he added, "Didn't you know?"

"I'm not sure I understand."

"Yamamoto came to this meeting wanting something."

"Sure." Jonas nodded. "He wanted a compromise."

Michael shook his head. "I don't think so, Uncle Sammy. He was bent on finding a nerve. He found it, and he exploited it to its fullest. He maneuvered the economist into insulting him. He lost face, but deliberately so."

"It was just an unfortunate incident," Jonas persisted. "The president will send a note of apology, and we'll be back at the negotiating table by the end of the week."

"By the end of the week," Michael predicted, "Yamamoto and the delegation will be back in Tokyo."

"I don't believe it."

"For some reason, he wanted these talks to break off. And he wanted the Americans to come off as being responsible for it." He looked at Jonas. "Can you think of a reason why Yamamoto would want that? I mean, how important are these talks?"

"They're crucial," Jonas said. He sipped at his coffee, stared meditatively out at the water. "You ever hear of the Smoot-Hawley Act? In 1930, Congress passed trade restrictions. Effectively, it made us an isolationist country. The result was an economic depression. No exports, no jobs, companies declaring bankruptcy right and left. It was a nightmare. A nightmare that is about to occur all over again if what you say is true and Yamamoto's delegation is returning to Japan. The bastard was telling the truth on one thing—our economy's shot to hell. We're as weak as a newborn kitten. This national deficit is sitting on our shoulders just waiting to squash us. The economy of the middle of the country is dying at a rapid rate, and there doesn't seem to be a damn thing we can do about it.

"And maybe you *are* right. The Japanese are like goddamn dogs. They can smell a weak negotiating position and they're quick to capitalize on it. If that's the case, we've really buried ourselves. Yamamoto Heavy Industries is working on the top-secret FAX jet fighter. They won't let us anywhere near it. We've been pushing the Japanese to increase their defense budget, but by buying American matériel. McDonnell-Douglas and Boeing make tens of millions of dollars selling off their Japanese sales. If Nobuo Yamamoto actually puts the FAX on-line anytime soon, it could blow our biggest aerospace firms out of the water."

"So this is the kind of thing you and Dad were involved in," Michael said. He was fascinated by what he had just witnessed, but after all, he had come here to discover how his father had died; that was uppermost in his mind. "I can't believe that after all these years I had no idea of what goes on at the bureau."

"What did you imagine?" Jonas said.

"I don't know," Michael confessed. "The name Bureau of International Trade Exports never meant much to me."

"But you must have been curious," Jonas persisted. "Every child wants to know what his father does. Surely you must have asked him."

" 'I travel, Michael.' That was what Dad said. 'I go to Europe, Asia, South America.' "

"And that was all?"

"Once he said, 'I serve my country.' "

"Ah." Jonas said. The emphasis he placed on that one syllable made it clear that he felt they had come to the crux of the matter. He produced a gray-bound folder from an inside pocket and handed it over.

"What's this?" Michael asked.

"Look inside," Jonas urged. And as Michael complied, he

37

supplied a running commentary. "Yesterday, you asked me how your father died. This is how. The photographs you are looking at were taken within an hour of the crash. As you can see, the fire did at least as much damage as the impact. Perhaps more. It's difficult to qualify such intense traumas."

Michael's hands were shaking; he had come to the shots of the charred remains of a body: his father's. He had come to the last photo, a close-up. He felt sick in the pit of his stomach. No child should have to see his father like this. He looked up sharply. "Why did you show me these?"

"Because you asked how your father died. This is not an easy question to answer, and it is important that you understand fully the consequences of your request." Jonas took the file back, closed the top, used a small metal object to seal the folder shut. "Your father was not lying when he said that he served his country. Nor was he speaking euphemistically." He put the file away. "It was a literal statement."

"He worked for the federal government," Michael said. "I know that." An echo in the back of his mind. Audrey's voice, soft and penetrating in the still of the night: *Do you know how Dad died?* What did she suspect? *You're the bogeyman. You tell me.*

"First, you should know that BITE is a name that I created long ago," Jonas said. "Second, the bureau does not exist. At least, it does not function in the world of international trade, budgets, tariffs and the like."

"Then what were you doing attending such a high-level meeting?" Michael asked. "And how were you able to get me in?"

Jonas gave him a small, self-deprecating smile. "After all these years, I believe I have some power in Washington."

Michael gave him a peculiar look. There was a hollow sensation in his stomach, as if he were in a plummeting elevator. "Who are you, Uncle Sammy?" he said. "I never asked you that. I think it's time I did."

"Your father and I built BITE," Jonas said. "From the ground up. We were soldiers, Michael, your father and I. Soldiering is what we knew. When the war ended, we thought our usefulness was at an end. We were wrong. We became soldiers of a different sort. We became spies."

There was much to be done that morning, and by default, Audrey was in charge of it. That it was all unpleasant would not have been so bad, she thought gloomily as she dressed, if the guilt she had exposed to Michael the night before wasn't weighing so heavily on her.

The arrangements for Philip Doss's funeral had to be made. Lillian had expressly forbade the bureau from handling it. Audrey had heard her mother on the phone, presumably with Uncle Sammy, her voice sounding shrill and sharp-edged.

Whatever Lillian was feeling, she would not—perhaps could not—express it verbally. But Audrey collected the minute manifestations of her mother's inner tension as a peeper will furtively hoard his glimpses of forbidden purience. And like a peeper, Audrey felt like an outsider with a compelling, almost shamefully intimate, connection to a dark interior. It frightened her as much as it fascinated her.

Audrey knew her mother well. Lillian Doss required the limitations of the supremely rational world in order to function properly. In it, death was as natural as life. One began, one ended. It happened to all living things. She was comfortable with the known: with set limits, boundaries with which one fended off the limitless dark of chaos. Rules and regulations were her communion and her confessional. And she would, Audrey had discovered, fight tooth and nail to preserve the sanctity of her rational world.

Lillian's self-possession was legendary both within the family and among its circle of friends. That was why there was no one to do the unpleasant things that had to be done today except for the two women. Lillian firmly believed that death—like sickness—was the province solely of the immediate family. In fact, to Lillian, death and sickness were very much the same. Save that the former lasted a good deal longer than the latter.

"Whatever has to be done," Audrey had heard her mother say to a close friend, "my daughter and I will do ourselves." Michael had been there as well, and Audrey had seen him turn his head in Lillian's direction. It was not the first time she had shut him out, Audrey knew. Nor, she suspected, would it be the last.

The funeral home was white on the outside, dark wood on the inside. Special arrangements had to be made because the body had to be flown in from Hawaii, and then the bureau had had the remains for several days.

It should all have been over and done with by now, Audrey thought, only half hearing the dreary intoning of the funeral director. The air was stultifying, as if whatever chemicals were used for embalming had seeped into the offices.

At last it was over, and as she had promised, Audrey took her mother out for lunch. In truth, her stomach was not interested, but she knew she had to eat sometime.

After the dark, cheerless morning spent with necrophagous men whose mournful expressions seemed as bogus as silk flowers, Audrey was ready for sunlight. Accordingly, she chose a new restaurant in Alexandria, not for its food but for its greenhouselike front room, paneled in great slabs of glass, which was perpetually bright and warm during the day.

She ordered Bloody Marys for them both, and set aside the menus. There was no point in giving her mother a menu— when she went out to lunch, Lillian always ordered chicken salad and iced tea with lemon, into which she put two packets of Equal. She kept the Equal in her handbag in case the restaurant served another brand of artificial sweetener.

"I'm glad that's finished," Audrey said. "What a relief to be out of there."

Lillian fished in her purse until she found a tiny mother-of-pearl box. She shook out an aspirin and, when the drinks came, downed it with her first swallow.

"Do you have a headache, Mother?"

"I'm fine," Lillian said.

Audrey watched her mother take the pain-killer. "It was a terrible morning."

"I felt as if I was choking in there," Lillian said. She looked around sadly. "Nothing seems the same anymore. It's as if I've come home from a long trip to find that nothing's left of the neighborhood." She sighed. "Too often it's not the neighborhood but oneself that's changed."

Audrey, listening to her mother, was becoming increasingly concerned. "Why don't you go away for a while," she said. "There's no earthly reason for you to stay here."

"There's my job."

"Take a leave of absence," Audrey said. "God knows you've earned it. And who's going to complain? Grandfather?"

"Just because I work for my father," Lillian said, "is no reason to take advantage of being family."

"Compassionate leave is not taking advantage," Audrey said. "Why not go back to France? You love it there. Remember that delicious place near Nice you told me about once? The place that had once been a cathedral?"

Lillian smiled. "A monastery."

"Well anyway, it was old. I remember your telling me about

it. What a wonderful time you had there. I wish you had been able to go with Dad."

"That is between you and me, it is our secret. I never told anyone else about that place," Lillian said. "Anyway, your father had no time for vacations."

"And now," Audrey said, "it's too late." She could feel the emotion welling up inside her again, just as it had at the funeral home. She put a hand up to her face. "Oh God, it was so horrible in there. Having to decide what kind of casket to put him in, looking at the prices."

"There's no use in talking about it, dearest," Lillian said. "What's done is done. We had a difficult job to do and we did it."

"You sound as if we're soldiers off to war," Audrey said, mystified.

"Do I?" Lillian evinced some surprise. "Well, perhaps we are, in a way. Courage and duty must guide us now. God knows your father can't."

Audrey began to cry. She had fought the tears back all morning, retreating into a kind of protective cocoon while the mortician took them through his macabre three-ring circus.

God knows your father can't.

She wept into hands cupped over her face.

"All right, now," Lillian said softly. She put her hand over her daughter's. "Be brave, dearest. That would be what your father would tell you if he were here."

But he's not, Audrey thought. Oh, I wish he were! She was abruptly angry. "I can't believe you're still spouting that nonsense! I don't even know what bravery means! Bravery is one of those mysterious terms men always talk about but can never explain either to themselves or anyone else." She was making a concerted effort to gather herself together. "That was always his hold over you."

"It was his hold over all of us," Lillian reminded her. "Including you."

But whatever control Audrey could summon was fast slipping away from her. The tears—or more likely, the swirl of primal emotion that had caused them—were lifting chunks of detritus from the dark pool of her unconscious. "He felt he had failed by siring a daughter, and I paid him back in kind. He wanted two sons," she cried. "Yes. Yes. He made that perfectly clear. Many times."

Lillian stared at her daughter. "Did you ever, *ever* hear him say that?"

"He didn't have to say it," Audrey said. "I could see the disappointment in his eyes every time he'd watch me swing a bat or throw a baseball."

"Your father was proud of you, Audrey. He loved you very much."

"Mother, don't you understand? I never got to know him!" Despite herself, she was weeping again. "And now I never will!"

"My poor baby," Lillian said, reaching across the table. "Oh my poor, poor baby."

"Spies," Michael echoed. He had said the word without really understanding it. Stunned, he had said nothing as they went down the wide staircase of the Ellipse Club, collected their coats from the steward and went out to Jonas's waiting limousine. During the short ride to BITE headquarters in Fairfax, Michael had stared mutely out the heavily tinted bulletproof windows. It was only after the car had deposited them inside the bureau's compound that he had said anything.

"BITE is an intelligence organization focusing on external threats to the United States," Jonas said.

"You're a spy?"

"Yes," Jonas Sammartin said. "Your father was as well. And a damn fine one, too."

Michael took a deep breath. He felt as if he had woken up one morning to find his entire world transformed into an alien landscape. Nothing around him seemed right or real. "What exactly did my father do?" he said at last. He had had to force himself to ask the question; his mouth seemed full of choking dust.

"Your father worked as a field operative," Jonas said. "He would never have been happy behind a desk. His field name was Civet. He was what we call a Cat. And like all Cats, he was involved in wet work." They were outside the BITE offices, walking down a tree-lined path. But they were still within the compound, still surrounded by chain-link fences, guard dogs, electronic sensors, perimeter trip wires. "It refers to a very specialized kind of field work." Plane trees interspersed with magnolia threw shade in their direction. It was already hot and muggy and the shadows were to be appreciated. "Only the most elite agents qualify to join the Cats."

"And what do Cats do?" Michael asked.

"I suppose," Jonas said, "that the term *wet work* derives its name from the literal spilling of blood that is involved."

"What are you telling me?"

"Cats are assassins, Michael," Jonas said. "They extract individuals who have been sanctioned by this office."

Stunned, Michael was silent. There was a knot in his stomach. Part of him wanted to run away and hide or break down and cry. Not my father, he thought. It couldn't be. But the truth fit his memory of his father's comings and goings. It fit so many little incidents, unexplainable until now. It was like a complicated jigsaw puzzle, incomprehensible until one missing piece—the key—was produced, linking all the pieces together.

Still, Michael heard himself say, "Not an assassin. That's a corruption of the Arabic *hashashin*. A *hashash* was a fanatic Muslim in the era of the Crusades who secretly murdered Christians and less fanatic Muslim enemies while high on dope."

Jonas Sammartin stopped beneath a magnolia. Its scent was so sweet it was almost cloying. His gray eyes regarded Michael shrewdly. "You hate me now, Michael. It's no good denying it. I can feel the force of it. You hold me responsible for your father's death. For his life as well, I expect. Well, you're wrong on both counts. Your father wanted to be in this line of work. He *needed* it. Yes, I recruited him. But only after I got to know him, got to know what it was he wanted."

Michael shook his head. "That would mean my father *wanted* to kill people."

Jonas's gaze was unwavering. "You know that's not the case, son. Philip did what he needed to do to keep his country safe."

Michael heard the heavy emphasis in Jonas's words and felt the truth of them at the core of his being. In that respect, he was his father's son all right.

"It was your father's choice. His place was not at home. That didn't mean that he didn't love you or Audrey or, God knows, Lillian. What it did mean was that he had a higher calling. Like a priest or a—"

"Priest!"

"Yes, Michael. Your father had a remarkable mind. Extraordinary, even. He saw the world in truly global terms. He knew what was important in the long run."

"All those trips, all the presents he brought back for us,

for the house. You're telling me that each one represents the death of a human being."

"He was doing a necessary job."

"Christ!" Michael said. He was still reeling from the shock of learning just what it was his father had been doing all these years. " 'It's a dirty job, but somebody's got to do it.' Is that it?"

"In a way. Yes."

"Oh Uncle Sammy!"

Jonas heard the despair in Michael's voice, and his heart went out to the younger man. "Your father was a patriot," he said. "You should never lose sight of that, Michael. On the contrary—you should cherish his memory all the more for it."

"I don't know." Michael shook his head. What was he going to tell Audrey?

"You asked me how your father died," Jonas said calmly. He could feel the force of Michael's rage; he knew what a dangerous position he was in.

"I didn't need to see that . . . atrocity. What was the point? Just like I don't need to see the catalogue of assassinations you say he—"

"Then you'll never learn why he died."

That stopped Michael. "You're not going to tell me?"

"I'm sorry to disappoint you," Jonas said. "But I can't. You see, I don't know why your father died."

"What do you mean?" Michael said thickly.

"That car crash your father was in on Maui," Jonas said. "It wasn't an accident."

"My father was murdered?"

"I'm sure of it," Jonas said. "Yes."

"By whom? Do you have any idea, any leads?"

"Just one," Jonas said. He kept his eyes on Michael. "But it's so tenuous I cannot afford to use any field personnel to follow it up. Besides, until we unravel the mystery of who killed your father and why, we can't know which operatives, if any, have been compromised."

The implications of that hit Michael hard. "You mean that he might have been tortured before—"

Jonas put his hand on Michael's shoulder. "I don't mean to imply anything, Michael. But it would be foolish to stumble blindly into a situation of unknown origin."

"Then your hands are tied."

Jonas nodded. "In a sense. Yes. But if I had someone with

your skills, Michael. Someone unknown by operatives and cutouts, well . . ."

Michael stared at him as if he had suddenly sprouted wings. "You want me to take over where my father left off," he said.

Jonas nodded.

"You don't want me," Michael said. "I'm a painter. I putter around a lab and concoct dyes."

"None of my people can touch your father's case," Jonas said. "Any of them could now be known to the adversary parties. I am not in the business of executing my own people."

"This is crazy, Uncle Sammy. I'm not six, and we're not playing cowboys and Indians."

"No," Jonas said seriously. "There is great danger here. I don't want to minimize that. Just as I don't want to minimize your background." He gripped Michael's arm. "Son, your training in the martial arts makes you just about perfect for this assignment."

"What you want is a Chuck Norris," Michael said. "But he only exists in the movies."

"I brought you to that meeting at the Ellipse Club for a reason, Michael," Jonas said. "I wanted to bring home to you how crucial a situation we find ourselves in. This is yet another kind of cold war we're fighting. And it's against a supposed ally. If Japan forces us into these protectionist laws, our economy's going down the tubes just as sure as I'm standing here. This country's in fragile enough shape as it is. There is so much national debt that we're already staggering. We're like a punch-drunk boxer who doesn't know when to quit. The protectionist legislation's going to deliver the knockout punch."

"But what's all this got to do with my father's death?"

"I don't know," Jonas admitted. "That's one of the things I need you to explore."

Michael shook his head. "I'm sorry, Uncle Sammy. I'm just not cut out to be your man."

Jonas pursed his lips, blew air out in a sharp burst. "Do me one favor, at least."

Michael nodded. "If I can."

"Think about what I've said. Think about your duty."

"To my country? That's what suckered my father into this game of yours."

But Jonas was already shaking his head. "No. I mean your

duty to your father. I think you owe it to him to finish what he started. And to find out who murdered him."

"That's your opinion," Michael said shortly.

"At least do as I ask," Jonas said. "As a personal favor. Then come and see me at the office tomorrow, or the next day."

Michael looked into the older man's eyes. He remembered that face, striped in warpaint, falling down in mock death as Michael shot him with his toy six-gun. He nodded. "All right."

It was only much later that Michael understood the ultimate implications of his promise.

A knock on the door announced Ude. The big man slid open the rice-paper screen, bowed until his forehead touched the floor, then came across the threshold on his knees. He knelt on the fragrant *tatami*, waiting.

Kozo Shiina was from the old school. He did not, as so many of his associates had, have a Western-style room in his house. There were no informal meetings, therefore. Each occasion at his house was formal, adhering to the strict code of etiquette centuries old. Here, it was as if the Westerner had never set foot on Japanese soil.

Looking at Ude, he sighed. Years ago, he knew, it was easy to recruit young people into the Yakuza. The lower classes, the disenfranchised, the outcasts, all were more than eager to become part of a highly disciplined machine such as the Yakuza. Here in the Japanese underworld they could make money, gain prestige, recover the face they had lost in various ways in the day-to-day world.

Nowadays, the outcasts were youngsters whose wildness was difficult, if not impossible, to contain. They seemed to have no ties to the past. They were only marginally interested in honor, in *giri*—that certain form of obligation that remained today one of the linchpins of Yakuza society. They most certainly were not concerned with discipline.

Shamelessly, they eschewed pain as a valueless commodity. These misfits were, in Shiina's opinion, the true criminals of his society, not the Yakuza, who lived by a strict code of honor and who had a long and illustrious history of altruism.

No, these young punks lived by night in a semidrugged stupor, spattered with music of mind-numbing volume. They were anarchic and, as such, totally alien to Shiina's way of life. They wanted money from him to feed their habits, not to build a family, a way of life for themselves.

46

Of course Shiina was not above exploiting them to achieve his ends. He had commissioned exhaustive studies of these punks and had discovered that they were not worthless after all. They, too, could serve a purpose, even if they themselves were unaware of it.

Shiina made absolutely certain of his psychological and emotional profiles before setting the last stage of his plan in motion. He saw at once the advantage these people would provide him, and he lost no time in discovering a way to use them. He did not feel remorse at what had become of the new generation. Only anger. The anger a great field marshal feels in war. The anger that burns inside him and ignites the courage to order his men into battle, knowing that blood will be spilled, lives will be lost. The anger of the righteous.

This burned inside Shiina with a force no reasonable man could possibly understand. But then it was said that war was not born of reason but of hunger. Those who longed for war often justified their action by saying that they were bringing order out of anarchy. But in fact they were merely replacing one reality with another. All of them—the righteous and just, the madmen and tyrants—had one thing in common: They hungered to imprint their conception of order on others. And Kozo Shiina was no exception.

"I am gratified that you stopped here on the way to the airport," he said now.

Ude knew what he meant. "I was not followed. I made certain of that."

Shiina gave no outward sign, but he was pleased.

"You do not trust Masashi, do you?" Ude asked.

"He is your *oyabun*," Shiina said by way of answer. "He is *oyabun* of the entire Taki-gumi now, the largest and most powerful of Japan's underworld clans. You must be loyal to him."

"I was loyal to Wataro Taki," Ude said. "He was magic. He was the one. Now that he is gone . . ." He shrugged.

"There is *giri*," Shiina pointed out.

"*Giri* is the burden hardest to bear," Ude said. "My obligation ended the moment Wataro Taki died."

"But surely your loyalty—your obligation—must lie somewhere."

"It is to the Taki-gumi," Ude said. "The clan is Wataro Taki's creation. Whatever or *whoever* ensures the dominance of the clan will have my loyalty."

Shiina broke out tea. For a long time, while he brewed it,

47

stirred it with the whisk and served it, there were no other sounds in the room. After they had both drunk—Ude before his host—the old man said, "Were it me, I would be thinking: How can I trust a man who rejoices in his own father's death and then orders his brother's demise."

"You ordered Hiroshi's death," Ude said pointedly.

The old man shook his head. "Remember clearly," he said not unkindly. "I *suggested* it. It was Masashi who ordered it." He shrugged. "It seems to me that my role was the minor one. After all, Hiroshi Taki was not my brother, he was Masashi's. And the decision was Masashi's to make."

"He did it in order to save the Taki-gumi," Ude said. The dregs of his tea had long ago grown cold. "Joji is weak. Now Masashi has taken Wataro Taki's place."

"And you said yourself that Wataro Taki was magic. He was the one," the old man said softly. "Can you imagine that Masashi is, also?"

Ude looked down at his cup. He was very still. The sounds of someone stirring in the corridor could be briefly heard. In time, he said, "The Taki-gumi must remain preeminent."

"I have promised Masashi that I will make him the first shogun of *all* the Yakuza clans."

"Masashi is not Wataro," Ude said. "He does not have the magic. He is not the one."

"But I am," Kozo Shiina said. Which was, after all, what this meeting was all about.

Ude considered carefully before he answered. "I will do what you wish."

Kozo Shiina nodded. "You will not change anything. You will continue to take orders from Masashi. But now you will report everything to me. On occasion you will do as I request. For this, I will protect you. I will elevate you." The old man watched him. "In return there will be an obligation."

"What kind of an obligation?"

"First," Shiina said, "you will take a later flight. This must be done because you must make a detour to Joji Taki's house."

"And what will I do at Joji Taki's house?" Ude asked, curious.

"I will tell you everything you must say to Joji Taki," Shiina said. "It is very simple."

"Nothing," Ude said, "is ever simple."

"Except for you," Shiina said forcefully. "From now on, the only thing you must keep in your mind is your obligation to me."

48

"Giri," Ude said.

"Giri," Shiina acknowledged.

The big man bowed his head before his liege lord. "So be it."

It was raining.

Her face was on the wall: a shadow, larger than life.

Michael was dreaming of Za.

He had begun a series of paintings of women, using a different model for each, but he had abandoned the project prematurely, not really knowing why.

Then he saw Za at a studio and understood immediately. It was one woman he wished to paint, not many. She was *the* woman. He hired her and began what was to become his most celebrated series of work: *The Twelve Inner Aspects of Woman.*

Michael made it a rule never to become involved with his models. But Za was different. He had fallen in love with her.

Za lived with a man, but that had no moral meaning for her. Za thought only of what was happening to her at the moment. Tonight—not to mention tomorrow—could not have meant less to her.

Having a relationship with someone, she said, was like owning something. Soon all the value one once saw in the object was gone. What was left was only the act of ownership.

It was raining. Blue rain. The streetlamps on the Avenue Élysée Reclus turned the rain blue. It clattered against the panes of the skylight in Michael's atelier.

The night Za finished her work and did not go home.

Her face on the wall, a shadow, larger than life.

Her flesh wet, as if she had been rained on.

Michael had not wanted to take her to bed. He wanted her here, in front of the half-finished painting. There was a sense that the primitive energy from the act they were about to perform would infuse the painted image with uncanny life.

Already he had the artist's intimation of greatness about this work.

His flesh trembled as it came into contact with hers. She had enormous eyes, black as pitch, black as her cap of hair. The shortness of her hair accentuated the sweep of her jaw, her long neck, the bone structure of her shoulders.

The hollow of her throat was filled up with darkness. Against her pale flesh, it possessed tangible weight. Michael felt as if he could drink the darkness from that hollow.

Za's eyes fluttered closed as his lips opened and his tongue licked the slightly salty sweat from the side of her neck. Her arms encompassed him, her fingertips stroking his muscular back.

His head lifted and his lips found hers, already open, waiting. Her legs were twining around him as if she sought to climb onto him, or into him.

They were still standing, and now she turned slowly in his arms so that her back was toward him. His hands slipped down from where they had cradled her head. They covered her high breasts. The nipples, large and full of color, were so hard she gasped when she felt his palms brush them.

She leaned her head back onto his shoulder and opened her mouth. Their tongues flickered and met again. There was an exquisite sensation in Michael's groin as she circled her buttocks against him. Her slim, firm arms were lifted over her head as she thrust herself into him, back and front.

He dropped to his knees and turned her slowly around to him. The spasmodic light, as lightning forked above their heads, illuminated the planes and dells of her body. The blue rain reflected down on her fully, shadows clothing her in transparent layers.

Her scent was strong as Michael put his hands between her thighs. She opened her legs, bent her knees so that the intimate forest of hair descended toward his upturned face.

He felt her give an involuntary shiver; the muscles in her lower belly rolled as they contracted. Her spread fingers pressed hard against the back of his head.

Her open mouth gave out little cries, but they were of a tone of voice Michael had never before heard her use. It was as if they were being wrenched out of some hidden depths, some private place she would not let the world see. Except now. With him.

"I love your mouth there," she whispered. Then the cries began again.

Perhaps it was then that Michael understood that it was not merely Za with whom he had fallen in love. It was Za the image; Za the icon. The Za that had been created in his mind—his painter's mind—when he had first seen her. He had wanted her then, in this way, but he had not known it; or if he had, he had pushed it deep down inside him. Into *his* private place.

I love your mouth there.

It was not Za the model who had said that.

I love your mouth there.

50

It was Za the icon. Za the painting that Michael was even now in the process of completing.

Her taste, the texture of her inner flesh, wetly flowering open to him, would find its way into the painting. Tomorrow or the next day or the next he would find a way to translate these aspects into color, form, a pattern. Sexuality existed on so many levels, could be expressed on so many more.

"I love your mouth there," she whispered. "There. Yes, there." Gasping now, bent over him so that he felt her breasts again. She wanted as much sensation as her nipples could take. Up on her toes, her hamstrings pulled tight, her pelvis bucking faster and faster. Nails scraping along his back as she approached the end.

He could feel her inner muscles beginning to spasm now, and this was a great spur to him. His penis was so hard. His testicles were drawn up tight, contracted as they were just before he would come.

"Now. Now. Yes, now!" Quick beats, her voice changing yet again, melting with an emotion stronger even than tenderness.

Pushing, pushing. Yes, pushing as her orgasm washed over her, squatting down, engulfing him in hot, hot wetness, urging him all the way in as she sat on his lap, as she felt around behind him for his aching balls and squeezed.

Her wet mouth on his. He was gripped by her, immersed in her wetness, his own spasms beginning. And he passed from dream state to wakefulness with the fluidity of the tide, as he always did. The dream evaporating at precisely the same point, as it always did.

Sadness welling, and an acute sense of loss.

Was there anything to counteract them?

"*Suigetsu.*"

It was not only at dawn that Michael incanted the *Shuji Shuriken*, cutting the nine ideographs.

Suigetsu. Moonlight on the water.

He also spoke the nine magic words when he was agitated.

Suigetsu was a tactic of sword fighting—*kenjutsu*—that he had been taught. It referred to the shadow cast by one's opponent. If one calculated the shadow's length and then stood just outside its range, one would be safe from harm no matter how aggressive one's opponent's attack might be. But moonlight on the water was a two-edged sword. It also referred to the tactic of stealing inside that crucial radius of shadow in order to attack one's enemy.

51

"Suigetsu." He had spoken the word, and it had formed within the room. A shadow within the shadows. Blacker. Moving.

Deep in the fugue state that was required for the incanting of the nine ideographs, Michael still felt the agitation. Za was a dimming memory. The effects of the dream had dissipated. But he remained deeply disturbed by the dream—or, more accurately, by its implications.

He remembered the pose Za had been in when he had entered the room that night. She had turned her head toward him, and in the blue light, with her hair pulled tightly back from her face, her features had taken on the aspect of a person long dead.

The spirit of Seyoko seemed to have risen from her unknown grave at the bottom of the valley. The moment was short-lived, but so intense that Michael had found his knees shaking, his belly turned to water.

Had he made love to Za because he desired her? Or because part of him had rejoiced in at last intimately connecting with his beloved Seyoko? That second thought terrified him enough so that ultimately he had been forced to push Za away from him, so that he would never have to answer that question. Not ever understanding that his fright of living in the past paralyzed him. The terror he himself devised made him powerless to exorcise Seyoko's ghost from his psyche.

It was no wonder, then, that he could not complete the incanting. Its end lay before him like a blighted path down which he dare not venture. For the *Shuji Shuriken* was far too potent to invoke in any but an unruffled state of mind.

Nothing worthwhile was ever accomplished without complete concentration, he had learned. Agitation was one of the two primary enemies of concentration. Confusion was the other.

Strategy dictated that either—or, ideally, both—be instilled in the enemy. Thus were battles won. This was true in business as well as in martial arts, since the former was merely an intellectual extrapolation of the latter. All truly successful businessmen were masters—*sensei*—in strategy.

Michael had always thought of his father as a *sensei* of sorts. Uncle Sammy had been correct in at least this one matter: Philip Doss had an extraordinary mind. Perhaps he was, in his own way, something of a visionary.

It had been his idea for Michael to go to Japan. Only there,

52

he had said, could his son be taught in the highest, purest levels of *kenjutsu*.

He thought of Jonas's request. Of how insane it was. And yet . . . something inside him wanted desperately to go wherever Jonas wanted. If only to keep hold of the tenuous thread that had been Philip Doss. To discover all he could about his father's life—and death.

Michael felt like an outcast who, years later, on returning to the place of his birth, finds that he has no home at all. In the back of his mind, he had always known that there were aspects of his father that he did not want to confront. But now confront them he must if he was ever to come to terms with his father's death. He suspected that he would have no sense of peace until he did.

In his mind, he returned to Japan. The seat of his peace. He recalled the night that Tsuyo had come home from his sad visit to Seyoko's family. It was late, but a lamp was still burning in Michael's room.

Tsuyo had come in. Michael had bowed, said all the proper words of greeting, but by rote. Time advanced slowly. Two shapes sitting cross-legged on the reed mats, shadows stretching away from their backs, mingling at their apex.

"How could it have happened?" Michael's hoarse whisper filled the room with contentious accusations.

In the ensuing silence, he swung around, stared into the *sensei*'s face. "You have all the answers. You tell me."

"I have no answers," Tsuyo said. "I have only questions."

"I have asked myself one thousand questions," Michael said bitterly. "And I come up with the same answer. I should have been able to save Seyoko." He put his head in his hands. "I have packed my bags, *sensei*," he said. "I am going home."

"Your home is here," Tsuyo said. "I do not understand."

"Don't you see?" Michael said. "Don't you get it?" There were tears standing in the corners of his eyes. "It was my fault! I should have found a way to save her! I didn't. Now she's dead."

"Seyoko is dead, yes," Tsuyo said. "No one will mourn her passing more deeply than I. But her death was her *karma*. Why do you feel that you are involved?"

"Because I was there!" The words seemed to choke in Michael's throat, so thick with emotion was he. "I had the power to save her!"

"You had the power to save yourself," Tsuyo said softly. "Which you did. What more can you ask of yourself?"

53

"Plenty!" Michael said hotly.

"Look at yourself," Tsuyo said. "The blood is pounding in your veins. It is rushing up to your face. You are burning with it. You are giving full rein to your temper. Temper is your false mind. You can accomplish nothing—not even speak intelligently or correctly—when you are controlled by your false mind. Your false mind throws up lies, deceits. It drains you of clear thinking and, thus, of power.

"Now your temper tells you that you must punish yourself. But your true mind, which you have managed to bury, knows the truth. It knows that you are guiltless for Seyoko's death."

"If only—"

"If only *what*?" Tsuyo said scornfully. "If only you were a lion, you would rend the flesh from my bones now. If only you were a gnat, I would reach out and slap you down. What nonsense it is you speak!"

"You don't understand!" Michael said helplessly.

Tsuyo, crouched, wrists on his knees, watched Michael carefully. "I went into Seyoko's room before I came in here," he said. "In my absence, someone has been placing a fresh flower in her vase each day." He cocked his head. With his white head of hair, it was he who looked like the lion. "Do you know who that someone might be?"

Michael bent his head, nodded.

"Now I see it all," Tsuyo said. "This has nothing to do with Seyoko." His voice had turned hard. "It has to do with your selfish feelings toward her."

Michael's morose silence was answer enough.

"Finish packing in that case," Tsuyo said, rising. "This school has no use for you."

But of course Michael did not leave. As Tsuyo foresaw, his words, acting as a kind of galvanic spark, shook Michael out of his self-pity. And in the future, it was only when those moods of passion—what Tsuyo called "temper"—arose within him that Michael would recall Seyoko and the ghost that still dwelled within the shadows of his spirit.

Philip Doss's death and the subsequent revelations of his life had shaken the moorings of Michael's meticulously un-planned life. Success—what others called brilliance—had allowed him to indulge this creativity as much as he wished. Now, he suspected, that freedom, which was so important to him, was being threatened. Now Jonas wanted to harness him to the same gritty engine to which Philip Doss had been strapped—and which had ultimately killed him.

Aren't I mad, Michael asked himself, even to contemplate such a thing? He wished that Tsuyo were alive so that he could speak to him, ask his advice. And then, tears burning his eyes, he realized that it was his father he most desperately wanted to communicate with. Where did the time go, Dad? he asked of the darkness. Where did *you* go?

In time, he rose from the lotus position and got back into bed. It was pitch-black in the room. The curtains barely moved. Heavy, moisture-laden air had come in off the Potomac. A low rumble. Somewhere, not far distant, lightning was flashing.

That was Michael's last thought before he dropped off into an uneasy sleep. It was only later that he would understand how severely his agitation had interfered with his concentration.

Surely that was the only explanation for his failing to notice what the pitch-blackness meant. That the security lights had not switched on.

Audrey picked up a gun, aimed it and shot her father through the left eye. But instead of falling, he spoke to her.

I can give you the world. His lips, as blue as the ocean, do not move at all. In fact, they have been sewn shut. A whistling sound accompanies his words.

He wears a three-piece suit that looks curiously like a suit of armor. It shines where moonlight strikes it. He wears metal gauntlets with spikes at the knuckles. In his right hand is a sword of some black substance that appears to smolder, as if it is very hot. In his left hand is a spear with an ivory handle and a blade cut from a translucent jewel.

Here is the earth and the sky. There is no more black hole gaping at her. Instead, a patch with an unblinking eye painted on it covers the ruined orb.

I have given them to you, Aydee. He stretches forth both arms and, in so doing, presents his weapons. Clouds billow and stream behind him, so close that the vapor appears to ruffle his hair.

"What have you given me?" she says. "What have you *ever* given me?" In comparison to his echoing shout, her voice sounds small. She is strangling on the anger she feels.

I have been blinded by my enemies. He moves with inhuman fury. *They have tried to kill me and, instead, have wounded me.*

"It was I who shot you, Father," she cries. "I hated you

55

for what you failed to do for me. You were never there when I needed you. You never thought of me. It was always of Michael. You sent him off to Japan. He was special to you. Always special. You lavished such attention on him, even when you were away from us. You created his schooling in Japan, you monitored his progress every step of the way. Why? Why? Why? Now you're dead and I cannot ask you. I can't even be angry with you without feeling so guilty I want to die myself."

But I am not yet dead, Aydee. Is it that he does not hear her? Or that he does not care?

Appalled, Audrey claps her palms to her ears. "Stop it!" But it does no good. His words penetrate her flesh and detonate in flashes of painful electrical energy. He raises the black sword and it is engulfed in fire. He raises the spear and rain flies off it.

I have much to tell you yet.

So that she jumps with each word he projects into her.

I have much to give you yet.

So that she feels like a fish on a line, jerking and twisting against a pain inside her that she can never be rid of.

Audrey is screaming.

His voice thundering. *Aydee, listen to me! Aydee, Aaaaaaaydeeeeeee!*

Heart pounding, Audrey shot up in bed. Put her hands over her heart as if the gesture could stop the painful pounding. She could feel the blood rushing in and out of her heart, the thump-thump of its beat.

She was bathed in sweat.

The darkness surrounded her like a shroud. Reached over and turned on the bedside lamp. Got out the postcard from her father. It had arrived days before. She had read it, then had put it away, not being able to bear thinking about it in light of her father's death. But now she seemed compelled to hold it again, to read it, as if it were a talisman against the terrible portents of her nightmare.

> *Dear Aydee,*
> *Here I am in Hawaii. For the first time in ages I am truly alone. There is only the golden air to talk with. It's not how I envisioned it. Life has a funny way of doing that to hopes and dreams.*
> *I still don't know whether I have done the right thing. It's the end, Aydee, that is all I know for certain. The*

end of whatever life has been for this family up until now. Is that good? Or bad? I don't know. I wonder if I ever will.

When this reaches you, like a message in a bottle from a far-off place, throw it away. I know that you won't want to. You won't understand that for some time, but please do as I ask.

It's time to go. There's work to be done, even here in paradise. It seems quite fitting, somehow, for it to end here in paradise.

Tell Michael, when you see him, to think of me when he next has his green tea. Tell him to use my porcelain cup. He always treasured it. I'm thinking of the place where you and he almost died. Even in summer, alas, there is not a single heron there.

Love,
Dad

Audrey read the postcard over and over until it was ingrained in her mind. She did not understand it, but it was the last vestige of her father. He was right; she did not want to destroy it. She took it, went slowly into the bathroom. Folding it carefully, she put it in the back of her medicine cabinet, behind a box of Q-tips. Then, quickly, almost convulsively, she took it out again and, before she had time to think about it, she ripped it into tiny squares and flushed them down the toilet.

Reading the postcard had somehow increased the panic the nightmare had engendered in her. Just as she had not been able to destroy the card when she first got it, she had not been able to share its contents with Michael. Now she knew that she must. She had already told Michael she had gotten a postcard from Philip. She resolved to tell him in the morning what Philip had written.

Audrey padded back into the bedroom, relieved at least that she had made that decision, and the light went out. She reached over, turned the lamp switch. Nothing happened. Oh God, she thought. What a time for the bulb to blow.

Drew her knees up to her breast and hugged herself, rocking a little. The blackness seemed overwhelming. It was so palpable it seemed to beat against her eyelids in the same tactile way her father's words had affected her. More than anything else, she wanted light. She wanted to get up, to make her way down the hall to the closet where the spare light bulbs were stacked. But the effort was too much. Just thinking of moving through the darkness seemed to paralyze her.

She gasped, looked up. Had she heard something? Or was it an insidious remnant from her nightmare? The darkness and her father. They seemed to Audrey to be one and the same. To be forged out of nightmare, born in a world so alien to her sensibilities that she had difficulty comprehending their physical shape, let alone their inner nature.

The night is a time for listening.

Isn't that what her father had said to her when she was a child? She remembered him coming into her room in response to her calling out. He would sit on the edge of her bed and she could feel his warmth seeping into her, making her sleepy. It made her think of Christmastime, when the fireplace was alight with sparking fir logs exuding their aromatic oils. When the house was warm and cozy and filled with presents.

"The night is a time for listening, Aydee," her father would whisper. "For listening and for dreaming of possums and hedgehogs out for a stroll, frogs and salamanders swimming in a lily pond, robins and thrushes basking on a branch. Listen for them, Aydee. Listen."

But years later, when she was older, the dark held other secrets of a dreadful nature. The devil would come by night. Vampires would seek the vulnerable necks of their victims. Psychotic murderers would creep over the window sashes to maim, rape and, ultimately, slaughter their . . .

"Ohhh!" Audrey gave a little shudder. What was she trying to do, scare herself to death? The aura of her nightmare continued to pervade the night air. Thick as woodsmoke, it swirled around her, a damp and clammy web that she felt helpless to dissipate.

The darkness. It was her nemesis. She had to overcome it. With a concerted effort, she got out of bed and went to the door. Opened it and went down the hall to the closet for a spare bulb. There, she told herself. That wasn't so bad was it?

With her hand on the knob, she froze. Oh God! Her head turned, questing. Yes, there it was again! A noise.

Her heart beating wildly in her breast, she went to the top of the staircase. Listened. Jesus! Someone was downstairs! Her fingers gripped the banister until all the blood was squeezed out of them.

Audrey gritted her teeth. She had to calm herself. Don't

be such a baby, Aydee, she told herself, unconsciously using her father's language. The house was locked tight. It must be Michael prowling around. She had seen how upset he had been after their talk. That must be it, she decided. He couldn't sleep, either.

Relieved not to be alone, she went down the staircase. Heard the noise again. She was at the foot of the stairs and could tell that the noise was coming from her father's study. Now she knew that it must be Michael. She smiled, went across the dining room and opened the door to the study.

The night is a time for listening.

"Michael—"

Breath cut short in her throat. A guttural sound, saliva drying. The inside of her mouth like cotton, swelling inward to strangle her.

Heard a sound in the darkness. An odd, ethereal whistling, tuneful, hard-soft, almost plangent. The chord of death.

And in the same instant, her nightgown was slit open from right shoulder to left hip. It slithered around her ankles. Like a ripe peach, she was utterly exposed, and supremely vulnerable.

Audrey uttered a little cry and cringed. She backed up, but something was impeding her egress from the study. It was so like her nightmare of a few minutes before that she felt all strength leave her. She moved in ungainly slow motion, as awkward as a racing mare imprisoned within a human-proportioned room.

She whirled around to see what was impeding her and slammed her elbow on the thick edge of the mahogany door against which she was pressed.

Something had hold of her. There was strength, a power of untold proportions, in the grip. Michael could grip her in just this fashion, she thought wildly. His, too, was a power beyond that of the normal. Felt a body pressed against hers and, unthinking, shot out with the heels of her hands.

Audrey was not a weak woman. Years in the family presided over by her father had obliged her to take up physical activity. She had worked out three times a week for most of her life. She had even spent the past several years lifting weights. Therefore, when she attacked, she was swift and powerful.

Freed, she turned, slipped to the carpet as she tripped over a small table. Cried out as the breath was knocked from her. Tried to rise, felt the darkness overwhelming her.

Terrified, she turned her head, saw the shadow moving, so close its heat suffused her. She searched for eyes, mouth, any feature, as if giving the figure some semblance of humanity would in some way allay her panic.

But there was nothing. Darkness within darkness. Body against body, the two struggled. So close they might have been mistaken for one form in terrible conflict.

Audrey could feel soft breath on her cheek. She felt as if she were entangled within barbed wire. Some primitive intuition guided her, and she stuck as close to the other figure as she could. She suspected that remaining in close quarters was her only chance of survival.

Felt an opening and used her knee, drawing it up suddenly between her assailant's legs. She heard the grunt, felt the force of the exhalation so close to her. But the normal gagging reaction never came, and she once again felt the welling up of panic. Now she had the distinct sense that she was fighting something supernatural. Her courage withered.

In some manner unfathomable to her, the figure knew of her change in attitude and took advantage of it. She was rolled over on her back before she had a chance to protect herself. Her mind, half numbed by fear, was several beats slow in reacting. That was all the opening her assailant needed.

Audrey tried to use her knee again, but it was already too late. A sharp blow to the inside of her knee sent fire up her thigh into her hip joint. A nerve nexus point. Audrey knew enough from Michael to understand that her right leg was now useless.

She used her arms, hands and fingers. Tried to gauge an eye, the underside of the jaw, the base of the neck. Thwarted at every turn. Felt a rush, and she thought, Oh God, I'm going to die.

Michael came fully awake within the space of a heartbeat. It was not what he had heard but rather what he had felt. Something had reached down into the delta layers and had given his mind the command to awaken.

He was up and across the pitch-black room in an instant. Took up his *katana*, his Japanese longsword, and, naked, went out into the upstairs hall. Instinct took him past Audrey's room. The door was ajar; he did not need to look in to know that she was not there.

Crept down the staircase on the outside edges of his soles. The wind would have made more noise. He held the *katana* sideways with both hands, elbows slightly bent. He advanced as he had been taught, with his left side forward. His fists, as they curled over the haft of the sword, were in such a position that they could be used as a shield if the sudden need arose.

Without sangaku *you are nothing*, Tsuyo had said. *Discipline. Concentration. Wisdom. These three constitute* sangaku. *Without the three elements you can attain nothing. You may learn to slash, to maim, to kill. But you will be nothing. Your spirit will wither. Your power will diminish, and surely there will come a time when you will be cut down. This will occur not by the sword of a more skilled opponent, but by the force of his enlightened spirit. Without the wisdom of truthfulness, survival is impossible. This is the tenet of the Way.*

Discipline. Concentration. Wisdom.

These were what Michael summoned when he assumed the wheel, the opening *tai* stance that would allow him to rotate his sword in any direction he chose. As dictated by the *Shinkage* school, the wheel was basically a defensive posture.

At the bottom of the stairs, he could see that the door to the study was open. There were tiny sounds . . . Audrey was in there!

Part of him wanted to rush into the study. Discipline. Concentration. Wisdom. He could hear Tsuyo's raspy, inhuman voice emanating between lips that barely moved. *To enter battle and prevail, you must do one thing only*, Tsuyo's mechanical voice whispered again through Michael's consciousness. *In your mind, in your spirit, you must relinquish life and death. They must cease to be of concern to you. Only then will you be a swordsman.*

Michael took it step by step. Through the dining room, to the verge of the study. Through the partly open door, he could feel the night breeze brushing his face. It was far darker in there than it had been in either the hall or the dining room.

He listened. The tiny noises began to coalesce into a recognizable pattern: the grunts and strainings of hand-to-hand combat. Michael recalled the prowler who had prompted his father to have the security lights installed and was about to put aside his sword, figuring to use his body.

He took one step, so that he was straddling the sill. And something stopped him. He could feel the aura of the intruder, and he knew—*knew*—that whoever was inside with Audrey also wielded a *katana*.

Shrugging aside his shock, he moved with absolute silence into the study. Nevertheless, he was overheard.

Eagles shrieked in his ear as a lamp just in front of him was sheared in two. Audrey! his mind shouted. Where are you? Are you safe? Or . . . Felt the appalling proximity of the keen blade, and he lunged forward and out with his sword. Immediately, he regretted it as the other blade struck the top of his, forcing the tip through the carpeted floor.

Michael cursed himself. His anxiety over Audrey's presence had caused him to lose concentration. *An inauspicious attack will fail and, having failed, will both alert your opponent and bolster his determination.*

In the instant it took for Michael to free his blade, he felt the presence of the other's *katana*, a predator's shadow amid a forest of shadows. Without looking, he knew where it was and, now that it was in motion, what its target was.

Tucked his head down into the pit of his stomach as he rolled into a ball. The hardest thing was letting go of his sword. But his life hung in the balance, for he had divined the intent of his opponent: to sever his head from his body.

Slammed into the shadow figure, felt its weight coming down, curling over him. An instant's claustrophobia as he felt a hand searching to cover his nose and mouth as the other's body folded down around him. Put pressure on the small of his back as well, trying to maneuver him into a position where a low-force kick could snap a vertebra or rupture his spleen.

Michael used his elbows to keep his momentum going, in order to roll past the vulnerable spot.

But now his shoulders were mashed against the carpet. The weight of another human being was pressing down on him, and he had no protection for his face. He smelled the chemical before the cold cloth made contact. Held his breath. Still, he felt the caustic fumes penetrating his nostrils.

He wanted desperately to use his hands, but there was so much pressure on him that he knew if he moved his elbows at all, he would be open to an instantly lethal kick. Rolled up in a ball as he was, his legs were of no use to him.

His training allowed him to hold his breath longer than most people, but even he had his limits. He could see nothing but distorted shadows, smell nothing but sweat and fear, hear nothing but the rushing of his own blood through his veins. In the physical stasis they were in, he could feel nothing but the singing inside his brain, the silent scream that presaged the fall into unconsciousness, the swift slide to defeat.

Struggling, Michael found himself thinking of the moment he struck out with his sword, of how that had been his mistake. Replaying the instant over and over, trying to fathom what would have happened if he had done what Tsuyo had counseled. *To meet the enemy with your mind settled in that spot where your fists grip your sword.*

And sinking deeper toward that twilight world where volition is subjugated, where the will cannot work. Where even the Way has no power.

Zero.

He did not want to be there.

"Audrey!"

Screamed her name even as a blackness deeper than the surrounding night lapped at his senses. He was no longer fully in control of his body. He continued to struggle, unaware of what he was doing. His mind, locked within the effects of the chemical-saturated cloth, created a world somewhere between nightmare and semiconsciousness.

Crashing of the sea where there was no sea, reaching for the sky where there was no sky, clawing out from the earth where there was no earth. This was Michael's new world.

One that dimmed, flickered and, at last, gave way to a sensation of falling that never ended.

When he was a boy, Philip Doss had lived on a farm in rural Pennsylvania. A small town in the westernmost section of the state near Latrobe, a beautiful area of dense woods, rolling emerald hills and sylvan lakes.

The Dosses raised chickens. Their days began at four-thirty in the morning and did not end until after sunset. It was a life of grinding work and little reward. Philip's father was continually fighting higher feed prices, disease among his stock and the growing intrusion of large farming combines. Chicken farming was the only thing the elder Doss knew, and while he just about managed to eke out a living for himself and his family, he figured it was better than the alternative—bankruptcy.

Philip hated the farm—the stink of the chickens, the smell of blood when they were slaughtered, the sheer sameness of the life. But he dearly loved the surrounding countryside. He spent the long afternoons staring out at the hills, blue-hazed by distance. He walked down to the way station to watch the Erie Lackawanna freight train rumble by, clickety-clack, riding the rails. He particularly loved that train, would dream about it at night, its headlight piercing the darkness, its long, hooting whistle echoing off the slumbering hills, the blackbirds clattering off the telephone wires in its churning wake.

It wasn't until he was far away from the farm that he understood the significance of its hold over him. The train emanated from an unknown destination. It was an absolute mystery to him, one which he needed to solve. It brought up yearnings inside him, unknowable things that made him toss and turn in bed at night.

Philip's father was a pragmatic man. Thinking back on it, Philip realized that he must have been made so by circumstance. A brown-faced man with leathery skin and eyes the sun had washed of all color, he was continually dragging Philip back from his reveries to do his chores around the farm. Philip's responsibilities were to gather the eggs from the layers' nests before he left for school and to clean out the hen houses after he returned home.

"You'll never amount to anything, son," his father would say to him. "The world's got no use for dreamers. World revolves around hard work; what else keeps it spinning?" He'd eye his son. "Man's got to know that what he wants for himself ain't important. A man's got better things to occupy himself. One day he'll have a family. He's got to provide for them. Make sure life's secure for his children." Philip's mother had died in childbirth less than two years after Philip was born. Philip's father, who had never remarried, did not speak of his wife—or any other wife, for that matter. "Family's what life's all about, son. No more an' no less. Foolish an' a waste of time to think otherwise. The sooner you learn that, the better."

Nothing anyone could have said to Philip could have terrified him as much as this—the thought of living out the rest of his life on this farm, working eighteen hours, seven days a week, doing the same rounds of chores month in month out; it was enough to make Philip break out in a cold sweat. He longed to hop the fast freight that came through town once a day but that streaked again and again through his dreams each night. He longed to climb those blue-hazed hills, to discover what was on the other side. He longed to meet people who were different from himself.

But when he tried to tell his father all this, the words stuck in his throat, and instead, he bowed his head and silently took his rake into the coop to complete his chores.

But in the end, it was the red fox—not the fast freight—that solved the mystery of what was in Philip's heart and changed his life forever.

During a long, particularly bitter winter, when Philip was nearing his fourteenth birthday, a red fox began to find its way into the hen house. It was Philip himself who first found the evidence: blood smears, caked feathers, pieces of the hens' carcasses.

For weeks, Philip and his father tracked the fox across snow-blanketed fields, whispering woods, into a rock-strewn stream bed silvery with ice. Philip, armed with an old but serviceable .22-caliber Remington rifle, watched as his father stopped periodically in their hunt to show him the red fox's

65

spoor: footprints here where the animal's weight broke through the snow's icy crust, here where it brushed against the bole of a tree and left reddish hairs, there where it left its droppings.

As the hunt progressed Philip found himself coming more and more alive, aware. His mind, quick to pick up the tricks his father taught him, began its own questing. So that by the third or fourth time they set out after the fox, it was Philip who led the way, Philip who spotted the animal's spoor.

And in the end, it was Philip who discovered why their trail always petered out in the stream bed. The red fox was more careful here. They had been constantly frustrated and mystified as to why they lost all sign of him in this area.

His father had told him that foxes generally slept in tall grass, their bushy tails curled around them for warmth. But some elemental instinct drew Philip to the banks of the frozen stream, where badgers, moles and similar creatures made their burrows. Sure enough, the fox had gone to ground in one of these recently abandoned holes.

The elation that filled Philip at the moment of discovery was like a white-hot fire.

He remembered his father's voice in his ear: "He's yours, son."

He remembered pulling up the Remington, sighting down its barrel.

Most of all he remembered that moment—as if it could be frozen in time precisely, like the pristine stream bed—when the fox was slammed backward against the burrow wall, the red clay smearing its red and silver back.

The fox was the raider: the killer, the invader, the destroyer. It was the Saracen among the Christians. Philip discovered a deep satisfaction in tracking it down and expunging it from the face of the earth. It was as if he had righted an essential wrong.

Philip sold the farm the day after he buried his father in the earth. The next day he stole a ride on the fast freight. He left western Pennsylvania far behind, but the red fox filled his mind. The memory of tracking that fox, of the moment he had caught up with it, pushed him onward through the streets of one town after another. He was caught up in a restlessness, in a need to feel again the straightening of the cosmic scales. Nothing else could satisfy the anarchic emptiness inside him. He went from towns to cities. And the larger the population, the more he saw the scales of justice as lopsided. In Chicago, he tried his hand at police work for a time. But his maverick personality continually ran him afoul of the political machine entrenched there.

He swung aboard another train, came east to New York. But it was 1940 now, and the war was on. This interested Philip in the most elemental way. Here was the greatest of wrongs that needed righting.

He enlisted in the army. During basic training, his unconventional nature got him into trouble. But luckily for him, he had a drill sergeant with a keen eye, who signed Philip up for special training: for intelligence work in the OSS. The DI's assessment of his charge was correct. Philip proved himself to be one of those special people for whom the armed services are always on the lookout. He never considered his own safety, never contemplated his own death. Rather, it was as if he was surrounded by an invisible aura that not only protected him from harm but kept those around him safe as well.

His superiors at OSS training took full advantage of this quality, putting Philip through the most rigorous and grueling of physical and mental training. He not only accepted what they threw at him, he welcomed the challenges.

And when they put him into the field, they hooked him up with someone they considered "compatible." By this, they meant someone who could get close to Philip, someone who had the "correct" background. Someone, in short, who could tame his maverick spirit.

Philip and a lieutenant named Jonas Sammartin followed the twin prongs of the Allied advance toward the Pacific Rim. They never saw action in the conventional sense. Rather, they used Jonas's forte—decoding ciphers—to intercept Japanese military communications. Using the information, Philip would lead a team of hand-picked men on nighttime forays into enemy camps, to inflict the maximum amount of damage without leaving any trace of who had been responsible.

In 1943, they were at work in the Solomon Islands. Less than a year later, it was New Guinea. Then, with increasing rapidity, the Marianas, Iwo Jima and Okinawa, heading inexorably for the Japanese islands.

So effective were their raids throughout the Pacific that the Japanese high command coined a phrase for them: *ninja senso*. Ninja warfare. While their exploits naturally never made it into the *Stars and Stripes*, the *ninja senso* had gained something of a reputation in the whispered scuttlebutt among the American troops.

In the last six months of the war, in that time after the fire bombing of Tokyo in March 1945, in which fully half the city was incinerated—and before the world changed forever in August of that year, when the *Enola Gay* dropped the atomic bomb on Hiroshima—Philip and Jonas found time to become more than combat buddies who had to rely on one another for their lives. They became friends.

Jonas was the last in a long and illustrious line of military men. His grandfather had been a New York City police captain in 1896, when Teddy Roosevelt had served as head of the city's police board. A year later, the two of them resigned. With mutual friend Leonard Wood, they formed the famed Rough Riders. Jonas's father had been a major in the cavalry during World War I. He had died in France, after having been decorated four times in the field.

Jonas was already living up to his family's reputation. He graduated first in his class from West Point. A strong-willed, by-the-book young man, he distinguished himself at the OSS, astonishing his mentors with his uncanny ability to solve seemingly impossible strategic puzzles. They put him to work in cryptography.

"There's so much death here," Jonas said late one night as they finished off a fifth of Russian vodka, "it's become unreal." They were on a destroyer, heading for Mindanao. The commander, flattered to be ferrying such famous men, had broken out his best liquor for them.

"Life is unreal," Philip said. "That must mean there's no longer a difference between life and death." He remembered the three of them laughing their heads off over that.

"I don't know what life is anymore," the commander said, refilling their glasses. "Jesus, one month is like a day out here. One part of the Pacific's like another, one island full of Japs looks like any other island. All I gotta do is make sure my guns hit what I aim at and be sure I keep my men as safe as I can."

Philip waved his arm, gesturing. "There's more than that out past the horizon. Gotta be."

"Maybe. But isn't that what war is all about?" the commander said. "Death and the compression of time?"

"No," Philip said, unaccountably angrily. "War is about winning."

That morning, the radiation ate Hiroshima alive.

Philip was in the business of death. He did it so well, he would come to understand years later, that he would have no reason ever to do anything else. He was not unlike the poor wretches who had survived Hiroshima and Nagasaki, watching their bodies being corroded by an invisible and incomprehensible force that had taken hold of their lives and would not let go.

Another form of radiation was affecting Philip. He had allowed his work to become his life. And in so doing, his work had become both strict definition and ultimate boundary. In that sense, was it so far removed from the chicken farm in western Pennsylvania that had enslaved his father?

When he and Jonas arrived in Tokyo in November 1946, the city was blanketed with an early snow. They hadn't seen snow for a very long time; they had even forgotten what winter was. The black kimonos stood out starkly against the virgin-white. It was only gradually, as the city dug out from under, when the snow turned ash-gray, that other colors began to be seen: the bright red of a kite, the deep blue of a porcelain cup, the intense green of a cryptomeria tree. Yet they were no more vibrant or memorable than that first startling contrast that had been their first sight of Tokyo that chilly November morning.

In Japan, Philip and Jonas were under the control of a colonel named Harold Morten Silvers. The previous October, President Truman had fired William Donovan, disbanding his brainchild, the OSS. In its place, the president—with the urging of close advisers such as General Sam Hadley—had created an ill-defined, temporary network, the CIG, the Central Intelligence Group. The CIG was, of course, composed of the dogs who had been leashed to the OSS. Silvers was one of the most important of those. He assigned to Philip and Jonas a young CIG aide named Ed Porter, who had come here with the first contingent of the occupation army. Porter was a fresh-faced, regulation-type kid who gave them an extensive tour of the vast, half-burned city.

Late in the afternoon, they arrived in the Asakusa district, north of Tokyo's center. A pale and bloated sun shimmered on the sinuous Sumida River. The place was odd. Tokyo was usually thronged with people, vehicles and energy that even the immediate aftermath of war could not affect. But around here there was nothing: no pedestrians, no traffic, no life.

"This is what's left of the great Asakusa temple," Porter said, pointing to the charred remains of what was now nothing more than a hole in the ground. He walked them through it while he talked in the practiced, dispassionate tone of the professional guide. "This was where thousands of Japanese fled during the fire bombing of Tokyo last March. Three hundred Superfortress bombers dropped over seven hundred thousand M29's. Ever hear of them, you two? Not in your line of work, I expect. M29's are an experimental type of bomb that contain a mixture of incendiary jelly and oil.* Explosions and raging fires ensued."

Porter pointed to the remnants of what appeared to be a couple of blackened pillars. "The temple was built in the seventeenth century. Ever since then, it had survived every natural disaster, including violent earthquakes and the great fire of 1923. The M29's took care of that.

"In all, almost two hundred thousand Japanese died in the fire bombing. That's maybe sixty, seventy thousand more than we estimate died—and will die—as a result of the atomic explosion in Hiroshima."

The Japanese people buried their dead. But they had been given a task: to forget the misery of the war, to turn their faces away from the mistakes of the past and begin a new life. To build a future upon the ashes of the old.

General Douglas MacArthur had also been given a task, that of "redirecting" the new Japan. This concept came straight from an Eyes Only memo from President Truman's desk. It meant not only helping to put Japan's economy back on its feet, but also making sure those feet stayed on the straight and narrow—American-style. This was officially known as the democratization of Japan. It included a new constitution, decentralization of the highly centralized Japanese government, an end to militarism, dissolving the huge *zaibatsu*—the family-owned industrial conglomerates that wielded so much power in prewar Japan—as well as an immediate purge of war criminals and all known and suspected left-wing elements from both the public and the private sectors.

The Tojo-controlled Diet, the Japanese parliament, was "liberated" of its militaristic members. Every day, Philip and

---

* The first experimental use of napalm.

Jonas expected to hear of the beginning of rumored purges throughout the *zaibatsu* hierarchy. But nothing happened.

Until one morning they were summoned to Colonel Silvers's office. As usual, they were greeted by David Turner, Silvers's administrative adjutant. Turner was a man approximately their age. He was tall, slender, bespectacled, with a handsome, ascetic face. Women apparently found him charismatic, for Philip had often seen him out with a variety of unattached WACs or female CIG administrative personnel. Unlike other single CIG men, he preferred American women to the staggering array of Japanese girls available in Tokyo's booming nighttime clubs.

They exchanged greetings with Turner, but from their side they were more than cool, since Philip and Jonas possessed the field man's inbred contempt for office-bound paper pushers, who lacked the courage to test their mettle in the arena of battle.

Turner led them into Silvers's inner sanctum, then he closed the door behind him, leaving the three men alone. They sat on the hard-backed wooden chairs in front of Silvers's desk, and he handed them coded files. During the war, the OSS had been a shadow organization. That was one of the main reasons it had been so successful. Now, in peacetime, there was an urgent necessity to lengthen and deepen those shadows.

"The *zaibatsu*," Silvers said, "still wield an enormous amount of power. That's not surprising since they are the traditional business conglomerates owned and operated by Japan's most influential families.

"According to my intelligence, the Japanese spent a lot of time rewriting log books, accounts, drafts and memos. While we were busy putting together the nuts and bolts of the occupation, their bureaucracy was in the process of getting rid of the incriminating evidence against their most important militarists.

"Of course, we have no proof of this. But the upshot is they did such a good job of it that the war-crimes tribunal can't touch a number of the worst industrialists who were directing the manufacturing of munitions and spurring on the war effort.

"Therefore, it is often . . . difficult if not downright unpolitic for the war-crimes tribunal to go after certain, ah, high-ranking *zaibatsu* members. As you will see from the files, there are a specific number of influential people from this sector of Japanese society who must be eliminated. We cannot—and neither can the Japanese—tolerate the existence of war criminals in this new society the president has committed us to building in Japan, not even those whom the war-crimes tribunal cannot touch."

Silvers brought out a pipe and leather pouch. "Sometimes the democratic process needs a bit of, er, unconventional assistance." He unzipped the pouch. "These individuals cannot be disposed of in the accepted, public procedural manner. That is to say the war-crimes tribunal is powerless to touch them."

He stuffed the pipe with tobacco from the pouch, got it going. "That's where you two come in. You will terminate each target detailed in those files and make each operation seem like an accident."

Philip considered this. "Can I ask why the war-crimes tribunal can't get at these men? If they are war criminals, they deserve to be brought to justice."

"You can ask," Silvers said, staring at the ceiling.

"Let's be creative," Jonas said. "Let's imagine the most banal of reasons. In this kind of bureaucracy, that would make sense. The men in these files still have too much influence within the government. Or they've got dirt on us we don't want aired."

Philip leafed through the files. "Arisawa Yamamoto, Shigeo Nakajima, Zen Godo." He looked up. "What I'd like to know," he said, "is how these targets were identified—if, as you said, elements within the Japanese bureaucracy did such an expert job of destroying the evidence of the war crimes these men committed."

Colonel Silvers puffed on his pipe. He seemed inordinately fascinated by the spider-web network of cracks in the ceiling.

"Just execute the directive," he said in a hard voice. "In the manner outlined."

Philip had the CIG to thank for his marriage. He met Lillian Hadley in Tokyo.

It happened on a late December day in 1946. He and Jonas had been in Japan for just over a month. It had rained all afternoon. The evening washed itself clean like a cat. The USO troupe was putting on a Christmas show for the American forces occupying the city. By show time, the skies had cleared and the crowd was dense.

Philip got his first glimpse of Lillian Hadley that evening:

72

spotlit, chrome microphone in one hand, backed by a sixteen-piece band. It is difficult to convey the profound effect Lillian had on him. Though she had a vibrant voice, it was never-theless unremarkable, which was in stark contrast to her aura. Her great gift was in playing to the crowd. She obviously adored being the center of attention of twenty thousand sol-diers. It showed in the way she sang to them, in the way she bent down, holding first this soldier's hand, then touching that soldier's cheek. She was wholly American, the epitome of the girl next door who appeared on magazine covers. In short, she reminded them of home, and they loved her.

So did Philip. Seeing her up there, he was reminded of where he was and just how long he had been away, not only from home—his house, his town, his country—but from any-thing that had a semblance of normalcy. Seeing her, he was swept away by the powerful nostalgia that causes the expatriot periodically to weep into his whiskey and get into fights for no good reason.

When the concert was over, Philip found himself heading backstage. His CIG credentials were more than sufficient to get him through the phalanx of guards.

Once backstage, amid the scurrying people in greasepaint and costumes, trunks and batteries of lights, snaking cables and instrument cases, he did not quite know what to do, until he saw Lillian.

She was standing by herself, a quiet, almost regal figure, drinking coffee from a paper cup, thoughtfully absorbing the controlled chaos around her. She reminded him of a home-coming queen at college, that unobtainable personage with the perfect face and body, smiling sweetly while all the horny men mentally undressed her. He had seen such a scene in the movies. Philip, of course, had never gone to college. The farm had seen to that. But that had not stopped him from educating himself. He had always been a voracious reader, for reading, like daydreaming, possessed that wonderfully unique quality of allowing oneself to escape into a whole new world.

Without being totally conscious of what he was doing, Philip went up to Lillian and introduced himself.

She laughed at his jokes, was pleased at his compliments, spoke at first shyly, then more openly. After a time, Philip realized how lonely and cut off from all she loved she was. She was the kind of girl you had always longed to take to the local hangout after a Saturday night movie, so all your friends could moon over what was yours.

Time would show that Lillian Hadley would age well and—perhaps even more important—gracefully. But in those days she was absolutely stunning. Her father was Sam Hadley, a three-star general on MacArthur's personal staff, who had a well-known reputation as a strict disciplinarian from the old George Patton school. Hadley was a brilliant career officer, capable of making instant decisions under the most harrowing of circumstances. He was the same General Hadley who had pushed for the creation of the CIG. He was one of the creators of America's top-level strategy in Japan. It was even said by some that the president relied on General Hadley more than on anyone else to formulate long-range policy in the Far East.

They spent the evening together, talking and staring into each other's eyes. Often he saw in her face everything that he had loved—and had fled from—in the rolling hills of western Pennsylvania. It was as if he could define her features by his tiny hometown soda shop that slaked his thirst on dusty summer afternoons, the red-sided wooden school in which he had learned to read and write, the sweet pealing of the bells of the church where on Sunday mornings he and his father went to pray and give thanks. For him, this all-American girl embodied all that was wonderful in his childhood—without any of the dark baggage that had caused him to run away. So perhaps it was not surprising that he should confuse this intense nostalgia with love.

"Sometimes," she said, "I miss my brothers so much I feel as if I can't breathe."

"Are they far away from here?" Philip asked.

Lillian staring up at the stars, their own private playground. Weeping silently.

"What happened?" he asked gently.

For a time, Philip thought she hadn't heard him. "My brothers," she said so softly that the wind took her words past his ear, "were both killed in the war. Jason was at Anzio, on the beach. I don't think he ever felt solid European ground beneath his feet.

"Billy was a tank commander. In Patton's division, no less. Father was so proud of him. Billy was all he could talk about for months and months. Well, Patton was a headline-maker, after all. And where Patton went, Billy did too.

"He made it all the way to Pilsen. Then a German land mine ripped open his tank and his belly."

She was shivering a little, and Philip put his arms around her.

"I still hate this war, even though it's over," she said. "It was cruel and inhuman. Human beings were not meant to bear such pain."

No, Philip thought sadly, on the contrary. Human beings gladly wage war, time after time, learning nothing from history, because they crave power above all else. And power, by definition, means the enslavement of others.

"They were so young," Lillian said. "So pure and brave."

Philip had never met a woman who so filled up his eyes and his heart. He couldn't think around her. He didn't want to. He wanted to hold her, touch her, kiss her. He felt drenched in her beauty.

It wasn't until much later that he found out how much she despised Japan and the Japanese. But by then it was too late.

In the autumn of 1946, the American government subsidies to Japan had finally ceased. Because, to an inordinate degree, they had been propping up the shaky postwar economy, it immediately began to crumble.

There was an air of panic among the top ministers, who foresaw that by March 1947, the Japanese economy would grind to a complete halt. The subsidies had come to an end at a time when Japanese stockpiles were virtually nil, when imports were almost nonexistent, when the country was facing an appalling coal shortage. In short, Japan would be producing nothing because there would be no raw materials from which to manufacture products.

Two weeks before the occupation forces would celebrate Thanksgiving, Prime Minister Shigeru Yoshida had handpicked a brain trust of top ministers to devise a way out of the crisis.

Of the six men making up the Coal Committee, all but one was either from the Ministry of Commerce and Industry— from its inception in 1925, the most powerful and influential of all the ministries in the Japanese bureaucracy—or the Foreign Ministry, with a degree in economics. The exception was a man by the name of Zen Godo. He was a newly appointed vice-chairman of the Bank of Nippon and was by far the youngest of the sextet.

Nevertheless, it was Godo who formulated the idea, adopted and endorsed by the committee, of prioritizing sectors of the economy to promote specific "high-speed" production. With-

75

out this great leap forward, he reasoned, there would very soon be no new Japan left to support its people.

Godo had the best education imaginable. He had graduated first in his class from Todai—Tokyo University, the most prestigious seat of learning in Japan. He had joined the home ministry in 1939 along with fifty-six other newly graduated lawyers. That, however, is where their bureaucratic careers diverged from the other thousand or so newcomers to the various ministries.

Godo and the select others were given very special training. By 1941, all were in place throughout the country. Godo's place was with the Tokyo Metropolitan Police Board.

Eventually, according to the files Silvers had provided Philip and Jonas, Godo became the chief of the city's *Tokko*—the thought-control police. *Tokko* was established to ferret out any and all anti-militaristic elements within the country who might sabotage or in some way undermine the strenuous war effort. Mostly this meant Communists and Communist sympathizers.

Because of the nature of their job, *Tokko* officials were accorded almost unlimited privileges. Around the country they could virtually do as they pleased. Their superiors were that only for the record. A *Tokko* official could not be fired or even disciplined by his superior. In fact, because the *Tokko* man was appointed from Tokyo, his superior was duty-bound to follow his instructions.

The best of the ex-*Tokko* men—such as Zen Godo—used their inside contacts to prepare themselves for the surrender of Japan. Thus, unlike many others, they flourished after the war. As vice-chairman of one of only three central banks, Zen Godo wielded almost unlimited power in the Japan of 1946. It was he who helped formulate the new economic setup: Guided by government policy, the central banks overloaned to specific companies to get them started up. These companies became so dependent on the banks that they were eventually engulfed by them. Soon these central banks would become the nuclei of the successors to the *zaibatsu*, the traditional family-run conglomerates. They themselves would run multibusiness *konzerns*, all within the most profitable sectors of the nascent, ready-to-boom postwar economy.

Zen Godo was also one of the foremost practitioners of *kanryodo*, the art of being a bureaucrat. *Kanryodo* was no less difficult to master than *aikido*, the art of hand-to-hand combat, or *kendo*, the art of sword fighting.

76

Only the Japanese could have the mind-set to elevate such a pedestrian pursuit to the level of an art. And consequently, it was the bureaucrat who was to the new Japan what the *samurai* was to the old Japan. Ironically, the rise of the bureaucrat was the American occupation's doing. By dismantling the military and severely crippling the *zaibatsu*, General MacArthur had left a power vacuum of such magnitude that it could not exist for long.

As the sector of the nation designated to rebuild Japan, the bureaucracy naturally moved into this vacuum, taking advantage of every opportunity with which it was presented.

Zen Godo had read about the death of Arisawa Yamamoto, and it disturbed him. Though the newspapers reported Yamamoto's death as an accident, something about its timing did not sit well with Godo. He had been a friend and close business associate of Yamamoto's since the old days. Yamamoto had been the director of the aircraft company that bore his name. It, along with Nakajima Aircraft, was the manufacturer of the Zero airplane engines. The company had made a fortune for Yamamoto during the war. But he, like Zen Godo, held no animosity toward the Americans. They— among the few—had seen the ultimate folly of their country's entering the war. On the surface, they did their duty to their emperor because for men such as they, there was no other course of action. But in their hidden hearts they secretly welcomed an end to the conflict. Now all they wanted was to get on with the rebuilding of Japan.

As recently as a week ago, Yamamoto had met with Godo and told him of his plan to turn over to the Americans the technology for a new type of jet engine his engineers had been working on during the last months of the war.

Now Yamamoto was dead. Run over by a truck, the newspapers reported. Zen Godo did not believe the newspapers. The timing was too fortuitous for Yamamoto's enemies. Yamamoto's enemies were also Zen Godo's enemies. They were in many quarters, they were superbly organized and they were industrious in their malevolent plotting. Thus, it paid Zen Godo to be cautious. And to seek out the real cause of his friend's death.

Accordingly, Zen Godo sent for his daughter.

Michiko was newly married to Arisawa Yamamoto's eldest son, Nobuo. It was a marriage arranged by the two fathers. Zen Godo thought of this marriage as his future. Nobuo was bright, presentable and reasonably handsome. And far more

77

important, he was the firstborn and would therefore inherit the company on the death of his father.

Godo thought Nobuo a perfect match for Michiko, who, while beautiful enough, was possessed of a vile and fiery nature, which Godo privately considered to be irredeemable. Nobuo was older than she, more mature. With a personality such as hers, Godo often found himself thinking, what young man in his right mind would chance wooing her for long?

The two men had talked of the physical bonding of their families much as two brokers will discuss an important business merger. Eventually they had agreed on the terms, and the marriage was consummated. This was six months ago. Now Michiko and Nobuo were together, although with what degree of success Godo had no idea. The couple had moved to Kobe soon after the wedding, as there were family-run factories near there that Nobuo had been assigned to oversee. The company was in the process of changing over to heavy-industry-machinery manufacture. The family intended to be at the forefront of the rebuilding of Japan. To that end, they formed a partnership with Kanagawa Heavy Industries.

It all seemed to be going smoothly. Until Arisawa Yamamoto died. Run over by a runaway truck.

"Michiko," Zen Godo told his daughter, "I suspect that we are under attack by our enemies. Accordingly, I must know the real circumstances of your father-in-law's death."

Michiko, kneeling in filial piety in front of her father, bowed her head.

"You have always been my strong right arm. Many of my business successes I attribute to your ingenuity. You have sought out the secrets of this city for me in ways only a woman could achieve. Now I fear that our enemies have begun to move against us. I am too much in the public eye to make any overt countermeasures. I cannot afford to bring the attention of either our enemies or the Americans to myself. I have only you to turn to."

Zen Godo could not bear to mention the name of his daughter Okichi, now gone from them forever.

"If Arisawa Yamamoto was murdered," Michiko said, "I will find those who killed him. What do you wish me to do when I discover their identities?"

For a long time Zen Godo did not answer her. He was contemplating the nature of revenge.

* * *

The night Philip proposed to Lillian, she was singing. Flooded in light, she worked the audience—boys, mostly, not more than eighteen years old—into a kind of ecstasy. What she gave them was more than sex appeal. It was entirely natural, and therefore highly potent. They watched her, rapt, without any real understanding of what they were hearing. That didn't matter. She reminded the boys of home. And she wasn't afraid to reach out to them.

With Philip it was another story entirely. Several times he had tried to make love to her. Always she demurred, though he was gentle, attentive and loving. Though they spent hours kissing and caressing, whispering endearments and holding each other close.

"I've never been with a man," she said, "in . . . that way." She put her head against his chest. "I want it to be special. Very special."

"Aren't our feelings for each other special?"

"Oh yes," she said. "Yes. It's just that I always dreamed . . . When I was a little girl, I dreamed of how it would be. None of my other dreams have come true, Phil. This is my last chance. I want it to be as I imagined it would be." Her eyelashes were wet. "You're the first man who . . . I think you could make me give up the dream. If you insisted." She held him tight. It was not her voice but something far more elemental that spoke to him, saying, But I'm asking you not to. Please.

He didn't.

But he did ask her to marry him. Which was, of course, what she had wanted all along.

Zen Godo had had three children by his now dead wife. Now only one, Michiko, was alive. He could not bear to think of his other daughter, Okichi. Tetsu, his lone son, had fervently believed in the war. He had seen it as a divine wind from which his homeland would emerge in powerful splendor.

To this end he had devoted himself in patriotic and most unselfish fashion for three years as a kamikazi pilot. Zen Godo carried within him the boy's death poem:

> The wild cherry blossoms of
> Yamato
> When they fall
> May dazzle even Heaven

79

Yamato was an old, poetic name for Japan. It was also the name of the unit of the *Tokkotai*, Special Attack Force, to which Tetsu had been assigned. He was twenty-two when he died.

Tetsu had believed in the *shokokumin*, the children of the rising generation. Had he not quoted to Zen Godo what the war hero Vice-Admiral Onishi had written, that "the purity of youth will usher in the divine wind"? Tetsu had been infused with *yamato-dama-shii*, the intense Japanese spirit. In the last days of the war, when desperation filled the air almost as thickly as the American bombs, it was assumed that *yamato-dama-shii* would bring victory where superior arms and manpower could not.

At the graves of his family, Zen Godo lit the *joss* sticks and dutifully said the prayers for the dead, knowing the agony of false beliefs.

When Zen Godo remembered the ultimate futility and obsessive behavior that defined *yamato-dama-shii*, he automatically thought of Kozo Shiina. Shiina was currently the most powerful minister in MCI, the Ministry of Commerce and Industry, which, through his maneuverings, had emerged as Japan's most influential postwar bureaucracy. Shiina was also at the heart of a dark and deadly clique of ministers.

Shiina worked diligently—almost, one could say, megalomaniacally—on polishing the image of the new MCI. He had calculatingly surrounded himself with ministers of the wartime ministry of munitions. These men, like him, were all former high-ranking military officers. However, Shiina himself had seen that his and their dossiers were altered during the first week of the occupation, when chaos reigned in Tokyo. Now these men were beyond reproach by the war-crimes tribunal or by anyone else. They were also forever in Shiina's debt.

The Japanese had learned from their terrible loss of face at the hands of occupation forces. Particularly Shiina, who so resented the MacArthur constitution being shoved down his throat that he resolved to make the Americans pay.

At MCI, it had been Shiina's idea to begin employing principle and practice. *Tatemae* and *honne*. This meant that within the Japanese bureaucracy, two courses would run simultaneously. *Tatemae*, principle, would be used when discussing policy with the occupation forces. *Honne*, the practice—that is, the implementation—of those policies, agreed upon among the Japanese ministers themselves, would be something else again.

The success of *tatemae* and *honne* was incalculable. It bestowed upon Shiina a kind of stature he had not had even during the height of the war. Yet because of Japan's humiliating defeat, because of Shiina's abhorrence of the occupation, this victory provided only a modicum of emotional satisfaction.

Philip worked only at night. By now it had become something of a trademark. Anyway, it was how he had been trained, how he worked best.

Jonas was the planner, the spider manufacturing intricately plotted webs. Philip refined the plans, taking them out of the realm of the theoretical, making them workable on a physical level, then carrying them out. Together, they made a formidable team.

Jonas had chosen a night before the new moon was set to rise. But that night turned out to be too clear, so Philip waited for the atmosphere to turn thick and misty. Two nights later, even car headlights seemed inadequate to the task of cutting through the blackness.

There were still many lights out in Tokyo, even on blocks where houses stood whole and undamaged by bombs. The parks, of course, were pockets of stygian blackness.

Shigeo Nakajima was the second target singled out in their directive. Arisawa Yamamoto had been the first. Philip had driven the truck that had run him over. According to the intelligence Silvers had provided Philip and Jonas, Yamamoto had run a prisoner-of-war camp in Mindanao that had had an extraordinarily high death rate among its inmates. Yamamoto had been in the habit of physically taunting the POW's. Those who could not take it were shot. Those who could were tortured.

Shigeo Nakajima was accused of leading a battalion of soldiers into battle on Okinawa, of defeating the enemy and of exhorting those under his command to defile the bodies of the enemy. The wounded were summarily executed. The corpses were stripped of all armament and valuables and, as an example to those who would find them, were then castrated.

The dossiers on both these men were damning, piling on fact after stomach-turning fact. "These aren't men," Jonas had said to Philip at one point. "They're monsters."

But the evidence was so abundant and extraordinarily detailed that privately, Philip had trouble believing all of this intelligence could have been covered up so completely. He had carried out the first termination with doubts nagging at him. Something did not feel right. Now, as he began the second mission, he felt those doubts surfacing again, more persistent now.

The house was in Matsugaya, near Ueno Park, north of Tokyo's downtown hub. It loomed up, invisible until Philip was very close to the outer gardens. He had left the car half a mile away, walking the rest of the way.

Breaking in was no problem. He left his wet shoes on the porch outside. An ironically polite gesture. *Tatami* mats were for bare or *tabi*ed feet only.

Philip was wearing *tabi*, those functional Japanese socks that divided the big toe from the others for ease of movement. It was conceivable that oils from the sole of the foot could leave a trace on the reed mats.

Philip slid open the rice-paper door into Nakajima's bedroom. He placed one foot carefully in front of the other. The *tabi* allowed him to feel with his toes, as well as to grip when the need arose. The darkness in the room was mitigated somewhat by the *shoji* screens out onto one of the gardens. There, Nakajima habitually left small votive candles burning so that the spirits of his family might not lose their way should they come to visit him during the night.

But it was another spirit who had come.

The small flames' illumination was dispersed by the rice-paper screens. Philip saw Nakajima asleep beneath the coverlet. He crept across the *tatami* until he was behind the man's head. He knelt down.

Nakajima was lying on his back. Philip leaned over and folded the cotton coverlet until he had tripled its thickness. Then he carefully lifted it until the tripled section was directly over Nakajima's upturned face.

Now all at once he rose up and jammed the coverlet down across Nakajima's face. Quickly, he used his knees to anchor it on either side of the Japanese's head. Kept his hands free as Nakajima gave a muffled cry. His torso began to arch upward. Stopped by the swath of the coverlet.

Philip leaned into his task as Nakajima's motions became more animated. The Japanese's hands scrabbled along the *tatami* as if searching for something precious. A weapon, perhaps? Philip glanced down. No. A slip of paper. He returned his attention to his task.

Nakajima's legs were thrashing now, the heels drumming against the resilient straw mats. He jerked and strained, his body's twitchings becoming desperate now. Nakajima was not easily relinquishing his hold on life.

Philip applied the final amount of pressure. Nakajima's fingers crackled the paper they were gripping. Then slowly, the arm fell. Philip removed the folded coverlet, stared down into the blank eyes.

Carefully, he unfolded the coverlet, placing it back precisely as he had found it. He was turning to leave when his gaze was caught again by the paper clutched in Nakajima's hand. Why had that paper seemed so vital at the moment of death? It was as if he was trying to protect it—or to destroy it.

Philip bent, took the paper out of the stiffening fingers. He went to the screens, used the candlelight to read the calligraphy.

It was a letter. Philip read it twice without pause. Ice water spread through his belly. All the incipient doubts about the directive he and Jonas had been given came racing to the foreground. And he thought, God in heaven, what have I done?

With a mounting sense of urgency, he pocketed the letter and, as a whippoorwill sounded its nocturnal call, disappeared from the house.

Only the votive candles remained, their flames flickering, casting numinous shadows upon the rice-paper screens.

Philip and Lillian were married the next day. It was crisp and clear, the heaviness of the previous night's weather cleaned out by a strong north wind. The breeze off the Sumida smelled of pine and ash—like Japan, a symbol of the new and the old.

Lillian was dressed in a plum-colored suit. A true wedding dress was out of the question; lace and taffeta were impossible to come by. But she had a hat with a veil that covered the top half of her face as she walked down the aisle arm in arm with her father.

General Hadley, a large, handsome man with a silver moustache and pink cheeks, was as dapper as could be in his dress uniform. His shoes were so highly polished Philip was quite certain he could have used them as a mirror to knot his tie.

The general's wife, a small, neat woman with a retiring temperament, cried when Lillian said, "I do." The general sat beside his wife in the first row, gloved hands in his lap, as still as a statue. If the ceremony affected him in any way, he failed to show it.

But at the reception afterward, he pumped Philip's hand energetically and said, "Congratulations, son. You're a fine addition to the family." The expression on Philip's face made him laugh. "Don't you think I had you checked out when I found out you were seeing my little girl? Hell, I had you so scrutinized I can tell you how often you wash your Jockey shorts."

He steered Philip into a corner, lowered his voice. "You and your friend Jonas Sammartin have done a damn fine job for us in the Pacific. And you're continuing to perform a much-needed service for your country here in Japan. Sure I know what you're up to now. Won't get much public recognition out of it, so I want you to know that your work is appreciated."

"Thank you, sir," Philip said. He could see Lillian, her mother at her side, amid a swirl of well-wishers. For hours after he had returned home from Nakajima's house, he could not sleep. He had debated with himself whether to show the letter to Jonas. Twice had picked up the phone to call his friend. Both times he decided against it. Jonas was clever in ways Philip could never hope to be. But he was a West Point man through and through. He followed orders to the letter. How many times had he railed at Philip for bending—or breaking—the rules by which he lived his life.

"Dammit, Phil, the world can't run without order," Jonas had said many times. "Rules are meant to be obeyed no matter what. Sometimes I think you're a goddamn menace to the armed services." Then he'd grin and say, "I don't think you'll ever learn."

But those episodes of rule breaking had been minor infractions. As far as Philip was concerned, they were the harmless result of his being a free spirit. This was totally different. If what Philip suspected was true, then everything he and Jonas had done in Japan was a complete lie. And taking it a step further, it was impossible to say whether Colonel Silvers himself, their commanding officer, was being duped or whether he was in on the falsification of intelligence.

Much as he loved and trusted Jonas, Philip knew that he could not take the chance that Jonas would pass on this information to Silvers. Not until Philip could ascertain which side of the fence Silvers was on. So Philip had decided to keep the information in Nakajima's letter to himself.

But how to act on it on his own? That was the question that plagued him. Now he had a thought. And, perhaps, the answer. "If you don't mind, General, I'd like to ask a favor of you."

"Call me Sam in private, son. You're part of the family now."

"Yes sir. Well, I was wondering. Regarding my current directive. I'm curious as to the origin of the intelligence on my targets. Do you think you could find out for me?"

Hadley snagged a couple of glasses of champagne from a passing waiter, handed one to Philip. "Why not ask your commanding officer? Silvers is a good man."

"I've tried, sir," Philip said. "But I've run up against a stone wall."

"Well now, Phil. You've been in the CIG long enough to understand the procedures. Information's extended on a strictly need-to-know basis. I guess Silvers has made that decision."

"But what," Philip said, "if the intelligence Silvers is passing down to me is false?"

General Hadley's eyes narrowed. "You got any proof to back up that allegation, son?"

Philip handed him the letter he had found in Shigeo Nakajima's hand.

"I don't read Jap," Hadley said, looking at it upside down.

"It's a letter," Philip said, turning it right side up. "From Nakajima to Arisawa Yamamoto. It talks about a radical-design jet engine that Yamamoto was about to hand over to us. That doesn't sound like the action of a war criminal hiding from American justice."

General Hadley sipped at his champagne, shrugged. "Maybe Nakajima was going to use it as barter."

"I don't think so," Philip said. "First, there's no mention of that in the letter." He pointed to the vertical lines of calligraphy. "Second, and more important, Nakajima mentions Zen Godo, a business partner of his and Yamamoto's. He says that the three of them have been made the targets of something called the *Jiban*."

Hadley frowned. "What is that?"

"I don't know," Philip confessed. "*Jiban* is the Japanese word for a local political machine. I'd say it's a group of some kind."

"And you suspect that this group, this *Jiban*, may have leaked the intelligence damning Yamamoto and Nakajima?"

Philip nodded. "What I now believe is that Yamamoto, Nakajima and Godo are not the war criminals the intelligence Silvers gave us would have us believe. Rather, it is beginning to seem as if those three men are political enemies of this *Jiban*. The *Jiban* wants them destroyed, and they have found the perfect way to effect that destruction: use the services of the CIG, which is hell-bent to ferret out Japanese war criminals who are beyond the reach of the war-crimes tribunal. It's the perfect crime: Hire people to kill for you by making them believe that they are meting out justice."

Hadley considered the ramifications of what Philip was saying. "Yamamoto and Nakajima have already been terminated," he said after a time. "What about Zen Godo?"

"He's next on our list," Philip said. "Sir, I've already got two murders on my conscience. I cannot tolerate a third."

"Put that away," General Hadley said, indicating Nakajima's letter. He eyed Philip. "Tell me, why didn't you go to anyone at CIG with this information?"

"I don't know that either, really," Philip said. He had been thinking about that all night. "Instinct, maybe."

Hadley nodded. "Trust is the most hard-won commodity in life, eh?" As a former field commander, he had a healthy respect for a soldier's instinct. "All right," he said. "I'll see if I can find out the source of Colonel Silvers's intelligence. But until I do, you are honor-bound to carry out any directive your CO gives you. I want you to understand that." Then he smiled, clapped Philip on the back, raised his glass in toast. "But right now, let's both enjoy ourselves. Here's to you and my daughter. May you both be blessed with a lifetime of happiness!"

If Zen Godo believed in one thing, it was in standing in the sun. That is, in business as well as in battle, always stand with the sun behind you. This was a figurative as well as a literal philosophy. Watch your enemies well, but do not allow them to see you with any clarity. If your enemies cannot see you well, they cannot attack, or at least attack with any degree of success.

This philosophy was taught to Zen Godo by his father, a man who outwardly never lost his temper or said a harsh word against anyone. Yet he was a ruthless businessman who would stop at nothing to achieve the goals he had set for himself. Many had died broken men in the wake of his mergers and lightning buy-outs, but none living would speak ill of him.

Zen Godo, a man of extreme filial piety, spoke to his father every week. His duty to his father's spirit would not end until Zen Godo's life itself was over.

At the graves of his family, Godo lit the *joss* sticks, bowed his head, said the Buddhist prayers for the dead. After waiting the proper interval, he spoke to his father. Perhaps it was only the tranquility of the spot that provided him with inspiration. Godo did not believe it so. Here, he felt the presence of his father's spirit floating, observing, commenting.

"Father," Godo said, his head bowed, "I am surrounded by enemies."

My son, his father's voice echoed in his head, *turn over the coin of success and you will find an enemy*.

"Father," Godo said, "they have already murdered Yamamoto-san and Nakajima-san. Now they seek to destroy me."

Then, his father's voice rumbled, *you must destroy them first*.

Nearly a week after his wedding, Philip met General Hadley in the austere precincts of the Meiji Jinja Temple. All around was Yoyogi Park, looking stark and barren in the sere winter. The temple, another of Tokyo's myriad Shinto shrines that seemed to girdle the city, had been built in 1921 to honor the Meiji Emperor. Its architecture was eclectic, an odd but affecting combination of Greek, Middle Eastern and Far Eastern styles.

"There seemed no point in your coming to my office," Hadley said. It would have been superfluous to say that meeting at the CIG headquarters was out of the question. "Let's walk."

They went up the wide stone steps toward the columned entranceway to the shrine.

"Did you find out the source of the CIG intelligence on Yamamoto, Nakajima and Godo?" Philip asked.

"Yeah," Hadley said. "I did." His cheeks were pink and well scrubbed. He looked at if he got a face massage daily. "Silvers's contact is a man named David Turner."

Philip waited while a pair of Japanese matrons in black-and-yellow kimonos went past them, into the temple. Between them they carried a garland of snow-white *origami* cranes, which they would place before the image of the temple's spirit to show the sincerity of their prayers.

"David Turner is a four-eyed paper pusher," Philip said. "What's someone like that, Silvers's administrative adjutant, doing with his finger in the CIG field intelligence pie?" he asked. "It makes no sense."

Hadley shrugged. "I can't say. As head of the Far East theater for CIG, Silvers is free to use whatever intelligence-gathering methods he chooses. Frankly, son, no one back home in Washington really cares that much. They're all too busy trying to find ways to fight Beria and his NKVD." Hadley was speaking of Lavrenty Beria, Stalin's chosen successor to Feliks Dzerzhinski, the creator of the Soviet intelligence apparatus the NKVD, *Narodnyi Komissariat Vnutrennikh Del*, the People's Commissariat for Internal Affairs, which eventually would become the KGB. "We believe that within the NKVD is an *apparat* known as the KRO. We suspect that officials of the KRO are responsible for training NKVD operatives for exportation into the United States as deep-cover spies. However, so far I have had little luck in persuading the president that any such apparatus exists, let alone poses an immediate threat to our security."

The general looked into the distance. "The problem is that elements within our government still see the Russians as heroic allies of the war. But that isn't anything new. Patton and MacArthur have been screaming about the Soviets for years. Trouble is, nobody listened. Anyway, we had to work with the Russians during the war. Hell, they fought like sonsofbitches. Got to give them that. But at some point we've got to begin looking beyond all that. I've no doubt that the Russians already have."

At the moment, Philip was unconcerned with the Russian NKVD. "If I'm to make any headway at all," he said, "I'm going to have to ferret out David Turner's intelligence sources."

Hadley looked at Philip. "You've got very little time left. From what I hear, Jonas is almost done with his proposal on the Zen Godo directive. When he's finished, you'll have to terminate Godo."

"Can't you order the CIG directive put on hold?" Philip asked.

"Negative, son. I've done as much as I can without awkward questions being raised. There's a limit to the amount I can meddle in CIG affairs."

Philip thought of the Japanese matrons, walking like a pair

of blackbirds into the temple. He wished he had the faith to follow them into the shrine and pray to the Shinto *kami* for guidance. He already had two deaths on his conscience that might have been wrongful. He could not countenance another.

"If you're still concerned that you're acting on tainted intelligence," Hadley said, "you'd better put a tail on this Turner, pronto. That's the only way you'll ever get to see who it is he meets with."

But it was Michiko whom Philip met.

It so happened that Ed Porter, the CIG aide, frequented Furokan, a bathhouse in Chiyoda. Because it was only two blocks from the Imperial Palace and central to the occupation force's headquarters, all the high-ranking American brass went there to relax.

They liked it because it was fully staffed by Japanese women schooled in the old, traditional ways. A man could feel like a king within minutes of putting himself in their capable hands.

Porter was one of Colonel Silvers's most successful lotus-eaters, CIG parlance for intelligence gatherers. He, like his commanding officer, was aggressive and slightly paranoid, two traits that served him well in the CIG, an aggressive and excessively paranoid organization.

Porter found the Furokan bathhouse a treasure grove of intelligence. It was here that three times a week he confirmed or dismissed every high-level rumor passing through the military.

Michiko also found Furokan a treasure grove. She worked there twice a week, ostensibly as a bath maid. It was assumed by the bathhouse's patrons that none of the Japanese employees understood English. This was, by and large, correct. Michiko was the exception.

As she moved from general to lieutenant colonel, she gleaned the cream of the intelligence that had allowed her father to prosper so magnificently in postwar Tokyo.

It did not take Michiko long to identify Porter. He was the youngest man by far at Furokan, and he did not have the expertise to act like an aide. The second time she noticed him at the bath, Michiko contrived to be his bath maid. She had already taken a peek in his wallet, memorized his name, rank, status, etc. Then she did some research on him and discovered the CIG connection.

It was through Porter that Michiko found Philip. Porter

had an ego that, as with most young men, responded well to being massaged. Being administered to by a totally submissive woman was a high Porter disliked coming down from. He was like an addict. And like an addict, he always craved more. It was not sex he wanted from Michiko. After all, he could get that on just about any street corner; there was no great thrill in that.

But having a beautiful female scrub him, oil him, massage him, relax him and take care of him as no one else had ever done brought him to a place beyond his wildest dreams. Still, it wasn't enough. He wanted her to know who he was, what he did. He needed her to know just how important he was. Then, all that she did for him took on an entirely new dimension.

He began to teach her English. It made Michiko secretly smile. Not only because she already was fluent in the language, but because his arrogance—the arrogance, she had come to believe, of all Americans—caused him to speak to her at a speed and with a vocabulary that, had she indeed been a beginner, would have precluded her from understanding most of what he said.

As it was, she learned a great deal. Including what it was Philip and Jonas were doing in Tokyo.

Her approach to Philip was totally different from the one she had used with Ed Porter. But that was dictated mainly by the fact that she met him at the Temple of Kannon in Asakusa. This was a Friday, the fifth day in a row that she had followed him here.

She had watched him from a safe distance, day after day, this tall man with the sad eyes, wondering what in the world he was looking at and why. In the end, she realized it was the remains of the temple that drew him. And this knowledge somehow absorbed her own cynicism about him—about his American heritage—so that when at length they did meet it was on a kind of equal footing, which startled her.

The fact was that Michiko herself came here to the ruined temple often. It was always to pray. And to remember.

"Am I disturbing you?" Philip asked on the day they met. It was a damp morning, the low clouds like slabs of wet rock cemented across the sky. Mist swirled about them as if called up from the center of the earth.

He spoke in idiomatic Japanese, and this too startled her. She lowered her head. "Not at all," she said. "Like all Japanese, I am used to being surrounded by people."

He stuffed his hands in his pockets, hunched his shoulders. He watched her out of the corner of his eye. The shadowless light, oyster-gray, as dull as lead, lent her features a lambent quality. The mist shrouded the lower part of her body. It was as if she were an extension of the elements all around her, as if she embodied their timelessness. The grace with which she moved and spoke was wholly natural. She seemed to Philip more an apparition out of some *kwaidan*, the ancient Japanese tales of the supernatural, than a flesh-and-blood woman. "I don't know why it is," he said, "but I find myself coming back here again and again."

"The Temple of Kannon is an important artifact for us," Michiko said. "She is the goddess of pity."

"Why do you come here?" he asked.

A Japanese would never ask such a question, which might cause embarrassment. "No reason," she said, "in particular." But her emotions got the better of her, and seeing this place again, she was overwhelmed by the agony of the spirits who had died here.

"You are crying," Philip said, turning to her. "Are you all right? Have I said something to offend you?"

She shook her head, not trusting herself to speak. A brace of plovers swooped and darted overhead, calling to one another. A dog barked, running at the heavy military traffic pouring through the streets several blocks behind them.

"There were high winds the night of March ninth." Michiko was stunned to hear herself speaking. Astoundingly, she was about to voice all the things that had been in her heart for so many months. Trapped there in darkness, never heard. And now that she had begun, she was powerless to stop. No, she did not want to! It was this tall stranger with the sad eyes who somehow had become her touchstone. Precisely because he was American, she did not feel the reticence to bring emotion to the surface that Japanese, brought up with many family members and only rice-paper walls to separate them, naturally felt. Now her heart, given wing, was speaking its mind. It was as if she stood outside herself, observing the two of them struck like an artist's rendering in a bleak and forbidding landscape. "My sister, Okichi, was hurrying home from the factory where she worked. She, like my brother, believed in the war. She would take neither my father's money nor his advice. After her husband was killed in Okinawa, she continued to work long hours for the war effort.

"That night in March, the air-raid sirens began to scream.

The fierce winds drove the liquid fire through the city. Okichi was in Asakusa, and she, like so many others, raced toward this temple, seeking safety in the arms of the goddess of pity. She found only death."

A long strand of blue-black hair had come loose. It whipped at Michiko's white throat, but she ignored it. It was as if, Philip thought, something over which she had no control was compelling her to speak.

"Okichi was dutifully wearing the hooded air-raid cloak the Japanese government had dispersed to the populace to protect their ears from noise. Unfortunately, it was not fire-retardant. Her hood caught fire as she was inundated with sparks and flame. Likewise the blankets wrapping her six-month-old son strapped to her back."

She was panting with the emotion running through her. Her breath clouded the chill air in front of her face. "The huge, ancient gingko trees surrounding the temple, splendid and full in summertime, were lit up like Roman candles. The temple's wooden superstructure, saturated with caustic chemicals, collapsed inward on those crowded into it seeking shelter from the fire storm. Those who were not crushed or asphyxiated as the oxygen rushed out of the interior were roasted alive."

The ensuing silence rang in Philip's ears like ethereal shouts. All the while Michiko had been recounting the horrifying death of her sister, he had been staring at the scarred earth, the burned-out pillars, the fallen walls. How different it appeared now than on his first afternoon in Tokyo, when Ed Porter had given them the statistics of the fire bombing. It had all seemed so impersonal then, so far away. And yet something had been drawing Philip back to this spot.

He crouched at Michiko's side, picked up a length of charcoal. There was no way of telling what it had once been. Staring out again at the gaping wound in the earth that had once been the ancient Temple of Kannon, hearing Michiko's choked words, he wondered all at once how he had come to this wasteland. And precisely what it had taken to turn beauty into nothingness.

There was a zone of emptiness here that gripped him in the same way he was gripping the length of charcoal. He found himself once again returned to the bitter winter twilight when he had tracked the red fox to its den. Saw again the furred body slamming into the red clay wall as the .22-caliber bullet struck it in the chest. But now, for the first time, he experienced what it was like to be the hunted. The death and destruction of this place were somehow changing him.

Now he could hear the screams of the burning women, now he could see the bright kimonos, crimson and gold, disintegrating beneath the sheets of orange flame. He felt the temperature of the air reach scorching levels. He gasped with them as the air was sucked out of the burning interior.

All at once, Philip Doss was weeping.

For the innocents who had perished so unjustly here. For the children who had lost life even before they had had a chance to understand it. But also for the lost child within himself who had suffered in boyhood, who had spent so many years hating life that he had never even said goodbye to his father.

It was hating life, he realized now, that had brought him to this spot, this zone of emptiness. It was what made him what he was. How much more wretched was he than the young ones who had been burned alive in the fire storm! It was one thing to have life abruptly taken away, quite another to feel that life was meaningless. And so he felt a kinship with the death and destruction that had been wreaked here. Now he understood that he had been drawn back to this ruined temple because it echoed so accurately that ruined place inside himself. Looking into that blackened pit where thousands had sought protection, and had found only death, was like staring into his own soul.

It was the hatred of life that had caused the wanton destruction that men knew as war. It was the hatred of life, Philip saw now, that allowed men to blindly obey other men not more mortal than themselves. He had been the good soldier, accepting facts as truth—and killing on the sole strength of those facts. Now he knew those facts to be lies. What was he to do about those lives he had taken without cause, without the mitigation of justice?

At that moment, he felt fully as dead as those poor souls who had perished in the fire bombing of the Temple of Kannon. And he heard their silent cries more clearly than he did the mundane street sounds that surrounded him. He felt more alone than he could ever have imagined. How could he go home and explain to Lillian what he was feeling or what he had done? She would never understand, and never forgive him for making her feel excluded from so private a part of himself. In a sense, he saw now that his marriage to Lillian

93

was just a dream, a fantasy that part of him needed to cling to in order to survive.

But there was another part of him coming to the fore now, a part that felt increasingly in tune with Japan—the sights, sounds, smells, customs. With its people. Philip was quite certain that at this moment he understood the Japanese way of life more completely than he did any other. And he began to despair further in his utter solitude. He was like a scarecrow, in the middle of a fertile field, calling out without anyone hearing him.

And then he felt a hand on his shoulder. He looked up into Michiko's eyes and saw that tears were trailing down her cheeks. Stunned, he realized that she was feeling lost as well. He wanted to catch those tears in his hands; they seemed as precious as diamonds.

He rose and took her fingers in his, realizing that this zone of emptiness might be inhabited by someone other than his own featureless ghost.

TENDO

THE WAY OF HEAVEN

TOKYO
WASHINGTON
MAUI

When he was young, Kozo Shiina had surrounded himself
with mirrors. When he was young, his muscles were firm, his
skin glistening; the river of life ran through him in a torrent.
When he was young, Kozo Shiina was proud of his body.

Once, the sweat of effort burnishing his supple skin had
provided him with a kind of exultation impossible to duplicate
by any other method. Once, the building up of his body had
provided the ultimate defiance of time and mortality. Once,
lifting weights had made him high. And afterward, licking
the sweat rolling off his lips, staring into the mirrors, seeing
an endless parade of Kozo Shiinas, naked and strong, he had
been convinced that he was a reincarnation of Ieyasu Tokugawa himself, the creator of modern Japan. He had stared
into the face of perfection and had thought himself a god.

Now that he was old, he had banished all mirrors from his
sight. Now the force of years, like breakers pounding the
shoreline, was too apparent to be denied. Now Shiina knew
with a certainty like an ice pick through his heart that he had
missed his opportunity to end life in the proper manner, at
the height of his physical beauty. Now he knew that he would
allow the decay of time to complete the act he had not been
heroic enough to perform when the blossom of his body was
in full flower. When death was still pure, when it would serve
the *samurai*'s ultimate purpose: to sow his death like a seed,
and use it as an example for others.

Now he must content himself with what was about to occur
and trust that it was reward enough for almost forty years of
suffering. Of course he had been right about the Americans:
their occupation of Japan, the new constitution they had drafted
in 1946, had forced the Japanese to become a nation of
middle-class businessmen with middle-class tastes and habits.

Because the Americans insisted that the new Japan make

97

no provision for defense in its own budget, Japan had no defense burden weighing down its economy. How it angered Shiina when the young, affluent merchants of his acquaintance lauded the Americans for allowing the new Japan to become so affluent that now even the burgeoning middle class was rich beyond the imaginings of their grandparents of a generation ago. It angered Shiina because they failed to see what to him was so obvious. Yes, America had allowed Japan to become affluent. But in return, Japan was America's vassal, totally dependent on America for its defense. Once Japan had been a nation of *samurai* who knew how to wage war, who created their own defense network. Now that was all gone. America had brought its brand of capitalism to Japan and, in so doing, had emasculated an entire culture.

Which was why Shiina had created the *Jiban* in the first place.

It was nearing summer. Less and less, the chill of the long winter invaded his home. The songbirds could be heard with increasing frequency as they flitted through the stand of quince trees outside his study.

Kozo Shiina, sitting with hands across his bony knees, remembered one particular summer more vividly than all the rest—1947, two years after the destruction of Japan.

The heat had been rising in almost palpable waves, and the air was very wet. Eight ministers had gathered at Shiina's summer villa on the shore of Lake Yamanaka. These eight, plus Shiina, constituted the *Jiban*. It was amusing to them, then, to be known as a local political machine, since their combined power was so far-reaching that they were anything but local. Secretly, however, the *Jiban* was known as the Society of Ten Thousand Shadows. This was a more serious reference to the sacred *katana*, symbol both of the traditional Japanese warrior's power and of his exalted status in society.

The *katana*, or longsword, was made by a Zen artisan who folded and refolded the heated steel ten thousand times in order to make a blade that was so strong it could pierce armor, so supple that it was virtually impossible to snap in two. Each folding of the steel blade was called a shadow.

The *Jiban*'s *katana* was a weapon of astounding design and quality, forged sometime in the fourth century by the most famous of Japan's legendary Zen swordsmiths for Prince Yamato Takeru, who slew his twin brother for imagined infractions of simple courtesy. He also singlehandedly destroyed the savage Kumaso tribes to the north of the capital.

This sword was by far the oldest, and therefore the most revered, sword in all of Japan. Because of its extraordinary history, it belonged in a museum. The soul of Japan resided in that blade.

"Here is the symbol of our might," the young Kozo Shiina had told the eight ministers, lifting the *katana* aloft. "Here is the symbol of our moral obligation. To the Emperor, and to Japan itself."

Behind him, in that summer of 1947, gusty rain was turning the lake as opaque as the inside of an oyster's shell. Mist rose off the skin of the water like perspiration off a *kabuki* actor.

We all wear masks, the young Kozo Shiina thought as he addressed the founders of the Society of Ten Thousand Shadows. If we are not actors, then we are nothing. He stared at the ancient sword. Here is the mirror of ourselves. We hold it up to the light, and call it life. "If we cannot animate the essence of our spirits," he said, "then we shall fail in returning Japan to its former glory."

It had been impossible that day to tell where gray water met gray sky. It was impossible, even, to tell where the zenith of heaven lay, so uniform was the color that spread across the countryside.

"We cannot—we shall not fail. We know our duty, and each of us will do what is necessary to purify Japan. Not for the first time has the sacred soil of our country been contaminated by the Westerner. Capitalism has come to Japan like a phoenix with a voracious appetite. Capitalism is destroying us. It eats us alive, transforming us until we no longer remember our heritage, until we no longer know what it means to be Japanese, to serve the emperor, to be a *samurai*."

And yet, where the lake waters failed, where the hills and the sky failed, the mountain did not. Mount Fuji rose in ghostly splendor, a deep and abiding shade, etched against the grayness as if with charcoal sweeps from some celestial palette, crowned at its majestic summit by a crescent of glistening snow. Fuji the sacred. Fuji the redeemer.

The young Kozo Shiina was naked to the waist. His magnificently muscled body commanded their attention. He wrapped a *hachimachi*, the traditional headband of the warrior in battle, across his forehead, tied it in back.

"Now, for the first time, I will draw the sacred blade of Prince Yamato Takeru from its scabbard," Shiina said. The mist seemed to shrink from the magic of that hand-forged steel so that, as he remembered it, a kind of aura, an aureole

99

of emptiness not unlike the Void, surrounded the weapon.

The young Kozo Shiina held the blade aloft in such a manner that, for an instant at least, he and the blade—both perfect beneath their sheens of oil—were one. "When next I draw this sacred sword, it will be to consecrate the successful fruition of the seeds we plant here today."

In a swift motion, he sliced the tip of his finger with the very end of the *katana*. Dark red blood dripped into a sake cup. He dipped an old quill into the cup and wrote his name in blood at the bottom of the *Jiban*'s charter.

"Here, for all time," Kozo Shiina told them, "is *kokoro*, the heart of our philosophy, the essence of our purpose, the details of the future to which we are this day dedicating our fortunes, our families, our very lives." He passed the document to the minister on his immediate left, drew the blade across the tip of the man's finger. As the minister dipped the quill into the mingled blood and wrote his name beneath that of his leader, Shiina said, "Here also for future generations to ponder are all the consequences of our actions, witnessed by all the unseen ancestors whom we revere beyond all else and in whose name the Society of Ten Thousand Shadows is dedicated." The document was passed on, more blood was spilled, another name was added.

"We have here a living diary of the *Jiban*'s work," Kozo Shiina continued. "Soon it will become both our banner and our shield." Now the last of the ministers was signing. "By its very existence it engraves on our brains this truth: We who have entered our names on this roll have in the same way entered into that state of virtue from which there can be no turning back."

The drip of blood, the scratch of the quill against the stiff paper. "This Katei document—named so because it is the curriculum of the Society of Ten Thousand Shadows—will constantly serve to remind us of our dedication of purpose, of the sacredness of what we do. For we seek nothing less than to preserve the purity of the emperor, the surety of the legacy of the unifying shogun, Ieyasu Tokugawa. We seek a fusion between past, present and future, a continuity for the greatness of the Land of the Rising Sun."

Now, in the spring of the present, Kozo Shiina sat in his study, contemplating the bower that the quince blossoms created outside his window. That summer, he thought, I believed, in my godlike immaturity, that the battle had already been won. Yet it had only been joined. I had not counted on Wataro Taki. His power within the Yakuza grew, and as it did, he directed all of that power against the *Jiban*. Where had he come from? Why was he my enemy? I did not know. But we fought in every arena: political, bureaucratic, economic and military. He foiled our plans time and again. Even when we hurt him, he rebounded, gathered his forces again and attacked once more.

Until two weeks ago, when I finally succeeded in destroying him. But I had not counted on his closest ally surviving him, if only for a short while. I underestimated Philip Doss's cunning. It had been he who had taken the *Jiban*'s sacred *katana* so many years ago. And what had he done with it? He had given it to his son, Michael.

Kozo Shiina's hands tightened into fists. It galled Shiina that he never would have known what had happened to the sword had not a *sensei* in Paris seen the sword and, recognizing it, telephoned Masashi. "Get it back," Shiina had told Masashi, "whatever the cost."

The trilling of the songbirds was sweet, but not to Kozo Shiina's ears. The food that had been laid out before him was fragrant, but not to his nose. The burst of pink of the quinces' first tender blooms was pleasing, but not to his eyes. He still did not have the *katana* of Prince Yamato Takeru.

But there was another matter, fully as pressing as the sword. The *Jiban*'s Katei document had been stolen. It detailed every step of the Society of Ten Thousand Shadows' plan to bring Japan into world prominence, to bring it slowly but surely back toward a firmly militaristic posture, its intentions—with the aid of allies both within and outside Japan—to launch a coordinated invasion of the Chinese mainland.

In the hands of the enemy—if it were, for instance, to appear on the desk of the president of the United States—it would sound the death knell for the *Jiban*. This he could not tolerate. If the *Jiban* was to fulfill its destiny, to lead Japan into a new era where the Land of the Rising Sun would never again be dependent on foreign oil or foreign energy sources of any kind, then the Katei document must be returned.

Kozo Shiina's powerful fingers tightened their grip on his knees. Still he was haunted by the enigma of who had killed Philip Doss. If Doss had survived, Shiina was certain that Masashi's people would have run him down. Ude had been so close, until Doss dropped out of sight. Then, in Maui, he had died. By whose hand? Kozo Shiina did not know, and this disturbed him because it meant that there was a force at play of which he was ignorant.

Soon, he thought, calming himself, with the unwitting aid of Masashi Taki, this sword will be returned to me. Just as the Katei document will be returned. Then the sword of Japan's soul will at last be freed from its scabbard, and my work will be done. Japan will be a world power in every way, to rival even America and the Soviet Union.

Michael was sure that the darkness would never end. And yet it did.

"Audrey!"

The clamoring of temple bells shaking him out of a long slumber.

"Oh my God! Oh my God!"

Head full of noise, reverberating on and on. Wanted to blot it out, go on sleeping for another hundred years.

"She's gone!"

Light like splinters of glass in his eyes.

"My baby's gone!"

Groaning, light-headed, he awoke.

Uncle Sammy was shaking him. "Michael. Michael! What happened?"

Temple bells and a bamboo flute, a reedy melody, a sonorous percussion accompaniment.

"Michael! Do you hear me?"

"Yes." Gauze pulling apart, the atmosphere inside his head clearing.

"Where is Audrey? For God's sake, Michael! What happened?"

"I—I don't know." His head hurt when he spoke or moved. Aftermath of the chemical.

"What do you mean you don't know!"

His mother's face was alight with feverish anxiety. "I called Jonas at home. He came right away. He said no police." Taking a step toward him. "Are you all right, darling?"

"I'm okay," he said. He looked at Jonas. "How long have I been out?"

Jonas was crouched down beside him. "It's been—what, Lillian?—forty minutes since you phoned me."

Lillian nodded.

Michael looked around the study. A whirlwind had come in through the window, or so it seemed. Lamps, overturned chairs, books looked as if they had been blown out of their neatly aligned rows. All scattered across the carpet.

"Christ!" he said softly. Began to rise.

"Michael!"

He saw the slash as he lurched off balance. Jonas caught him, and he steadied himself. The slash went all the way through the carpet, as neat an incision as a surgeon makes in his patient. Where is my *katana*? Michael thought. What in God's name has happened to Audrey?

"*Michi*," the woman said. "It is the path I chose. And now I have been humbled by it."

Michiko was weeding her garden. "There is danger everywhere these days," she said. "In the mysteries inside the Takigumi. In the tenor of Japan itself. The younger generation has grown up disaffected. They no longer understand short- and long-term goals. Everything is viewed in extremes.

"They do not even understand what it is they want. They are for the most part inarticulate, uninterested in anything save their own fleeting pleasure. They only know that they do not want what *is*. This makes them exceptionally vulnerable. To suggestion. They join the Yakuza but openly flaunt its strict code. They join radical splinter groups, or even anarchic revolutionary cells which, quite ineptly, manufacture homemade missiles, which they fire, also ineptly, on the Imperial Palace. Meanwhile our ministers become more and more intractable in their reactionary views. They see America as becoming inflexible, no longer willing to extend its magnanimous support to Japan. They see America reneging on its unspoken oath to keep Japan strong, as Japan keeps the Pacific Rim safe from communism.

"Is America truly our friend or our enemy? they ask. I feel as if we have returned to the emotional state before the war of the Pacific."

Joji Taki shook his head. Lately, Michiko seemed obsessed with the deteriorating trade relationship between Japan and America. True, recent developments indicated that Japan was unwilling to change its ground rules for another country. So what? Why should she? It was this mare's nest of restrictions against outside intervention or investment that had built Japan up from the ashes of the war in the first place. Why weaken them now? For the United States? What had it done but try to recreate the new Japan in its own image? So it could become America's steel fist against communism in the Far East.

"Michiko, my stepsister," he said, waiting patiently for her to finish, "though you were adopted by my father, Wataro Taki, I consider you no less my family."

Michiko paused in her gardening. Her hands were streaked gray and brown from the earth. Her hair, which was piled atop her head and set with *kyoki* wood combs in the ancient fashion, was dotted with strands of wildflower clippings. "You have not come here to flatter me, Joji-chan," she said softly. "I know you too well."

Joji glanced around at the burly young men standing a discreet distance from Michiko. Michiko's husband, Nobuo Yamamoto, did not allow her to go anywhere without being accompanied by servants. But, oddly, Joji did not recognize any of them. And they certainly were not dressed like servants. They seemed more like bodyguards. Joji shrugged. Well, why not? he thought. There was no lack of wealth in the Yamamoto family. As the president of Yamamoto Heavy Industries, Nobuo ran one of the largest conglomerates in Japan. "As usual, Michiko-chan, you have seen through my poor facade," he said. "You were always able to see into my mind."

Michiko gave a rueful smile.

"It's about Masashi."

Michiko sighed, and her face clouded over. "It is always about Masashi these days," she said. "First, he clashed with Father about the direction the Taki-gumi should be going in. Now what?"

"I need your help."

She lifted her face to him, and the sunshine bathed her features in light. "You have only to ask, Joji-chan, you know that."

"I want you to help me against Masashi."

There was an unnatural silence in the garden. A plover, hopping along the ground, paused to cock its head and stare at them. In a flutter, it took off.

"Please," Michiko said, the unnatural terror turning the breath hot in her throat. All these days since Masashi had come to see her, to show her why she must now do whatever he asked of her, she had tried to hide away from the awful danger he presented. Otherwise, she would have ceased to eat and to sleep. As it was, she was plagued by nightmares from which she would jerk awake, filled with dread and panic. "Do not ask that of me."

"But you're the only one I can turn to," Joji pleaded. "You have always helped me before. When Father sided with Masashi, you always spoke up for my side."

"Ah, Joji-chan." Michiko sighed. "What a memory you have. That was a long time ago."

"It's no different now."

"But it is," she said. There was a great sadness in her voice. "Listen closely to my counsel. Whatever the problem is, forget about it. Forget about your brother Masashi, I beg of you."

"Why won't you help me?" Joji cried. "We always joined forces before to keep Masashi in check."

"Please do not ask me, Joji-chan." There were incipient tears in the corners of Michiko's eyes. The sunlight turned them to jewels. "I cannot intervene. I can do nothing."

"But you do not know what has happened." Joji hung his head in shame. "Now Masashi has deposed me as *oyabun* of the Taki-gumi."

"Ah Buddha!" she cried. But she already knew this. Just as she already knew what Joji had not yet begun to suspect, what, if he remained uninvolved, and therefore safe, he would never come to suspect: that it had begun. The final phase of a strategy so vast, so terrifying that there was no hope of stopping it. And yet she had committed herself to the destruction of that strategy.

"Now Masashi is free to twist the entire resources of the Taki-gumi to his own ends. The clan business has already changed radically. Masashi has his drug networks in place. Already the first of the money is flowing in. Soon it will come so fast it will be like a tide. The Taki-gumi will be inextricably involved in the filth—the last thing Wataro Taki, our father, wanted."

"But how is this possible?" Michiko said. "I thought matters were settled between you and Masashi."

"They were," Joji said. "Or so I thought. But at the clan meeting, Masashi moved against me. You know what a speaker he is. I had no chance once he opened his mouth. The lieutenants were frightened. The death of our father made us terribly vulnerable to incursions from the other clans. Masashi cleverly played upon that fear. Now the Taki-gumi lieutenants feel safe again. They would follow Masashi into hell if he asked them."

Before this is over it may come to just that, Michiko thought. Impulsively, she reached out, and Joji put his hands in hers. "Forget all of this, Joji-chan," she whispered fiercely. "There is nothing you or I can do. The changes have already been made. Leave him alone; you do not have the power to defeat him. Neither do I, now. *Karma*."

"But these changes you speak of," he said, "will affect not only us, but others in our family. Your daughter, for instance. And Tori, your granddaughter. How is she? I miss her little smiling face."

"She is fine," Michiko said. "Just fine." Pressing her cheek against his. "Tori asks about you all the time." She did not want him to see the fear in her eyes. Masashi is playing a terrible game, she thought. For the highest possible stakes. Masashi is in control of the Taki-gumi. And this time, the call to battle will be the final one.

"The time has come," Jonas said, "for me to tell you the truth."

Michael blinked. "The truth." He said it as if it were an Urdu word that he could not quite fathom.

They were sitting in Jonas Sammartin's office in the BITE building.

"Yes," Jonas said, unperturbed. "The truth."

"What is it that you have been telling me up until now?"

"My dear boy," Jonas said. "You are closer to me than any nephew could be. I never married. I never had children. You and Audrey are as dear to me as if you were my own blood. Surely it isn't necessary for me to tell you this."

"No, Uncle Sammy," Michael said. "You were always our protection. I told Audrey recently that I thought of you as Nana, the Darlings' sheepdog in *Peter Pan*."

Jonas Sammartin smiled. "I take that as a great compliment, son."

They were both quiet for a time. It was as if invoking Audrey's name had made the dread return, of not knowing where she was or what had happened to her.

The phone rang and Jonas picked it up. He spoke in low tones for a moment. When he cradled the receiver, the bleak atmosphere had dissipated enough for him to continue. "The fact is," he said, "I believe that your father knew that he was going to be killed—or at least that the possibility of his imminent death existed.

"The day before we received word of his death, I was sent

a packet by courier. It had originated in Japan. So far, we have not been able to trace it farther than the Tokyo office of the air-express company. The packet was delivered to them by a Japanese man. That's all they know. We have no name and only the vaguest description, which is worse than useless."

Jonas took out a stiff oversize envelope and a folded sheet of paper. "In any case, the packet was from your father. In it was this letter, instructing me to speak with you in the event of his death."

"Speak with me?"

"I've done what he requested."

"Let me see the letter, Uncle Sammy."

Jonas emitted a deep sigh. He handed the sheet over, passed a hand over his face, as if he could scrub away the events of the past several days. He looked tired, his face gray-tinged.

Michael looked up from the typescript. "It appears it was my father's idea for me to take his place if he died."

Jonas nodded.

"He refers here to a private will," Michael said.

"This is it," Jonas said, holding up the envelope. "It's sealed and, following your father's instructions, it will be opened only if you agree to take his place."

Michael had a flash of impending dread, then it was gone. "I see you have the will handy," he said. "Pretty sure of yourself."

"No," Jonas said. "I'm sure of you, Michael. You're here, aren't you?" He gave Michael a weary smile. "Your father always said you were precocious. I can just hear his voice. 'Mikey's smarter than the two of us put together, Jonas. I know it now. But one day you'll see.' Prophetic words, son, considering the circumstances." He handed over the envelope. "I believe it's time you opened this."

Michael took it but did not open it. "What about Audrey?" he said.

"That's what that call was about," Jonas said. "There's nothing—so far. But it's early yet."

"Early!" Michael cried. "For God's sake, we don't even know whether she's alive or dead!"

"I think—I hope to God—that she is alive, son. Your father was on a piece of work for us. In the midst of it, he stumbled upon something very special. So special, in fact, that it was impossible for him to make regular reports. He was that far undercover. His enemies tried once to get to him through

Audrey. I found that out only after I had read the letter your father sent."

"You mean that the supposed break-in wasn't anything of the sort. It was an attempt to get at my father through Audrey!"

Jonas nodded. "Of course we did not tell Audrey or your mother the real reason for the aborted break-in. That Philip's enemies planned to abduct your sister. I wanted to put her into protective custody, but by the time I found out about the attempted kidnapping, your father was already dead."

"And now they have succeeded," Michael said. "But my father is dead. And yet they went after Audrey anyway? What earthly good could she be to them now? It doesn't make any sense."

"It's another piece of the puzzle to which I don't have an answer," Jonas admitted. "It's another urgent reason that I need you, Michael. You can find out what's happened to Audrey, as well as discover who killed your father."

"Who are my father's enemies, Uncle Sammy?"

"Yakuza."

"Yakuza!" Michael exclaimed. "Japanese gangsters. Then you *do* know what my father was up to. It should be easy to—"

"The fact is, your father kept me entirely in the dark on this matter. I have no explanation as to why. I just hope to Christ there was a compelling reason."

"I want Audrey back," Michael said. He was dimly aware that he was gripping the leather armrests of the chair with clawed fingers.

"As do I," Uncle Sammy said. "I want her home safe and sound with all my heart. Follow your father's footsteps. It's our only chance of finding her."

Michael felt emotionally drained. His muscles were giving little twitches, as if he had just finished a marathon run. He exhaled, aware that he had been holding his breath. "I think," he said, "that I had better open this letter now."

The call could not have come at a more inconvenient moment. Joji Taki had just lifted the white kimono with the salmon chrysanthemums embroidered on it and was peeking between coyly parted thighs.

Joji Taki had waited all evening for this glimpse. Through an elaborate tea ceremony, a smoke-filled dinner, endless talk about the rise and fall of the yen and, finally, seemingly interminable farewells.

Through it all, Kiko had been an exemplary hostess. She had performed the tea ceremony with uncommon grace. She had skillfully kept Kai Chosa entertained all dinner long, then had engaged Kai's wife in girl talk while the men spoke of business.

And in the end, it had been Kiko, seeing her master making no progress, who had given the tiniest, most demure yawn behind the back of her hand. Kai Chosa's wife had taken the cue, touched her husband's sleeve and the couple had departed.

The evening had been a disaster, Joji thought disconsolately. He had approached Kai Chosa, the *oyabun* of the Chosa-gumi, the second largest Yakuza clan, in the hopes of enlisting his aid in an attempt to regain control of the Taki-gumi from Joji's brother Masashi.

Kai Chosa had all but ignored Joji's offer of an alliance. Perhaps, like the Taki-gumi lieutenants, he did not believe that Joji possessed the strength of determination to dislodge Masashi. And he seemed peculiarly reluctant to enter into any negotiations that would bring his clan into a confrontation with the Taki-gumi.

This Joji found both puzzling and dispiriting. He had been so sure that Kai Chosa would jump at the chance to take a bite out of the Taki-gumi. What was it about his brother Masashi, he wondered? Had he underestimated Masashi's power? If so, what was he missing?

Joji found his mind spinning around. What I need, he told himself, is a godfather. A man with enough power, a man who is not afraid of Masashi.

All through dinner, Kiko had stolen infinitesimal glances at Joji. Her gaze had caressed him, urging him to caress her in the same manner. But even when he took in the curvaceous line of her shoulder and breast beneath the silken folds of her kimono, the tiny sliver of fire-red at the nape of her neck where she allowed her underkimono to peek sexily out, it had had no effect. Kai Chosa had filled Joji's mind.

But now that he and Kiko were alone, Joji found himself in need of distraction from his woes. In fact, Kiko was just beginning to get his attention when there was a discreet knock on the sliding door. At just that instant, his eyes were locked with Kiko's. The intimation of delights to come seemed infinite.

Joji saw something in Kiko's eyes and dropped his gaze to where his hand lay on the inside of her leg. She had parted her thighs even more, so that the fire-red underkimono had fallen away. He saw with a leap of his heart that she wore no other garment. Her intimate flesh, dark hair rising up the center of her mound, wisping like a beckoning finger where it ended on her lower belly.

"Ah Buddha," Joji murmured.

The discreet knocking came again.

"Leave me alone!" Joji called thickly. "Have you no manners at all!"

Kiko was subtly lifting her buttocks off the *tatami*. As she did so, she tilted her pelvis forward and upward. The heart-stopping result was to expose the underside of her mons. In this hairless area he could see every fold and pucker of her most intimate flesh. Her hips, off the *tatami*, began a sensuous circling. On the third pass, the petals of her lips opened of their own accord.

Joji thought he was going to faint.

The sliding door opened a sliver and he could see the shaven head of Shozo. His face was carefully averted.

"I will take out your eye for this," Joji said angrily. His avid gaze was back locked on the vision at the juncture of Kiko's thighs.

"Oyabun," Shozo whispered, "you would take out my eye if I failed to tell you at once."

"Tell me what?" Kiko had begun further movements of her pelvis that did unbelievable things to that which Joji desired above all else now.

"There is a visitor."

"At this late hour?" Joji felt the heaviness in his belly. "Most inconsiderate."

"Oyabun," Shozo whispered, "it is Ude."

Despite what Kiko was doing, Joji felt his manhood deflating. A cold chill swept through him. Ude, the man who performed executions for his brother Masashi. What could Ude want? Joji asked himself. With a chill of dread, he wondered whether Masashi somehow knew about the subject of Joji's discussion with Michiko this morning.

"You did well to inform me, Shozo," he said, trying vainly to keep himself calm. "Tell Ude-san that I will be just a moment."

The door slid shut. It had a center panel taken from an *obi*. Woven into the silk was a scene of hunters killing a wild boar. Joji stared at it now as he began to ready his mind.

Kiko was too well trained to open her mouth at a time such as this. Instead, she occupied herself with rearranging her clothes until she appeared just as she had throughout dinner.

Without a word, Joji opened the door, went through. In the next room, he saw Ude's huge bulk in the center of the *tatami*. Joji forced himself to smile. "Good evening, Ude-san," he said, his heart fluttering. "Shozo," he called, "have you offered our honored guest tea?"

Ude brushed away the invitation. "Pardon this intrusion," he said in his rumbling voice, "but I am in something of a hurry. I have a plane to catch."

Joji took a deep breath, let it out all the way. He came across the *tatami*, sat facing the huge man. "Ude-san," he said, "this is an honor I had not anticipated."

"I find myself in the peculiar position of having to get right to the point." Ude's voice was as hard as granite. It made it seem as if he was not sorry at all to be impolite. "One must be mutable to events as they occur."

"Hai." Joji waited, breathless.

"I did not choose this hour to speak with you," Ude said. "So we must both make do with haste."

"This is not the way my father would do business," Joji said.

"Ah, your father," Ude said. "The most honorable of men. His death is still mourned. He will be forever venerated in my household."

"Thank you," Joji said.

"But your father is gone, Joji-san. Times change."

Joji put a hand to his forehead. It came away slick with sweat. What did Ude want? Joji could not help but be aware of the enormous power of the other man.

"As to business," Ude continued. "Your brother is, well, uncomfortable with the strain in his relationship with you. He knows how this would have hurt your father. It has occurred to Masashi-san that you would be better off discussing whatever lies between you."

Joji was stunned. "Pardon me for saying so, Ude-san, but I know my brother. I do not think that Masashi would have any interest in talking matters out. He and I feel that the future of the Taki-gumi lies in different directions."

"On the contrary, Joji-san, Masashi has only the best interests of the Taki-gumi in mind. As well as the wishes of your esteemed father, Wataro Taki."

111

Joji was elated. If Masashi was willing to give back a portion of the Taki-gumi to Joji, Joji was all for it. On the other hand . . . Joji did not want to think about what lay on the other hand.

He nodded. "All right."

Ude smiled. "Good. Shall we say tomorrow night?"

"Work while all others sleep," Joji said.

"Precisely. To Masashi's mind, the sooner this is settled between you, the better."

"A public space."

"Yes," Ude said. "That was Masashi-san's thought as well. Well, at that hour, your options are limited. Would someplace in the Kabuki-cho be suitable?" The Kabuki-cho was in Shinjuku but on the wilder side of the area of Tokyo, where the densest construction had gone on for the past ten years. Originally, a new *kabuki* theater was scheduled to be erected there, hence the name. It stuck, even when those plans were abandoned. Now it was packed with cheap restaurants, *pachinko* parlors, X-rated movie theaters, nightclubs and brothels. "There are any number of *no-pan kissas* to choose from." These were night spots where the waitresses wore no underwear.

"How about A Bas?" Joji said.

"I know it," Ude acknowledged. "It's as good as any."

After Shozo showed him the way out, Ude climbed into his waiting taxi. He smiled into the darkness. All had gone just as Kozo Shiina had predicted.

Settling back in the seat, as the cab lurched ahead into traffic, Ude imagined Shiina on the phone, talking with Masashi.

"How will you get Masashi to the meeting?" Ude had asked Kozo Shiina, his new master. "He despises Joji as a weakling. Masashi hardly considers Joji a brother."

And Kozo Shiina had replied. "I will suggest to Masashi that it is important for the Taki-gumi's image for it to present a united front. The politicians and bureaucrats with whom we deal have never gotten over their innate nervousness when it comes to the Yakuza. To see the two remaining brothers of the Taki-gumi feuding will only unnerve them, I will say. Just yesterday, Minister Hakera asked me if any trouble could be expected from the Yakuza quarter now that the Taki brothers have quarreled. Of course not, I assured him, I will tell Masashi. Everything is under control. But you see, I will tell Masashi, as long as you and your brother are apart, there is the potential for trouble. At least in the eyes of those who aid us."

"But a meeting between Masashi and Joji cannot help but end badly," Ude pointed out "They have never agreed on anything. You can hardly expect them to do so now."

Kozo Shiina had smiled that odd, reptilian smile that made even Ude uncomfortable. "Don't worry, Ude. You just do your job. In the end, Masashi Taki will do his."

"It's not a will at all," Michael said.

Jonas held out his hand. "Let me see that, son."

Michael handed over the contents of the envelope from his father. There was one sheet of airmail paper on which were written six lines. There was no greeting, no signature.

Jonas read what was on the sheet. He looked at Michael. "What the hell is this? A riddle?" He had been expecting, at the very least, a clue to what Philip had uncovered in Japan.

"Not a riddle," Michael said. "It's a death poem."

Jonas blinked. "A death poem? You mean like the crazy kamikaze pilots used to write just before they went on a mission?"

Michael nodded.

Jonas grunted, handed back the sheet. "You're the Japanese expert. What does *shintai* mean?"

" 'In falling snow/Egrets call to their mates/Like splendid symbols/of *shintai* on earth.' " Michael quoted his father's death poem. "In a Shinto shrine," he said, "a *shintai* is a symbol of the divine body of the particular spirit the priests believe inhabit the sanctuary."

"I didn't know that your father was a Shintoist," Jonas said.

"He wasn't," Michael said. "But my Japanese master, Tsuyo, was. Once I remember my father visiting me in Japan. Tsuyo and I were at the Shinto shrine where Tsuyo made his second home. My father was in awe of the place. He said that he could feel the place breathing, just as if the entire structure were a living creature. The priests were very impressed with that when Tsuyo translated it for them."

Jonas waved his hand impatiently. "Then what's it all mean, Michael? The poem, I mean."

Michael got up, walked across the office to peer out the window. He could see the compound, the beautifully manicured lawns, the carefully tended gardens. And beyond, a twelve-foot-high wall rose, filled with the most sophisticated

113

electronic sensors and deterrents to break-ins of any kind. As he watched, one member of the three squads of specially trained German shepherds bounded into view, roaming a three-foot-wide perimeter just inside the wall.

"Obviously, the poem is supposed to mean something to me," Michael said. "But I don't know what it could be."

"Does snow have any significance for you?" Jonas asked. "Or egrets?"

"Not really."

"What could they be symbols of?"

Michael shrugged.

"Oh come on, son," Jonas said. "Think!"

Michael returned to his chair. "All right." He raked his hair with his fingers. "Let's see, snow could be purity of purpose—or death. White is the color of mourning in Japan."

"What else?" Jonas was busily writing this down.

"Egrets. Symbols of eternal love, of singular beauty."

Jonas stared at Michael, pen poised, waiting. "And that's it?" he asked eventually. "Purity, death, love and beauty?"

"Yes."

"Oh Jesus!" Jonas threw down his pen. "Your father loved his secrets. But I'll tell you, I've got no time for riddles. You were right on target. Nobuo Yamamoto took his negotiating party back to Japan. The bunch you saw at the Ellipse Club were stunned.

"At midnight, I got word that the Japanese prime minister announced that twelve percent of his country's new budget is being allocated for defense. That's unheard of. Ever since the end of the war, defense spending in Japan has never gone beyond three quarters of one percent. Do you understand the dire significance of such a change?"

Michael looked at him. "Why dire? It seems to me that the more Japan spends on her own defense, the more self-sufficient she'll be."

"We won't have the kind of power over them we have now," Jonas said. "We're their knight in shining armor. We have been ever since the end of the war. And that monetary commitment to them has kept them as our outpost in the Far East. Hell, in some places, Japan's less than a hundred miles from the Soviet Union."

"Maybe the Japanese are tired of the role we have given them," Michael said, "as America's vassal in the Pacific."

"The morals of defense aside," Jonas said, "there's the fact of Japan's rearming to consider. For more than forty years, they have had a steadfast reluctance to the kind of militarism that goes hand in hand with a large defense budget. They still remember Hiroshima and Nagasaki. So much so that they've refused to allow even American nuclear-powered armaments in Japanese waters.

"The combination of aggressive militarism and the overreaching of economic ambition is what got them into a world war. It damn near destroyed the entire country once. I'd have thought they would do everything in their power to keep it from happening again.

"So what are we to make of this new budget? And of the Japanese arrogance in the economic sphere? It seems to me as if the Japanese are beginning to resonate to the same dangerous chord that caused them to declare war against us forty-odd years ago."

"You're jumping at shadows," Michael said. "Just because Nobuo Yamamoto and his party don't want to play by the American rules anymore, you start waving the flag all over the place."

"Michael," Jonas said quietly, "an independent Japan is a disaster waiting to happen, take it from me. The bastards are crazy. They are obsessed with freeing themselves from dependence on foreign oil."

"Perfectly understandable," Michael said. "If you were stuck on the far side of the Pacific with no natural energy resources, you'd feel the same way."

"I don't like it," Jonas said. "What was merely a barely detectable drift in unofficial sentiment six months ago has suddenly become a very official series of major policy shifts."

Michael said, "Get me over there and—"

"You're going to Hawaii," Jonas interrupted. "I told you that we had one lead to your father's death. That lead is on the island of Maui. He is a man named Fat Boy Ichimada. He's the *oyabun*, the head, of the Taki-gumi Yakuza family in the Hawaiian Islands. Hotel records show that your father called Ichimada the night before he was killed. I want to know why."

Jonas opened a file, passed four photos over to Michael. "Here's as much as we know from this end. Ichimada's boss— the *oyabun* of the Taki-gumi—is Masashi Taki." He pointed to a black-and-white photo of a wolf-faced man. "He's the youngest of the three Taki brothers. Their father, Wataro Taki,"—he pointed to another photo—"died recently. The consensus on Wataro is that he was the godfather of the

115

Yakuza. He brought them out of the twilight world of small-time hoodlums and gamblers into the legitimate—and not so legitimate—arena of big-time conglomerate business.

"I must admit, of all the Yakuza *oyabun*, Wataro was by far the best of the bunch. He was legitimately against communist encroachment in Japan, and ever since the Communist-instigated '48 riots along the Kobe docks, his clan helped the Tokyo police on many occasions."

Jonas pointed to a third photo. "Just after Wataro died, his eldest son, Hiroshi, was killed under suspicious circumstances. One rumor has it that Masashi ordered the assassination to move him closer to taking over his father's position. Another, more persistent rumor attributes the death to someone named Zero. No one knows who Zero is, only that he's a kind of *ronin*, a masterless warrior operating within the Yakuza sphere, yet apparently not a part of it, not bound by any of its rules or laws of *giri*. There are, apparently, many stories about Zero. So many, in fact, that it is doubtful all of them could possibly be true. Yet the Yakuza firmly believes them. Even the clan bosses are afraid of Zero."

At the first mention of Zero, Michael felt a little chill run down his spine. *Zero*: the absence of law; the place where the Way of the warrior has no power. No wonder the Yakuza were afraid of this *ronin*; he was well named.

Jonas snapped the edge of the last photo. "That leaves Joji, the middle brother. Masashi has already thrown him out of the Taki-gumi. We can discount Wataro's adopted daughter, Michiko Yamamoto. She's far older than the boys and hasn't been active in Taki-gumi affairs for years. Now, maybe your father knew more than this. It wouldn't surprise me. He had dealings with these people years ago, and as far as the Japanese are concerned, with such ties and obligations, time doesn't exist."

Jonas threw a thick folder across the table. "Everything you'll need is in there: tickets, passport, Japanese visa, files on Ichimada and the Taki-gumi, maps of Maui. You ever been there? No? Well, it's a piece of cake compared to some other places. Easy enough to get around, virtually impossible to get lost, except on the wild side around Hana. But you're going to the other end of the island: to Kahakuloa. The area's lush and mountainous, but manageable.

"You'll find maps of Ichimada's compound, details about his security system, the number of men he employs and the like. You can trust the intelligence one hundred percent. But it'll be up to you how to get inside. Don't count on him inviting you. And getting close to him when he's on the outside is too risky. His men are all armed, and they're not afraid to shoot first. Okay?"

Michael nodded.

"A Jeep will be waiting for you at Kahului airport. Your hotel room's been paid for. There is five thousand dollars in there, but an account has been opened for you at the Daiwo bank in Kahului should you need more."

Michael hefted the packet. "You said something about a passport and a Japanese visa," he said.

Jonas grunted. "I haven't been reading your tea leaves, if that's what you think. I just like to have all the bases covered."

"Well," Michael said, "if I *do* get to Japan, I'll do a little poking around about Yamamoto and his business associates. I've still got a lot of friends over there."

Jonas held up his hands. "Don't do me any favors, Michael. Please. You're going to have your hands full just tracking down your father's murderer and Audrey's abductor. Your father's area of expertise, the Yakuza turf, is your territory now. Get used to it, and stick to it. All right?"

Michael had returned to studying the death poem his father had written. "Maybe I spoke too soon," he said. "Maybe this *is* a riddle—a kind of test my father is giving me." He closed his eyes. Something flashed through his mind, something Audrey had caused him to remember that night of reminiscence. "There *is* something. When Audrey and I were younger, we were caught in a snowstorm." *Falling snow.* "I built a shelter out of the snow. Audrey wanted to run, but I stopped her. I pulled her into the shelter, and we huddled together until Dad found us. Afterward, he said that shelter saved our lives."

"Sure," Jonas said. "I remember him telling me how he brought you home. He was proud of you, son." He shrugged. "But I don't see what that's got to do with this poem."

"That's just it." *Falling snow.* "I can't quite explain—" *Egrets call to their mates.* Michael's head snapped up. "That's it! It must be!"

"What?"

"Egrets don't call to their mates," Michael said excitedly. "They call to their families."

"Yes?" Jonas still didn't see it.

I called and called, Mike, Audrey said. *I thought Dad would*

hear me all the way back at the lodge. Do you remember?
Michael remembered.

He stabbed at the letter. "This is only half of it!" he said.
"Whatever is in here, whatever clue's been left for me, it's
only part of the message Dad left me."

Jonas spread his hands. "Where in God's name is the other
half?"

"Audrey has it."

"What?" Jonas almost leaped out of his chair. "What the
hell are you talking about?"

"Don't you see, Uncle Sammy? We're the egrets, Audrey
and I. Calling to each other."

"I don't understand."

"She told me Dad sent her a postcard."

"Listen, son, my people were over the house from top to
bottom. There was nothing of a recent nature from your
father."

Michael stared at Jonas. "Then she's got it on her," he
said. "Jonas, don't you see? This could be why Audrey was
kidnapped now. To get the information my father sent her."

Jonas said nothing.

Michael looked down at the letter from his father, wondered if someone else had read it. "Uncle Sammy?"

"We're looking at an awful lot of ifs. But it is possible,"
Jonas admitted finally.

"Who could have intercepted this letter?" Michael asked.

Jonas shook his head. "Any number of people. But really,
we don't know if anybody did."

"Dammit!" Michael said. "Give me a better explanation."

Jonas stared bleakly at Michael. "I understand your frustration, son. And right now I'm in the dark as to why your
sister was kidnapped." He drummed his fingertips against the
desk top. "For now, we had better assume the worst. The
fact is, Audrey is in the gravest danger. We also have to
assume that there is a very strict time limit. *If* whoever kidnapped her knows she's got information that Philip passed
on to her in some manner." He looked at Michael. "Of course,
the corollary of that assumption is that they'll come after you
next."

"We've got to save her," Michael said. "Besides, I know
I'll never understand the message my father left until we do."

Jonas turned to stare out the window. The sun was coming
down, sending deep gold shafts slanting into the office. At

last he said, "Follow your instincts, son. Right now they seem to be our best—our *only*—offense."

Michael rose.

"One more thing," Jonas said. "Don't underestimate this Ichimada character—or any of the Yakuza you're likely to meet. They're tough, and they have no compunctions about taking a human life. Watch your back from the moment you get off the plane. Ichimada's people monitor everyone's comings and goings.

"By the way, you'll find a Beretta in the glove compartment of the Jeep."

"No gun," Michael said.

"Michael, you can't drive around there unarmed."

"Get me a *katana*, then. A good one."

"I can't promise it'll be as good as the one your father gave you."

"That would be impossible," Michael said. "Just do the best you can."

Jonas hesitated, then nodded. "It'll be waiting for you." He gave Michael a quick smile, stood up. He stuck out his hand and, as Michael took it, said, "Good luck, son. Godspeed."

"I can see you."

Water lapping.

"I'm the only one who can."

Lapping at pilings.

Masashi smiling into the gloom, at the shadows. "I'm the only one who knows who you are." He gestured. "Zero."

At their backs, the Sumida River pulsed with the vehicles of constant commerce. Ancient pilings creaked; rats squeaked, running like acrobats along hawsers.

"My Zero." He laughed. A passing boat sprayed brilliant shards of lights through the pilings, into their intimate meeting ground. It seemed to illuminate the cruel cast to Masashi's expression. In a moment the gloom returned, and Masashi felt the movement. He drew the *tanto*, the Japanese dagger, from its hidden scabbard at his waist.

He could see Zero moving, and flicked the tip of his weapon in that direction. Before he could react to his error, he felt a blow numbing his left hand, so that the *tanto* dropped to the rotting timbers at his feet.

The razor-sharp blade of a *katana* glinted.

119

"Will you kill me now?" Masashi asked. "Well, all right, get on with it. Do you imagine that I am afraid of you?"

Then the *katana* was coming for his throat. Masashi, standing his ground, clapped his hands together. The blade was caught between his palms. For a moment they struggled, each one trying to wrest away the other's grip. Even though Zero had the advantage, the blade stayed between Masashi's powerful hands.

Masashi spat. "Fear is for others to feel, Zero. You know what will happen should you hurt me—or try to foil me in any way. I've made that quite clear, haven't I?"

Masashi relaxed, let go of the blade. In a moment, Zero had handed it over. It was coercion, not strength or strategy, that decided this contest. Masashi held the *katana* up so that it was hit by one of the shafts of moving light. In this manner, the sword appeared as if it were piercing the darkness. The worked silver and gold on its guard sparkled like a burst of stars in their enclosed world.

Prince Yamato Takeru's legendary blade, symbol of the *Jiban*, soul of Japan. "You brought it back," Masashi said.

Zero turned away so as not to witness the expression of sheer avarice on Masashi's face. "You left me no other choice."

Masashi tore his gaze away from the shining sword. He nodded. "Yes, that's true. The calls come regularly. Michiko keeps you informed. She talks to the child every day. 'I am alive and well,' the tiny voice says, or something to that effect. So Michiko knows. The child is perfectly fine. So long as you do everything I say. That is our arrangement, yes? And it will remain so until I have no more use for you—until I have nothing else to fear from Michiko."

Masashi nodded. "There is a lesson to be learned from this, dear Zero. Power is so ephemeral, so fleeting. Michiko was always feared in Yakuza circles, almost as much as my father was. Just as you are feared."

"I am feared," Zero said, "because Wataro Taki used me to keep the other Yakuza families in line."

"My father used you to strike fear into the hearts of his enemies. He used you to paralyze them. It is only right that I, who have inherited my father's place in the Taki-gumi, should have inherited your skills as well."

"How the Taki-gumi has changed since Wataro's death!" Zero said. "You are destroying the family—everything your father built—through your overriding ambition and greed."

"My father was living in the past," Masashi said. "His time

120

had gone; he was too stubborn to see that. His death was a merciful blessing for all of us."

"It was neither merciful nor a blessing," Zero said evenly. "Your father died in great pain. His death benefited only those filled with an evil venality. You and Kozo Shiina. It is Shiina, your father's enemy for decades, who will have the last laugh. The Taki-gumi will soon be riven by greed and blind avarice. The lieutenants cannot help aping their *oyabun*. They will fight with one another over power and territory, just as you and your brothers have fought. They will make the family vulnerable to the other families, who were held in check by the force of Wataro's will."

"A fanciful—and totally inaccurate—reading of the future." Masashi shrugged. "But in the event that there is a grain of truth to what you say, I always have you, Zero. Whosoever defies my will shall be destroyed."

"That is what happened to Hiroshi, isn't it?" Zero said. "I had no hand in Hiroshi's heinous death, but I'll bet you did. Was it Ude, your executioner, who murdered poor Hiroshi? Hiroshi was the eldest son, he was Wataro's choice to succeed him, to become the new *oyabun* of the Taki-gumi. Hiroshi was too strong for you to throw out, as you did your other brother Joji. Hiroshi was strong of will and popular among the lieutenants. Hiroshi would have controlled the future of the Taki-gumi had he lived. He would have continued the family in the manner Wataro had wanted. Therefore Hiroshi had to be eliminated."

"My brother is dead," Masashi said quickly. "What matter the method of his demise?"

"It is where the bloodstains dry that concerns me."

"That is quite amusing," Masashi said, not in the least bit amused, "considering what you do for a living."

"I do nothing for a living," Zero said enigmatically. "Because I am not alive. Not now. Not since your ascension. Not since you took from me that which is most precious."

The shadowed figure turned partially away from Masashi. "Once," Zero continued, "I was an extension of the will of Wataro Taki. Wataro was a great man. He used the Yakuza as no one else had. Yes, he made enormous profits from illegal activities. But he never preyed on the weak and the helpless as other *oyabun* do as a matter of course. And he gave back much of his profits to the needy in communities throughout Tokyo. He believed in the common man, and he did all in his considerable power to help those people.

121

"That was why he refused your request for the Taki-gumi to get involved in drugs. Drugs are a destroyer of life. Wataro loved life too much."

"I am tired of hearing what a great man my father was," Masashi said. "He is dead, and I am *oyabun* now. I will show everyone who so reveres the god Wataro Taki what the true meaning of greatness is. He turned his back on the enormous profits the drug trade—and only the drug trade—would bring in. Now I am making these profits a reality. Soon the Taki-gumi will be wealthy beyond the imaginings of even the god my father, Wataro Taki.

"I am preparing to lead all of Japan into a new era, so that every human being on earth will at last turn his face toward the Land of the Rising Sun."

"You're mad," Zero said. "You are but the head of a criminal family."

"You insignificant insect!" Masashi sneered. "How little you know of the vast reserves of wealth and influence I am even now amassing!"

"You'll bring ultimate destruction to the one thing that meant more than anything else to your father: the Taki-gumi."

"Shut your mouth!" Masashi snarled. "I'll tell you when to talk, just as I tell you where and when to go. Why was I unable to contact you last week?"

"I was unavailable."

"That is not in our understanding!" Masashi shouted. "You are to be available to me day and night. At all times. Where were you?"

"I was . . . unwell."

"I see that you have made a recovery." Masashi glared in Zero's direction, thinking. "Well, no matter," he said in a calmer tone. "It has come to my attention that Michael Doss is on his way to Hawaii. Maui, to be exact."

"Why would that be of any concern to us?" Zero asked.

"We intercepted a letter Philip Doss sent to his son," Masashi said. "It was very touching, a kind of passing of the torch. Our good *karma*. I let the letter go because what could be better than to have Philip Doss's son brought into this. You have returned the *katana* to us, but the Katei document is still missing. Though Philip Doss is dead, I'm betting his son will lead us to the document. It is the very heart of the *Jiban*, detailing its entire strategy, as well as the networks of its power throughout the Japanese business, bureaucratic and governmental sectors."

A barge hooted, and for a moment their coffinlike compartment was flooded with bars of probing light. Zero moved further into the shadows. When the sound of the engines had faded sufficiently, Masashi resumed. "So Michael Doss is your quarry. I don't want you involved in anything else until this matter is resolved. It will not be long now. No more than the space of two weeks at the outside. My schedule is both demanding and unyielding."

Zero was silent.

"Well?" Masashi said.

"I will do as you ask."

Masashi smiled at last. "Of course you will."

Fat Boy Ichimada felt oppressively hot. It was like the jungle here. Or like Japan in August. The trees stifled all air coming in off the ocean. These wild mountains of Kahakuloa, within which he had chosen to work, had their drawbacks. But these very drawbacks, Fat Boy Ichimada reminded himself, were part of the reason his solitude was rarely breached.

On breathless days such as this, it was important to remind himself of every positive aspect of his work. Like the little house he had built for himself in Hana, on the other side of the island, hidden away from everything and everyone. When the pressures of his world became overpowering, he took his helicopter and flew to Hana. His hideout. Few people knew about the house. Wataro Taki, Ichimada's *oyabun*, had known about it. But Wataro was dead. Now only the two Hawaiians who Fat Boy had hired to find the Katei document knew of its existence, since Fat Boy had lost patience with checking up on the house himself. He certainly did not want anyone in his clan to know of its whereabouts.

It had not been Fat Boy Ichimada's idea to come to Hawaii. Others far more inexperienced than he would perhaps have seen it otherwise, thinking themselves fortunate to have a job—to be in a position to become top man in the Islands.

But Ichimada knew better. Being top man in what he considered to be the asshole of the universe was no honor.

Not that Ichimada had anything against Hawaii. After all, he had been here for seven years. But in the Yakuza, anywhere but Japan was nowhere. Japan was where the real power resided, no matter what anyone back home assured him.

Once Fat Boy Ichimada had been a favored lieutenant in the Taki-gumi. Wataro Taki had seen his bravery and his

123

loyalty and had rewarded him. Then Masashi began to gain in prominence. Masashi had seen to it that anyone with a modicum of power within the Taki-gumi was swept aside. Except in Ichimada's case it had not been so easy. Masashi had trumped up charges against Fat Boy. They were totally false, but evidence that Masashi had obviously planted had been found in Ichimada's house.

Fat Boy Ichimada was missing the little finger from his right hand. It still resided, he suspected, in a jar of formaldehyde in the Taki mansion. Fat Boy Ichimada had taken a knife, and to atone for a sin he had not committed, a sin created by Masashi, he had sliced off the finger.

He had been sitting across the table from Wataro Taki at the time. In Tokyo, seven years ago. Bowing, he had wrapped the finger in a white cloth and passed it across the table. Bowing, Wataro Taki had accepted the gift.

Being banished from Japan to Hawaii was the other part of his atonement.

Nowadays, Fat Boy Ichimada thought, the new Yakuza asked for a shot of Novocain before they put knife to their flesh. But Ichimada was from the old school. Honor and *giri*, the burden hardest to bear, were his watchwords. It was *giri*, after all, that had led him to cut off his finger. He had done what Wataro Taki, his *oyabun*, had asked of him. Now that Masashi was *oyabun* of the Taki-gumi, Ichimada no longer felt any obligation to his boss. Quite the opposite, in fact. His heart burned for revenge, and the years had not cooled that ardor.

Therefore, when Masashi Taki had signaled Ichimada that an American named Philip Doss was on Maui, that Doss was carrying something that belonged to Masashi, that Masashi wanted it back and that Ichimada was to use any and all means to get it, Fat Boy had made his own plans; he had hastened to comply. But for his own ends, not Masashi's.

Masashi had made it clear to him that the Katei document was invaluable. Ichimada had no idea what the document contained. But he was certain that if he should become its possessor, he could buy his way off of Hawaii, buy his way back to Japan. Masashi was so determined to get the Katei document back that Fat Boy was convinced that Masashi would give Fat Boy his own subfamily to run, as thanks for its safe return.

That had been Fat Boy Ichimada's plan. Hence the use of

the two Hawaiians. They were supposed to bring Philip Doss and the Katei document to Ichimada.

Instead, Philip Doss had crashed and burned. But not before he had phoned Ichimada. "I know who you are," Philip Doss had said. "And I know where your loyalties lie. I know you will do the right thing. You and I both loved Wataro Taki, didn't we? If you are still loyal to the old ways, you will find my son. Ask him if he remembers the *shintai*. I have left a key in his name—Michael Doss—with the concierge at the Hyatt in Kaanapali. With it, he will be able to open a numbered locker at the airport."

"What?" Fat Boy had said, stunned to be hearing from the very man who was his quarry. "What are you talking about?" But there was only dead air on the other end of the line.

Ever since the call, Fat Boy Ichimada had wondered what was in the airport locker. In the meantime, Masashi had phoned him to expect Ude. The news had put Fat Boy into a panic, and he had sent the two Hawaiians to pick up the key and bring him the contents of the locker. What was in there? The Katei document? And what was the significance of the *shintai*?

At the same time, he had driven out to the airport to pick up Ude. Ude, who had come, was hot on Philip Doss's trail. And with him, an icy fist clamping Fat Boy Ichimada's heart. Fat Boy was certain that Ude had not come just to retrieve the Katei document. Masashi had plenty of other people he could have sent to do that. Ude was Masashi's executioner. That planted the suspicion in Fat Boy's mind: Had his two Hawaiians talked? He had been a fool to trust them. But he had had no alternative. If he was to have any chance of escaping this paradisiacal prison, he had to make a grab for the Katei document. As soon as he was free of Ude, he would have to find the Hawaiians and punish them.

For now, though, he would have to deal with Ude. The problem, as Fat Boy Ichimada saw it, was not so much how to retain possession of the Katei document he had sent the two Hawaiians in search of but how to stay alive long enough to make use of it.

Ude was a member of the new breed. In Tokyo, no doubt, he would hang out at the Wave or the Axis in Roppongi, eat at Aux Six Arbres, dress in Issey Miyaki outfits. Try to make it with the *gaijin* blondes busy gobbling hamburgers and french fries.

Like all of his ilk, Fat Boy thought, looking at him now, Ude wore his desires on his face. Like a Westerner.

Fat Boy Ichimada told himself that he was not scared of Ude. Why should he be? Ude used drugs, and that made one careless. The key, Fat Boy knew, was not to make any precipitous moves. That was what Ude would try to make him do.

Now Ude and Fat Boy were down in the lower lea of Fat Boy Ichimada's property; it abutted on acreage that had been a cattle ranch for decades. Horses, cows and flies abounded, and not much else. Ude walked down along the cliffs and then back into the cow pastures. Fat Boy huffed beside him, always a pace or two behind, hurrying to catch up. Fat Boy liked Ude to think of him as a rather stupid fat man. The less sharp Ude believed he needed to be around Fat Boy, the better.

Ude strolled through the grazing herd. Their enormous brown eyes regarded him with bovine somnolence, while their tails switched at the horseflies. Ude's gaze, however, was not on the spectacular scenery or the bucolic inhabitants. He watched where he was walking.

He passed over those pies, steaming and glistening like oatmeal. These were too newly excreted. Those cracked and grayed from age, half leached into the grass, he passed up as well. What he was searching for were cowpies crusted over but still gravid with nutrients—the fertile mound of creation for the mushroom. Not any mushroom. *The* mushroom. The one that, when Ude ate it, would paint the sky orange and red and turn the universe inside out.

Mushrooms were the object of Ude's pilgrimage onto the lea in Fat Boy Ichimada's field: slender white stalks with buttonlike heads, slightly brownish, growing in small clumps.

When he found what he was looking for, he knelt and, using a penknife, clipped the mushrooms. Fastidiously, he circumcised the septic bottoms. Then he popped them into his mouth and, rising, chewed reflectively.

In a moment, he felt the first changes beginning. He could discern the blood pumping through his veins and arteries. A pulsing in his lower belly, a *geisha*'s delicate fingers plucking the strings of a *samisen*. Time extruded through the Third Eye.

He began to hum as he walked. "Sayonara No Ocean," a pop tune from more than a year ago that had stayed with him. The notes, as they rumbled out of him, twirled in the air like clouds of breath on a frigid morning. Spent, the vi-

126

brations dying one by one, they burst like a line of crystal goblets striking a tile floor.

The sunlight covered him, some viscous substance that stuck to him in tender globules, heating his flesh. He nodded his head, slipped off his black polo shirt.

Blue, green and black double phoenixes rose amid a bed of crimson flame. Wings spread wide, their long, powerful necks twined as they stared into each other's faces. Below the pyre that had spawned them, a thick serpent curled and slid through rock and foliage. Its fanged jaws opened wide, its jeweled eye omniscient, its forked tongue eternally questing.

Naked to the waist, Ude's *irezumi*—the traditional Yakuza tattoos—rippled and danced in concert with his musculature. Muscles invariably made him think of Masashi Taki. Masashi was a nut about fitness. Often, he and Ude would work out together, hour after hour, until even Ude's superbly toned body ached. It was at those times that Masashi frightened Ude. Ude, who was frightened of no one.

Ude would stand, exhausted, watching Masashi continue his strenuous workout, sweat streaming off his glistening hide, and Ude would find himself thinking, He is not human. He has more stamina than a dozen men.

Finally, when Masashi was finished, they would move to the *dojo* mats, there to take up longswords so that the *oyabun* could practice his *kendo*. It was all Ude could do to keep up with him. At every turn, it seemed, Masashi gained in strength. He was indefatigable.

In the lea, the ocean's froth streamed from the corners of Ude's mouth. Ude laughed as he saw another deluge of froth. Finally, he recognized the bubbles as words. He was talking to Fat Boy Ichimada.

"Consider," Ude realized he was saying, "that the Katei document is everything."

"I know only what Masashi has ordered me to do," Fat Boy Ichimada said.

"Philip Doss was here," Ude went on, ignoring him. "Philip Doss stole the Katei document. He fled here with someone's assistance, *neh?*, since he had dropped out of sight in Japan. He eluded me in Japan. Then here on Maui he is mysteriously killed. Not by me. Not by anyone who works for Masashi Taki. Then by whom, Ichimada? You know everything and everyone. Here." He showed Fat Boy Ichimada the photo of

Michael Doss. "Have you seen him? This is Philip Doss's son, Michael. Has he been here?"

"The son is not on Maui," Fat Boy Ichimada said, thinking how much the son resembled the father.

"No? Are you sure? Maybe Doss gave his son the Katei document for safekeeping."

"This man hasn't been on the Islands."

Ude, his black pupils unnaturally dilated, laughed cruelly. "Perhaps it's just that you can't handle a situation like this anymore." He gave Fat Boy Ichimada a nasty smile. "Incompetence—that *is* why you were sent here, isn't it?"

"You're here for a day," Fat Boy Ichimada said, "and you think you know everything." But he was stung. He did not like being reminded of why he had been sent away from Japan.

"Seven years," Ude said mockingly. "If I had been here for seven years, I'd have built a clan that would have made the old boys in Japan blanch. I would even have thought of keeping a plum such as the Katei document for myself." His grin was so broad it was a leer. "But you're too stupid ever to have thought of that, aren't you, Ichimada?"

Fat Boy Ichimada said nothing. He knew Ude was trying to bait him into making an admission of guilt. Masashi could suspect from the Hawaiians' information what he was planning. But without proof, he could do nothing. For now, face protected Ichimada. Masashi needed a reason to remove him from his position in Hawaii. That was why Ude was here: to get that reason. Masashi knew that was going to be difficult, so he sent Ude to bait Fat Boy. If Ude's insults proved sufficient for Fat Boy to strike back, then Ude could kill him with impunity. None of Ichimada's family on the Islands would protest. Therefore, Fat Boy resolved to remain calm.

"I don't blame you for not talking about it," Ude went on. "I certainly wouldn't. You see, the difference between us is that I would have made the best of being an exile. I'd be out from under the thumb of Tokyo. This is the land of plenty. The United States. They don't know what we're about. Rich, virgin territory. Ripe for the picking. A man can make his reputation here, as well as amassing a fortune! Yah!"

Ude's face turned to stone. "You knew Philip Doss in the old days, *neh*?"

"We both knew Wataro Taki," Fat Boy Ichimada said, thinking, That's why Masashi sent Ude to put pressure on me. He's suspicious that Philip tried to contact me. I must be very careful.

For Ude, the world was swimming in color. It was alight with glimmerings of an astounding nature. "I want the Katei document," Ude said, concentrating. "Masashi Taki ordered you to get it. If you don't hand it over to me, I must assume that you are holding out on me."

Ichimada had an answer for that. "I am loyal to the Taki-gumi. Masashi need have no fear about that. As to the where-abouts of the Katei document, I am working on that right now. I have been at it from the moment Philip Doss was killed. He was not carrying the document when he burned. I am checking all the places he stayed or visited on the island." Fat Boy felt the maddening tickle of a line of sweat as it rolled down the side of his temple. Ude peered at it with the intense interest a lapidopterist devotes to an exotic butterfly.

"You?" Ude said, examining the droplet of sweat. "You are handling this personally?"

"Of course," Fat Boy said, trying to keep one mental step ahead, wondering now if Ude knew about the two Hawaiians at all. Had Ude's bluster been just a ruse after all? "I would not trust this delicate a matter to anyone else."

"You have a reputation for never getting your own pudgy fingers dirty." Ude threw his head back and laughed. "I saw your finger, by the way. It was in a bottle filled with brown liquid."

"*Giri*," Fat Boy said, struggling to keep himself calm. "But that is a concept Japanese like you no longer understand, *neh*?"

Ude's eyes were suddenly fierce. "I have been given total autonomy to settle this matter in any way I choose." He sneered. "Unless you deliver the Katei document to me within forty-eight hours, Ichimada, you will die."

Fat Boy Ichimada stared at Ude as if he were mad.

"I advise you to do whatever you have to." Ude cocked his head, making an exaggerated show of listening. "Do you hear that? It's the sound of your life running out."

Fat Boy Ichimada listened to the insane laughter and ground his teeth in impotent fury.

A Bas was alight with gold-and-green neon.

"It's like being in a fishbowl," Joji Taki said.

"The night has a thousand eyes," Shozo said, recalling a

line from an old American film. "And every one of them is here."

The nightclub was decorated in a style that could only be described as minimalist chic. Down a steep flight of steps from a street awash with people, glossy gray-and-black tables and chairs were scattered about a floor that seemed to shimmer with tiny lights. Astoundingly, there seemed to be no less of a crowd here than on the floors above. The nightclub was on several levels, connected by acrylic stairs in which had been embedded neon tubes, twisting like futuristic serpents.

The walls were a series of thick sheafs, acoustically arranged, covered in a woven material that was neither gray nor brown but that borrowed from both hues. They rose in separated tiers toward a ceiling filled with a firmament of metal scaffolding lit by a series of spotlight clusters, all of which were in constant movement. The result was not unlike being inside a stomach in the process of digestion.

The intimation of anatomy was well founded. The girls who roamed the narrow aisles between tables flashed their semi-nakedness in the same systematic manner that sides of beef are hung in a slaughter-house.

That this kind of mechanical sexuality appealed to so many males had ceased to amaze Joji years ago. It might be a truism of modern life that mechanical sexuality was better than no sexuality at all.

He thought briefly of Kiko, waiting with the patience of Buddha for his return. Then, having allowed himself this minute treat, he turned his full attention toward the meeting at hand.

Masashi had entered A Bas. He stood in the doorway, his head surveying the scene by increments. This was Masashi's way. When he walked into the interior of any place, he would stand just inside the doorway. He would not fully enter until he had a clear picture of the area in his mind.

He was dressed in a black pin-stripe suit, pearl-gray shirt and a white-on-white-patterned silk tie. He wore gold cuff-links and a plain gold band on his ring finger.

The man he had brought with him was unfamiliar to Joji, an older Yakuza with clever eyes.

Masashi spotted Joji and Shozo and made his way slowly toward them. His man, quite deliberately Joji was sure, remained where he was beside the door. This was by way of an admonition to Joji. A silent reprimand that Masashi wanted this meeting to be solely between principals.

130

The two men bowed to each other, performed the ritual greeting. Joji dismissed Shozo. Drinks were ordered.

On the small stage, a young male Japanese in sunglasses was singing a current pop song to a prerecorded accompaniment blasted out of a phalanx of speakers suspended from the ceiling. Light jumped and sparked. The reflections off his smoked lenses were dazzling.

"I admire punctuality," Masashi said, "above all other virtues. A punctual man is a reliable man."

The waitress returned, delivering the drinks. From all sides Japanese men, suited and sunglassed like the singer, ogled every exposed inch of her.

"I asked for this meeting because since you left the Takigumi," Masashi went on, "it occurred to me that perhaps I had been unfair to you."

Masashi took a long swallow of his Suntory scotch. Having been recognized as Yakuza, Masashi and Joji had been served stiff drinks rather than the normal watered-down bar drinks.

"I wish," Masashi said, "to minimize whatever misunderstanding there may be between us. My wish is for the Takigumi to maintain its position of preeminence. Whatever is required for that to take place, I am willing to do."

"I appreciate your candor," Joji said, relaxing. "I, too, would welcome an equitable solution to our differences. There is no earthly reason for there to be tension between us."

"Good," Masashi said. "There is much money to be made— for all of us." He lifted his glass.

"Oh yes," Joji said. "Bad blood is for men without honor. Men who belong to another, lesser, world than ours, *neh*?" He laughed, immensely relieved, as he clinked his glass against Masashi's.

"We are a rare breed, Joji-san," Masashi said expansively. "Our father was a simple orange farmer. He was casteless, an outsider whom society neither wanted nor could tolerate. Yet here we are. We own more, make more, control more, than ninety percent of the population of Japan. We regularly meet with the heads of the largest business concerns, with the top vice-ministers—even, on occasion, with government officials.

"But what good is any of this? We are all of us squeezed into centimeters of space. In America, the poorest member of the middle class may buy a moderately priced house on an acre of land. An *acre*, Joji-san! Can you imagine such a thing? How many dwellings would we put on an acre of land

131

here? How many families would occupy that space? I tell you it no longer matters how much money one has in Japan. We are all humbled by our own lack of space. We live like insects, continually climbing over one another."

The anger in Masashi's rising voice intrigued Joji because it had an odd element to it. Joji had been listening hard, not only to what Masashi was saying but to how he was saying it. The bitterness was unmistakable, a corrosive core that went beyond philosophy. That masochistic undercurrent of self-hatred. If so, it fit the memories Joji had of their childhood. Masashi had been the baby of the Taki brothers. He had always been the most difficult, the most headstrong; the willful one, the contrary one. It was entirely conceivable that Masashi, having been coddled by Wataro Taki, grew up resenting that very attention.

"Do you really hate our country so much?" Joji said. "I cannot believe what I am hearing. It is the place that has given us life, the place that nurtured us."

"Drivel," Masashi said contemptuously. "Well what else can I expect from my mouse of a brother? Your timidity was always your worst fault. You cannot see that the only way for Japan to be great in this new atomic age is to expand its boundaries."

"The greatness of Japan," Joji said, "is in our hearts, where the spirits of our ancestors dwell. It is in our minds, where the memories of our history remain eternal."

"Japan has rebuilt itself from ashes," Masashi said. "But it has gone as far as it can. Now it is up to men with vision to take it farther." He downed his drink. "I speak only the truth," he said. "And the truth is often not what a man wants to hear."

"Do you want the truth?" Joji said. He spread his hands. "Look at these suckers, my brother. Here is where you find your new recruits, *neh*? They come here to be voyeurs. They stare the night away. Then they go home and masturbate." He made a sound deep in his throat, as if he were going to spit. "There is nothing real in looking beneath the skirt of a woman who leaves her underwear off for a living."

The waitress removed their glasses, placed fresh ones on the table. The sunglassed singer was crooning.

"Listen to that insipid garbage," Joji said. "It's what your new recruits listen to for hours on end. Do they care about *haiku*, the poetry of their own great heritage? No. They have lost touch with the past, with all that makes Japan great.

" 'We sit and stare for hours/At the smoke in each other's eyes,' " he mimicked the sunglassed singer. "It's meaningless. Like the manufactured violence in the movies, where audiences root out loud for more and more mutilation. Like the manufactured grotesqueries of television news shows. The violence they bring us is as contrived in its way as that in films. Why? Because all of it is meant to manipulate us. The viewer is titillated but never made to feel any real emotion, such as outrage or disgust. The electronic world has no place for such realities. Simply because its business is fantasy."

Joji was aware that he was talking too much, that his brother was staring at him, but it seemed he could not stop himself. He felt the anger like a knot inside himself; it was as if he had become infected by his brother's rage. "The new breed of Yakuza you are bringing into the Taki-gumi is without honor, without a sense of tradition," he continued heatedly. "And this is why. They were raised on electronic junk food. They were manipulated since birth. It's mother's milk to them. Consequently, all they know is how to manipulate. Each other. Themselves."

Joji gestured. "Look at their pleasures. They require bombardment for any reaction to surface. Their spirits are decayed and callused. Extremism is the banner they hold high. Because the extreme is the only thing that has sufficient power to move them. All the rest falls on deaf ears and sightless eyes."

"Extremism," Masashi said, "is often misunderstood." He leaned forward. "Today it is extremism—and *only* extremism—that will wrench Japan from the hands of the Westerners—the *iteki*! If you were not so soft-bellied, you would see this truth as I do. If only our father had understood. The only good he did was use the Taki-gumi as a weapon against the Russians."

"How can you speak this way about our revered father?" Joji said.

"I say what has to be said. I am the only one with enough courage to do so. As usual."

Masashi has not changed, Joji thought wearily. All the elation he had felt at the beginning of the meeting washed out of him. Joji realized that he was on a fool's errand. Masashi had not changed one iota. He was still contemptuous of the old traditions. It was Masashi who had argued at clan meetings that the Yakuza were mired in the past, that their code of honor—though once useful—was now more of a detriment. "We are nearing the year two thousand," Joji recalled Masashi saying. "If the Yakuza is to have any chance at all of surviving the new century, then it must look to expand its base of operations.

"We are wholly local, as we have been for centuries. We have done nothing to better ourselves. We are, essentially, where we were in the days of our grandfathers.

"The world is rapidly passing us by. In order to remain strong, we must seek new horizons. The Yakuza must do what our government has done. Compete on a global scale."

But going global would take an enormous outlay of capital. And there was only one way to fund such expansion in an ongoing manner. Drug running. Wataro Taki had vetoed any such involvement. And that had been the end of it. Or so everyone had believed.

Then Wataro had made his retirement announcement. And Masashi had made his move. Into the twentieth century. The age of thermonuclear nightmare and electronic dissemination.

Profit without honor was a life better left to corporate businessmen, Joji firmly believed. Honor was what set the Yakuza apart. It was what made them special, it was their link to the greatness of the past. The splendor of the *samurai*. Masashi would, no doubt, sneer at such a comparison. But this kind of continuity was the only protection against the disconnection rampant in society. That was the difference between them.

He was wrong. It was not the mutilation served up daily on TV and films that had crippled the spirits of the new breed. It was the electronic media's murder of the past. According to the postmodern credo, the past was as disposable as last week's fashion trend. It had been made irrelevant.

"Learning is difficult enough for the young and inexperienced," Joji said. "It is impossible for your new Yakuza recruits to *un*learn this explosion of fallout from the atomic age. What's bred in the bone," he added, quoting Shozo.

"What's that?"

"An American aphorism," Joji said. "But it is apt for us in this instance. You are resigned to the necessity of employing the young and inexperienced, for whom learning is impossible. Garbage is their mother's milk."

"Are you questioning my methods? Again?" Masashi said. "The problem is universal among us. Only the solutions differ."

"And what is yours?" Joji asked.

"An alliance," Masashi said. "Between the Yakuza, the bureaucracy and the government."

Joji laughed. Surely his brother was drunk on Suntory. "Who has been filling your head with such nonsense?" he cried. "The Yakuza are outcasts. They are beyond society at large. We are who we are because essentially we are misfits. We cannot survive in the highly stratified society of Japan otherwise."

"Perhaps that was true once," Masashi said. "But no more. Now the Yakuza will join the mainstream of society."

"Impossible!" Joji could not believe what he was hearing. "We are outlaws. We will always be viewed as undesirable by the ruling powers. You cannot change what is."

"I can change it," Masashi said. "And I am. I am taking the Taki-gumi out of the shadows. For one thing, I am planning to make public the heroic deeds performed by the Taki-gumi over the years in defense of Japan; our history of work against the Russian KGB should be a matter of public record. I am stepping up our involvement in Yamamoto Heavy Industries' businesses. Nobuo Yamamoto and I are planning several new ventures in which Taki-gumi members will participate more fully. The clan will soon be as great and legitimate a force in Japan as any business conglomerate you can name."

"Listen to yourself," Joji said. "The businessmen and bureaucrats with whom you seek an alliance will spit on you. They would sooner commit *seppuku* than grant Yakuza entry into their strata of society. Your self-delusion would be a source of humor were it not so sad."

"Enough!" Masashi shouted. Heads turned as he was heard even above the electrified music.

Joji persisted. "Don't you see that the very presence of your new breed of recruits spells utter disaster for the future of the Yakuza? They are ungovernable because they are rootless. Without a heritage, they cannot be committed to anything. Certainly not to a Yakuza *oyabun*. They will not submit to discipline, because the only thing they believe in is anarchy. You are an out-and-out fool, unfit to be *oyabun* of the Taki-gumi, if you believe otherwise."

Masashi leaned across the table, grabbed Joji by his shirt-front. Glasses crashed to the floor. Two bouncers moved in the table's general direction but were stopped by Shozo and Masashi's pockmarked soldier. "Listen! You may be my brother, but I don't have to tolerate this kind of discourtesy!

I am *oyabun* of the Taki-gumi. I took pity on you and was going to offer you a post back inside the clan for the sake of appearances.

"There will never be a chance of that now. You're like our father. You've got your head back a hundred years. I want no part of you. Do you hear me? Get out of my sight, weakling!"

Ude found the two Hawaiians drinking beer at a local place in Wailuku. They were not difficult to find. Ude had put a tap on Fat Boy Ichimada's private line before they had had their little chat down in the lea. Ude had frightened him so badly, it had not taken Fat Boy long to get on the phone. The tap Ude had used was a TN-5000, one of the new generation that Fujitsu had designed. Using an ROM microchip, it stored the computer tones coming into and going out of the phone base to which it was attached. That gave Ude the phone number Fat Boy had dialed. Ude was hooked into everyone and everything on the Islands; it had taken Ude only a short time to get the name and address that went with the phone number.

Ude sat down at a table near the front door. Took a chair at a ninety-degree angle from them, so he could keep an eye on them without having to face them directly. He had pulled up just as they were getting into their van. He had followed them here.

Ude ordered a club soda. He never touched alcohol or tobacco. Saving himself for the mushroom. He smiled. These Hawaiians, he thought, relaxing now, have got the life. They'll never amount to anything, but they sure are happy.

While he waited, he had plenty of time to think about Fat Boy Ichimada. In many ways the *oyabun* reminded Ude of his own father. Know-it-alls who couldn't see a foot in front of their face. They were the center of everything; they held the past in their hands.

Fah! Ude thought now. The past is meaningless. It is baggage that saddles you with its useless weight all through your life. Ude had no such compunctions. He saw only the future, brightly lit, overheated, eternally beckoning. The future was what set his juices running. Ude would do anything he was told in order to have a piece of it.

Now he had to find out what these Hawaiians were up to. He did not believe a thing Fat Boy Ichimada had told him; he could not afford to. Fear had its advantages, as Masashi

Taki was ever pleased to enumerate. But it also made liars out of even the most honest of men. More often than not, you were told just what you wanted to hear. Which was why Ude had come to the source.

Eventually, the two Hawaiians got bored with drinking beer. It took them a very long time. Their capacity for liquid astounded even Ude, who had been with many prodigious drinkers in his time.

There was no problem following them. All they had on their mind was girls. They picked up a couple of locals in another hangout, which was obviously familiar to them. Ude waited outside. There was no need to get out of his car because he had a clear view of the place through the open door.

The four of them emerged and got into the Hawaiians' van. Ude took off after them. They had a place in Kahului near enough to the airport so that the rumble of the jets' engines was a permanent fixture of the neighborhood.

He was going to wait until they were alone. But then he thought, What the hell. Fat Boy Ichimada had pissed him off, holding out on him when Ude had expressly warned him not to. The quicker this was done, the quicker Fat Boy Ichimada would get wind of it. Ude dearly wished he could be with the *oyabun* when that happened, impossible though that would be. Ude laughed, thinking of Fat Boy's expression. Sometimes, he knew, the dream was better than the reality.

Take now, for instance. Ude sitting in his car, the engine off but the engine of his mind chugging along. Feeding images of the death and destruction in which he would participate moments from now.

Images of a surreal quality. Sometimes he would see the two Hawaiians. Looking into their eyes at the moment of their deaths. Watching for the transition. To see the spark go out.

In reality he never did, of course. It was impossible, no matter how concentrated one's mind was. That instant remained elusive, save in the images of Ude's brain.

In those images he would reach out and grasp the spark as it lifted free of the body, a blister excised. Open his mouth and swallow it. Would this impart to him a power sublime?

In another image, instead of the two Hawaiians in the shabby house, Ude saw his father. It was his father's body beneath his. His father's face that he watched for the jump of the spark. It was his father he was going to kill.

Ude got out of the car. Crossed the street and went toward

the house. The grounds were a mess. Grass that hadn't been cut; shrubs that had needed pruning three years ago were now as wild as a lion's mane. Ude felt a surge of revulsion at human beings who could be so unconscious of their surroundings.

Ude's own home outside Tokyo was fastidious in every respect. Especially the grounds, which to Ude were sacred. To plant, he felt, was to take on a holy trust. Gardens were a matter of considerable complexity. They required élan in designing, skill in planting, care in maintenance.

That was another thing, Ude thought as he picked the lock, of which my father was ignorant.

He entered the semidark house. Hearing noises, he paused in the hallway. Listened to the grunts and groans, as if he were nearing the ape cage at the zoo. He could hear a box spring squeaking rhythmically.

He produced four lengths of cowhide rope. He preferred cowhide because it was supple yet strong. He moved forward.

It took him just over a minute to ascertain that the two Hawaiians had moved from separate quarters into one bedroom. The door was open. It was easy to look inside.

One of the Hawaiians had the bed. He was on top of his girl, humping away at breakneck speed. The other Hawaiian was lying on his back on the floor. His girl knelt over him. She was rising and falling, her hands on his chest. His eyes were closed.

Ude was wearing lightweight crepe-soled shoes that he had had made for him in Tokyo. They made no sound as he crept into the room and silently shut the door behind him.

Five people in the room, and he was the only one perfectly still. From this stillness he erupted into motion without warning.

At the bed, he grabbed the Hawaiian's wrists, twisting them backward. With a flourish he could only have learned watching Hollywood westerns, Ude whipped a length of cowhide around the Hawaiian's crossed wrists. The knot he made was slip-proof. In fact, the more the Hawaiian struggled, the tighter it got.

In almost the same motion, he turned to the couple on the rug. He kicked out. The steel toe of his shoe caught the girl in the throat. She coughed, gagged, sank all the way down on the supine Hawaiian's penis.

Ude pushed her violently aside as the Hawaiian's eyes flew open. They were still filled with her, his reflexes dulled by lust. Ude punched him hard just below the rib cage and, as he began to double over, pushed him onto his stomach. Used the second length of cowhide to lash his wrists together.

Heard someone scrambling behind him, turned, lashed out with his right leg. Caught the first girl as she was attempting to dash for the door. Connected with her hip, heard her heavy grunt, turned away from her before she had fallen to the floor.

By this time, the Hawaiian on the bed had gotten to his feet.

"Who the hell are you?" he shouted. Fear lent a shrill note to his voice.

With a leg strike, Ude crashed him to the floor. He used the respite to tie up the girls. When he was finished, he contemplated the two Hawaiians writhing.

The one Ude had hit in the rib cage used both legs, striking Ude on his thigh. Ude grunted, swung forward and down, jamming the toe of his shoe into the side of the Hawaiian's neck. That was unfortunate. It broke the man's neck, and by the time Ude knelt down beside him, took his head in his hands and stared into his face, there was nothing to see.

"You've killed him!" the second Hawaiian screamed. The girls began to whimper.

"The same thing will happen to you," Ude said, "unless you tell me."

"Tell you what?" the Hawaiian said.

"What Fat Boy Ichimada sent you to do."

"Who's Fat Boy Ichimada?"

Ude used the edge of his hand. It was a neat, clean calculated blow to the heart, which terrified the Hawaiian. His face went white; he gasped. His eyes watered. Ude waited.

"Answer," he said.

"A hearse!" The Hawaiian's eyes were squeezed shut. He was panting. "The woman was driving a hearse!"

"A what?"

"At the airport in Kahului!" the Hawaiian screamed. "A hearse drove up to take charge of a coffin flown in from the mainland!"

"Where on the mainland?"

"New York, Washington. I'm not sure."

"Why were you at the airport?"

"Because of the red cord."

"What red cord?"

"Untie me," the Hawaiian said, "and I'll show you." He

rubbed his wrists when Ude untied the rawhide. Ude went with him to a chest of drawers. The Hawaiian opened one, rummaged through his underwear.

"Here it is." He produced a short strand of braided cord of a red so deep it was almost black.

Ude took the cord. "Where did you get this?"

"At the airport. A locker. Ichimada told us to pick up the key. At a hotel. Under the name Michael Doss."

Doss! Philip Doss's son! Ude could smell the truth. "That's when you saw the hearse?"

"Yeah. I was waiting for my brother. He went to take a leak. I noticed the woman right away because she knew about Fat Boy's men. The ones he uses to monitor everyone who comes in and goes out of the airport. She avoided them."

"Then what happened?" Ude asked.

"Are you going to kill me?"

Ude smiled. "Not if you tell me what I want to know."

The man swallowed, nodded. "I went over to the hearse while she was signing the papers to get the casket through, and that's when I saw it. There was a hand-drawn map on the front seat. I leaned in. It showed the way to Hana. There was a circle drawn around a spot in Hana. It was Fat Boy's house. The one he uses maybe once or twice a year, when he wants to get away from business and the family."

A casket being brought to Fat Boy's house? Ude thought. What was going on? "Isn't Hana on the other side of the island? Very remote, very wild. Where exactly is this house?" The Hawaiian told him.

Ude thought it was time to take the hard edge off. "What has Fat Boy got going?"

"Oh, he doesn't know about this."

"How do you know that?" Ude asked.

"Because he's gotten lazy. He said he used to take care of the house himself. Now he has us doing it. We were there not more than a couple of weeks ago, getting rid of the roaches. They come in from the mountains. But there was no electricity on, no water. Nothing. He was not expecting anyone."

Even more interesting, Ude thought. He considered. "Did you tell Fat Boy any of what you saw at the airport?"

"You mean with the woman? Not yet." Tears were streaming from the Hawaiian's eyes. "My brother said no. Fat Boy locked him outside—with the dogs, you know? The Dobermans. Ever since then, my brother hates Fat Boy. 'We take his money,' my brother says. 'That's all.' "

"Who was the driver?" Ude asked. "The woman?"

"I don't know," the man said. "Please! I've told you everything. Let me go!"

"All right," Ude said gently.

He crashed the edge of his hand into the Hawaiian's throat, then knelt down beside him. For a moment their eyes locked. The cricoid cartilage had ruptured. The Hawaiian began to suffocate.

Ude continued to stare into his face even though the Hawaiian's eyes, opened wide, were darting wildly here and there as if they were seeking escape from the inevitable.

With a kind of devotion, Ude's hands covered the Hawaiian's face. Now Ude spoke in Japanese, as if to his dead father. "You left your wife. You left your son. There was no time to make you pay for the suffering you caused those who once loved you."

Thumbs curling into claws. "Those."

Lifting away from the already graying flesh. "Who."

Ligaments raised as tension came into them. "Once."

Moving over the trembling eyelids. "Loved."

Thumbs plunging downward in concert with a scream.

The murderer's or the murdered's?

"You."

Ude, his forehead pressed against the Hawaiian's, was weeping.

"Father."

Two hours later, Ude was in Hana. There were no roaches left in the house, but there was something alive.

Or rather, someone.

Like a stone skipped across a lake, Michael was winging his way across the Pacific. The continental United States was behind him, but Uncle Sammy's words would not let him be.

Michael's mind was wrapped around the enigma that was Philip Doss.

Up swam a memory. Philip Doss coming to Japan. To Tsuyo's school for Michael's graduation.

Michael saw his father enter the *dojo*, carrying a long, thin package wrapped in multicolored Japanese paper. Philip had come just in time. Michael was called to the center of the *tatami* mats. He, like all the other students, was garbed in padded suit and a mask with a metal grill over the face. This served as protection against the *bokken*, the wooden swords the students used.

"Tendo," Tsuyo said, "is the Way of heaven. It is the Way of truth. It is how we here live our lives. *Tendo* gives us our understanding . . . of the world around us . . . and of ourselves. If we do not grasp *tendo*, then we understand nothing."

Tsuyo moved to where Michael stood, handed him a *bokken*. He returned to his place at the edge of the mats.

"Understanding nothing, we are evil and will eventually slip into evil ways, whether or not we mean to. This is simply because in turning away from *tendo*, we have lost the ability to recognize the face of evil."

Two students, also armed with *bokken*, approached Michael from opposite sides. They attacked in tandem as if acting on an unspoken cue.

But Michael was already in motion. This was what Tsuyo called the Zen chance. He clashed his *bokken* against that of the first opponent, applying pressure in order to force the two weapons down and away from him.

At that instant he disengaged and, drifting to his left, brought his wooden sword in against the fists of the second student. Immediately, Michael attacked again and again, beating down the hastily erected defenses of the surprised pupil, until the *bokken* flew from his hands.

The first student had recovered sufficiently to race at Michael's back. Michael twisted, narrowly missing a blow to his spine. He engaged, sword against sword.

As he did so, Tsuyo signed for a third armed student to attack. Tsuyo was standing, watching the action with a practiced eye. His hands grasped his steel *katana*. There was no expression on his face.

Michael felt the strike from his opponent all the way up his spine. He knew this boy well. He was an attacker. He was stronger than Michael, but perhaps not as determined.

The student held his *bokken* before him, made a rush at Michael. Michael held his sword end downward and slightly to his left. He let his opponent's blade come at him, moving at the last instant so that the student's momentum took him past Michael. Michael pivoted, slashing the boy across the back. The student fell flat, his weapon rolling away from him.

Now the third student was almost upon Michael. As Michael turned, he saw that there was no defense, no offense he could offer. He was defeated. And he remembered the Zen saying "Beat the grass, surprise the snake." He threw down his sword.

For an instant, the third student did not understand the

142

gesture, and he stopped. In that moment of indecision, Michael struck, using the edges of his hands in *atemi*, percussive blows, on the student's nerve meridians. The student collapsed.

Now Tsuyo strode to face Michael. He was in the *ken-tai* position, the master's battle stance. What could this mean? Another test? The assembled students held their breath.

Tsuyo attacked, and there was no time for thought. The steel blade whistled through the air toward the weaponless Michael.

Who reached out, capturing the *katana*'s blade between the palms of his hands.

For the first time, Tsuyo smiled as he said, "It is always thus. *Tendo*, the Way of heaven, shows us the nature of evil. It shows us not only how to confront evil, but when."

Afterward, Philip spent the afternoon with his son. It was the first week of spring. In Yoshino, where Tsuyo's school was located, the hillsides were thick with cherry trees bursting into bloom. As they walked the country paths, tender white petals drifted about their faces like windblown snow.

"I came," Philip said, "not only to be at your graduation, but also to give you this." He handed over the wrapped package.

Michael opened it. The ancient *katana* glinted gold and silver in the sunlight.

"It's beautiful," Michael said, stunned.

"Yes. Isn't it," Philip said. "This was the sword made for Prince Yamato Takeru. It is very old, Mike. Very precious. There is a great responsibility in owning it. You have become its guardian, therefore you must take care of it every day of your life."

Michael began to withdraw it from its elaborate scabbard.

"It's as sharp now as it was on the day it was forged," Philip said. "Be careful. Use it to fight evil, only if you have to."

Michael looked up, a sudden intuition flooding him. "Is that why you sent me here, Dad? So I will be able to recognize evil?"

"Possibly," Philip Doss said thoughtfully. "But these days evil is adept at wrapping itself in many disguises."

"But I have *tendo*," Michael said. "The Way makes me strong. I have passed all of Tsuyo's tests today."

Philip looked at his son, smiling sadly. "If those were the most difficult tests you will face," he said, "I'd be content." He ruffled Michael's hair. "Still, I've done the best I can."

He turned, bringing them around so that they were headed back toward the *dojo*. "Now you know that first you must recognize evil. Then you must combat it. Finally, you must guard against becoming evil yourself."

"It's not that hard, Dad. I did it today. I stopped Tsuyo's attack without attacking him myself. I knew that he had no evil intent."

"Yes, Mikey, you did. And I'm proud of you. But knowing these things for certain gets harder the older you grow."

Audrey . . . Oh God! Poor Audrey! Michael thought now. He buried his face in his hands. His cheeks were wet with tears. He had not been able to recognize the evil that had come for Audrey. The magnificent *katana* that his father had entrusted to him could not save her. And in any case, now it was gone, too.

Where was Audrey now? Was she alive?

"Father," Michael whispered, "I swear on your grave that I'll find Audrey. I swear to you that I'll find whoever took her. I'll find whoever took the *katana* you gave me."

The shining bosom of the Pacific was flat and steely below the patches of thick cumulus. It seemed infinitely peaceful, an entire world unto itself. At this moment it seemed to Michael to be impossible—and unfair—for there to be teeming civilization plunked down in the middle of it.

First you must recognize evil.

"*Tendo.* The Way of heaven is the path of righteousness." Tsuyo's voice echoed in his ear. "The Way of heaven is truth. Those who deviate from the Way have already embraced evil."

Then you must combat it.

"Your father sent you to me for one purpose," Tsuyo said on the first day they met. "To learn the Way. He wishes you to have the opportunity that he never could. Here in Japan, there is a chance that you may learn. But first you must shed everything else in your life. If this seems distasteful to you, even harsh, so be it. The Way is difficult. The Way—not I, not you—will decide whether you are suited for this study."

Finally, you must guard against becoming evil yourself.

"The Way of heaven abhors weapons," Tsuyo said. "However, just as a gardener must rid his garden of weeds and vermin in order for the flowers he tends to grow, so there comes a time when the Way of heaven calls for eliminating destructive evil. The evil of one must be expunged so that ten thousand may live in peace and harmony. This, too, is the Way of heaven.

"Now you may think that the Way is everything. Yet defeat is possible even after you have come this far. Even a master of the discipline, a *sensei* such as myself, may know defeat. In that dread place where the Way cannot tread, where the Way is powerless.

"In *zero*."

Michael swallowed now, clearing his ears. With a bump, the plane was down. The jet engines screaming beyond the Perspex windows until the brakes took hold.

He looked out the window at palm fronds rippling and, beyond, the sapphire jewel of the Pacific Ocean.

Maui.

Michael was already in the air when Jonas entered the offices of General Sam Hadley. Hadley, in his eighties, had been retired from the Army for some years. But by special commission, he had retained his strategic advisory capacity to the president. It was not to the general's assistant that Jonas went, however, but to Lillian's.

The young major was a severe-faced man. He ran Lillian's section with a fierce competitiveness. He showed a serious lack of a sense of humor, but Lillian said that he could be forgiven that fault.

The major asked if Jonas would like coffee, Jonas assented, and it was brought into Lillian's office moments after Jonas himself had gone in.

Lillian had asked about Audrey as soon as Jonas arrived. But there was no news, nothing he could tell her that might give her some solace. She was controlled enough not to stay on the subject, and for this Jonas was grateful. Now that he had sent Michael off following Philip's trail, he was uncomfortable in Lillian's presence. He knew that she would not take it well when she found out what he had had a hand in doing.

"I'm glad you could come," she said, trying to smile.

"It seemed important when you called," Jonas said.

They sat in the end of her office that was more like her home, away from the desk. There were no file cabinets, no credenza. But half her desk was taken up with a phalanx of phones that at a moment's notice could connect her with every area of the government, from the White House to the Pentagon to just about anyone on Capitol Hill. General Hadley's

145

lines of power ran long and deep into the fertile soil, not only of Washington, but also of the major capitals of the world.

Over coffee, Jonas took a long hard look at Lillian. She wore a black dress. She had abandoned all jewelry save her plain gold wedding band and a pair of diamond stud earrings Philip had given her for their tenth wedding anniversary.

"The vault is no place for jewelry, Lillian," Jonas observed.

"My memories are there," she said tonelessly. "My jewelry is no more beautiful than those." She stared at her left hand. "What I choose to wear now I do so out of necessity." As if there were no longer a place in her life for personal luxury.

"Philip is dead," he said gently.

Lillian closed her eyes. "Do you suppose that his death has caused him to disappear? As if he never existed?"

"Certainly I didn't mean to imply that."

She stared at him. "Whatever Philip was, whatever Philip did, cannot be altered by his death."

She looked very pale. The lack of sunshine on her flesh had turned her skin translucent. It seemed to Jonas that she was as beautiful now as she had been when he had first met her. She had lost none of her luster; she was still desirable.

But not to Jonas. He wondered how long it would be before the unattached men in Lillian's circle would come nosing around. Her job as her father's assistant brought her into contact with the most high level diplomatic personnel from around the world.

All of them would want a piece of Lillian now. Jonas smiled inwardly at that. He had kept his personal animosity toward her carefully in check all these years. But now, in the intimate moment that her grief created, he could allow it to come up, he could turn it over and over like a precious artifact.

It had always been a question of the life he shared with Philip or the life Philip had shared with Lillian. It seemed to Jonas that Lillian had never understood the men's need for secrecy. She had wanted to be a part of everything that had been Philip. And when she couldn't, she had blamed Jonas for it. And because of her anger, he supposed, she had driven a wedge between Philip and himself.

It occurred to Jonas, sadly, inexorably, that his friendship with Philip never had been the same after Lillian's appearance.

And still, knowing this, after all this time, he could not hate her. She had loved Philip. And out of his own love for Philip, Jonas had made her part of his adopted family.

146

It was difficult to believe that he was sitting across from her and that Philip would not at any moment walk through the door. Lillian and Philip. Much to his dismay, Jonas discovered that he could not think about the one without thinking of the other.

"The consequences of Philip's life," Lillian was saying now, "will surely outlast the consequences of his death."

Too bad she knows nothing of either, Jonas thought. Or is it? In this case, maybe not. That last blow would no doubt crush her entirely. Impulsively, he reached out, put his hand over hers. Her marriage band disappeared beneath his palm. "Of course they will," Jonas said. "Philip was responsible for great things. Who should know that better than the two of us?"

"I'd prefer that you didn't patronize me," Lillian said. "You're well aware that for years I knew nothing about what Philip did. That was something that was always between the two of you. I never liked that, but I came to accept it. Eventually."

Lillian smiled. "But don't concern yourself, Jonas. The secrets you and Philip kept are in no danger from me."

He frowned. It had always amazed him, the transformation of Lillian Hadley Doss from USO singer to a mover within diplomatic and military circles. She seemed out of place in this office of power, attended to by the stern-faced major, every inch the strict disciplinarian that Lillian's father still was. Was the incongruity of it, he asked himself, because of her beauty? Because she was a woman? "What do you mean?" he asked.

Perhaps she heard the uneasiness in his voice. She kept her smile. "I work here, for my father, remember, Jonas? General Hadley is still your boss as well as mine. He runs all the bureaucratic interference for BITE. He's had the ear of every president since Truman, and with good reason. He's the finest military strategist this country's seen since the turn of the century.

"There are no secrets anymore, Jonas. Not from me, at least. I have gotten a measure of satisfaction from that. It was always you and Philip. I was always left out."

"That was business, Lil."

"It still is, Jonas." Her smile widened. "Only now, secrets are my stock-in-trade too." She put down her cup. "That's why I asked you to come as soon as you could." She held out a red-bound folder. It was stamped TOP SECRET and EYES

147

ONLY. Across one corner were the double black stripes that cautioned that the material contained inside could not be duplicated or taken out of the office of origination.

"What is it?" Jonas said as he took the folder from her. But there was already a sinking feeling in his stomach.

"Read it," Lillian said. She poured herself more coffee as Jonas flipped open the file. She took out her Equal, emptied two packets into the black coffee. With a silver spoon she stirred it around and around.

"Jesus!" Jonas said. "Jesus Christ Almighty!" He looked up. "Lillian—"

"It's true, Jonas," Lillian said. "That's the two-year report my father's been doing on BITE."

"I knew nothing about this!" Jonas said.

"Neither did I. Until now." She stared at him. "Is it true, Jonas? What the report says? About the intelligence leaks? The breakdown of networks over the past six years?"

"Certain ones, yes," Jonas said. "But that's the nature of the game, Lil." He hit the folder with the back of his hand. "But this! Christ, your old man wants to shut us down!"

"Permanently," Lillian said. "That's the recommendation of the report. And it's the recommendation my father will make to the president when they meet next month."

"Your father has seen the report, then?"

Lillian shook her head. "Not yet. He's scheduled back from Poland next week sometime. Right now, because of negotiations, his itinerary's a bit vague."

Jonas sat back, took a deep breath. "Why are you showing this to me, Lil?"

She sipped her coffee, silent.

He cocked his head. "What is it you've been trying to prove all these years in competing with Philip and me? That you're our equal? Because you're not, you know."

"Contrary to the male's mistaken way of thinking," she said, "women do not want to be men."

"No?" His tone was skeptical. "Then what is it they *do* want, since equality isn't in the cards?"

She contemplated him for a time before answering. "Just a measure of respect, Jonas. That isn't so much to ask, is it?"

"Respect."

"Yes." Lillian's glance took in the red file on his lap. "No one else could have gotten that, Jonas. Let alone got you a peek at it."

"What is it you want in return?"

She shrugged. "Nothing. We're family, aren't we, in a way?"

When she was finished with her coffee, she held out her hand. "I'll have to take that."

Jonas gave her the damning report.

"Do you know where your secrets are going?" she asked.

"To the Russians," he said. "But that's about all we've been able to find out."

"Well," she said, "you'd better find out who's selling you out before my father returns. He reads this report and BITE will be chopped up, shipped out in so many pieces you'll never recognize it again."

The major came in, delivered a sheaf of reports to Lillian's desk. He left without a word. When they were alone again, she said, "Where has Michael gone?"

The question he had dreaded. "Away."

Lillian's back stiffened. "He's my son, and you know where he is."

"Do I?"

"He came to say goodbye. He wouldn't tell me where he was going or why. But I can guess. You've swallowed him up," she said. "Just as you swallowed Philip up."

"I don't understand that," Jonas said. "Philip did what he wanted to do. He always did."

"Without you," Lillian said, "he would have found something else."

"Like what?" Jonas was openly contemptuous. "Computer programming?"

"Perhaps. In any case, he would be alive now."

"Don't blame me for Philip's death. I have enough responsibilities to bear."

"I'll just bet you do," Lillian said.

"What does that mean?" he said slowly and carefully.

"You have Michael," Lillian said. "You are the only person he could turn to." She was trembling with anger. "If you turn him into another Philip, I swear to you, Jonas, I will make you pay."

"Calm yourself," Jonas said, alarmed. "I've done nothing of the sort." He told her about what had taken place in his office. About Philip's "will," Michael's induction into the world of espionage, where Michael had gone. He had not wanted to tell her any of it, of course, knowing how she felt about his role in Philip's career, knowing how vulnerable she was now, after her husband's death. But he had had no choice. She had told him as much when she had allowed him to see

149

her father's Eyes Only report on BITE. He was grateful to her for that.

Now he watched for any signs of a breakdown. He knew that his sending her son out on the same path that had gotten her husband killed was a gamble. But it was a gamble dictated by desperate times. Besides, he told himself, it was what Philip seemed to have wanted.

Try telling Lillian that. He did.

"Lil," he said after he was finished, "are you all right?"

Lillian was very pale. He could see her teeth beneath her parted lips. They seemed to be chattering. She held her elbows in against her body. Now he could see that she was rocking gently back and forth.

"It's happened." Her voice was a feathery whisper, but it chilled him just the same. "My worst nightmare has come true. Oh Jonas, look what you've done!" Her voice suddenly rose in volume to a kind of pain-filled wail. "You stole my husband from me. Because of you, we don't know whether Audrey is alive or dead. Now you've put my son in the same deadly jeopardy! My God! My dear God!"

Audrey awoke with a start into darkness.

She was swimming through a dream, a diver, down in the depths too long, reaching upward toward the watery sunlight high above her. Even while the cool quiet of the ocean tried its best to hold on to her.

The ocean of sleep.

She had been dreaming that she was bound to a chair.

Wrists and ankles were blue and bloated from the cruel bite of wire flex. She had trouble breathing because wire was wrapped around her torso, over and under her breasts. Her back was arched; there was tension in every muscle.

The darkness was like velvet, thick, soft and impenetrable.

It began to move. To swirl, to shift, to coalesce. And as it did so, Audrey felt a fear crawling inside her, making her breath come fast and hot, making her mouth dry and her armpits wet.

Dear God, she thought in her dream. Make it go away. Not knowing what *it* was.

The darkness possessed shape now, though she could not say just what that shape was. The darkness pulsed with life, and it was drawing closer to her.

In her mind, an echo: *There is no escape.*

She had always been certain that she would live forever.

150

At her age, fifty years was forever. Now she knew that she was going to die. Her teeth chattered, her mind jabbered. Some elemental animal inside herself was trying hysterically to get out, to escape the doomed mortal coil in which it was trapped.

The darkness was upon Audrey now. She could feel its steeping heat on her thighs, could feel its warm breath on her lips. The presence was unmistakably male, and she felt another kind of heat. Her own sudden arousal terrified her even more.

Then the darkness began to penetrate her, and she began to die . . .

Awakening with a start into darkness.

She shuddered, still partially inside her dream. She wanted to wipe the sweat from her forehead, could not.

She found herself bound to a chair.

Michael thought: If Paris is a city of dusty browns, greens and blues, then Maui is an island of pastels: turquoise, pinks and lavenders. What surprised him was that it was a place where the color umber was impossible to imagine.

As opposed to Japan, where, among the slopes of Yoshino, where Tsuyo had taught him about life, umber was the dominant color.

He did not think that another spot on the globe could affect him as deeply as did Paris and Yoshino. In Paris, his work matured. In Yoshino, it had begun.

And this is the essence of what remained: that one employed strategy in every aspect of one's life. There was strategy in putting brush to canvas, in weaving cloth or planting a garden. When conflict arose—as it invariably did—one automatically sought a strategy first. Using a weapon was the strategy of last resort, which was why he had refused Jonas's offer of a gun.

It was early afternoon. The sun, still high in the sky, caused golden light to cascade across the enormous expanses of the sugarcane fields. To his right, the West Maui Mountains rose, haloed by misty cloud. His guidebook, read during the long flight, told him that within that shadowed crevasse lay Iao Valley, home of the ancient Hawaiian gods.

Michael picked up his rental Jeep. As he stowed his luggage in back, he felt for and found the canvas satchel containing the *katana* that Uncle Sammy had promised would be there.

In accordance with the strategy Michael had worked out

on the plane, he stopped in Kahului to make a number of purchases, the first of which was a cheap black satchel. An hour later, he was driving onto Honoapiilani Highway. He was near Maalaea Bay, heading south. Very soon, he knew, the highway would swing around what the locals called the Beautiful Woman's Chin and begin heading northwest. Maui, seen from the air, had the aspect of the bust of a woman. Southeast, where the enormous dormant volcano Mount Haleakala rose two miles into the air, was the upper torso. Kahului, where Michael had just landed, was one side of her neck, Maalaea Bay, the other side. Where Michael was headed, Kapalua and, ultimately, Kahakuloa, formed the woman's head.

The highway ended up past Kapalua. A vast twenty-five hundred-acre pineapple plantation surrounded a secluded resort with a pair of remarkable golf courses. As Michael turned left at the end of the highway, he saw evidence of these golf courses in the superbly manicured greens, the rippleless sand traps, curved like perfect wounds under a plastic surgeon's scalpel.

It was difficult to imagine that barely a mile ahead, the road—what there was of it—wound treacherously across the spine of another in the chain of volcanic mountains that dominated northwest Maui.

Past Fleming Beach Park, the road narrowed considerably. There was no sign of human habitation, no manicured and terraced lawns, no tile-roofed villas climbing amid fragrant sprays of bougainvillea.

Instead, thick, tangly foliage overgrew the margins of the road. Massive outcroppings of rock, ocher and steely-blue, pushed their way toward the center of the road.

When the pavement gave out altogether, what remained was a heavily rutted dirt track no more than a vehicle's width wide. Muddy and slippery, it wound vertiginously close to the parapet edge of the cliff face. At places there was close to a quarter of a mile drop to the churning ocean below.

Now the road had barely enough room for two cars to pass side by side. On one side was the sheer face of the cliff rising upward, on the other, an equally sheer drop downward to the sea.

Michael had put the Jeep into four-wheel drive. All about him the twitterings of birds could be heard, behind which he could just perceive, now and again as he jarred around this hairpin bend or that, the musical tinkling of a waterfall.

Glimpses of rolling meadows straight out of Scotland where brindled cows lay or stood in stultified poses as if they had not moved in centuries.

This was a landscape for which Michael was unprepared. No guidebook, no travelogue, no picture postcard, ever depicted this facet of the Islands. Without emerald palm trees, sapphire lagoons, black sand beaches. Instead, gathering slowly a quality of light—heavy, rich as cream, clear as crystal—like no other in the world.

He was reminded of Provence, in the south of France, and its unique light. It was as if the leaves of the plane trees acted like a time machine, altering the sunlight filtering through them. The remarkable result patinaed each indigenous hue so that it appeared just as it had for centuries.

Here, too, the illumination was unique, but in a wholly different way. The sunlight lent the landscape a lambent quality. Greens became so translucent foliage seemed to float in midair; yellows had a marvelous incandescence, as if exploding with energy. Mysterious blues were by turns iridescent in shadow, lustrous in sunlight.

In these two disparate terrains Michael felt he could discern the active hand of God. For surely the power to move the human spirit so was solely the province of a divine presence.

It was all he could do to keep control of the Jeep. The oncoming Jeep, careening around a snaking hairpin turn, had already slammed into him. A shockwave tore up his spine.

Metal tore into metal even as Michael ran the off-side wheels of his Jeep up the rock-strewn slope. The concussion almost flipped his vehicle over.

He was aware of the other Jeep slewing around as a result of chewing up the headlight and fender on his side of his Jeep. Then beginning a slow swing as its wheels fought for purchase along the dangerous outer edge of the roadway.

The driver was furiously applying the brakes in the correct on-and-off pattern, but this was only good for a road that was there. Abruptly, this one had given way to open space.

Michael's Jeep was already in neutral. He slammed on the emergency brake, scrambled over a door that had been jammed shut in the collision. The other vehicle was overhanging the cliff face, the drive in the rear wheels seeking to grip the road. But there was no tarmac, only sprays of muddy rock undermining its position. The Jeep teetered closer and closer to plunging the fatal distance to the rocky scree below.

Michael leaped from one vehicle to another. At the rear end of the other Jeep, he whipped his upper body forward, dragging the other driver back toward him.

Heard the grinding of the transmission, felt the Jeep slew badly as it continued its skid toward oblivion. With a heave, he threw the other driver clear of the Jeep, then sprang off it himself.

The loss of weight on its rear end sent the vehicle toppling off the cliff. One instant it was there, howling as if in frustration. The next, the empty air was singing in its place.

Sound, echoing, seemingly a long time after.

It was only then that Michael got a good look at the other driver. Saw that she was a woman, and a beautiful one at that.

She was Japanese. She had that golden skin that is very rare and highly prized in Asia. Her eyes were Oriental: long and almond-shaped. Her hair had a bluish luster when the sun caught it. It was thick and straight. It was woven in a wide braid that swung to the small of her back.

She had a wide mouth with sensual lips that seemed perpetually curved in the suggestion of a smile, a long neck and rather square shoulders over which clothes draped just as one saw them modeled in posters fifty feet high.

"Are you all right?" Michael finally said, helping the woman to her feet. In the process he was able to determine that she was well muscled.

"Yes," she said, brushing herself off. Her jeans were old, Michael noticed, faded almost all the way to white. They had no designer name on the pocket. "I guess I'm not used to these roads."

"What roads?" Michael said, and they laughed, more from relief than from anything funny.

"Eliane Shinjo." She extended her hand.

"Michael Doss." He took her hand. With his other one, he plucked twigs and leaf shreds from her hair. Later he remembered thinking, she's not only the most composed woman I've ever met, but also the most unselfconscious.

"Thank you," she said. "I've never been involved in a collision before. This one could have been my last."

"*Our* last," Michael said.

She looked away from him for the first time since he had pulled her off the ground. There was a cooling sensation, as if her eyes radiated heat. "I guess the Jeep's totaled," she said.

"We'll be lucky if mine still works." He was reluctant to

154

move. "I'm sorry if I hurt you. I had to get you out of that Jeep."

Her head swung around; he felt the heat return. "You didn't hurt me." Then she smiled. "At least I don't feel anything resembling pain."

"We both nearly went over with it."

"Was it that close? Really?" Her expression returned to enigmatic. He wondered whether she might be excited by the thought. The proximity to death often did that to people. Especially one's own death. Either it gave one a new perspective on the value of life, or it provided the intense thrill that only defying the inevitable could bring.

"The road was so eroded, there was no purchase left for it. You were already over the edge when I got to you."

Eliane watched him. He wished he could tell what she was thinking.

"You're very strong," she said. "I didn't feel a thing. It's as if nothing at all happened."

"Except your Jeep is scattered all over the base of the cliff."

"It's only a piece of metal," she pointed out.

There was an absurd kind of logic to what she said. Except that her statement precluded any recognition of the concept of action and reaction. It was as if consequences did not exist for her.

Michael went over to where his vehicle stood. It was at an acute angle, the right side canted upward. "Okay," he said, climbing behind the wheel, "let's see where this goes."

He took the emergency brake off and put the Jeep in gear. It rumbled and rocked and almost toppled onto its side before he maneuvered it back onto the dirt road.

"Climb in," he said.

Eliane came warily around the front, stepped up on the running board. He took off, and she swung in just in time.

"Where were you headed?" she asked. Even now she did not pull her hair out of her eyes.

"Just sightseeing. You?"

She immediately regretted having spoken as she did. "I was on my way to Kapalua to play some tennis."

"Sorry," he said. "We're going in the opposite direction." He seemed wholly concentrated on the road.

"No problem," Eliane said easily. "How far are you going?"

"Civilization," he said. He beat at the horn as they went around a hairpin turn. "We've got to get you home. That is, unless you want to hike."

She laughed. "No. I'm a bit of an athlete, but I have my limits."

"Which hotel?"

"I've got a house in Iao Valley," she said. "Do you know how to get to the valley?"

"I make a right up here instead of going straight into Kahului, right?"

"Yes."

Eliane was startled by the effect he was having on her. She knew there was no rational explanation. This disturbed her. The irrational, Eliane believed, was what manipulated events. Like currents in a stream, unseen but felt, the forces of the universe worked to a purpose. Were these forces trying to tell her—warn her?—of something?

If so, what?

"Since you're not a tourist, you ought to know if the courts are good at Kapalua."

"What?"

"The tennis courts," Michael said. Solitary houses, a cemetery. They were nearing civilization.

"Oh." She had to reorient her mind. "Yes. They're very good." A gas station, a church, a phone booth. And just like that, she had the answer. "Would you mind stopping just up there? I've got to make a call."

"Sure."

"My tennis partner will wonder what happened to me," she improvised.

In the phone booth, she dialed her own number, carried on a mythical conversation over the ringing at the other end.

"He's okay," she said, climbing back into the Jeep. "Just a little worried."

"Your steady partner?" Michael asked.

"My boyfriend," she said easily.

"Doesn't he work?" Michael asked. "It's the middle of the work day."

Eliane laughed. "He doesn't have what you would call normal hours. He works for the biggest *kahuna* in the islands." She turned to look at him. "Do you know what that means?"

Michael shook his head.

"It's Hawaiian. Originally, it meant a kind of witch doctor. A shaman who was in touch with the ancient spirits and gods of Hawaii."

"And now?"

She shrugged. "Modern times. Like most old words, it's often misused. So much so that many of the younger Hawaiians have forgotten its true meaning. Today *kahuna* means big shot. A powerful person."

"Like your boyfriend's boss."

Eliane could hear the curiosity in his voice. She looked at the mountains looming out through the mist and thunderheads before them.

"What's this *kahuna*'s name?"

"It wouldn't mean anything to you." She gestured. "Turn here. Yes. Now straight ahead."

They drove into the valley. Thickly foliated ridges snaked away from the winding road on either side.

"Make a right here," she said.

When he pulled up outside the house, Eliane got out. She turned to him. "Would you like a bite to eat? Or a drink, at least?"

"I don't think so."

That smile again. "But you must." She extended her arm to him. "You've saved my life. Good *joss* for me; maybe bad *joss* for you."

"Why bad?"

She laughed. "Because now you are obligated to protect me for the rest of my life." Was there a mocking undertone to her expression? "There is a Japanese word for it. Do you know it? *Giri.*"

"Yes," Michael said, taking her hand, wanting now very much to come inside, to spend more time with her. Because *giri* was a Yakuza term. Fat Boy Ichimada is the head Yakuza here, he thought. If this woman is hooked into the Yakuza through her boyfriend, I can use that. Employing strategy again. Tsuyo would have been proud of him. "It means the burden too great to bear."

"Yes and no," Eliane said, leading him toward the house. "Some say that *giri* is the burden too great to bear alone."

When Fat Boy Ichimada got to the front door of the shabby house in Wailuku in which the two Hawaiians resided, he felt his blood turn cold. He had called the Hawaiians on his private line in his office; he had come alone. No one within his family knew that he was employing the two Hawaiians. Which was, of course, the point.

He stood breathing in the smells, listening to the sounds of the old neighborhood. He could smell *poi* stewing. A brief burst of children arguing came to him from down the block, the blast of a TV set, Jack Lord's voice saying, "Book 'em, Dano. Murder One . . ." A door slammed, breaking off the sound.

Fat Boy's hand hanging in midair, not more than two inches from the doorknob. Staring down at the dusty floorboards. And the dark stain that had crept out from beneath the door.

The stain glistened as if it were newly applied lacquer. Only Fat Boy Ichimada knew that it wasn't lacquer. He glanced around, then, grunting, he squatted down, put his finger into the center of the stain. Brought the tip up, rubbed the substance. It turned from dark brown to dark red. But Fat Boy had already known that it would, in his heart.

He rose, took out a handkerchief and used it when he twisted the doorknob. No prints. The door was unlocked.

Fat Boy drew a snub-nosed revolver with his free hand, then pushed the door all the way open so that it banged hard against the wall of the Hawaiians' apartment.

He crossed the threshold, went silently through the house. In one bedroom, he saw the girls first. He ignored them, stepping over their pale forms. He was careful not to touch or disturb anything or anyone. Or anything that used to be anyone. He marked the grotesque distortions of the corpses and thought, The man's a monster.

Fat Boy left after having found out the only two things worth knowing in there. One: The two Hawaiians were dead. Two: Whatever they had retrieved from the airport locker was not in the apartment.

Across the street in his parked car, in approximately the same spot that Ude had sat several hours before, Fat Boy went carefully over his options. There was no doubt in his mind that Ude had gotten to the Hawaiians. That meant that Ude was now in possession of whatever Philip Doss had hidden in the locker.

No matter what it was—the Katei document, the *shintai* or something else altogether—the consequences were dire for Fat Boy. Ude now knew that Fat Boy had held out on him. He might not yet know what Fat Boy had been up to, but knowing Ude, that would not matter much. Ude had said that Masashi Taki had given him full control over the situation here, and Fat Boy believed him.

There was now no doubt in Fat Boy Ichimada's mind that in order to survive, he was going to have to kill Ude. Philip Doss had entrusted Fat Boy with vital information. Fat Boy now knew what he had suspected all along: that he should have kept that information solely to himself. He was just now realizing the enormity of his error. Sending the Hawaiians to get the key and open the locker had been a grievous tactical mistake. But the presence of Ude had so unnerved Fat Boy that he had panicked.

He closed his eyes. It was as if the carnage in that grubby little house across the street was tattooed to the inside of his eyelids. He felt abruptly sick to his stomach.

He remembered all his years with Wataro Taki. He remembered when he had gone to see his *oyabun* to seek his forgiveness. Wataro Taki would have been within his rights to ask Fat Boy to commit *seppuku*. But instead, he had asked only for Fat Boy's little finger.

Wataro Taki was not like the *oyabun* of other Yakuza clans, who lived only to amass wealth, to bleed their countrymen dry. Wataro Taki had a vision for the future of Japan. And he had made Fat Boy a part of that future.

Now the vision was gone, lying six feet beneath the earth with Wataro Taki's corporeal remains. But Fat Boy Ichimada's mentor still lived, if only in Fat Boy's memory. What was it that Philip Doss had said over the phone on the day he had been killed? *I know where your loyalties lie. You and I both loved Wataro Taki, didn't we?* And: *I know you will do the right thing*.

Now is the time, Fat Boy thought, to repay Wataro Taki for all the kindnesses he showed me.

Fat Boy would have to rectify matters. He had already received a call from his airport spotters that Michael Doss had arrived on Maui. Fat Boy knew that he would have to find Philip Doss's son and give him all the information he had concerning the *shintai*.

Ask my son if he remembers the shintai, Philip Doss had said.

And then Fat Boy Ichimada said, "Buddha!" out loud. Because suddenly he knew how Ude had found out about the two Hawaiians. Ude had tapped Fat Boy's phone lines. That meant he also knew that Michael Doss was on the island. And Fat Boy had had to tell the two Hawaiians that the key was under the name of Michael Doss. Which meant that Ude also knew that the contents of the locker were meant for Philip's son.

Fat Boy started his car, pulled out into the street. Now it's going to be a race, he thought. And the finish line is Michael Doss.

It was raining.

Her face on the wall: a shadow, larger than life.

Michael was staring at Eliane.

"I came here," she said, "because I was tired of cities. Cars, apartments, offices. They were exhausting me."

The last thing he wanted was to be attracted to this woman. He found that he had to keep reminding himself that he was here to discover her link to the Hawaiian Yakuza. If her boyfriend was in Fat Boy Ichimada's clan, he might provide a nonaggressive way into the *oyabun*'s compound.

"I was becoming ill all the time," Eliane was saying. " 'Your resistance is down,' my doctor said. 'Your adrenal glands are depleted,' my chiropractor said. The city was polluting me."

"Which city?"

"It doesn't matter," she said. "They're identical. At least their pernicious effects on human beings are."

It was easy for him to show nothing on the surface. As he moved with her through the rooms of the house, he made all the appropriate noises. The place was undeniably spectacular, even in the rain, nestled as it was between two volcanic mountains.

"Here I can renew myself. In the home of gods beyond time."

The rain, cascading down the emerald-and-sapphire mountains. It was extraordinary. Akin to being sited in the valley between a pair of the giant earth dragons the Chinese believed crisscrossed all terrain. In such a setting, her overt mysticism was contagious.

"Can you feel them, Michael? Can you feel their power? The energy of these mountains?"

The odd thing was that he could.

The rain drummed against the skylight in Eliane's bedroom. What was difficult was to damp down on his inner feelings. He stood in this space and was reminded—despite his best efforts—of his atelier on the Avenue Élysée Reclus. Of the night when Za came to stay.

"You're so quiet." Turning to him. "I'm talking too much." She laughed. This, too, she did unselfconsciously.

"No," he said. "I'm enjoying it. It's difficult to speak in the face of these mountains."

"Yes. I felt the same way when I first came here. They're awesome without being intimidating."

At first it was impossible for him to fathom the link his mind had forged between Za and Eliane. He found that he did not want to leave this place that Eliane had made into her home. Some people can live in a house for years without ever giving any sign that it had been theirs. Just the opposite seemed to be true for Eliane. She told him that she had been here less than a month, but already she had managed to make this house hers. It smelled like her, felt like her. Her presence suffused the rooms like perfume.

"Time seems to slow down here. You know, Michael, the Hawaiians claim that their hero, Maui, climbed to the top of Mount Haleakala, reached up and grabbed the sun, slowing its progress across the sky so that his island home would be sun-drenched forever. Sitting here, it's possible to believe that story."

"Even in the rain?"

It was when they were sitting on the lanai, drinking iced tea, that he felt the blow on his heart. He remembered the moment his eyes had opened that night with Za. They had just made love. The rain was running down the skylight panes, reflecting onto their twined bodies.

"Oh yes," Eliane said. "Especially in the rain. See there?" She pointed. The magnificent rainbow, its colors so vibrant they made the eyes ache, arched across mountaintops still obscured by swirling cloud. "It means that the sun is out even while it is raining."

Back then, he had looked at Za's face for the first time in many minutes. Her eyes were closed, her face in absolute repose. Perhaps she had been asleep. There was not a line to be seen. Not the hint of a crease. Because her face was without expression, it was possible to see all the way inside her.

"Here," Eliane said, "rain has the power of drama."

"In Japan as well."

Eliane did not turn her head. "In Japan," she said, "rain is beautiful, stately, perfect in the angle at which it strikes the ground or the water. In Hawaii, it is wild, full of energy and light. Free of all constraints."

Lying next to Za, he had discovered that what he had fallen in love with was not Za at all. She was aligned with no ideology, no person, no philosophy. It was as if her spirit were composed of clear crystal. It shone. It refracted light into

161

varying colors depending on the nature of the light and the angle at which it was struck.

But at its core, it possessed no color of its own.

Then Za had opened her eyes and, filled with love, had said, "I want to stay. Not just tonight. Not until tomorrow. I want to be with you forever."

It wasn't just that he had seen her as more than human, this model of his mind's ideal. He realized with a painful lurch that he had mistaken the crystal of her spirit for the purity of Seyoko's soul. It saddened—and frightened—him that he should still be searching for what had already been denied him. Seyoko was long dead, but he could not give her up. The memory of her was insufficient to sustain him.

Thus, when Michael closed the door behind Za the next morning, it was for the last time. She was gone. Her image on his canvases remained. But that was all.

It was wholly his doing, his inadequacy. In her pain he had briefly found a weapon to use against himself. Her tears had awakened him to the agony of unassuageable longing he would carry around forever.

"Did you live in Japan?" he asked.

"For many years, yes." Eliane said. "After a while, Tokyo's furious energy only made me want to sleep."

It's not that she reminds me of Za, he thought now, his heart beating faster. She reminds me of Seyoko.

"Don't you miss it?" Michael said thickly. "Japan."

"I belong nowhere," Eliane said. "I have no ties, no affiliations. Like cities, ties to people, to causes, exhaust me. The crosscurrents of responsibility are like shackles. Have you ever read *Gulliver's Travels*? That is how alliances make me feel. Like Gulliver bound to the ground in Lilliput. I am content to be."

Now came Eliane. Her mysticism drew him. Her unconditional surrender to the forces of nature spoke to him on the most profound level. Because she was wholly uncivilized in an elemental way, she was unaffected by any of the manmade restraints that so disturbed him.

Michael would not understand this until much later, but his attraction to her mirrored his father's affinity to the clandestine life afforded by the Seventh Service, and then by BITE.

It was apart from the rest of the world, yes. It reinforced his sense that he was someone special, yes. But more than anything else, it represented the ultimate freedom.

For Philip the ability to do anything, to be anybody, to choose from this bewildering multiplicity, was something that he had worked on all of his adult life. In his own mind, it had been his ultimate achievement.

For Michael, it had come more naturally. His training in Yoshino had taught him to embrace life—to appreciate its unending diversity. Possessing the freedom to choose was essential to his nature.

"The sun," Eliane said. "Oh look! Here come the mountaintops!"

Michael had forgotten why he was here. Transfixed by nature, he watched with an artist's eye as the white smoke, the bannered remnants of the rain, tore itself to shreds along the snaking peaks. Like the unseen fingers of a prestidigitator, the wind plucked the riven fragments away. Golden sunlight streamed down upon the mountainsides, revealing treelines, sparkling, slender cascades of water. Birds, trilling sweetly, streamed by overhead.

He had to get up, he knew. Otherwise, the pull would never allow him to leave.

But just as he was about to move, Eliane turned toward him. The sunlight transformed her hair into spun copper. In an instant he saw a painting, the pose perfect, her expression cutting through the masks that all people wore. Masks that temporarily turned off animation, spirit, life.

"You can't leave now," she said.

And he knew that she was right.

Michiko went through the same ritual every morning.

It began an hour before the call was scheduled to come in. Bathed and dressed, she would go out into the garden. There was always someone at her side, always a man, always big, always with a gun hidden under his jacket. Someone loyal to her stepbrother Masashi. He would hold a parasol above her head. On clear days it protected her from the sun, on stormy days it kept the rain off her face.

She would walk slowly down the stone path until she reached the large, flat rock from which three separate paths diverged. Taking the right-hand one, she would listen for the woodfinch that made its nest in the cherry tree that grew beside the high stone wall. In the spring, she liked to sit within the bower of the tree and listen to the frantic cheeping of the woodfinch's hungry chicks.

Just past the cherry tree, near the far wall of the garden,

was the weathered wooden shrine she had transported here and erected to Megami Kitsune, the fox-goddess. With the help of her companion, she would kneel, light *joss* sticks, bow her head in prayer.

Always, she prayed for two things. One, that the call would come. Two, that her granddaughter was still alive. Always, when she returned from her prayers, her hands and feet were as cold as ice.

She would sit in her house, the telephone beside her, and shiver as if with the ague. She refused anything to eat, though her cook would beg her to take even a mouthful of food. She refused tea. Nothing would pass her lips, not even water, until she heard the shrill *briing!* of the phone and, snatching the receiver off its cradle, would wait with fluttering heartbeat for the sound of her granddaughter's little voice.

"Granny?"

Michiko would close her eyes, weeping silent tears. Her granddaughter was alive for another day.

"Granny?" Like the voice of a wood sprite in her ear.

"Yes, darling girl."

"How are you, Granny?" The sweet voice Michiko knew so well at the other end of a phone line, emanating from—where? If only Michiko knew where Masashi was holding her.

"I am fine, little one. And you? Do you have enough to eat? Are you getting enough sleep?"

"I am bored, Granny. I want to come home. I want—"

And the line would go dead, every time.

Despite herself, Michiko screamed at the dead line: "Little one! Little one!" Weeping bitter tears.

Masashi had left instructions to disconnect in the middle of the child's sentence. It brought home with an irrational finality the scope of his control over the situation. In this instance, he was god: the bringer of life, and of death.

Three times a week, Masashi Taki spent mornings at the warehouse at Takashiba Pier. Almost precisely in the center of the western bank of Tokyo Harbor, Takashiba was a high-density enclave within a high-density city. Here, shiploads of produce, hardware, software, drygoods, were continually being offloaded for consignment to thousands of companies throughout the country. At the same time, goods of all kinds were being transshipped to virtually every nation in the world. The result was a maze of interweaving consignments that dizzied even the efficient Japanese Customs machine.

The Takashiba warehouse was a joint venture between the Takis and the Yamamotos. Increasingly, the activities there were taking precedence over all other Taki-gumi clan activities. Which was, Masashi thought, just as it should be.

The men with whom he met were always the same: Daizo, the big soldier who Masashi had put in charge of training the new recruits; Kaeru, the small, heavily tattooed adviser left over from Wataro Taki's regime; and Kozo Shiina.

After the initial period in the late 1940s when Masashi's father had come to power, Wataro Taki had outlawed such vicious strong-arm tactics as Masashi now routinely employed. Wataro had been content to allow the threat of violence to speak for him and instill loyalty in those who made his profits. Masashi was not so benevolently inclined. Besides, he had something to prove. Much as he disliked to admit it to himself, Wataro Taki had made an indelible mark on the history and development of the Yakuza. It was incumbent on his successor to reach for new heights, to surpass the achievements of the past generation.

Masashi liked to have his meetings in the workout room he had had built onto a section of the wooden catwalk that ran a dizzying forty-five feet above the underground warren beneath the warehouse. This basement was large enough to contain laboratories filled with Yamamoto Heavy Industries' most sophisticated equipment, storerooms, as well as workrooms as large as entire factories.

The workout room was dominated by gleaming Nautilus machines backed up against packed earthen walls that had been part of the foundations of buildings dating back almost four hundred years, to the time of the Tokugawa shogunate.

Masashi liked to meet the men bare-chested. Sweat ran in thick runnels over his hairless chest. Muscles bulged as he worked on one machine after another. He spoke while he pushed his magnificent body to its limits. He was never short of breath, and he never ceased his activity no matter how long the meeting went on.

"Daizo," he said when they were all gathered, "your report."

"The boys are coming around," the big man said. "They are a wild pack of dogs, as you can well imagine. They came to us as dope smokers, hopheads, motorcycle riders." He laughed shortly. "They called themselves outlaws. But they were just a bunch of punks. They lacked discipline. Huh! They had never heard the word."

"All fighting machines must have discipline," Kozo Shiina said. He looked neither at Daizo or at Kaeru. Rather, his gaze was fixed on the play of Masashi's ropy muscles as his mind remembered when his own body had been as strong and elastic. "The armies of even the crudest of history's military commanders possessed discipline. A war cannot be won otherwise."

"The recruits will be disciplined," Masashi said easily. "Daizo will see to it. They are like sheep, these rough boys, *neh*, Daizo? They have no self-image, so they look to a leader to give them what they themselves cannot." He climbed off one machine, mounted another. "Where is their leader now, Daizo?"

The big man grinned. "Hanging upside down in the center of their sleeping quarters."

"Is he dead?" Kozo Shiina inquired in much the same voice he used to ask his fishmonger if his catch was fresh.

"The place is beginning to stink," Daizo said, and laughed. "They asked when I was going to cut him down. I told them I was letting him cure. I told them when I'm ready to feed him to them, I'll cut him down."

"Already the new ones fear Daizo more than they ever did the man who was their leader," Kaeru said. He was an older man, taciturn, seemingly without any ego at all. He was a master strategist. It was he who designed the method by which the mountains of hardware were being transshipped from their diverse points of origin, passing through Customs unsealed and arriving day by day in this warehouse. "Already I can see emotions behind their eyes. I see the coalescing of an army."

Kozo Shiina nodded. He, too, appreciated Kaeru's mind. In the bald man he perhaps recognized a kindred spirit. Shiina was not one to underestimate the value of human thought.

"It is space that we desperately need," Shiina said. "Our forefathers knew that when they went to war with China. In this land of plenty, we have no space to move. We are like ants milling about a single hill, black with our bodies. Already we crawl all over one another and think nothing of it. We have become inured to this horror of a future that is already upon us.

"The war and its immediate aftermath have shown us that this nation can be mobilized. That it can, indeed, work miracles. And it can do so again, if given the opportunity.

"This is our goal. Now we do not have far to go, and we

166

are relying on your expertise, Daizo, in turning this rabble into an efficient army."

"They will be ready," Daizo said.

"What about the hardware?" Shiina asked Kaeru.

"As you know," the bald man said, "our recent dealings in the drug traffic had allowed us to use the same complex networks to smuggle hardware into Japan. The real danger was Customs. If any of those packages were discovered, the resulting furor would make it extremely difficult for us to continue assembly."

"More than that," Shiina said, "the army would be swarming all over the docks looking for related items."

"Correct," Kaeru said. "Therefore, after setting up the drug networks, I set about taking care of Customs. There are many avenues of persuasion open to me. I merely chose the most advantageous ones."

"The coerced officials," Shiina said. "What do they know?"

"The magic word," Kaeru said. "Opium. They have no idea what those packages really contain."

"And Nobuo Yamamoto," Shiina said, staring at Masashi. "Is he living up to his end of the bargain?"

"The Yamamotos and the Takis have been friends for years." Masashi used a word for *friend* that connoted that kind of lifetime association that is rare outside of Japan. "You leave Nobuo to me."

"Without him we cannot move," Shiina reminded Masashi.

"I said leave Nobuo to me."

"Good," Shiina said. "All is going according to schedule. Within ten days, we will be ready. Japan's new era will begin."

The men bowed ceremonially. Then Daizo looked at his watch. "I must get back to the men." He took Kaeru with him, leaving Masashi and Shiina alone.

"If I had a son," Kozo Shiina said, still gazing at Masashi's musculature, "he would look just like you."

"You," Masashi said. The place stank of sweat. His black-gloved hands gripped the gleaming chrome of the weighted bars. He grunted as he flexed, pushed the weights up their track. He let out a breath as he eased them down. His muscles easily held one hundred pounds off the stack. "You are my father's enemy."

"I *was*," Shiina corrected. "Your father is dead."

"I am the heir to his legacy," Masashi said. He licked at the sweat coating his lips. "I am *oyabun* of the Taki-gumi. I am what Wataro Taki left behind."

Kozo Shiina watched him without moving. Being in such close proximity to Masashi recalled the physical power of his own youthful body. Time was his only enemy now. But he had known that long ago.

Masashi let the weights all the way down, climbed off the Nautilus saddle. He took a towel off the rack on the wall, wiped himself down as he moved. When he was standing in front of Shiina, he pushed the towel into the old man's face. "Here," he said, "drink that in. Remember what I have that you no longer do."

Masashi threw the towel away. "You're old, Shiina. And you're weak. You need me to be your arms and your legs. Without me you're just a helpless old man filled with dreams of glory. Without me your dreams won't come true." He bent over the seated man. "I urge you to remember that the next time you think about taking over my meetings. These are my men. They are loyal to me. Perhaps you have forgotten that you are here on my sufferance."

"I make my contribution," Shiina said calmly. "As does everyone else."

"Just make sure," Masashi said, "that you don't overstep the boundaries of that contribution."

Outside, on the docks, Kozo Shiina stepped into the interior of his waiting car. He could still smell Masashi's sweat on his face. The agony and shame of his own body's inadequacies were never more apparent to him.

With a small grunt, he settled himself in the back seat, signed for his driver to go. When they were back in the main hub of the city, Shiina began to give directions to the driver.

In the Shinjuku district, he said, "Pull over here and wait. I'm expecting someone."

The driver got out of the car, stood on the crowded sidewalk. Kozo Shiina glanced at his wristwatch. It would be a while before he could get to someplace where he could wash off Masashi's sweat. The rage that he had deliberately suppressed at the warehouse now emerged. Shiina's hands closed into fists. Masashi's arrogance was sometimes difficult to take, even for one so disciplined as Kozo Shiina. In his youth, Shiina had never tolerated any form of insult. He recalled a time at college when he had been taunted by an upperclassman. He had been rash, then. He had gone after the man immediately and had been thrown into the mud outside the classrooms for his efforts.

But that had not been the end of it. Shiina had bided his

time. He had considered many alternatives. In the end, he had chosen the most elegant—and therefore the sweetest—one. Near the end of the term, when that upperclassman, along with the most promising seniors, was scheduled to take the all-day examination that would dictate whether or not he would be considered for a position at the most prestigious bureaucratic ministry, Shiina had crept into the upperclassman's room and had reset his alarm clock. The boy was three hours late for the exam and was thus disqualified. Even his wealthy father's pleas for leniency fell on deaf ears. His son's career was ruined.

Now Shiina saw the man emerge from the building and head toward the car, and his fingers relaxed. He smiled to himself. All at once, Masashi's crudeness was forgotten; the sweetness of elegant revenge suffused his mind like a rare perfume.

As instructed, the driver had the rear door open as the man approached. He ducked his head inside, sat down beside Shiina. A moment later, the car was heading out into the noonday traffic.

"As I said when I received your call," Shiina said to the man beside him, "I am entirely at your disposal." He smiled easily. "We will go to a teahouse I know. Very private and comfortable. There we will drink tea and eat rice cakes. And you will tell me how I can be of service to you."

"That's very kind of you, Shiina-san," the man said. "I'm certain that I can outline an arrangement that will suit both of our desires." He shifted in his seat, and a shaft of sunlight illuminated his face.

It was Joji Taki.

At 8:22 A.M., Lillian was picking up a public phone on M Street in Georgetown. She dialed a local number, waited for the clicking, then the computer tone. She dialed an overseas number she had committed to memory.

After the third ring, a voice with a distinct Parisian accent answered. Lillian identified herself, but not by name.

"I must speak with him," Lillian said in fluent French.

"He is not here," the male voice on the other end of the line said diffidently.

"Then contact him," Lillian snapped. She glanced at the pay phone, read off its number. "I will be here for the next ten minutes," she said. "Have him call me."

"I will see what I can do, *mad*—"

She slammed down the phone. She immediately picked up the receiver, but surreptitiously kept the engage lever down. She pretended to talk while she watched the window-shoppers strolling by.

While she waited, she attempted to keep her thoughts calm. But all she could think of was Michael heading into the midst of terrible danger. She was just barely able to hold herself together as it was, what with Philip's death and Audrey's abduction. Now this. It was too much to bear. She closed her lids tight against the tears burning her eyes.

Within nine minutes of her call, the phone rang. Startled, Lillian jumped, heart pounding. She lifted the engage lever.

"Allo?" Still in French.

"Bonjour, madame," the cultured voice said. Unlike the first voice, this was not that of a native Frenchman. "How are you?"

"Terrified," Lillian admitted.

"This is to be expected," the voice said. "You're not having second thoughts, are you?"

"I am thinking of the danger," Lillian said. "At last."

"It means that you are alive," the voice said. "Revel in the acuity of sensation danger brings."

"What time is it where you are? I can never get it straight."

"Just after four in the afternoon. Why?"

"You will soon go home to your wife," she said. "I want to picture that right now. It is important, sometimes, to summon up unpleasant feelings."

"Nothing will happen, Lillian."

"Nothing will happen to you. How easy it is from your vantage point."

"From my vantage point," the voice said, "nothing is easy. I want you to remember that."

Lillian watched the traffic slide by as if it were a television show. She was already distancing herself from the humdrum of life.

"When will you have it?" the voice said in her ear.

"Tomorrow night." Why was her heart hammering so? "But it will still be a long way from you." Was it because she knew how dangerous this man could be? Not to her, of course. But to others.

"You will take care of that," the voice said softly. "I have complete confidence in you. And as for your family, I have assured you that I had nothing to do with your husband's murder."

"Have you heard any word about Audrey?"

"I'm afraid not. Her abduction is still as mysterious as Philip's death."

For an instant, he sounded like Jonas. But then these two men had so much in common. Lillian put her forehead against the phone box. "I'm tired," she said. "I'm so tired."

"It is almost the end now," the voice said. "In three days we will meet, and it will be all over. Forever."

"And what about my children?"

"I will do all in my considerable power to keep them safe from harm. Like God, extending His arms around them."

"Shall I put all my faith in you, then?"

He laughed easily. "Why," he said, "I thought you knew. You already have."

"Do you want to go to bed with me?" Michael asked.

Eliane laughed. "Possibly. Yes." They were in the kitchen, where she was preparing dinner. "What makes you ask?"

"I wondered why you invited me here."

"Because I wanted to," she said simply and directly. This was something she did so well. She went across to the refrigerator, got out some greens.

"What about your boyfriend?"

"What about him?" She tore off a sheaf of lettuce leaves.

"He's Yakuza," Michael said.

She turned, stopping what she was doing. "How do you know that? I didn't tell you."

"Sure you did. You mentioned *giri*, a Yakuza term. Or is *giri* something from your other life in the big city?"

"What do you know about the Yakuza?" Eliane said, resuming her cutting.

Michael got up. "Enough that I'd be nervous if your boyfriend walked through the door right now."

Eliane smiled. "After the way you saved me this afternoon, I wouldn't imagine anything would make you nervous."

"Guns make me nervous," Michael said, taking a bite of raw vegetable.

Eliane watched him while he ate. "The papers are full of Yakuza. But where did you learn about *giri*?"

"I studied in Japan for several years," Michael said. "My father sent me there. He served in the American armed services in Tokyo just after World War Two."

Eliane looked down at the vegetables she was chopping. "What did you study in Japan?"

171

"I learned how to paint," he said.

"But that's not all," she said. "I saw the *katana* in the back of your Jeep. Do you know how to use it?"

"I learned many things in Japan," he said. "But the most important was how to paint."

"Is that what you do for a living? Paint?"

"Partly. It's what makes me the happiest. But I also have to earn a living." He told her about the fine-arts printing business he had created.

She smiled as she resumed her chopping. "It must be wonderful to be able to take a brush in your hand and create something." She laughed. "I envy you. Blank anythings terrify me. Blank pages, blank canvases. I always have the urge to paint them solid black."

"If you do that," Michael said, "they disappear."

"They lose their threatening quality that way, don't they." She pushed the pile of chopped shallots aside, began on the mushrooms. "Their anarchy is controlled—or at least contained."

"Anarchy?"

"Yes. Don't you ever find a blank canvas intimidating? I mean, there are so many directions in which you can go. It's bewildering."

"Unless," Michael said, "you know what you're going to paint before you ever get to the canvas."

Eliane frowned. "Do you always know what you're going to do before you do it? Isn't that boring?"

"Have you already answered your own question?" He smiled. "I know how I'm going to *begin*. After that . . ." He shrugged.

She appeared to be considering something. "How well do you know the Yakuza? I know you said you lived in Japan for a while. Did you ever meet any Yakuza?"

"Not that I know of. But perhaps they're not so different from other people I met in Japan."

"Oh they're different, all right," Eliane said. "Yakuza are a breed apart. Japanese society considers them outcasts, and they revel in the role created for them. The word *Yakuza* is composed of ideographs for three numbers. Added up, it is a losing number in gambling. Yakuza think of themselves as doomed. Fated to be heroes within their own tightly knit cosmos."

"From what I know of them," Michael said, "they're too dangerous to be so romantic."

She nodded. "They're very dangerous." She put down her

172

cleaver, turned on one of the stove's gas burners, on which she had put a pot. "Maybe I shouldn't tell you this, but"— she gave him a fleeting smile—"you *are* bound to protect me forever, right?" When Michael said nothing, she went on. "The truth is, my boyfriend makes me nervous. You're right. He's Yakuza. For a while it was a kick dating him, you know? No, I suppose you don't."

"He's a big shot," Michael said. "A *kahuna* himself. Sure I know." He took another slice of vegetable. "What happened?"

"He's a boor," she said. "Likes to throw his weight around, get into fights. I can't stand it."

Michael shrugged. "Tell him."

Eliane laughed. "I did. So what? It doesn't matter. He's deaf to those things. He does what he wants. He's used to the power. I can't stop it."

"Sure you can," Michael said. "If you try."

"Guns make me nervous, too," she said, then, "Ow!" She dropped the pot of scalding water, sucked at her hand. "Damn!"

Michael took her hand, turned it over. It was red where the pot handle and then the water had burned it. The skin was raw. "You have any disinfectant?"

Eliane shook her head. "No bandages, either." She sucked at the burn again. "Don't worry, I'll live."

Michael looked at her. "Is that what your boyfriend did," he asked, returning to the subject, "wave a gun in your face?"

"Eventually," she said. She picked up the cleaver again, wincing a little as she tightened her grip on the haft. "He hit me first."

"Jesus." Michael was thinking of Audrey and Hans. Thinking of what he had done to the German.

"He's very . . . physical."

Right there he should have said, You got yourself into this, get yourself out. But he didn't do the smart thing. Why? Because what if this boyfriend worked for Fat Boy Ichimada? Playing the jealous lover would buy Michael a lot of time inside the compound if he was discovered. That time could be critical to getting out again. Sure, Michael thought. That's all it is. A child's game of strategy to get inside the bad man's castle.

"Who does he work for, your boyfriend?" Michael asked.

"What are you going to do?"

"If you can't get satisfaction from the hired help," he said, "go straight to the top."

Eliane laughed. "That's pretty funny."

"I wasn't joking."

"I don't believe you."

"Try me. Who does your boyfriend work for?"

"A guy named Fat Boy Ichimada. He's the head Yakuza *kahuna* in the Islands."

"Where does Ichimada live?" Michael asked. Knowing already.

"Just past where we ran into each other this morning. In Kahakuloa, remember?"

"I have to go," Michael said, walking to the door.

"Where are you going?" She wiped her hands on the cotton apron. "Dinner's almost ready."

"You said I had an obligation to take care of you."

She came around from behind the kitchen pass-through. "Are you serious?"

Michael looked at her. "Weren't you?"

"Oh come on." She laughed, trying to make a joke of it. "Besides, there are guns there. Lots of guns. Ichimada doesn't like uninvited guests."

Michael walked to the door. "That's okay," he said. "I'll avoid them."

"Just why in the hell are you doing this?"

"I told you."

"And I don't believe you for a minute. For one thing, we just met. For another, why would you be doing this now, when you could go tomorrow during the day, like any normal human being?"

"In the daylight," Michael said, "Ichimada will see me coming."

"You're not going for me," she said. "You want something from Ichimada for yourself."

"Maybe." He shrugged. "So what?"

"Why lie to me? Why this nonsense about this obligation to take care of me?"

"It's not nonsense," he said.

"You're half serious." She shook her head in confusion. "I don't understand you."

"Don't try so hard to understand me," he said. "I'm something of an enigma even to myself."

When she saw that he was about to leave, she took off her apron. "Okay then, we'll go together."

"Not a chance."

174

She put on a jacket, shook her hair out. "Just how do you intend to get into Ichimada's compound in the dark?"

"I'll get in," he said.

"Is that so? Do you know about the dogs, the trip wires, the spotlights?" She scrutinized his face. "Besides, you don't even know my boyfriend's name or what he looks like."

Michael saw the bind she had put him in. He did not want to take anyone with him when he infiltrated Fat Boy Ichimada's compound, but now he had no choice. This woman knew that he had lied to her, that he had an ulterior motive for getting into Fat Boy Ichimada's compound. If he left her behind, she could very well call her boyfriend the moment Michael left. Michael had no desire to have Ichimada's men waiting for him when he arrived at the compound in Kahakuloa.

"All right," he said, opening the door. "Come on. But keep your mouth shut, and do what I tell you, okay?"

"Sure, boss." Eliane grinned. "Anything you say."

"Does your hand hurt?"

"Not much," she said.

But he had seen it as she climbed into the Jeep. He pulled off the highway at the main light in Lahaina. She directed him to a pharmacy, where he purchased bandages, burn salve, a roll of surgical tape and a small spray can of Bactine.

Back at the Jeep, he sprayed her burned hand, pocketed the can. Then he applied the salve, wrapping the bandages over the burn, fixing it in place with the tape.

"How's that feel?"

"Better," she said. "Thanks."

They set out again, still heading northwest. On their right were the West Maui Mountains, as crenellated as a castle's bulwark. To the left, the Pacific was lit by moonlight that painted a shimmering brushstroke across its calm bosom. Black crosshatching delineated the masts, spars and rigging of fishing vessels at anchor in the harbor. Further out, it was possible to see a cruise liner lying to. Bright strings of lights beribboned its deck and, once, a gust of wind brought the sound of a band to their ears.

"I think you need a new boyfriend," Michael said.

"I didn't need him to begin with," she said.

They were zooming past Kaanapali, the large resort area, filled with hotels, condos, restaurants and the only movie theater for miles.

Ten minutes later, they were into the golf courses of Kapalua, heading down toward the ocean when the highway ended. Rolling past the small general store. Turning right onto the old road. Soon they would be at the extreme northernmost part of Maui. Swinging around to head back south. To Kahakuloa.

The moonlight that, before, had illuminated Eliane's face now dappled the road. The inconstant light obliged him to reduce speed. His shoulders were hunched with the concentration required to negotiate a road that he knew at any moment would become a deeply rutted dirt track.

The Pacific crashed against the saw-toothed rocks five hundred yards below them. They had left Fleming Beach behind them and were now beginning the torturous navigation along the Honokohau cliffs.

Michael turned off the Jeep's headlights, slowed considerably. He was obliged to drive without headlights to ensure that Fat Boy Ichimada's guards would not see their approach.

The hills of Kahakuloa.

Not a quarter of a mile farther on, Eliane's Jeep had gone over the cliff. Michael passed a closed gate. A moment later he pulled into a rocky wayside carved into the edge of the cliff. There were many of these roadsides scattered along a road whose snaking turns were impossible for two cars to negotiate at once.

Michael turned off the engine.

"Okay," he said. "You've gone far enough. What's your boyfriend's name?"

"Bluto."

"And yours is Olive Oyl. Eliane, what's his name?"

"If I tell you, you'll leave me here."

"That's the idea."

"I want to go with you," she said.

"Why?"

"It was me that he hit, remember? Can't you understand that I can be of some help?"

"That's why I'm asking you to give me your boyfriend's name."

She shook her head. "You didn't come here to get Fat Boy Ichimada to keep my boyfriend away from me."

"You didn't come here for that reason either, did you?"

She peered into the shadows that shrouded his face. "I guess neither of us trusts the other." She shrugged. "That's

176

natural, I guess. I don't know you; I don't trust what I don't know."

This is crazy, he thought. I can't involve a civilian. It never occurred to him that yesterday he himself had been a civilian. "Stay here, Eliane. I mean it."

He grabbed the satchel and the *katana*, got out of the Jeep. He went up to the gate. Producing a pair of wire cutters from the satchel, he went to work. When the hole was large enough, he went through bent over.

On the other side, in the Jeep, Eliane sat still. Between them, the torn barbed wire seemed to glow in the moonlight. The crickets droned, and night birds swooped, unseen, above their heads.

"Michael," she whispered, "take me with you."

He started up the slope, paralleling the dirt track.

"Michael," she said, turning the key in the ignition, "don't leave me." The Jeep's headlights came on.

"Jesus!" he said. "Are you nuts? Turn those off, Eliane!"

"Take me!"

"Eliane, for Christ's sake, everyone will see—"

"Take me with you! I can help. Do you know about the boar traps?"

Michael paused. He didn't. There was nothing about boar traps in the BITE file on Ichimada's compound.

She saw his expression. "I didn't think so. They were put in last week. I know where they are."

Michael stared up at the stars, weighing the options. Was she telling the truth? "All right," he said at last.

Somewhere far ahead, a dog began to bark.

Fat Boy Ichimada, heading into the compound in his helicopter, saw the lights down by the main gate. Ichimada had been searching for Michael Doss all day. Tired of the car, he had spent the afternoon in the copter. Away from the dusty roads. And from a possible tail from Ude. Ichimada was tired and disgusted that Michael Doss seemed to have dropped from sight as surely as a stone thrown into the Pacific.

The pilot, a Yakuza soldier named Wailea Charlie, said, "Want me to radio the compound to let the dogs loose? You're not expecting company, are you?"

"Not yet." Fat Boy Ichimada was already looking through his infrared night glasses. He could see the woman in the Jeep. And then, as the headlights flicked off, he followed her

177

as she scrambled off the road. Through an expertly cut hole in the fence, where she joined another figure. A man.

"Get me down there," Ichimada said. "One sweep."

Wailea Charlie banked the helicopter, and Fat Boy Ichimada felt his stomach trying to reach his feet. He concentrated, keeping the image of the man in his binoculars. The resolution was superb, but the man was turning away. Ichimada gave instructions to Wailea Charlie, and the copter banked further.

Now Fat Boy Ichimada got a clear look at the man's face, and his pulse jumped. Buddha, he thought as he recognized the face. Even without having seen the photo Ude had showed him, Ichimada would have known that face. It could have been Philip Doss's face twenty years ago.

"Forget the dogs." Gave Wailea Charlie orders to set the copter down on the landing pad beside the rambling house that sat in the center of the compound, thinking of the irony of it. All day he had been searching for Philip Doss's son, and now the man was coming right to Fat Boy Ichimada's front door.

The race has been run, Fat Boy Ichimada thought as the dust whirled up all around them, the copter settling onto its pad, and I've come in first.

But when he had walked, doubled over, from beneath the diameter of the still *whopp-whopp-whopp*ing rotors, he saw that someone had released the Dobermans from their screened-in runs. The pitch of their barking told him that they had already caught the intruders' scent.

Fat Boy Ichimada began to run.

They were still far from the house when Michael heard the Dobermans' yelping. He had already identified the sound of a helicopter.

"They know we're here," he said, taking her arm and beginning to run.

"Not that way," she said, pulling him off to the left. "It's thick with traps." Holding on to him. "Careful right here." Guiding him around a nasty-looking contraption. A well-camouflaged boar trap.

Now Michael was glad that he had taken her with him. He reached into his satchel, threw several small cotton bags to their right, then he pulled them left.

"What were those?" Eliane asked.

At least she isn't out of breath, Michael thought as they charged up a long rise. She's not the liability I had feared she'd be. Into a copse of trees, where he held them in the dense shadows for a moment. "Dried blood," he said. "Gardeners use it to keep pests like rabbits away from their flowers. Hopefully, the blood will confuse the dogs."

"Not for long, it won't," Eliane said.

"I don't need very long. Come on." Michael took her by the hand. Crouching, they moved on across the lush heath. He could make out the lights of Fat Boy Ichimada's house through the swaying branches of the trees. He did not approach their illumination directly, but rather began to circle to the left, away from the baying Dobermans.

The layout of the compound was a live thing in Michael's brain. He had spent most of the plane ride memorizing everything Uncle Sammy had given him about Fat Boy Ichimada. He knew now that he would need every scrap of information in the BITE file.

The trip wires were not difficult to negotiate once he had located them. He was careful to keep Eliane directly behind him, so that there was no chance she would blunder into one while he was working on disengaging another.

They moved on, circling nearer the house now. But it had taken longer than he had anticipated to put the trip wires out of commission. The baying of the Dobermans changed pitch, and he knew they had found the bags of dried blood. Frustrated, they had begun to pick up a new scent.

Michael pushed Eliane onward, ignoring the spotlights. His plan had called for him to take them out; there wasn't time. Out from the inky shadows of the trees, across a lush lawn, urging her onward.

Realized his mistake too late. The spotlights coming on all at once, spangling the night, eating up the darkness in great, awful swatches. The dogs with sight now, bounding out of the still-black woods and onto the lawn, where Michael and Eliane were silhouetted against the white clapboard of Fat Boy Ichimada's house.

Michael thinking, There are three Dobermans. *They're full-grown males*, Uncle Sammy had said. *They've been attack-trained, son. Do you know what that means? Once they are given the specific command, nothing can stop them short of death. They'll go right for your throat and do their best to rip it out.*

"What the hell is going on?" Fat Boy Ichimada bellowed. "Who set the dogs loose?"

At that moment, the spotlights came on. Buddha, Fat Boy thought, with all that illumination Michael Doss doesn't have a chance. The dogs will tear him to shreds.

He saw one of the Dobermans' trainers, began to yell at him.

"Save your breath," a voice said. "He's through taking orders from you."

Fat Boy whirled, saw Ude step out of the darkness of the eaves.

"They all are."

"This is my house!" Ichimada screamed. "These are my men!"

"Not anymore." Ude was grinning. He was enjoying this immensely. "I told you Masashi gave me complete control over this situation. I am *oyabun* here. I give the orders from now on."

Fat Boy Ichimada took a step toward Ude, checked as Ude swung up the Mack-10. It was a compact automatic machine pistol.

"I wouldn't do that," Ude warned. "I'm not about to let you within arm's length of me. I know what those hands can do."

"Let's negotiate," Fat Boy Ichimada said. "We can work a deal."

"Yeah? What do you have that I don't have already?"

"Money."

Ude laughed. "Someone's coming, Ichimada. Maybe you'll tell me who it is."

"I don't know. A local kid, probably."

Ude scowled. "I've had enough of your lies." He gestured. "Get in the house."

"How are you going to take care of me *and* the intruder?"

Ude grunted. "I'll let someone else take care of you." He made a movement with the Mack-10, and Fat Boy Ichimada turned. He saw Wailea Charlie aiming a pistol at him.

The pilot gave him an apologetic smile. "Sorry, boss," he said. "But when Tokyo talks, I gotta listen."

"Take him into the house," Ude said to Wailea Charlie.

He was already turning his attention back to the sound of the dogs.

Michael had sent Eliane off in an acute diagonal away from the arc-lit perimeter of the house while he headed into the light. The dogs were closing in on him; there was not much he could do about that.

Passing the shadows of a tall tree, he turned and heaved his small satchel up into the lower branches. Then he drew the *katana* Uncle Sammy had given him. It was old, well made. Though the wrapped leather grip was shiny and worn, the blade had marvelous heft and balance, both of which were crucial.

They came out of the shadows in a pack, as they had been trained to do. Michael faced them sideways. His right hip was toward them. He held his *katana* in the prescribed two-handed grip. His left elbow was lifted. His weight was on his right leg and hip.

Two dogs leaped at him. They hit the light at once. Coming at different angles, they were illuminated oddly, so that they seemed two halves of one monstrous creature.

Itto ryodan. Splitting an opponent in two with one blow.

Michael erupted into motion. He was tracking the arcs of their leaps. Now his *katana* swept up, and in that preliminary motion, the blade—so razor sharp that it disappeared when looked at head on—slammed into the rib cage of the first of the Dobermans.

Michael was still moving, his left shoulder twisting away from the hurtling thing. His downward strike—the second half of the wheel maneuver—swept through the torso of the second animal.

Michael whirled. The third Doberman was crouched just outside the reach of his sword. It growled, bared its teeth. Its muscles were spasming continuously beneath its glossy black fur.

When it took off, the talons on its back feet scored deep furrows in the ground. Instead of springing, it tore to Michael's left. As he pivoted away from it, it leaped. Using *usen saten*, Michael ducked. Lifting his blade at the same time, slashing left. Sliced the Doberman open along its left side.

The creature crashed to the ground at Michael's feet, lying on its side and panting as its eyes glazed.

Michael lowered the *katana*. Took a deep breath. Then the sword was flying from his hands.

He hit the ground on top of the dying dog. Tried to turn, felt a great weight on him, the gnashing teeth. Pain as nails raked him. What? The first dog! Somehow it had gathered the remainder of its strength and had attacked again.

He had pinioned its forepaws, but its rear legs began to work on him. There was nothing in Michael's arsenal to deal with the animal fury of the Doberman at close quarters. He was losing his hold.

He saw his sword lying out of reach. He was using all his muscle just to keep the frantically snapping jaws from his throat. Meanwhile, the powerful hind legs were doing their best to rip open his belly.

The feral eyes glowing yellow in the semidarkness, the animal stench of the dog, the stench of blood. Both instinct and pain told him that he could not hold on much longer.

Already the jaws were closing in on his face. It was becoming increasingly difficult to turn aside the furious attack.

There was a chance, but it meant having to free one of his hands. And using only one to fend off the thing's head. Had to try it. Now!

Freed his left hand, the right going to work on the Doberman's muzzle to keep it at bay. But the jaws were snapping faster now. It was as if the animal could sense that its own end was near. The knowledge increased its frenzy, and now it had gotten through, the jaws opening, the teeth, dripping saliva, blurring inward toward Michael's unprotected throat.

The fingers of his left hand closing around cool, curving metal. Bringing it up, spraying the Bactine antiseptic directly into the eyes, nose and mouth of the dog.

The Doberman howled and jerked away. Michael was up, lunging for his longsword. The dog, blinded, was on him immediately. He fell, twisted his torso as he did so. Slashed down, severing the dog's spinal column.

He threw the corpse aside and rose. People coming.

Stood with knees bent. Held his *katana* over his right shoulder so that it stretched out and back, as one might carry a parasol to defeat the rays of the late afternoon sun.

Two men armed with M-16 assault rifles plunged out of the shadows from which the Dobermans had emerged moments before. Michael stepped forward, slashed down once, then, pivoting, struck horizontally. The men joined the dogs.

For some moments he stood still as stone, listening. When he was certain that there was nothing hostile in the immediate environment, he picked up his scabbard, slid the *katana* home.

Sticking it through his belt, he climbed the tall tree and retrieved his satchel.

He dropped to the ground, then headed toward the house.

Ude was within the perimeter of the spotlights' illumination when he heard the Dobermans cease to bark. He waited for precisely a minute and a half. When he heard nothing louder than a moth's fluttering, he spoke softly into his walkie-talkie. There was no response to his repeated callings.

Ude ordered everyone inside—there were five, not counting Fat Boy Ichimada—to arm themselves with M-16's. Wailea Charlie was already armed. Ude told them to shoot to wound, though none of them knew who it was they were supposed to aim at.

He instructed Wailea Charlie and Fat Boy Ichimada to follow him out to the living room.

"What do they want?" Wailea Charlie asked.

"Shut up," Ude said. "Just make sure Ichimada here stays in one place, and keep him away from the weapons." He was checking the load when the front window ballooned inward. A rain of glass flew at them.

The Yakuza opened fire with their M-16's, completely shredding the incoming object.

The moment the bolt was off, Michael dropped the compact hunting crossbow and was sprinting around to the east side of the house. Pried open a window to a bedroom and climbed through.

He hoped the vinyl float he had shot through the front window by tying it to the crossbow bolt had provided him enough time.

The bedroom was empty. Drew his *katana*, opened the door cautiously. Caught the stink of cordite fumes. In the darkness, there was more shooting. Maybe, he thought, they'll kill each other off.

Turned left down the hall. Fat Boy Ichimada's master suite was next. Burst through the door, the longsword held in front of him. Ran through the bedroom and attached bath. Empty.

It was imperative that he make a sweep through the rooms in order to determine who was left and where they were.

A bathroom, also deserted.

Now he came to a fork. To his left lay the office, to the right, the kitchen and, beyond, the living room. The kitchen was the obvious place to go now since the lack of large windows made it a probability for defensive tactics.

He stood to one side of the swinging door, lifted his blade until its very tip made contact. Then he pushed inward, opening the door.

Two Yakuza, one firing immediately.

But Michael had come in rolled in a ball. He came out of it, swiping sideways with the blade. Cut through one man. He screamed as the other whirled.

Michael chopped down, immediately slashed again, and the man collapsed.

Up and running along the hall as machine-gun fire erupted through the kitchen's other door. Another Yakuza in the dining area, his M-16 hammering away as the door into the kitchen disintegrated.

Michael took him down with one powerful slash. Dodged back as more fire spewed out. Retreating down the hallway, drawing them after him.

When he heard them coming, he turned and ran to the spot where the hallway branched. Went five steps in the direction of the kitchen, dug into his pocket, pulled out a lighter and a half-dozen long-fuse firecrackers.

Headed down the opposite fork, toward Fat Boy Ichimada's office.

When Ude saw the slashed remnants of the vinyl float, he sent two men into the kitchen, another to the other side where the hallway began off the dining area. He kept the rest of them where they were.

But within minutes, he was obliged to alter his tactics. For one thing, three of his men were down. For another, they had all gotten their first glimpse of one of the intruders.

Ude immediately ordered the three remaining Yakuza down the hallway. As they began to move, he began to follow them, not reluctantly but cautiously.

The firing of the weapons was deafening. Ude could see the three men advancing at an even pace. But when they reached the fork in the hallway, something happened. The men hurled themselves down toward the kitchen. What were they up to? Ude shouted to them, but they could not hear him.

Then he saw the blur of a shadow pass across the open space at the head of the hallway. The glint of polished steel. A *katana*! Slashing forward and down.

184

"Ah!" Ude breathed. "Michael Doss." He spent a precious moment assessing the situation, then he went back down the hall. He smelled a trap, and he had no intention of walking into it himself.

When he returned, it was with Wailea Charlie. With a massive push, Ude sent Wailea Charlie stumbling forward.

Onto the point of something sharp, shiny and seemingly endless. It went all the way through Wailea Charlie while he screamed. Then dizziness supplanted the agonizing pain, and he fell forward.

Michael withdrew the blade and retreated down the hall. He kicked open the door and went into the last remaining room. The office. It contained an ornate desk, an oversize chair and, behind that, an open window onto the now-floodlit compound. Banana-leaf prints were on the walls.

Where was Fat Boy Ichimada?

Michael whirled, and stopped dead.

Ude was filling the doorway. "Put down the *katana*," Ude said, leveling the Mack-10 in Michael's direction. He had been set to pull the trigger and not let go until the intruder was in ribbons. "Michael Doss." He advanced into the room. "I think that's good. For me." He began to laugh.

"I'm going to kill you, of course," he said, watching Michael carefully as he prepared to lay the *katana* at his feet. Shook his head. "No. Slide it onto the desk, hilt first. I don't want it near you." He nodded when Michael had complied. "That's much better." He grinned, waving the Mack-10; he loved the power the machine pistol gave him. "You have much to tell me before I get around to the pleasure of killing you." The smile seemed plastered on his face. "I think I will enjoy the prelude even more."

"Who are you?" Michael asked.

Ude raised his eyebrows. "I am a member of the Takigumi. Have you heard of my *oyabun*, Masashi Taki? Of course you have." Keeping the Mack-10 trained on Michael, he brought out the length of red cord the Hawaiian had given him. "Look familiar? This was meant for you. Your father left it here on Maui. Now you're going to tell me what it means and where the Katei document is hidden."

"What are you talking about?" Michael was genuinely baffled.

But Ude was shaking his head. "No, no. You have it wrong. I ask the questions."

185

"But I don't—"

"This red cord." Dangling it. "What is it?"

It does seem familiar, Michael thought. Where have I seen it before? "You killed my father," Michael said. "Do you think I'm going to tell you anything?"

"Eventually you will," Ude said. "I have no doubt of it." Beginning to squeeze the trigger of the Mack-10.

"You're not going to kill anyone."

Ude whirled.

Fat Boy Ichimada was in the doorway, a pistol seeming almost lost in his great hand.

The two men shot at once. Fat Boy Ichimada's heavy frame spurted blood as it tumbled backward into the hallway.

Ude's Mack-10 was still firing when Michael lunged for his *katana*. Ude smashed the bottom of the machine pistol onto Michael's wrist.

Pain ran up Michael's arm and he grunted, slipping to his knees.

Ude clucked his tongue. "No," he said. "It's not going to be nearly that easy." He shoved the Mack-10 into Michael's face before retreating to a safe distance. When he saw the blood begin to stream from Michael's nose, he laughed. "You're going to tell me what I want to know." He hefted the weapon. "I have a lot of time now—all the time in the world. There is no one around to disturb us—or to hear your screams of pain. Which will surely come when I shoot off one foot. An hour later, I'll shoot off the other. Then I'll begin on your hands. Think about that. Going through life without hands or feet. It'll be a challenge at the very least, *neh*?"

"Go to hell," Michael said.

Ude shrugged and laughed. "More fun for me." He aimed the Mack-10 at Michael's right foot.

A sound was already forming in the room. All in a split second, Ude hesitated, began to turn toward the window.

Michael saw the blur, could not believe his eyes.

Eliane had climbed in through the window. Now she wielded Michael's sword as only a master could. The edge of the blade slashed into the Mack-10, and it spun out of Ude's grip. Blood spurted.

But Eliane was already into her second strike and Ude, scrambling desperately, just missed being decapitated. He slammed into the corner of the desk, grunted heavily, then threw himself headlong into the hallway.

Michael grabbed the Mack-10, hurtled after Ude. He had

to leap over Fat Boy Ichimada's body. He could see the shadow of Ude's form disappearing around a turning, and by the time he reached the front door, there was no sign of him.

Behind him, he could hear Eliane calling his name. He returned to the office. He found her kneeling over Ichimada. She had turned him over, seemed to be talking to him. A railing sound came from his open mouth. His gaze went from Eliane to Michael.

"You are Philip Doss's son," he said with some difficulty. "Truly?"

Michael knelt down beside Eliane. He nodded. "I am Michael Doss."

"Your father called me . . . on the day he died." Fat Boy Ichimada began to cough. He sighed, and his eyes fluttered closed for a moment. "He and I knew each other . . . in the old days. When Wataro Taki was *oyabun*. Before the madman Masashi wrested power from his brothers."

Ichimada was panting. It was becoming difficult to look at him. "He knew that I was still loyal to his old friend Wataro Taki. He asked me to find you. He wanted me to ask you if you remembered the *shintai*."

Michael recalling his father's death poem: *In falling snow/ Egrets call to their mates/Like splendid symbols/of shintai on earth.*

"What else did he say?" Michael asked. "Who murdered him?"

"I . . . don't know." Fat Boy Ichimada was gasping, as if his lungs had forgotten how to work. "It wasn't Masashi."

"Then, who?" Michael asked urgently. "Who else would have wanted my father dead?"

"Find Ude." Ichimada's eyes were already fixed on something only he could see. "Ude found what your father wanted you to have."

Michael leaned closer. Ichimada sounded like a grandfather clock in need of repair. "The Katei document," he whispered. "What is it?"

"Your father stole it from Masashi." Perhaps Ichimada could no longer hear anyone but himself. "Masashi will do anything to get it back. Sent Ude here."

"Who is Ude?"

"Ude shot me," Fat Boy Ichimada said. "Did I get him?"

"He was bleeding," Michael said. There wasn't much time left. "Ichimada, what is the Katei document?"

187

The big man's gaze moved back from Michael to Eliane. "Ask her," he said. "She knows."

"What?"

Fat Boy Ichimada smiled at something that only he could see. A glimpse, perhaps, of the world beyond? "Faith," he said, "and duty. Now I know their meaning. They are one and the same." Then all the breath—what life was left—went out of him.

Michael closed the Yakuza's eyelids. He felt tired; he felt as if he could sleep for a week. But there was so much to think about, so many questions to answer.

He looked at Eliane. Who is she? he wondered. Another question to which he must get the answer. But not now. They had to get out of here first, get some first aid and then get some sleep.

Eliane rose, handed him the *katana* in ceremonial fashion.

Michael, taking it, realized that he had never thanked her for saving his life. He wiped the blood from his face. "How's your hand?" he asked.

"It probably hurts as much as your nose," she said.

"It didn't seem to hurt your grip any."

She gave him a little smile. "You're welcome."

Then, together, they began the slow, painful walk back to civilization.

The truth was that Lillian Hadley Doss hated her father. She had joined the USO troupe that had brought her to Japan solely because of General Hadley's unrelenting badgering.

While it was true that she loved the attention lavished on her while she was onstage, it was also true that she hated every moment she spent away from home. She missed her friends, she missed knowing what the latest trends were. She no longer had any idea what was in fashion or whether any of the American slang phrases she used were now out of style. She had a recurring nightmare that she was home talking to a circle of her closest friends and they were all laughing at her.

She hated her father for shaming her into coming to a place she despised. But she hated him even more for what she saw as his role in her brothers' deaths. It was Sam Hadley who had instilled in his sons their sense of duty to their country. Duty! Was it their duty to die? Where was the sense in that? But, Lillian knew, there was no sense left in the world. The war had seen to that.

We were such a close family, Lillian thought. She remembered their laughter at Easter time, and how she waited through the long summer for her brothers to come home from military academy at Thanksgiving.

At Christmas, they trimmed the tree together, placed brightly wrapped presents beneath it, drank their mother's egg nog and sang carols. Was that corny? Lillian did not think so. Ever since she could remember, she had waited all year for that tradition. Wherever the peripatetic Hadleys happened to be, their holidays were immutable. They provided unwavering comfort in a world filled with military precision. They were the family's own pomp and circumstance. After a time, these oases came—at least in Lillian's mind—to stand for the family itself.

Now, with her brothers dead, that was all gone, swept away by the tides of the stupid, stupid war. Now there was no stability, no comfort, nothing to look forward to. There were only Sam Hadley's endless, intolerable dinnertime lectures on the theories of war.

"Death," General Hadley said over dinner one night several weeks before Lillian was to meet Philip for the first time, "is a necessary—and quite beneficial—byproduct of war. In a way, it is akin to natural selection; the survival of the fittest. War is a shaking out, a condition that did—and certainly should—occur periodically throughout history. Like the great flood in biblical times, war cleanses the earth, makes it ready for a new beginning."

Lillian could not take it anymore. "No, you're wrong," she said, for the first time raising her voice in anger to her father. "War is vile. It's nothing more than oblivion for the dead and despair for the survivors. You sound just like our minister. Both of you talk about monumental—terrible—events that are a matter of life and death as if they were—well, children's exercises!"

She was shaking. She was aware that both her parents were staring at her dumbfoundedly. What had gotten into their fun-loving, cheerful little girl? they must be wondering. "Don't you realize what your war—your precious agent of natural selection—has done? It's killed your two sons! Daddy, according to you, that means Jason and Billy weren't fit to live, to carry on the race—or whatever idiocy it is you believe!"

Lillian saw Philip as her way out, her knight in shining armor. The St. George who would, if not slay her particular dragon, then take her out of its kingdom. If he was a soldier, like her father, it was only the profession they shared. Their personalities and their temperaments could not have been more different. Besides, there was a sadness about Philip that Lillian felt rather than understood, and this drew her as surely as a magnet will find the North Pole.

It was this sadness which, Lillian immediately felt, could give her a purpose, if only she could discover its source and somehow replace it. In this way, she told herself that Philip needed her fully as much as she needed him. It was not a monstrous deception. But marriages based on lies—in any age—cannot long flourish. They can only dissolve. Or survive in a kind of rusting isolation. Like reluctant explorers who

190

prefer to roam aimlessly in a desert that is familiar to them rather than strike out for unknown territory, Philip and Lillian inhabited the cooling corpse of their marriage without knowing that anything might be amiss.

Except that Philip had found Michiko.

And where did that leave Lillian?

On a sunny, blowy day a week after they first met, Philip and Michiko were in his car. He had invited her to a picnic. Of course, although spring was coming it was still too cold to dine outside, but the heated interior of the car would do nicely.

Halfway there, Michiko put a hand on his arm. "There is a place I wish to take you before lunch," she said. She gave him a series of directions. The streets were crowded, and it was slow going until they were clear of the city's hub.

At length, Michiko directed him to pull over and park. They were in the Deienchofu area, a section of the city Philip was unfamiliar with. It was filled with enormous villas, all built in the traditional Japanese style. Lush gardens, ancient cryptomeria trees, stone-and-bamboo walls lined both sides of the street.

"Where are we?" Philip asked as Michiko led him up a stone pathway toward a massive mansion, so heavily foliaged on the outside that it was completely hidden from the street.

"Please," Michiko said, taking off her shoes in the entranceway. She indicated that he should do the same.

The slate floor gave way to pale green *tatami* mats. The scent of new-mown hay they gave off permeated the house. Behind him were a pair of massive *kyoki* wood doors, set in slabs and ribbed with wrought-iron bars. Thick, rough-hewn wooden beams crisscrossed the ceiling in an intricate pattern. The place had an ancient, almost feudal air about it, giving the impression that it had materialized whole from out of the seventeenth century.

At the end of the hall, a line of sliding doors barred their way. The doors' center panels were made of embroidered silk depicting circular winged phoenixes in reds, oranges, golds and yellows.

Michiko knelt in front of the sliding doors and opened them. She indicated that Philip should enter.

As was the custom when coming into *tatami* rooms (for these were invariably the formal areas of a Japanese house), Philip went across the threshold on his knees.

191

"Welcome, Mr. Doss."

The sight of the man sitting across from him snapped Philip's head up.

"What—?"

"You are surprised," Zen Godo said. "That is as it should be, don't you think?"

Philip tried to still the hammering of his heart. This is the man I have been ordered to terminate, he thought.

He was a lean man, with a long, wolflike head, extraordinary eyes that held one's attention like magnets. His hair was brush-cut, dark and thick. An impeccably manicured moustache that was already colored salt-and-pepper lent him the air of a pirate. "My daughter Michiko," Zen Godo said. "You have already met."

Philip turned to stare at Michiko. "You're *his* daughter?" He could not recognize his own voice.

"I know who you are, Mr. Doss," Zen Godo said. "I know that you are responsible for the death of my friends. Arisawa Yamamoto and Shigeo Nakajima."

The names detonated in the air like bombs.

Michiko said nothing. She stood with her hands behind her back, as demure as a schoolgirl. Philip felt trapped, betrayed.

"You cannot keep me here," he said, beginning to rise. "I am a member of the American—"

He felt a weight against his neck, saw that Michiko was holding a *katana*, a Japanese longsword, with its wicked edge at his flesh.

"Michiko will not hesitate to use it, Mr. Doss," Zen Godo said. "She is a *sensei*, a master, of *kenjutsu*. Are you familiar with this word?"

"Yes," Philip said. He was staring at the shining length of the steel blade, at Michiko's unwavering gaze. "*Kenjutsu* is the art of swordsmanship." He had no doubt that Zen Godo was telling the truth about Michiko's skill.

"Believe me, I wish you no harm," Zen Godo went on. "But please keep in mind that Michiko will not hesitate to protect me from harm."

Philip sat back down. He did not see that he had any choice. "You say that I killed your friends and business associates, yet you want me to believe that you wish me no harm. I don't think I can believe that."

"As an answer, allow me to relate a story from the past, since all we learn in life emanates from there." Zen Godo was wearing a formal kimono. It was of black silk, with a glossy black wave pattern woven throughout. An embroidered snowy egret flew over each breast. Their eyes and the tips of their beaks were a bright crimson. "My father taught me that I must destroy my enemies before they destroy me," Zen Godo began. "He was an utterly ruthless man. He was honorable in every way. But he never failed to use the advantage of circumstance to his own ends. And there came a time when my father's ruthlessness caught up with him. Through his endless dealings, he had made many enemies, and now they were too numerous for him to destroy them all.

"My father was a devout Shintoist. He believed fervently in animism. He used to point out trees, sections of brooks and lakes, escarpments of wooded hillsides shimmering in the dusk, and swear to me that spirits dwelled in those places. Now it happened that there was a spirit who my father said lived within the shadows of the rafters of our house. This spirit was possessed of a remarkably evil temper save where it came to my father. It was my father who gave this spirit succor when no one else would—or so my father said.

"It was to this spirit that my father went. 'My enemies surround me,' he told it. 'You counseled me to destroy my enemies before they destroy me. I cannot now. What am I to do?'

"The shadows above his head stirred as if a gentle wind was blowing. In a moment, a gruff voice said, 'You must find an ally who can aid you.'

" 'I have tried,' my father said. 'But none have the fortitude to stand with me.'

" 'Then you must look elsewhere,' the spirit said.

" 'I have searched everywhere.'

" 'Not everywhere,' the spirit said. 'For allies may sometimes be found in the most unexpected places.'

" 'But I have no allies left with stomach for such a battle as this. I have only enemies.'

" 'Then,' the spirit said, 'it is among your enemies that you must discover an ally.' "

Zen Godo smiled. "My current circumstances, Mr. Doss, mirror those of my father in a most uncomfortable manner. I too am surrounded by enemies who wish to see me destroyed. They are numerous, exceptionally well organized. And they are quite powerful."

"Why should I believe any of this?" Philip asked reasonably. "You are a persuasive speaker, but after all, these are words only. And I have a sword at my throat."

Zen Godo gave an almost imperceptible nod, and Philip felt the pressure lifted from his neck. In a moment, Michiko had reversed the *katana*. She placed the hilt in his hands.

Then, to his astonishment, Philip saw Zen Godo bend all the way forward until his face touched the reed mat at his feet.

"Here is your chance, Doss-san," Zen Godo said from this position. "One swing of the *katana* on the back of my neck will sever the spinal cord completely. Your task will be accomplished, and you will not have had to think on your own. You will merely have had to follow orders."

Philip glanced at Michiko. She stood unmoving. Her face was white and rigid. She glared at him from out of eyes filled with ice and fire.

But he needed to know what they both meant by this, and he rose on one knee so that he was above the prostrate man. He lifted the *katana* so that the blade was directly over Zen Godo's exposed neck. He took a deep breath, brought the blade swiftly down.

Zen Godo did not move, and neither did Michiko.

Philip stopped the blade inches short of the flesh. He exhaled deeply, took several breaths before resuming his former position opposite Zen Godo on the mats.

There was a profound silence. Philip imagined that he could hear motes of dust falling. In time, Zen Godo brought his head off the floor. He stared at Philip. There was no expression on his face.

Philip saw his opportunity and seized it. "These enemies you are talking about," he said. "Are they known as the *Jiban*?" Now was the time to see whether he was right, whether he and Jonas were being duped into terminating the wrong people.

Zen Godo watched him with glossy ebon eyes. "Yes. But I would be most pleased if you were to tell me how you came to know that name."

"Only if you tell me who, or what, the *Jiban* is," Philip said.

Zen Godo nodded. "An equitable exchange of information. My father always told me that that was an excellent method of beginning a relationship built on mutual trust."

Philip handed over the letter he had taken from Shigeo Nakajima's corpse. Zen Godo read it through, then passed it on to Michiko. He looked up. "What does this letter tell you, Mr. Doss?"

Philip shook his head. "First tell me about the *Jiban*."

"*Jiban*, as you might already know, means a local political machine," Zen Godo said. "That was meant as a rather ironic comment. The *Jiban* is a closely knit clique of high-level bureaucratic ministers who have banded together under the leadership of a man named Kozo Shiina. Shiina is a particularly odious individual. He was a mass murderer during the war. Oh yes, there were many of them, I suppose. But Shiina was by far the most hideous of the lot. He enjoyed his work—the business of war seduced him, then enslaved him.

"It was Shiina who first pushed for Japan's military expansion into Manchuria. It was Shiina who helped whip up popular support for the aggressive stance needed for imperialism. He had—and still has—a great deal of influence within both the political and the industrial spheres.

"Since the war's end, Shiina has seen to it that he and his cronies have clean slates. The Americans cannot touch him. He has so cleverly rewritten the dossiers, they aren't even aware of his role in the war. Now, ironically, he and his ministers are advisers to the Americans. Ha! He gulls the Americans into confiding their policies to him. He agrees to help implement these policies, and then he and his ministers go about secretively undermining those very directives."

"What does this Shiina have against you?" Philip asked.

"Yamamoto-san, Nakajima-san and I were against the war from the very beginning. I joined *Tokko* in order to fight communism, which I cannot abide. We fought against Shiina, and he has never forgiven us. Now, after the war ended as we predicted it would, we see the opportunity America's help can afford us. We believe that Japan can emerge stronger, more self-reliant, from this disaster if we provide it with the right direction and momentum. Shiina and his *Jiban* want something else entirely."

"Which is?"

Zen Godo's eyes were dark, depthless, like a still lake at evening. "Shiina wishes to return Japan to its prewar militaristic state. He wants the Manchuria Japan never had. He wants more. He wants the mainland of China. He wants to expand our country. It is Japan's destiny, he says. It is our *karma*. Japan can never be great, he believes, until it is a nation of a physical size comparable to that of America or Russia."

God in heaven, Philip thought. What have I stumbled into? I was right. We *have* been fed tainted intelligence. It was now

195

clear to Philip that David Turner must be a conduit between the *Jiban* and Silvers. Still, the question remained: Whose side was Silvers on? A terrifying image was beginning to form in Philip's mind, but he needed confirmation.

Philip told Zen Godo how Nakajima's letter had planted grave doubts in his mind about his directive. He told him about his meeting with General Hadley, and what Hadley had found out—that Silvers's intelligence source for the directives to terminate Yamamoto, Nakajima and Godo was through Silvers's adjutant, David Turner.

Zen Godo absorbed this information impassively. At length, he said, "After she met you for the first time, Michiko described you to me as 'the special American.' This interested me intensely because it indicated that you understood many of the basic underlying precepts of the Japanese Way. I should tell you that Michiko is married to Nobuo Yamamoto. He is the eldest son of Arisawa Yamamoto. When she discovered that you were responsible for the death of her father-in-law, she was understandably distraught." Philip imagined Michiko wielding her longsword against him, and shuddered.

"In fact, I believed she harbored a desire to see you dead, Mr. Doss," Zen Godo continued. "But this was all before she met you. Then you became 'the special American,' and everything changed. That is why I had her bring you to me." He touched the edge of his moustache. "It was you who put me in mind of the spirit's advice. It saved my father's business. Now I pray that it will save mine." He held out his hands palms up. "To be fair, it is time I tell you why you are here." He laughed. "I want you to kill me."

Now it became imperative that Philip discover just what was going on inside CIG headquarters. The information Zen Godo had provided him dictated that. Once he knew that the *Jiban* was deliberately feeding tainted intelligence into Silvers's CIG files, everything else followed in logical progression. If, further, he supposed that Silvers knew about the nature of the intelligence and was not merely being duped by an unrelentingly clever foe, a number of otherwise inexplicable elements fell into place. For instance, why Silvers was so secretive concerning his source. For another, why he was using David Turner, an office hand, to carry out delicate field work in the first place. On the surface it made no sense to entrust such hazardous duty to a monkey like Turner. But viewed in this new and different light, it just might. Philip considered: As Silvers's administrative adjutant, Turner was tied to his CO in very direct ways. Silvers—if he *was* working for the *Jiban*—could both control the flow of tainted information (thus, making it security-proof) *and* have a perfect scapegoat—Turner—if the quality of the intelligence was ever called into question.

The more Philip thought about it, the more it seemed that Silvers was not what he appeared to be. What his motive might be was another story entirely. Frankly, Philip did not much care. As far as he was concerned, a traitor was a traitor. Whether he betrayed his country for money, blackmail or ideological reasons made no difference. Pragmatically, the result was the same, and that was all that mattered.

Accordingly, Philip made plans. Methodical as he was, he stole into the CIG headquarters first. He did not believe that Silvers would be foolish enough to leave implicating files in the office. But he would be foolish himself if he did not check out the possibility.

As he suspected, he found nothing of an incriminating nature. Then it was time to infiltrate Silvers's personal quarters. The head of CIG lived in a small, neat house near the Imperial Palace. It was not difficult to get into. Not for a specialist such as Philip.

The place was paneled in dark woods. Oriental carpets lay on the floor, muffling all sound. Philip had chosen a night when Silvers was attending a formal banquet at MacArthur's residence. Such affairs of state inevitably proved lengthy, since the general was fond of using these occasions to treat those in attendance to a substantial helping of his famous bombast.

Philip had been to meetings here twice before. His memory was virtually photographic concerning such things. Consequently, he required no illumination to make his way through the place.

He began with Silvers's study. There was an old rolltop desk, a wooden swivel chair, a leather settee, a couple of matching wing chairs scattered around in front of walnut bookcases. In short, a quintessentially Western room.

The contents of one drawer after another came under Philip's scrutiny. As he drew the beam of his flashlight over the papers, he prayed that he would be able to find something substantive, something conclusive. Philip was certain that with proof, his father-in-law would move against Silvers.

And then he had it! Hidden beneath a false bottom in a lower drawer was a slim, black-bound notebook. He could scarcely believe his luck. The evidence confirmed his every suspicion. Excitement mounting, he read over the pages of the notebook again. Yes. It was all here: times and dates of meetings with *Jiban* ministers whose names Philip recognized, accountings of payments made, records of where those payments had been deposited, along with the bank account number. Everything Philip needed to nail Silvers as a traitor in the employ of the *Jiban*.

The next morning, Philip presented himself at a downtown bank. Using his CIG credentials to get in to see the vice-president, he requested all pertinent information on account number 647338A. The depositor's name was not Harold Morten Silvers. But of course Philip had not expected that. Instead, he brought out a photostat of orders signed by Silvers. He compared the handwriting with that of the account's depositor's. It was the same.

The blueprints of Zen Godo's house arrived right on time. David Turner delivered the packet to Philip's apartment. It was the moment Philip had been dreading: It meant that Jonas had solved the question of how to make the termination seem like an accident without Philip's needlessly putting the CIG at risk. This was not an easy puzzle to solve, since Zen Godo possessed a high degree of visibility.

Because Jonas—ever security conscious—did not want Lillian around while they talked, Philip suggested that Turner take her to see *Across the Pacific*, a film she had been wanting to see. He knew that she had failed to make any friends, either among the army wives or among the locals. Lillian and Turner departed without a word, and Philip and Jonas got on with their plans.

Philip and Jonas pored over the blueprints, went over once more the intelligence each had memorized about Zen Godo. Losing himself in the minutiae of facts and figures, Philip was able to hold in abeyance the cramps lurking in the pit of his stomach. But when Jonas began to outline the nature of the scheme, the reality of the situation once more flooded over him.

He knew that he had reached a staging area. Now, like seeing the first sliver of the sun emerging from the darkness of night, he began to glimpse the full nature of what lay before him. It terrified him.

"Jonas," he said, glancing at his watch, "let's take Godo out tonight."

"Tonight?"

"Sure," Philip said, keeping his voice level. "Why not? We have all the materials." He had already turned the evidence he had discovered in Silvers's desk over to General Hadley. Tomorrow, Hadley would present his evidence to MacArthur. Then the shit would really hit the fan. All this had to be over with by then. Philip forced himself to grin. "Sure."

We need a witness to my complete demise, Zen Godo had said. *Who more perfect than your partner?*

"We can do this one together," Philip said.

"You must be joking," Jonas said.

"Isn't it time the spider emerged from his web?" Philip poured them both drinks. Jonas, at least, was going to need fortification before this night was through.

Jonas shook his head. "I don't know."

"But this plan is your crowning achievement," Philip said. "I, for one, think you should participate in it." He watched Jonas take a gulp of his scotch. "Besides," he continued, "remember that hazing you once told me about?"

"At Pickett?" Pickett was the military academy Jonas had attended in Kentucky before he went to West Point.

"Yeah," Philip said, warming to his topic. "At Pickett. You all used your swords. Your ceremonial swords. It was a kind of brand you inflicted on the candidates, right? Hurt like hell. Those blades were sharper than rat's teeth. Isn't that what you said? Sharper than rat's teeth?"

"Yeah." Jonas remembered it as if it were yesterday.

"If you cried out, if you made any sound at all, that was the end of it. You didn't make the hazing. Right?"

"Right." Jonas downed the rest of his drink, and Philip replenished it.

"Sure, Jonas. That hazing was your favorite time. In the night. Under a full moon. Hoods and black robes. Incantations to the spirit of General Pickett himself. All that adolescent claptrap." Philip watched as Jonas finished off the liquor. "Now you can live it all over again. What do you say?"

In the night.

Rain dripping dolefully from the wooden eaves. Philip and Jonas standing between rain-slicked cedar pillars.

"This is his bedroom," Jonas whispered.

A whippoorwill sang from its dry perch within the thick cryptomeria.

"Put your mask on," Philip said, positioning the black cloth over his head. They were dressed all in matte black.

There were no other sounds in the night now but the rain. Even the whippoorwill was quiet.

"You're certain there's no one in the house with him," Jonas said. Out of his element, he was nervous. "The files said that once a week, Godo allows his people to visit their families overnight. That's not for two days."

"This is February eighth, a holiday," Philip said. "*Harikuyo*. It's the needle mass, in Buddhist religion, the day when songs are sung for all the needles broken during the past year. You're smiling, but after all, nothing would get sewn or mended without the needle. Besides, think of the damage a broken needle could cause sticking up from a *tatami* mat. Don't worry. No one but Godo will be here."

"Speaking of needles," Jonas said, "do you have yours?"

"Right here," Philip said, patting his pocket. "Stop worrying. This'll be a milk run."

He led the way up onto the wooden porch. They stood very still, listening. Drip, drip, drip. Nothing more.

Crossing to the *shoji*, Philip knelt. He slipped a narrow metal blade between the rice-paper screens' wooden frames. Moved it upward, freeing the catch. He turned, nodded to Jonas.

Cautiously, they slid back the screen. The room within was very dark. Zen Godo was asleep on his *futon*.

Philip left his shoes on the porch, crept across the *tatami*. He was acutely aware of Jonas right behind him.

He was very close to the sleeping form now. He took out a box. Nestled inside it was a glass syringe filled with a chemical Jonas had obtained that would simulate a coronary embolism. Philip took the syringe out, pushed the plunger to free the needle of air. And inadvertantly hit a porcelain sake cup that had been left on the edge of a low table.

"Shit!" Philip said, making more noise than the cup falling onto the resilient *tatami* mat.

Zen Godo stirred, rising up.

Philip jabbed out with the syringe, but Godo slapped it away.

"Goddamnit!" Jonas said. "Do it!"

Philip took out a length of wire with wooden handles at either end. He whipped the wire around Zen Godo's neck, began to pull it tight.

Heard the distinctive rasp of the *shoji* out into the hall sliding back. Turned his head. "Watch out!" he cried.

The *katana* blade was whistling toward Jonas. Who wheeled and leaped at the same time. The edge sliced into the reed mat.

Philip continued his work. Pulling, pulling. While Jonas was busy feinting, ducking, weaving.

Blood covered Philip's hands in a warm stream, and he thought, That's it! Whipped the wire free, and dived for the syringe, pocketing it. He leaped up, grabbed at Jonas, who had pulled his service pistol. "I'm gonna kill this fucker!" Jonas said. The *katana* was whistling again. Slices in the *shoji* and the cedar walls attested to the rapidity with which the longsword was being wielded.

Jonas leveled the gun, and Philip slapped it away. "Are you crazy?" Pulling Jonas back across the threshold.

Out onto the porch. Stuffing his and Jonas's shoes into his jacket. Leaping off the porch, dragging an unwilling Jonas with him. Out into the rain, the black, black night.

"Godo?"

"Dead," Philip said. He wiped the blood onto Jonas's hand before the rain washed it all away. "The wire went halfway through his neck."

"Good," Jonas said. "Good." Philip noticed that he was trembling.

In the car, speeding through the city, Philip said, "That was insane what you almost did back there."

"What?"

"The gun, Jonas. The fucking gun. It's U.S. Army issue. If you'd used it, what do you think a ballistics check would've produced?"

"They couldn't trace it back to us."

"Maybe not all the way. But it sure as hell would've put Silvers in an awkward position. 'What are U.S. Army issue bullets doing inside a Japanese national, Colonel Silvers?' Do you think he'd care to field that one from his superiors?"

Jonas was silent. Streetlights streaked his face in furious colors. The residue of the rain dripped off them in concert to the *whick-whick-whick* of the windshield wipers.

"Christ," Jonas said after a long time, "but this was a nasty one." His tone gave Philip the impression of elation. He was flushed, his eyes alight. Then he turned. The pale, greenish streetlights lent his face an unearthly aspect. "But who the hell was that with the sword?"

201

"Who cares?" Philip said. "Godo's dead. Whoever it was didn't get a look at our faces."

"Yeah." Jonas ran a hand through his hair. "I've got to thank you for that one, buddy." He blew out a breath of air, relaxing. He was beginning to enjoy the aftermath. "Jesus, that goddamn sword almost decapitated me!"

When Philip thought back on it, the scene had possessed the quality of a film wherein the lead actor stares into a set of mirrors so that his reflection is repeated endlessly . . . That day, when Michiko had brought him to see Zen Godo. When Zen Godo had said to him, *I want you to kill me.* And Philip had said, *Why?*

But he had needed time to absorb not only what was being asked of him, but also what was to come. Having watched Michiko through every minute phase of the exquisite ritual of making tea, he had allowed the heat to seep into his palms as he closed them gently around the porcelain cup; the one he would, later that week, deliberately knock off the edge of the table. The gentle tendrils of steam rose toward his face like the last remnants of a dream.

Only after Philip had sipped all the tea out of the cup did Zen Godo begin. "I want you to understand the situation in its entirety." Michiko, at right angles to him, leaned forward to fill the emptiness between Philip's cupped palms. "By 'dying' I will win nothing but time."

"The power of the *Jiban* is such that it has forced me into giving up my name, my business, my life as Zen Godo. I will disappear from the bureaucratic scene. Dead, I will lose whatever power I might now have."

He sipped his tea, encouraging Philip to do so as well. "Accordingly," he said, "I must be reborn. This is a difficult and perilous undertaking. It cannot be accomplished alone. I have only my daughter. Cut off from everyone I know, I am terribly vulnerable now. If word that I still live should reach any member of the *Jiban*, I would certainly be executed within hours.

"Rebirth cannot be achieved overnight. Therefore, I will be going away. To Kyushu, the southern island. There I will live with the orange farmers. I will dig my hands into my native soil with enthusiasm and a free mind. I will work, I will eat, I will sleep. And time will pass.

"Meanwhile, here in Tokyo my daughter will take care of

202

my affairs. I have much money, many investments. There is a great deal to do."

Michiko pulled back the sleeve of her kimono, poured them both more tea. She looked neither at her father nor at Philip, but rather at what she was doing. She had, Philip thought later, the most extraordinary powers of concentration.

"But alone, she cannot complete what must be done," Zen Godo continued. "She needs assistance. And only you, Doss-san, can provide that."

Philip, drinking his tea, wondered at the change that had come over him. Like a thief in the night, it had appeared when he wasn't looking, transforming him. He thought about how he used to be, about how Jonas still was: My country right or wrong; I will follow orders unhesitatingly—unthinkingly. The United States *über alles*: That still might be Jonas's motto.

"Naturally, I do not expect this extraordinary service to be rendered without adequate compensation. Tell me, Doss-san, do you believe in futures? Yes, of course you do. You would not be here now, otherwise. In return for your work, I will give you a one third share in all future revenues."

"Revenues in what?" Philip had asked.

Zen Godo smiled. "I am a *kanryodo sensei*. The Way of the bureaucrat has defined my entire adult life. Even our defeat in the war of the Pacific could not alter that. Neither will my 'death.'

"Certainly, I cannot return to the ministerial arena. Nor can I enter any legitimate sphere of business without the distinct probability of coming to the attention of members of the *Jiban*. So what are my alternatives? I have only one. I must go underground. I must become Yakuza."

"Why Yakuza?" Philip had asked. "Yakuza are gangsters. By controlling gambling, prostitution, *pachinko*, they prey on the weak and defenseless. I will not be a party to that."

"Life is infinitely mystifying," Zen Godo had said. "I wonder how such idealism can be reconciled with the cynicism of the business you are in."

"I only know what I can and cannot do."

"In the beginning, it is said that the Yakuza protected the farmers in the countryside from the bands of marauders prevalent in those days." Zen Godo shrugged. "Legend it may be. Or fanciful notion. Who can say? In any event, I have no choice. If I will have any chance of defeating the *Jiban*, I must have power. I must control the actions of bureaucrats, politicians, bankers and manufacturers. If you can tell me how I may accomplish this any other way, I would be pleased to hear it."

"I cannot," Philip had said after a time. "But I am no criminal."

"There is much an honest man can do within the Yakuza, Doss-san. I do not pretend to be a—what do you Westerners call it? A saint? Yes. But saintliness is not within the province of man. There is much good that can be accomplished for my people. If I do not do this—and, Doss-san, let me say that you alone have the power to stop me—then surely the *Jiban* will triumph in eventually bringing on another world war. They desire space for Japan. They believe that it is the emperor's will—Japan's destiny. I do not say that this will be accomplished next week or even next year. But it does not matter to the *Jiban*. They are patient. Westerners are not. That is what the *Jiban* members are relying on. In thirty years, or forty, who will remember there was even a clique of ministers with that name? Hardly any. At that point, their time will have come. Unless I can somehow find a way to gain enough power to oppose them."

"Forty years from now?" Philip was incredulous.

"Yes, Doss-san. In the time span of this world, that is but a single breath. It is nothing. You must learn that."

Philip had stared at Zen Godo for a long time. At last he said, "I do not want the money."

"Then," Zen Godo said, curious, "what is it you want?"

When Philip did not answer, Zen Godo said, "Excuse me for saying this, but I believe you *do* want what your conscience mistakenly dictates you put aside. Believe me, Doss-san, it is not necessary for you to make up your mind about this now."

"I don't want it."

"But one day," Zen Godo said, "you will."

Michiko stayed with Philip long after Zen Godo had left them. "There are certain specific details my father wishes you to understand," she said. Beneath the ash-gray kimono, she wore an ice-white underkimono. The glow of her firm, dusky flesh warmed the color in spots.

"I don't understand," Philip said as she shed her ash-gray silk skin. "This can't be what he had in mind. You're married."

"The marriage to Nobuo Yamamoto, eldest of the Yamamoto sons," she said, "is my father's undertaking. It is not mine."

Philip watched her. "He forced you into it?"

"Forced me?" Michiko did not understand him. "He created the liaison. It is business. The Yamamotos are in the process of building a network of companies specializing in heavy-industry manufacturing. My father, during his tenure as head of the Bank of Nippon, was instrumental in creating a local bank that will, in time, become the central hub of the Yamamoto *konzern*.

"This is the way the future of Japan will be constructed, my father believes. The bureaucracy designates certain specific industries for high-speed growth. To induce new companies to enter the designated fields, loans of a highly beneficial nature to the borrower are extended through the Bank of Nippon to regional and local institutions. However, new industries take time. Money runs out all too quickly. My father has realized that once committed to lending these new companies capital, the local banks will have to continue the policy.

"Overloaning, my father calls it. Because eventually, the local banks will have lent so much money that they will end up owning a majority of the businesses that have borrowed from them. This will happen in the Yamamotos' case, as well. Except that thanks to my father's foresight, they will already own the bank."

Having the future of Japan predicted by this exquisite, half-naked creature had about it the aspect of the mythological. For an instant, Philip imagined himself a great hero on an epic quest. And now, at its end, coming face to face with an oracle of extraordinary powers. He was reminded of how he had first met Michiko, in the mist of the ruins of the Temple of Kannon. And this, too, seemed to reinforce the eerie mythic feeling she engendered within him. It was as if she had been resurrected from out of the temple's ashes, as if she were the reincarnation of all those lost souls whose bodies had been burned by the fire bombing, whom he had heard crying out.

"In that event," Philip said thickly, "you will be a wealthy woman."

"Money," Michiko said with a sneer. "If money and power did not go hand in hand, I would not care about money at all."

"Nobuo Yamamoto will have a great deal of power," Philip said.

"No," Michiko said, moving in her ice-white underskin so that Philip was unable to take his eyes off her. "He will have a great deal of money. He does not understand the nature of power. He knows neither how to acquire it nor what to do with it if he had it. Money is what Nobuo craves. So he can have his parties for his business friends. So he can provide girls for all of them. So they can get drunk, be sung to, fondled, caressed, coddled like babies at their mothers' breasts. 'Goo goo,' I say to Nobuo when he comes home in the morning after such a night. 'Don't you understand me when I speak your language?' "

She had such beautiful shoulders, such a graceful neck. Her small, pointed breasts rose and fell against the silk with her breathing. Her waist was so narrow he was certain that he could put his hands around it. Undressed, she seemed tiny, and tremendously vulnerable.

"Whatever power we accrue," she said, "will be my doing. Though I suspect that he may be unaware of it, it is my father who is responsible for my learning how to amass power."

Utterly desirable.

"Do you want me?" she whispered. The lamplight in her hair like gold thread glinting in a coal mine.

Philip found it difficult to speak. "I would not be a man if I did not."

"That is what I need," Michiko said, rising. "A man. Not a child."

As she rose, the silken folds fell away from her hips. Shadows stroked her powerful thighs, curving inward to keep from him still her secret delta.

"You must want," she said, moving toward him over the reed mats, "for me to give." With a natural grace that could only be termed sinuous. "You must, in your wanting, give." Stood over him for a breathless instant, before bending her knees. "I think that we must both be selfish people to be here now, alone, together. Two married people, not married to one another." She knelt before him. Her eyes glowing in the low light. "But I do not want to come together with another selfish human being. I would prefer permanent abstinence to that. I do not wish to be selfish myself."

Opening the buttons at the cuffs, down the front of his shirt. Spreading it apart. "Tell me, Philip-san, do you think that selflessness can take the place of love?" Running her palms across the flesh of his shoulders, biceps, forearms, until

206

the shirt dropped into his lap. "Do you believe—as I do—that it can make of lust a more noble emotion?"

"I believe in what we are doing."

She gave a little laugh. "In my father's selflessness at wanting a better Japan?" Her fingers deftly slid his belt through the buckle, unzipped his trousers. "Or in our selflessness in wanting each other?"

She took the shirt off his lap.

Philip felt an exhilaration in being here. Ever since the night when he had wrapped the wire around Zen Godo's neck and had felt the freshly killed animal's blood washing over his hands, he had experienced a sense of freedom that was dizzying.

He had gone underground yet again, he realized. He had moved from one subterranean passageway to another. And now he would begin to play for real the game that so fascinated and obsessed him. Now he could be the red fox *and* the hunter, all in one. It was the unique role for which he had been searching all his life.

"When I return from Kyushu," Michiko's father had said, "I will no longer be Zen Godo. Zen Godo is dead, eh, Doss-san? You killed him. I am now and will henceforth forever be Wataro Taki. It is my pledge that nothing I will ever ask of you will compromise your patriotism. I know how you feel about your country. Perhaps better than you do yourself. As I said, in the *Tokko*, the special police, during the war of the Pacific, I worked at weeding out the Communist elements that, had they been allowed to flourish, would certainly have been a devisive force inside Japan. I plan to use my new Yakuza clan to continue that battle. You see, Doss-san, there is nothing I want for my country and yours that you do not as well."

They had sat facing one another. Two people from opposite cultures. Two individuals drawn to one another precisely because of that gulf. Two human beings so alike they might have been twins. Warriors who might have been sent here from the edge of time. It was as if they had been born for this moment, born to fight this particular battle.

"No one has ever loved me," Michiko said, bringing his thoughts back to the present. "Others have known only parts of me. Is that my fault? Perhaps, yes." She was concentrating on the space between them with an intensity that made it come alive. "Our culture dictates restraint. In a society that lives with rice-paper walls, privacy is unknown. There is no 'I' in Japan. Only 'we.' "

She sat quite still, studying him. Or some quality she found inside him. "But I open my mind. I think. And I feel 'I.' How is that possible? I cannot understand it. I cannot bear it. Because that 'I' is impossible to share with another Japanese. I must keep it forever locked away inside the deepest part of me.

"Except with you." Using the pads of her thumbs on his nipples until they stiffened. "My flesh melts like wax next to you." Then her tiny tongue. "The compressed air inside my head can escape." Licked under his arms. "I can close my eyes." At the base of his belly. "I can think 'I' and not feel like an alien crawling across the moon." Teaching him that it wasn't only his penis that could feel during sex.

She stopped abruptly, put her hand against her pursed lips. "I did not think that I wanted to talk."

"You wanted to talk," Philip said, reaching for her, "as well."

He bent all the way over, lifted the last layer of ice-white silk off her. Tongued her until her moans filled the tiny apartment. Her thighs spread and spread. Then, rock-hard, he climbed over her, felt her fingers curl around him, guiding him into her hot, liquid core.

He thought that he might go insane. He was caught up in a madness that seemed to encompass the universe. He felt sensations all through his body. He opened his mouth over hers. Felt the fiery points of her nipples pressing with exquisite sensation against his own. Tried to merge himself with her.

And almost succeeded.

One thing you could say about David Turner: He knew how to treat a lady. It became his habit to take Lillian to the U.S. Officers' Club that Silvers frequented. Perhaps he used credentials that his CO would not have approved of; Turner was adept at such deceptions. But it was all in a good cause.

For her part, Lillian loved the Officers' Club. It was within the U.S. ambassador's compound, a white stone building that had been entirely refurbished inside. MacArthur liked his brain trust to be comfortable, and the black market in meat, vegetables, fruit, wine and whiskey did a booming business behind the scenes here.

But over and above anything else, she felt, it was so *American*. And perhaps because of that, perhaps because she was sick of Japan, tired of doing nothing and longing to be home again, she spoke of everything. Because she was at ease in these rooms that so reminded her of home. Everything that was in her heart.

As they ate steaks from Omaha, potatoes from Idaho, greens from Long Island, as they finished off one bottle of vintage Bordeaux and broke open another, Lillian found herself relaxing in a way she had not done since she had come to Japan. Part of it, she was certain, had to do with her own agitated state of mind: The longer she was in Japan, she found, the more she hated it. She could not adjust to the customs, the layers of formal, semiformal and intimate ways of speech that dominated Japanese life. She found their religions—Buddhism, Shintoism and Zen—not only impenetrable but somehow vaguely threatening. The Japanese did not believe in heaven or in hell, but rather in a kind of reincarnation that to Lillian at least smacked of the supernatural. In fact she found, to her horror, that the supernatural was everywhere in Japan. The Japanese were basically animists—they saw spirits in every nook and cranny of their surroundings.

But just as much, she found that her new mood was engendered by something within David Turner himself. For one thing, he was a terrific listener. He possessed a natural empathy. She did not find herself fighting—as she often did with Philip—to understand an essentially mysterious personality. Also, he was a terrific teacher. She found his face handsome, yes. But also—and far more important to her—sensitive. What Philip saw as asceticism in Turner, Lillian recognized as intellectual. She was astounded by the scope of his knowledge, the plethora of philosophies and ideologies he had within his grasp—all of which he was able to convey to her.

Without having any clear idea how, Lillian found herself telling him what she had never told anyone in her life. About the time when, as a senior in high school, her best friend had been stricken with leukemia. Lillian had been terrified. Afraid to be witness to how the disease had altered her friend, she had put off going to the hospital as long as she was able.

But guilt and shame finally overtook her, and she went one morning. She remembered her teeth chattering with fear and anxiety as she rode up in the enormous elevator. On an intervening floor, two male nurses swung in a patient on a wheeled stretcher, and Lillian thought she would faint. She could remember, with an eerie iteration, the bottle of clear liquid, suspended above the stretcher, swinging and dripping, swinging and dripping.

Stepping out into the white, white corridor, Lillian had felt a giddiness not unlike the sensation just before she was overcome by ether when she had had her tonsils out. She needed some time to catch her breath, to allow the vertigo to subside. At last, she found the room.

She pushed the door inward and entered. She remembered that the window was open. The curtains were fluttering like the wings of a bird. She could hear street sounds wafting in.

But there was no Mary. Only an empty bed, neatly made. Awaiting the next patient.

Lillian heard a sound behind her and whirled. "Mary," she said wildly, but it was only a nurse. "Where is Mary?"

"Do you mean the young girl who—"

"Mary Dekker!" Lillian was shouting.

"Oh my dear, but she expired early this morning," the nurse said.

"Expired?" Lillian had said, thinking it was such an odd, antiseptic word.

"Didn't they tell you at Admitting?" the nurse continued. "They should have—"

Lillian was screaming.

In the end, they had put her in the bed that had been Mary's. They gave her a sedative and called her home.

Sam Hadley had come to the hospital to fetch his daughter. "You've got to understand, Lil," he told her as he drove her home, "that Mary's fought her war. She lost, but she was no less brave for that."

The sedative had worn off. Lillian could not stop weeping.

"You could learn a thing or two from Mary, I think," her father said. He did not look at her. He did not like tears. He could not see what purpose they served. "She was your best friend. She deserved your support when she needed it most. Don't cry for her, Lil. Mary certainly doesn't need your tears now. And crying for yourself is merely a sign of weakness. What earthly good will it do you? Now that you've wept, will it make you stronger? Will it give you courage?

"You've got to have courage, Lil, to survive in this world. Life's not all candy canes and rainbows. Your friend Mary could have told you that. But you chose to hide your head in the sand. I can't say that I understand that kind of reaction. Nor condone it. I'm disappointed in you, Lil. This isn't how

210

I expect a child of mine to act. Bravery is to be rewarded, celebrated. Not shunned and hidden from."

Then, years later, there was her brother Jason's last night on American soil. She had spent it with him. He was filled with the onset of battle. His face was flushed, alight with a frightening glow she had seen many times in her father. His anticipation was such that it strangled the list of arguments she had composed ahead of time. She had promised herself that she would use this last night together to try to persuade him not to go off to Europe. But when the time came, her words froze in her throat. Instead, she allowed his enthusiasm, his strength, to dominate her. So the next morning she watched his transport lift off into a sky as gray as lead, without ever having tried to dissuade him from going.

"It was what happened with Mary all over again," Lillian said to a concerned David Turner. "I lacked the courage to do what I had to do. And seventy-two hours later, Jason was lying dead on the beach at Anzio."

Turner leaned forward. His thick black hair caught the light, giving it a bluish sheen. "Don't you think," he said gently, "that you're putting a bit too much responsibility on yourself, Lillian? I mean, let's imagine for a minute that you *had* spoken up that night with your brother. Do you think that anything you could have said would have changed his mind?"

Lillian looked at him.

"Besides, his orders had already been cut. Even if you had managed to change his mind—which is highly unlikely—what could he have done about it at that late date? Gone AWOL?" He shook his head. "Events had already taken their course."

"But it would have meant something to *me*," Lillian insisted.

"Such as what?"

"That I have the courage of my convictions."

"Despite what your father the general says, life is lived by cowards. Wisdom, Lillian, comes not from making war on one's fellow man, but from an understanding of the necessities of history." Turner took her hand in his. "Don't you see that you needn't live your life by the dictates of your father? He is a militarist. He has based his life on impressing his will on others. That is his function, after all. His twisted philosophies have got you tied up in knots. You cry, and he tells you you're weak. You cannot confront death, and he tells you you're weak. It's happened so many times when you were

211

young that now you yourself believe the lie. Surely you don't need me to point that out to you."

But, of course, she did. It wasn't until this moment that Lillian understood her motivations. Or the depth of her loathing for her father and all he stood for. She told Turner all this. It was such a relief to do so. Turner—bless him—had seen it and, by gently pointing it out to her, had freed her from what she had always seen as a weakness. Because she had been told so by her father!

Oh, how her hatred of her father burned inside of her! And all because of David Turner.

"You've changed."

"Really?" Philip said. "How so?"

Lillian closed the book she had been reading. "It's hard to say." She pursed her lips. But, of course, she knew. He was somehow, mysteriously, no longer vulnerable. Though she still needed him—or, more accurately, needed something she had glimpsed within him—she suspected that he no longer needed her.

They were sitting across from one another in the living room of their small apartment. Streetlights sifted across the ceiling like spun sugar. Occasionally, a passing vehicle dusted the rug between them with moving light. "When I first met you," she said, "I felt as if I had squeezed through the bars of a cage and was standing very close to a beautiful but wild creature. I mean deep down, I felt . . . there was a strength I wanted to hold on to and never let go of."

"Like your father."

"No!" she cried, alarmed, and then laughed when she saw his face and knew that he was joking. "Oh God, no. Nothing like my father." Or Jason, she thought, my brother, whose strength was so like my father's it froze me at just the time I should have acted. Jason, flying off into the last sunrise, the good soldier. But Jason's death wasn't my fault, right? David said so.

"And now?" Philip asked. "What's changed?"

She put the flat of her hand on the book cover. "Do you know," she said, not wanting to tell him, because that would mean admitting it to herself, "that I think the thing I hate most about my father is his purity of purpose. His strength is the strength of the righteous. He had a sword at home that he took me to see one day. It had belonged to *his* father, who was a cavalry officer in the First World War.

212

" 'Do you see this blade, Lil?' my father said, taking the sword out of the sheath. 'It's made of a solid sheet of steel.' He slammed it down onto a block of concrete. 'It won't bend, Lil. It is strong. It is indomitable. Have you ever asked yourself about the meaning of life? Well, here is the answer.' "

She kissed Philip's cheek. "That is not your strength. When I met you, it was the first time I had come in contact with a strength that, well, that flowed. I guess that's the only way to describe it. It wasn't a solid sheet of steel. It wasn't indomitable."

Philip closed his eyes. "Have you ever seen a Japanese longsword? A *katana*?"

"I must have. But I don't remember."

"Then you haven't seen one," he said. "You'd remember it, all right. The *katana* is forged from a piece of steel that is heated and beaten. It is folded and refolded upon itself ten thousand times. The result is the finest blade the world has ever seen. A true *katana* can pierce armor. It would shear through your grandfather's cavalry blade as if it were cheese. So much for your father's concept of indomitability."

She watched his face as if he were asleep. "I wish," she said at last, "that I could understand what it is you love about this country."

"It's the people as much as the country."

"Sometimes I'm convinced that you must be crazy. These are the same people who bombed Pearl Harbor. Who sneaked up on us in the middle of the night."

"That's how they do things here, Lil," he said in such a reasonable tone that she shuddered. "Even war. It doesn't make them evil. Not all of them, at least."

"You see?" she said. "When you talk like that I don't know what you're saying."

"I don't see how I can make it any plainer."

"But I can't fathom anything about the Japanese," she protested. "They think in a wholly different way from me. They give me the creeps."

"I can't teach understanding, Lil," he said. "No one can."

Not true, she thought, pressing her hand against the book. David teaches me understanding. Each day I feel as if I know more. As if I'm blossoming open, like a flower. "I feel as if— as if we're two ships sailing on separate seas," she said. "Sometimes, Phil, you seem very far away from me."

He opened his eyes. "I'm right here." What else could he say? Who could explain the unexplainable? he asked himself.

How to explain what had gripped him at the edge of the ruined Temple of Kannon? How to describe Michiko's rising from the mist of that day? Because that was what Lillian wanted him to do. For better or for worse, he had fallen in love with Japan. Now he felt a stake in seeing that it not only grew again—like the Temple of Kannon, which was being rebuilt from the ashes of its destruction—but that it grew in the right direction. That meant fighting Kozo Shiina and his *Jiban* in any arena they chose.

She tried to smile, but what she said next was so important to her that the expression died midway. "I can't tell you how much I miss the States, Phil. It's like I've died here. Or I'm in limbo waiting for life to begin again."

"Life is all around you, Lil," he said. "If only you weren't so frightened of it."

If only you would take the time to teach me, she thought.

"You see?" she said. "You *are* different. You're content here now."

Perhaps, he thought, she's right. Because it's Japan that has changed me. Now she is aware of my purity of purpose, of my commitment to the future here.

It didn't occur to him until much later that as far as Lillian was concerned, Japan had very little to do with it. That it was Michiko whom she felt, as close beside him as his own shadow.

The phone rang, and Philip reached for it.

"I'm at Silvers's." It was Jonas. "You know where it is?"

"Yeah. Sure." Philip rolled out of bed. Not a "Hello" or a "How are you?" "What's going—"

"Get down here, buddy." Jonas sounded out of breath. "Right fucking now."

There was not exceptional activity on Silvers's block, except that the front of his house was cordoned off. Military police were guarding the area as if the president and the entire cabinet were inside.

Philip flashed his credentials. Even so, a square-jawed sergeant patted him down. "Sorry, sir," he apologized. "Orders."

Philip went up the stone stairs, opened the door.

"That you, Phil?" Jonas's voice. "I'm in the library. It's just to your right."

Philip went in and stopped in his tracks.

"Jesus."

"That's just how he was found."

There was blood all over the place. The rug was soaked in it; rivulets of it glistened along the polished wooden floor. Following them backward, one came to the nexus point.

Colonel Harold Morten Silvers lay twisted on the floor. Or what was left of him, anyway. It looked as if he had been hacked to ribbons.

"Who found him?" Philip asked.

"I did," a voice sounded.

Philip glanced at the other figure in the room. He saw the freshly scrubbed face of General Sam Hadley.

"This how you found him?" Philip asked.

His father-in-law nodded. "Silvers and I had a meeting. The door was unlocked but not open. I came in, called Silvers's name."

Despite the bizarre circumstances, Philip found himself wondering what Hadley and Silvers had to discuss. "No one else was in the house?"

"No one else responded," Hadley said.

"That's not what I asked." Philip had seemed to take over the investigation.

The general shrugged. "I can't really say. I found Silvers just as you see him. I touched nothing. I informed CIG command immediately."

"And they called you, Jonas?"

"David Turner did. He's giving his statement to the military police."

Philip went closer. It was difficult because of all the blood.

"What do you think got him?" Jonas asked.

"You mean the murder weapon?" Philip was bending over the mutilated corpse.

"So far, we've found nothing of a suspicious nature," Jonas said.

Philip stared in disbelief. What flashed through his mind as he stared at the wounds was the *katana* that Michiko had put at his throat the first time he had met Zen Godo. "It appears Silvers was killed with a Japanese longsword," Philip said.

"A Japanese killed Colonel Silvers?" David Turner had entered the room. "Lieutenant Doss." He smiled. "I know that you're somewhat of an expert when it comes to things Japanese. So now we have a place to start."

Philip was going to say that though it appeared as if a *katana* had been the instrument of death, he doubted that a Japanese

215

had wielded it. The deep slashes that ribboned Silvers's corpse, which had brought a froth of blood as a result of the frenzied attack, were crude, administered in haphazard fashion. No one with even the least bit of *kenjutsu* training would have killed in such a sloppy manner. General Hadley did not give him the chance to voice his thoughts.

"This is almost like a retribution," Philip's father-in-law said. He saw the expression on Philip's face, made a placating gesture. "It's all right, son, both Jonas and Turner know about the evidence you handed me against Silvers. I told them about it last night. It was so overwhelming, I thought it best they know about it before I went to MacArthur with it. I think you'll agree they deserved that courtesy, at least. I'd hate to have seen someone from outside give them the news, eh?"

Hadley circled the corpse. "I'll send these military policemen on their way. This is no business of theirs." He looked at each of them in turn. "I believe we're all agreed on that point."

Hadley nodded. "Good. As far as Silvers is concerned, he has found his final reward. The fewer people who are made aware of his perfidy the better. MacArthur agrees. He's given me full reign in this matter. He—and all of us, surely—wants this cleared up quickly and quietly. Therefore, I think it's best if this incident be reported as a suicide. In that way, all evidence can be put to the torch, and nothing more need be said concerning the matter." He looked around the room again. "Agreed?"

Jonas and Turner nodded solemnly. Philip was about to protest. There were a number of points about the murder, small but nagging, that disturbed him. But looking at General Hadley, he knew that this was not the time to bring them up. In one sense, his father-in-law was correct. The CIG was on tenuous ground with President Truman anyway. If any hint of this matter should cross the Oval Office desk, the future of the service most certainly would be in the direst jeopardy.

Reluctantly, Philip nodded his assent. But why, as he did so, did he feel like one of the Roman senators conspiring to assassinate Julius Caesar?

Philip could not wait to sink himself into Michiko's tender flesh. The heat she generated caused him to tremble long before he even touched her. The fact that they were both married seemed not to exist or, perhaps, to belong to another world far outside their own.

Michiko, the fierce, implacable *samurai*, wielding her *katana* with uncompromising skill, was, with him, in their most private moments, the docile and feminine lover. Docile, not in the normal sense. She did not lie still with her legs open wide waiting for him to mount her. But rather docile in the way a Japanese woman learns to be, almost from birth: to be attentive to the desires of her man, and to herself fully enjoy those pleasures.

This was what Philip meant when he said to Lillian that he could not teach her an understanding of the Japanese ethos. It was not something one could be taught. Rather, it had to be absorbed, a slow seeping that comes from stillness, observation, patience and acceptance. None of these concepts was in a Westerner's emotional or intellectual vocabulary.

What quirk of fate—of *karma*—Philip wondered, had allowed him to be born with this affinity? He could not say. The very qualities that had caused him to feel an outcast as he was growing up—to actively seek the outlaw's status as soon as he was old enough—were what bonded him to the inaccessibility of Japan. He was known as "the special American." The kind of recognition that he had been unconsciously seeking all his life. The way out of the inevitability of his father's vision of life.

He said a prayer—to what God? Christ? Jehovah? Buddha?—that he had been allowed to find his way to this exalted state. Buried in the center of the cosmos, hidden for all time from his father and his father's spoken curse. From everyone.

Here, he was beyond the law: He was the creator of the law.

BOOK THREE

HA GAKURE

HIDDEN LEAVES

"*Chinmoku*," Kozo Shiina said. "In architecture, silence and shadow are the same. One stands for the other. Do you see this, Joji?"

"Yes, Shiina-san," Joji said. It pleased him that Kozo Shiina, one of the most powerful men in all Japan, used the form of speech that indicated an equal talking with an equal.

They had come to the Kan'ei-ji Buddhist shrine in Ueno Park, in the northeastern sector of Toyko. The Kan'ei-ji possessed great significance for the Japanese. Following the ancient principles of geomancy—originally, a Chinese art based on the five cardinal elements of the world: earth, air, fire, water and metal—the northeast part of the city was the most vulnerable to invaders from both the corporeal and the spirit worlds.

"Outside these gates," Shiina said, "the hordes race by, intent on their daily chores. Inside the Kan'ei-ji a semblance of the old Japan remains intact, unadulterated. The ancient silence creates its own space in a metropolis with none to spare."

Accordingly, when the Kan'ei-ji was built, it included a powerful *kimon*, a demon's gate, which would protect the city. Gradually more *kimon* were constructed not only in this sector but throughout Tokyo. Until, at length, the city was completely encircled by demon gates. By their shadow silence, they kept the evil spirits at bay while at the same time providing, for the city's inhabitants, spiritual sanctuaries where the elemental concepts of the past could cleanse, renew and, for a time at least, deflect the growing modernization that threatened to rip the heart of Japan from the fabric of its unique past.

"The shadow silence," Shiina said, "is what thrusting rock, rising wood and the gardens of sand artfully create." He stared through the dust motes dancing in the sunlight. Joji had the eerie sense that Shiina could see the true heart of this sacred place. "*Yama no oto*. Here, enwrapped by the silence, I can hear the sound of the mountain."

"I hope it has some words of wisdom for me," Joji said.

"Calm yourself, Joji. Instead of striding nervously about, sit here beside me. Listen to the shadows creep along the walls, engulf the rocks, slide across the raked sand. Allow the silence to penetrate your impatience, to deflate your anxiety."

"Shiina-san," Joji said, "I have come to you because there is no one else I can turn to. I need help. My brother Masashi has wrested the power of the Taki-gumi from me. I am the rightful heir now that my eldest brother, Hiroshi, is dead."

Shiina waited until Joji was seated next to him before he said, "Do you know the true definition of war? No, I think not. It was given not by a *samurai* or a great general, but by a poet and a sculptor named Kotaro Takamura. He said that war was 'a very deep silence attacked.' "

"I don't know what that means."

"It is why I chose to come here instead of to the teahouse."

"I want to understand, Shiina-san."

"Just as architecture can create silence," Shiina said, "so does the human psyche: thought. Without silence, thought is impossible. Without thought, strategy cannot be formulated. Oftentimes, Joji, war and strategy are incompatible. The generals who congratulate themselves on the winning strategy are most likely deluding themselves. Unless one actively seeks out the silence in the midst of war—as I seek out this sanctuary in the midst of the cacophany of this gleaming modern-day metropolis—one has not won. One has merely survived."

Joji was struggling to understand.

"You are in the midst of a war, Joji. Either you will win that war, or you will merely survive. This is the choice that you must make."

"I believe I have already made the choice," Joji said. "I have come to you."

"Now you must explain something to me. I was your father's enemy. How is it that you expect me to aid you?"

"If you back me, if you help me plan my strategy," Joji said, his heart fluttering with anxiety, "you will have one half of the Taki-gumi the day I am declared its *oyabun*."

"One half," Shiina said meditatively.

Joji, wondering if he had made the offer rich enough, said

222

hastily, "That is what you have always wanted, Shiina-san, isn't it? And now, through me, you will have it. Together we can defeat Masashi, and we will both get what we desire most."

Shiina closed his eyes. "Listen to the silence, Joji. You must be able to interpret its many meanings. Then you will be able to learn. If you cannot learn, then you are of no use to me."

"Shiina-san, I am trying."

"So," Shiina said. "An earthworm, ripped from his underground home by an earthquake, tries to find his way in the light. But the light is not his milieu. Unless he can find his way back underground, he will surely perish."

"Is that how you view me, Shiina-san?" Joji said stiffly.

"You," Shiina said, "or your brother Masashi. As I see it, the problem is that your brother has cut himself off from the past. And the past, Joji, is where the threat to Japan began. In the invasion of the Americans.

"It seems to me that Masashi seeks the future somewhat like a bat venturing out of its cave at noon. He is blind to the forces of nature that were set in motion years ago. He believes that history is the cynosure of old men simply because they are old, fossilized, that history is all that they have now to hold on to.

"How smug he is! How secure in his avarice! And because of that, he is being used. By people older, wiser, who possess the strength of history on their side. He wishes to control the currents of industry, bureaucracy and government by his brute strength. But without the knowledge history can provide, he cannot even identify those currents let alone hope to turn them to his advantage."

Joji, watching the inexorable march of the shadows across the temple rooftops, along the sheltered groves of bamboo, the stark rocks, the swirled gardens of sand, felt Shiina's words as if each one was a drop of acid on the center of his forehead. "Explain yourself, if you would, Shiina-san," he said.

Kozo Shiina's eyes were closed against the afternoon sun. "It is simple, Joji. Through my contacts in the government, I have learned that your brother has made a number of alliances among a sector of rather, ah, radical elements within the various ministries."

"Yes, yes," Joji said. "He told me some of this."

"Did he?" Shiina's eyes snapped open, impaling Joji on their unwavering gaze.

"Yes," Joji went on. "Masashi seeks to gain entry into society. He wants to accomplish what our father could not, to become a true member of Japanese society. He craves respect. And because he is haunted by the accomplishments of Wataro, he has become incautious. I believe he will lose the Taki-gumi if he continues on this course."

A line of bald-headed priests walked along a path. A slow, even chanting began to fill the air. Rather than disturbing the slow silence of Kan'ei-ji, it deepened it.

When, at length, the chanting died away, Shiina said, "Tell me, then, why should I do anything to stop him?"

Thinking, Now I have him, Joji said, "Because if you help me, you will own part of the Taki-gumi. Isn't that far better than seeing it destroyed?"

"When you put it that way," Shiina said, "I don't see how I can refuse."

Joji frowned. "Your intervention will mean great changes for the Taki-gumi," he said, as if thinking this through for the first time. Up until now he had always had Michiko to help him reason complex matters through.

"Do not be sorry, Joji," Shiina said benevolently. "Think of the Meiji Jinja. The shrine to the first Meiji Emperor was erected in 1921. It was destroyed during the war of the Pacific and rebuilt in 1958. This is true of a great many of our institutions. They have a history of destruction and regeneration. Yakuza clans as well." He smiled. "And think of the good you can do."

"For the moment, I can think only of how I will be able to deal with Masashi," Joji said.

"Listen to me," Shiina said. "Here, within this temple, we can observe the war like gods. In seeing both sides, we will be able to divine a strategy that will defeat your brother. But I warn you: We have little time. The alliances Masashi has formed grow stronger every day. If we delay too long, even I will be unable to help you."

"I am ready, Shiina-san," Joji said, like a *samurai* preparing for battle.

Shiina breathed a deep sigh of contentment. "I can see that, Joji. And I have no doubt that you will make a worthy champion."

* * *

"Hello, Granny."

Listen, Michiko thought. You must pull yourself together and listen. But her heart was breaking, and all she could think of was her poor Tori held captive like an animal.

"How are you, my darling?"

"I miss you," Tori said. "When can I come home?"

"Soon, little one."

"But I want to come home now."

That plaintive little voice. Michiko could imagine her tear-streaked face. Stop it! she told herself. You are not helping your granddaughter by acting like a weakling. Michiko listened to the background noises, just as she had every time Tori called. Sometimes Michiko heard the voices of men in the background. Sometimes she could even hear snippets of what they said: They were as bored with their vigil as Tori was.

Michiko remembered an episode of a TV show where the hero's girl friend was being held against her will. Every time the kidnappers called to make their demands, the hero heard a peculiar sound. He finally identified it as that of a pile driver and, checking city records of construction sites, was able to find his girl friend. Now Michiko strained to catch any aural nuance that might give her a hint as to where Masashi had hidden Tori.

There were no sounds other than those of conversation, nothing she could identify. She could not even say for certain whether Tori was in Tokyo or somewhere in the surrounding countryside. Michiko bit her lip. It was an impossible task. Only in movies was it possible for good to triumph over evil every time. This was real life. In real life one never knew the final outcome.

"Oh Granny, I want to see you so much. I want to come home."

She had pledged herself to fighting evil, but now, as she heard her granddaughter weeping, Michiko began to think that the price she was paying was far too high. Tori was an innocent. To have her dragged into this battle was unjust and terrifying.

"Listen, little one," Michiko said, making one last attempt. "Tori, do you hear me? Good. Are the men listening to you? No, don't look at them. I want you to tell me what you can see out the window of the room you are in."

"I can't see anything, Granny," Tori said. "There is no window."

"Then you are under—"

"If you try that again, Mrs. Yamamoto," a harsh voice she did not recognize said in her ear, "I will have to hurt your granddaughter."

Michiko lost control. "Who are you?" It was too much: the threats, the thought of the cruel man behind that harsh voice, images of Tori being beaten. "Where are you keeping her? Why don't you let her go?"

"You know why we can't do that, Mrs. Yamamoto. We are ensuring the cooperation of your entire family. Don't make me remind you again."

"Let me speak to my granddaughter. I want to—"

She heard the click of the receiver at the other end of the line. The sound turned Michiko's blood to ice.

"Here there is power," Eliane said. "Here on Maui, here in Iao Valley." In the semidarkness, only her eyes were visible, luminous pinpoints, a panther's eyes in the night. "I believe that there are places of power in the world. Stonehenge is one, the pyramids at Giza and Les-Baux-de-Provence are others. When I was little, I thought there were only one or two power places. But as I grow older, the list gets longer."

"I want to know about the Katei document," Michael said. He had come out of his bedroom, had seen Eliane curled up on the couch, a mug of steaming tea between her hands. "Fat Boy Ichimada said that I should ask you what it is."

It was nearing dawn. Somewhere a bird was calling. The sky behind the volcanic mountains was already pearlescent. They had slept for a few hours. But, exhausted as they had been, the excess adrenaline pumped out by the battle at the compound in Kahakuloa had robbed them of slumber.

Michael's nose was bandaged. The flesh was bruised and swollen, but the cartilage had not been torn.

"But of all the power places I've been," Eliane said, "the energy here is the strongest. The Hawaiians say that it was in this valley that their ancient gods gathered. Here, those gods loved and fought, hurling lightning, thunder and great cascades of rain at their whim."

Michael sat on the couch next to her. He took the mug of tea out of her hands, turned her to him. "Eliane," he said, "who are you? Where did you learn to handle a sword like a *sensei*, a master?"

Her eyes caught the first of the morning's pale light; her cheeks were pink. She disengaged herself, stood up. She went

226

across the room to where a pair of faded jeans was draped over a chair. She began to pull them on.

"Don't you think there was a meaning to why we met?"

She ran her fingers through her hair, turned to look at herself in a mirror hanging on the wall.

"You can't tell me you believe it was coincidence," Michael continued. "I came here to find Fat Boy Ichimada. Your boyfriend worked for him—"

"I know you meant to get into the compound all the time. To find out who killed your father."

"Yes."

"As long as you've decided to begin telling the truth," she said, "I'll admit to you that I wanted to get into the compound too. I don't have a boyfriend." She came back to the couch, sat down.

Michael looked at her. "Who are you, Eliane? Ichimada knew you."

"I am Yakuza," she said. "Or at least I come from a Yakuza family. My mother is Wataro Taki's daughter. Well, step-daughter, really. He adopted her a long time ago, many years before I was born."

Michael watched her with the utmost care. She must know who I am, he thought. She must have known all along. "Did Masashi send you?" he asked.

"I don't work for Masashi," she said. "I despise him. As does my mother."

"But you came here nonetheless. Why?"

"I came to try to find the Katei document. Before Masashi's people do."

"Ichimada said that my father stole the Katei document from Masashi Taki."

"I heard that. Yes."

"What is the Katei document?"

"It is the heart of the *Jiban*, a clique of ministers formed just after World War Two. A clique Wataro Taki was dedicated to destroying. The *Jiban* had a long-range plan for the future of Japan."

"What kind of plan?"

"No one knows," Eliane said, "except the members of the *Jiban*. And now perhaps Masashi. Because he's made some kind of deal with the *Jiban*."

"And what does this *Jiban* want?"

"Independence for Japan. They want freedom from the

oil-producing countries. But most of all, they want freedom from American dominance."

A warning bell went off in Michael's head, but he could not think why. Too much had happened all at once. His head was filled with a thousand unanswered questions. Such as his father's message: *Do you remember the* shintai? And where had he seen the red cord that Ichimada had mentioned?

"Why did you come to Maui?" Eliane asked.

"Because my father apparently made a call to Fat Boy Ichimada the same day he was killed."

"Is that what Ichimada was talking about just before he died?"

"I don't know," Michael said, not altogether truthfully. He was sitting by the side of a half-naked woman to whom, he had to admit now that he was surrounded by silence and peace, he was attracted. But could he trust her? That was another matter entirely.

"Why didn't you tell me you were Yakuza right away?" he asked.

"Maybe for the same reason you didn't confide in me." She was watching the sunlight streak the volcanic mountains of Iao Valley as if they were the canvas of a godlike painter. "I couldn't trust you. Your motives. I still don't."

It was a kind of confession, but it did not make Michael feel any more comfortable. *The cleverest of your enemies,* Tsuyo had cautioned him, *will seek first to become your closest friend. With friendship comes confidence, trust, and a lessening of vigilance. These are the most effective allies of your enemy.*

"How was your father killed?" Eliane asked. "That was a terrible thing."

"I don't know," Michael said. "That's what I've come to Hawaii to find out. I was hoping Fat Boy Ichimada could tell me. Now I'll have to find Ude and ask him."

How can I guard against the clever enemy, sensei? Michael had asked.

In the same way that the badger protects itself, Tsuyo had said. *By testing your environment constantly. Test, too, those who seek to be closest to you. There are no other ways.*

"Did you love him?" Eliane asked. "Your father?"

"Yes," Michael said. Then: "I wish I had taken the time to know him better."

"Why didn't you?"

I was too busy learning my complex lessons in Japan, Mi-

228

chael thought. He shrugged. "He was away a lot of the time when I was growing up."

"But you respected him."

Michael wondered how he should answer that question. It was so complex. Philip Doss was not the vice-president of a successful company to whom his child could point with pride. On the other hand, he was certainly a self-made man. "For most of my life," he said, "I never knew what my father did. So in that respect it's hard to say." The mountains were all lit now, the fire of a new day across the tops of the dense foliage. "Now that I know, I still find it difficult to understand. I admire him. He had great strength of conviction."

"But?" She had heard something in his voice.

"I'm not sure that I approve of what he did."

"What was that?"

"What about *your* father?" Michael asked, changing the subject.

Eliane had taken up the mug again, and she was holding on to it as if it were a life preserver. "I respect him."

"But?" Now it was his turn to hear something.

"But nothing." Eliane was staring straight ahead.

"All right," he said. "If you don't want to talk about it."

But she did. Very badly. The trouble was she had never had anyone to tell it to. Certainly, she could never have unburdened herself to her mother. "My father never paid much attention to me." She stared into the dregs of her tea. "I was always my mother's responsibility. Running the family business was his. He resented it every time she spoke up. He never saw her as having a business head. But, of course, she does. She always did." She put the cup down. "I never spent much time with him until I was much older." It was hard doing this, Eliane realized. Harder than she ever could have imagined. But she needed to do this so badly. It seemed as if she had spent her whole life searching for someone in whom to confide. "But there was someone else. A man who was a friend of my mother's. He came and saw me. I used to think it was because my mother asked him to. I imagined she was trying to make things easier for me. But gradually I came to realize that he loved me, that he came to see me on his own." Eliane had to close her eyes. She felt tears burning behind her lids, and she fought to keep them back. "My mother always wanted me to believe in this man. In *someone*. But especially in him."

"Why?"

Eliane was hunched over, her arms tight against her sides. "Because *she* did. Because it was so very important after my grandfather died to have someone to believe in." In the slow sunlight seeping into the room, he saw that Eliane was weeping silently. "I don't want to talk about it anymore."

"Eliane—"

"No," she whispered. "Leave me alone."

A strange separation had stolen in along with the sunlight and pushed them apart. Oddly, it was as if their reminiscences about their fathers had driven them apart rather than drawing them closer together.

That should not happen with shared truths, Michael thought.

Yvgeny Karsk was smoking a cigarette. While he waited for the phone to ring, he watched his wife. She was packing his bags with the precision with which she did everything.

"I want you to use the *dacha* while I am away," he said, blowing smoke into the bedroom. "It will be good for you to get away from Moscow for a while."

"It's still too cold for the country," his wife said. She was a handsome woman: dark-haired, slender, neat, well dressed. And she had borne him three sons. He had chosen well.

Karsk ground out the butt and immediately lit another cigarette. "So? What do you have your fur for?"

"The sable," she said with efficient practicality, "is for the opera or the ballet."

Karsk grunted. He liked the way she looked on his arm. He especially liked the way the younger officers looked at him jealously. Yes, he decided, he had chosen well. "Do as you wish, then," he said. "You always do in the end. I just thought that with my leaving and the boys away in school, it would do you some good. The winters are always so bleak in Moscow. And so long."

"It is you who longs for Europe, Yvgeny, not I," she pointed out. She brushed down a suit before packing it in his hanging bag. "I am perfectly content here."

"And I am not?" Said a bit angrily? Or a bit defensively?

His wife zipped up the hanging bag, turned to face him. "Do you know something, Yvgeny? You are having an affair and you don't even know it."

"What do you mean?" Now he *was* angry.

"You have a mistress," his wife said, "and her name is Europe." She came and stood in front of him. Then she smiled and kissed him. "You're such a little boy," she said. "I think

230

that's because you're an only child. Psychologists say that only children need more than those who have brothers and sisters."

"That's nonsense."

"Judging from you," she said, "it's quite true." She kissed him again to show him that she meant what she was saying. "Don't be guilty about having your mistress. I'm not jealous."

After she left the bedroom, he stood by the large window, looking out at the Moskva River, which ran through the city. As one of the four chiefs of the KRO, the Counterintelligence Department of the First Chief Directorate of the KGB, Yvgeny Karsk was afforded many privileges. One of which was this rather large apartment in a new high-rise overlooking the Moskva.

The view, though spectacular, with sparkling lights and gilt-covered onion domes, did not please him. There was still ice on the river, though it was well into April. Winter, which gripped the city in a stranglehold, was loath to relinquish control even after its time had passed.

Karsk lit another cigarette even before the last one had burned all the way down. His throat was raw and aching, but he could not seem to make himself stop. His smoking was a kind of penance, he thought. But for what?

For not believing in God. His mother had believed in God, but his training for the KGB had taught him to ridicule God as a concept for the weak of spirit. Religion was the opiate of the masses, an ephemeral concept at best, by which a small group of people—priests—were able to control the many. Organized religion—*any* religion—was potentially dangerous and counterproductive to the scientific dialectics propounded by Marx and Lenin.

It was the same with reforms, he mused. They were all well and good—in their place. No one would dispute the need to make the Soviet economy more efficient. Or the need to abolish the abuse of perquisites within the government. But one had to consider the ramifications of reform very carefully. Once one opened the door to such radical thinking even a crack, as was being done now, was it then possible to keep the door open only that wide? Won't the reforms, by their very nature, tend to swing the door open to its widest?

And then, Karsk wondered, where will we be? In the end, one will be hard pressed to differentiate us from the United States.

Karsk leaned against the window frame, feeling the cold

231

seep into him from the chill Moscow spring, waiting for Europe.

The telephone rang. He could hear his wife in the kitchen, beginning to prepare dinner. He glanced at his watch. The phone continued to ring; she would not pick it up. She was at the other end of the apartment and could not overhear the conversation. He heard the water in the kitchen begin to run. He picked up the phone.

"Moshi moshi?" Hello?

"I called the office," Kozo Shiina said. "Your duty officer had the call transferred."

Sergei is very efficient, Karsk thought. He was never worried about leaving the day-to-day running of the office in Sergei's capable hands.

"What news of Audrey Doss?" Karsk asked.

"Nothing yet," Shiina said.

"I must know of her whereabouts," Karsk said, frowning in annoyance. "It is essential."

"I am doing everything I can," Shiina said. "I will let you know as soon as I hear something. Do you have any information on who killed Philip Doss?"

"No," Karsk said. "I have drawn a total blank."

"Hmm. It bothers me," Shiina said. "Who killed him? I don't like unseen players. All too often they turn out to be enemies."

"Do not be concerned," Karsk said. "Whoever it is cannot stop us now."

"Does that mean we can expect delivery of the item on schedule?" Neither of them would dare use its name, even over a secure line such as this one.

"Yes. Within a day or two," Karsk said. "It is being shipped now. You understand how difficult that is, given the circumstances."

"Completely," Shiina said, relieved that the final piece of his plan was ready. "And I appreciate the care you are taking." They spoke in Japanese. Shiina may have thought that it was out of courtesy to him, but it was because Karsk liked to get every nuance of a conversation. Karsk had made a career of languages, believing that when contacts offered verbal reports in a second—or a third—language, valuable sub-rosa information was invariably lost. Accordingly, Karsk spoke twelve languages, and twice that many dialects, fluently. "Just remember to keep all Russian lettering and numerals off the item," Shiina continued. "I don't want anyone to know the origin of the item." Especially Masashi, he thought, recalling how much Masashi hated the Russians.

"Have no worries about that," Karsk said. "We have no desire to let that particular secret out." He did not want to contemplate the disastrous consequences of such an eventuality. "Now, about the rest?"

"The destruction of the Taki-gumi is at hand," Shiina said, and the pleasure in his voice was unmistakable. How good it is, Karsk thought, to have those who are working for you think as you do. Especially those who did not believe they were working for you at all, because you had deluded them into believing that they were your equal, your partner. Like Kozo Shiina.

"Hiroshi Taki is dead," Shiina was saying now. "Through my instigation, though, as we planned, it was Masashi who gave the order. Now, also as we discussed, I have set the two remaining Taki brothers, Joji and Masashi, against one another."

"Sometimes I wonder," Karsk said, watching the ice floes in the Moskva throw dull light back at the cars passing along the highway, "whether you will take as much pleasure in your country's coming new status in the world as you do in the destruction of Wataro Taki's creation."

"An odd thought," Kozo Shiina said, "since I assumed you would understand that the two are inextricably linked. With Wataro alive, the *Jiban* would never achieve its goal; Japan would never have her proper place in the world. And you would never bring America to its knees."

"Perhaps," Karsk said. "But we would have found another way."

"No, no, Karsk. Remember your history. The only way you Russians ever invade a country is with the Red Army."

"We don't want to invade the United States," Karsk said. "Such an endeavor—even if we were to be successful without devastating the entire earth—would quickly bleed Russia dry. Contrary to what you might think, I have read my history. I know that the decline of the Roman Empire was due to its spreading itself too thin. The Romans were too good at their trade—warfare. They defeated everyone. That was the easy part, as it turned out. What was difficult—impossible, according to history—was to keep all one's possessions under control. Too many people, too many local rebellions. Funding the burgeoning Roman army eventually bankrupted the Empire. We do not intend to make the same mistake."

"Then what is it that you want to do to America?" Shiina asked.

Karsk, watching his smoke dissipate against the window pane, saw that it had begun to snow. His shoulder seemed frozen from its contact with the frame, the Moscow spring. Grinding out his cigarette, he wondered why it was that he smoked only when he was in Russia. "Something that you are providing as your part of our long-standing bargain, Shiina-san," he said. "The destruction of the American economy."

When Ude returned to Hana, he was bleeding. He recalled a vision he had had some time ago. He was the sun, and he was afire. The light he generated was enormous, incalculable. He pulsed with light, with heat, with life. Until he had begun to bleed. What godlike ichor does a star ooze when it is wounded? Plasma? Magma? Never mind. Ude, the sun, was bleeding. And as he bled, he could feel the light, the heat, the life, ebbing from him.

He had begun to scream. Until the woman who had been with him had forced twenty-five cc's of Thorazine down his throat.

Now, in the darkness of Fat Boy Ichimada's shuttered house in Hana, Ude's fingers scrabbled at the wire binding Audrey to the chair. Her chin lolled against her chest, and he slapped her cheek repeatedly. "Help me," he shouted at her. "Help me! I'm bleeding!"

Audrey's eyes opened. She did not know where she was, she did not know who was shouting at her. Starved, dehydrated and terrified, she screamed and passed out.

Ude watched her, panting. He thought of how she had been, sleeping peacefully, when he had broken into the house. She had not been tied up, and there had been food and water at her bedside, which he had consumed as he read the unsigned note lying under the pitcher of water. *Audrey,* it had read, *do not be afraid. I have taken you to Hawaii in order to save you. You are safe from those who wish you harm. Stay here until I return for you. Trust me.*

Ude had destroyed the note. It was he who had bound Audrey to the chair, to keep her from wandering off while he attended to other business.

Now he attended to the drip of his own blood.

Audrey awoke sometime later to the sound of birds. A gekko lay atop one breast, asleep. Seeing it, she screamed. Her hand snapped out, flinging the small lizard from her body.

She sat up. Where am I? she wondered. Her head ached as fiercely as if it had been squeezed in a vise. There was an odd, acrid taste in the back of her throat. Her mouth was dry; she was burning with thirst.

All around her were trees—thick, lush, overgrown. Sunlight and shadow played across her body. She was clothed—blue cotton shorts, a white T-shirt, purple Jellies plastic sandals on her feet. None of them new, none of them hers. Something printed on the shirt. She plucked the material away from her body so that she could read: KONA IRON MAN TRIATHLON, 1985.

Kona? Where was Kona? She racked her brain. Wasn't that in Hawaii? She looked around. Felt the warm breeze on her bare arms and legs. Heard the birds calling, the insects droning. Is that where I am? Hawaii?

And then: What happened?

She put her pounding head in her hands, squeezed her eyes shut against the glare of the sunlight. The brilliance made her headache worse. Oh God. Oh God. Please make the pounding stop.

Now she recalled being at home in Bellehaven, hearing noises in the house, going downstairs. Assuming it was Michael downstairs in their father's study. And instead . . .

Who? Why?

Questions without answers flew around inside her head, like panicked birds. The headache grew sharper. With a groan, she turned over and threw up, mostly dry heaves because there was almost nothing in her stomach.

Dizzy, she lay back down on the grass. Just breathing was a terrible chore. But her body kept on, and eventually she began to feel better.

She put the heels of her hands on the ground and levered herself up. Her legs were weak; she felt like an invalid. On her hands and knees, her head hanging down, she became aware that she must have blacked out again for an instant.

Now she began to feel frightened. What has happened to me? Judging by the angle of light slanting in through the treetops, it was late afternoon. Apparently, she had been unconscious for a long time.

She remembered hearing Michael calling her name. Coming into the study. The flash of his *katana*. The clash of blades colliding. Over and over again . . .

And then?

Michael! Michael!

On the verge of tears, she stopped herself. She could hear her brother's voice admonishing her, *That won't do any good. Pull yourself together, Aydee.*

Drawing strength from his voice inside her head, she tried to do just that.

Which was when she saw Ude. She was aware of the *irezumi*, the tattoos covering his bare torso, first. Then his massiveness. She saw the bandages covering his left shoulder, the dark brown smear of dried blood.

The man was Oriental. Japanese or Chinese—she could not tell; Michael would be so angry with her.

"Who are you?" she asked. It seemed inordinately difficult to speak even those few words.

"Here," Ude said, pouring water into a plastic glass from a Thermos. "Drink this." When she began to gulp the water, and choke, he added, "Slowly."

Audrey felt dizzy; she sat down in the high grass. "Where am I?" she asked. "Am I in Hawaii?" Her head felt as if it were made of lead. She rested it on her crossed forearms, but not for too long, because her swollen wrists also throbbed terribly.

"It doesn't matter where you are," Ude said. "Because you're not going to be here very long."

Audrey continued to drink slowly, even though her body was aching for its thirst to be slaked. Ude refilled her glass several times. She looked into the sunlight. "What's happening to me?"

"All right," Ude said. "That's enough." He took the glass out of her hand, pulled her to her feet. She almost collapsed into his arms, and he was obliged to half carry her back down a rock-strewn path. She got a glimpse of a house—the house in which she had been tied up?—and then she was bundled into a car.

The next few hours were a blur of inconstant images. Although she tried her best to remain alert, she repeatedly slipped into unconsciousness, only to start awake painfully, as if even a peaceful sleep was to be denied her.

She was aware that the going was slow, because the terrain turned out to be quite mountainous. Without having a direct view of it, she was nevertheless aware of the steepness of the ground. At times, the car was obliged to pull over and wait. She heard engines, as of other cars passing in the opposite direction.

At length, the incline became less extreme, and finally it

leveled out. Now the way was easier, and at last, exhausted beyond her endurance, she passed into a deep slumber.

Nobuo Yamamoto's palms were wet with sweat. For perhaps the tenth time in as many minutes, he wiped them on a linen handkerchief already gray with the grime of the city.

This was an unaccustomed symptom for a man of his rank and personality. In his chauffeur-driven car, he sat forward, his body tense, his nerves taut.

It had been many months since Nobuo had slept well at night. When he did sleep, he dreamed. And his dreams were full of death. The terrible, flesh-searing death both quick and agonizingly slow that was the result of the flash. The flash is what Nobuo chose to call it. Not detonation. The flash was a term he could live with—just about.

Because he was Japanese, Nobuo knew the horrendous danger better than most. There was a history here. In Hiroshima and Nagasaki. And the Japanese possessed a special abhorrence for anything nuclear, especially a weapon.

My God, he thought, how did I ever become involved in this? But of course he knew. It was because of Michiko. She bound him to the Takis body and soul. That was how his father and Wataro Taki—Nobuo had long since forgotten Wataro's original name, Zen Godo—had envisioned it when the two men had worked out this alliance. Two family businesses, wedded for all time, strengthening one another.

But now Wataro Taki was gone, and so was Hiroshi. Masashi had gotten everything he ever wanted. Masashi became *oyabun* of the Taki-gumi, and Masashi was a madman. A madman to whom Nobuo was now bound in a unique way. I am building him what he wants, Nobuo thought, nauseated by the prospect of completion, but I am dragging my heels every step of the way. Still, the end is near; I have reached the limit of procrastination. I must complete the project. With my granddaughter's life in jeopardy, what else can I do?

Still, the nightmares persisted. Still, the walking dead, rotting flesh stinking, haunted his nights, turning them into an abattoir of guilt.

Nighttime Tokyo was emblazoned across the horizon limited by the width and height of his window onto it. The great neon signs and advertisement billboards coruscated off every shiny surface, every blackened window, every curved form, of which there were so many even within his limited range that they were impossible to count. Staring out at Tokyo was like gazing up at the star-filled sky. Standing, perhaps, as a symbol of Japan's apparent contradictions, the commingling sense of endless clutter and of enormous space was as dizzying as it was edifying. For it was an affirmation of the essence of the culture's ability to transform very little into magnificent excess.

"He's here, sir," Nobuo's driver said.

Always late, Nobuo said to himself. An unsubtle reminder of the nature of our relationship.

He watched Masashi emerge from the car, sweep into the theater's entrance. Time to go, Nobuo thought. Wiped his palms one last time, stuffed the limp handkerchief away.

Inside, the theater was stark, severe, minimal. There was an area for the audience, a stage, and that was all. Except, of course, for the monitors. Banks of TV screens—now dark—studded both side walls. There must have been more than a hundred fifty in all, blank windows to nowhere. They increased the bleakness of the setting exponentially. One had the feeling of entering a section of space where even the stars had died. Whatever reflections were hinted at here and there in the screens were from the audience itself, settling in.

Masashi, as was his custom, waited in the doorway until just before the performance was scheduled to begin. By this time, all the seats were filled save one. But more important, he had had a chance to scrutinize each entrant.

He took his seat. On his left was a young Japanese woman in oversize clothes, layered in so many shades of gray that the distinction between hues blurred. Her cheeks were blushed with blue and purple. Her lipstick glittered. Her hair, short everywhere but in front, seemed as stiff as if she had brushed glue through it. On his right sat Nobuo.

Without fanfare, or even warning, the performance began. The banks of monitors sprang to life all at once. A forest of phosphors darting and pulsing in electronic imagery.

At that moment, the dancers entered the stage. They were naked or seminaked, many of them smeared with white body paint. This was *buto*, a kind of primal modern dance form, created out of the urbanized, Westernized angst of the post-nuclear Japan of the late fifties. It was both politically subversive and culturally reactionary, relying as it did on mythological archetypes. *Buto* was rigid and fluid at the same time, employing patterns that revealed it as both a physical and a mental experience.

Stage center, the sun goddess, from whom the Emperor

238

was descended. Anguished by what she sees about her, she retreats into a cave and the world is plunged into darkness.

Only the hedonistic sounds of carousers, only the sight of wild, erotic dances being performed as primitive rites can induce her to emerge, bringing with her the eternal harbingers of spring, light and warmth.

As the dancers reenacted, in stylized fashion, this ancient agricultural myth, the video monitors projected what could only have been a dress rehearsal of the dance. It began just after the live one, so that the rather startling effect was of a visual echo.

At intermission, Masashi rose and, without saying a word to anyone, went into the outer lobby. In a moment, he could make out Nobuo coming toward him.

"Can you make head or tail of this filth?" Masashi said when Nobuo had reached his side.

"I wasn't paying attention," Nobuo said. "Were the dancers any good?"

"You mean those contortionists?" Masashi said. "They belong in the circus. If this is art, then creative talent is dead, and here is the murder weapon. There is no grace, no silence, no *yugen*." This last, a concept from the time of the Tokugawa shogunate of the early 1800s, meant a kind of beauty so restrained in its outward manifestation that it allowed the inner side to show through.

Nobuo knew enough not to fall into the trap of debating with Masashi; it was a pastime Masashi enjoyed because Nobuo could not win.

"The parts' shipments are not arriving fast enough."

"This is the best I can do," Nobuo said. "There is the manufacturing process to think of. We're not making cars, you know. Everything must be manufactured to the most demanding tolerances."

"Keep the advertising pitch for someone who will appreciate it," Masashi said contemptuously.

"It's the truth," Nobuo said stiffly. "Do you know how much energy is released by a nuclear explosion?"

"I don't care what the difficulties are," Masashi said. "I have a schedule to keep. We must be finished in two days."

"Damn your schedule," Nobuo said angrily. "I care only for my granddaughter."

"If you do," Masashi said, "then you will be ready when we meet at your factory in two days' time. It is imperative. The fate of Japan hinges on your technical expertise, Nobuo-san. The fate of the whole world, if truth be known. What does the life of one little girl mean in the face of that?" Nobuo blanched, and Masashi laughed. "Calm yourself, Nobuo-san. I am not planning to harm Tori. I gave you my word."

"And what is that worth?"

Masashi's eyes glittered. "You had better hope that it's worth a great deal."

"I am in no position to offer an opinion," Nobuo said curtly. "Consult the spirit of your dead father. Surely he knows."

"My father's death was *karma, neh*?"

"And *karma*, I suppose, killed Hiroshi." Nobuo shook his head. "No. You killed your eldest brother, despite all your protestations to the contrary. And now that you are *oyabun*, I am allied with you. But it wasn't Hiroshi's murder that created our alliance. You know what it is. You have taken my granddaughter. I will hate you to the day I die for what you have done."

"I?" Masashi asked innocently. "But what have I done except put together an extremely efficient machine? More efficient than even my father could have imagined. Why look so glum, Nobuo? You are part of history. With what you are helping me to build, we will soon rule the new Japan."

Or, Nobuo thought, we will be wiped from the face of the earth, along with every man, woman and child in Japan.

Birds sang in a glade rippling with light. Golden beams, thick as slabs, slanting through the gaps in the trees. The murmur of a brook as it meandered its way down a gentle slope, insects thrumming.

And Eliane walking toward him, looking only at him. She smiled. Coming toward him, slowly, deliberately, confidently.

A crack as of a rifle shot, and Michael screaming her name as she disappeared from view along with the collapsing mountain ledge. Hurled into the valley's shadowed abyss.

The echo of the ledge shattering, rumbling on and on.

Michael awoke knowing that the name he had screamed was not Eliane's but Seyoko's.

A profound depression swept over him. In the darkness, he heard a railing. His own breath. For a moment he could not remember where he was. Eliane's house. He must have slept all day.

He rose and padded into the bathroom. Turned on the tap and stepped into a cold shower. Three minutes later, he emerged and toweled off. He did not turn on a light, but with the towel wrapped around his waist, he went out onto the lanai that ran the length of the house.

Michael heard the wind moving through the palm fronds. Small lights illuminated the garden path so close he could reach out and brush the foliage. Beyond, in their eternal vigil, the mountains rose. The night smelled of plumeria and pineapple.

It's tomorrow already, he thought. Where did Ude escape to? He did not know, but he knew where he must look: Tokyo. Tokyo was where he would find Audrey, where he would find out who killed his father and why.

The *Shuji Shuriken*.

He squatted down and began his slow breathing. His voice whispered the chant: *"U."* Being. *"Mu."* Nonbeing. *"Suigetsu."* Moonlight on the water. *"Jo."* Inner sincerity. *"Shin."* Master of the mind. *"Sen."* Thought precedes action. *"Shinmyoken."* Where the tip of the sword settles. *"Kara."* The void. *"Zero."* Where the Way has no power.

Suigetsu. Moonlight on the water was a phrase that meant deception. *Everything you absorb here*, Tsuyo had said, *is based on deception. In Shintoism, the deception that becomes truth is called* shimpo, *mystery. It is said this* shimpo *causes people to have faith, simply because it is hidden. In the Way of the warrior*, shimpo *is known as strategy. As an example, let us say you pretend that your right hand is hurt, and by that method you draw your opponent out, you change his own strategy, and by so doing, you defeat him. Can you not say that your deception has become truth?*

When you can alter the way your opponent perceives his environment, you have mastered the art of strategy.

Was Eliane practicing *shimpo*? Was she deliberately cloaking herself in mystery, or was she really the pure elemental she presented herself as being? Michael remembered his graduation from Tsuyo's school again. How easy it had seemed then to divine his *sensei's* motives. And his father had told him, later, *First you must recognize evil. Then you must combat it. Finally, you must guard against becoming evil yourself. Knowing these things for certain gets harder the older you grow.*

The house slept on, devoid of answers.

The Way is truth, Michael thought. It is *tendo*.

He abruptly rose, went inside. In the kitchen, he went to the phone, dialed the airport at Kahului. He made his interisland reservation, then called the number for Honolulu International Airport. Then he dialed Jonas's private line.

Jonas picked up after the first ring.

"Uncle Sammy?"

"Michael. How are you?"

Michael had called Jonas the moment he and Eliane had gotten back to her house from Fat Boy Ichimada's. Yesterday? Michael had told Jonas everything that had transpired since he had landed on Maui.

"Is there any news of Audrey?" he had asked.

"Nothing yet. But don't give up hope. We're doing everything we can." And to take Michael's mind off the subject of his sister, Jonas said, "I've seen to the Feds on Maui. You won't be involved in any investigation into the massacre at Ichimada's."

"I think your hunch about our own investigation leading back to Japan was right," Michael said. "I'm taking the first flight out to Tokyo later this morning."

"Do what you have to do, son," Jonas said. "I have a crisis here that looks as if it will be impossible to handle. After spending over a year negotiating a mutual import-export agreement with the United States, Japan has shifted its attitude. The Japanese prime minister informed the president yesterday that all existing individual trade agreements between us and Japan have been declared null and void. No explanation was given for this action. And there seems no hope of a resumption of talks.

"I've been up all night at Capitol Hill. The Congress has retaliated by passing an export-tariff act similar to the Smoot-Hawley bill of decades ago. I tell you, son, ten years ago America might have been able to withstand such a blow. But not today. No one here seems to give a damn about the severe economic depression that will result from this protectionist trade bill."

"It sounds as if you have your hands full," Michael said.

"As if that weren't enough," Jonas said, "there's a possibility that BITE will be out of business permanently." He told Michael about the report that Lillian had shown him and what it meant.

"Uncle Sammy," Michael said, hearing something in the other man's voice, "are you all right?"

"To tell you the truth, son," Jonas said, "for the first time, I'm beginning to think that we're not going to win this one."

When Michael hung up the phone, he was more disturbed

242

than ever. He returned to the lanai. Being here in Iao Valley was like standing in the keep of the most formidable of castles.

He heard a noise and turned. Eliane had come out of the glass doors that led to her bedroom. She looked at him in the moonlight. She was dressed in jeans and a man-tailored long-sleeved shirt.

"I heard you out here," she said.

"I didn't mean to wake you."

"I was already up." She turned her head to look out across the valley. "The nights are so beautiful here," she said, moving along the lanai. "Even more so than the days, if that's possible."

"With that full moon," Michael said, "you can see every inch of the valley."

"Not all of it," Eliane said. "There are places in there that haven't been explored in centuries."

"Because they're so overgrown?"

"No," she said. "Because no one will enter them. They are sacred places, points in time as well as space. The old gods still inhabit those places. Or so the Hawaiians believe."

He saw that she was quite serious. He was not much of a skeptic. Tsuyo had said, *Physicists tell us that gravity—or the lack of it—rules the universe. But faith rules the mind. In any event, there are certainly places where faith, not physical principles, is the ruler. These are places which you will find, in time, either with my help or on your own.*

"Will you show me one of these places," he said now, "where the gods of Hawaii still live?"

He watched her face, knowing that she was working out whether or not he was making fun of her.

"All right," she said after a time. "But the place is high up. It's a long climb."

Michael hesitated, remembering his dream, the accident in Yoshino at Tsuyo's school. He remembered Eliane disappearing into the abyss, and calling out Seyoko's name. It all gave this an eerie ring.

"I don't mind," he said, not altogether truthfully. But he recognized in the fluttering of her movements an element of his own restlessness. It would be hours before he could board his flight to Honolulu.

Were they fated to go on this hike? he wondered. Was he fated to see her die in the same way Seyoko died? What an idiotic idea, he told himself.

She followed him inside, watched as he pulled on jeans

243

and a sweatshirt. Starlight seeped into the room like a billion unfulfilled wishes. Eliane moved about the room as if uncomfortable within its confining space.

"Here," she said, handing him a pair of powerful field glasses. "The views from where we're going are spectacular, even at night."

She led him out of the house, down a winding path that quickly petered out into grass between rocks and foliage. The cicadas were calling. There was a symphony of infinitesimal sounds.

They went across the valley. Eliane had taken a flashlight, but between the moon- and starlight, it wasn't needed. Then they began to ascend into the mountains that had reared up from the ocean's floor in one lunatic spasm centuries before.

Fifteen hundred feet up, they took a rest. Michael got out the field glasses, had a look around. In the starlight, the world was stark, flat, hard as granite, but no less beautiful for that. In fact there was an added sense of wonder, a slow accretion of knowledge of the distance in time between man's lifespan and that of the earth. Now, without color, depth or the distraction of any fauna, Michael thought, there was no escape from coming face to face with the humbling grandeur of the world.

"What do you see?" Eliane asked him.

"Myself," he said.

"If only mirrors could tell us what we need to know about ourselves," she said.

She stared at him for a long time with a peculiar intensity. It was as if, he thought, she were trying to drink in the essence of him. As if she were trying to inhale his spirit.

At last, she said, "When I was little, there was a prayer I said before I went to sleep each night. It was taught to me when I was a small child, by a friend of my mother's. He told me to say it only when I was alone and to tell no one that I knew it. Not even my mother. It went, 'Yes is a wish. No is a dream. Having no other means of crossing this life, I must use yes and no. Allow me to keep hidden the wish and the dream so that someday I may be strong enough to do without them both.' "

The moonlight draped her in silver. The cool blue light cascaded over the strong features of her face. It simultaneously drained her of her natural color and infused her with an energy possible only from the concentration of monochromatic illumination.

"Michael," she said, "I've done terrible things in my life."

"We've all done things we aren't proud of, Eliane." He put aside the binoculars.

"Not like these."

He came close to her. "Then why did you do them?"

"Because," she said, "I was afraid not to. I was afraid that if I did nothing, the anarchy—remember that blank canvas?—would overwhelm me. I was afraid that I would be nothing."

"You're intelligent," he said. "You're clever, adept and powerful." He smiled. "You're also beautiful."

Her face was impassive. He had wanted to make her smile. "In a word," she said, "I'm perfect."

"I didn't say that."

"Oh, but you did. And you're hardly alone. I've been told I was perfect ever since I can remember. It was required that I be perfect. I had no choice. I could no more throw off the responsibility engendered by perfection than I could renounce being a female. That terrible responsibility robbed me of my childhood. I have been an adult all my life, Michael, because if I wasn't, I knew that my whole life would fall apart."

He watched her, a mixture of sadness and anger welling up in him: the one emotion for her, the other at those who forced the lie on her. "You really believed that?"

She nodded. "I still do. Because, in the end, that rigid responsibility came to be the one and only thing that defined my existence. What was I if I was not this? Nothing. Anarchy, again. An anarchy that I could not face."

He shook his head. "But you *are* something." He held out his hand. "Come on. Let's go."

It seemed a long time before her fingers touched his.

"That stupid Ichimada," Ude said, finishing his report. He was in a phone booth outside of Wailuku. His skin was covered in volcanic dust. "He had big plans. They did not include you." Every few seconds he glanced over to the car, where Audrey was bound and gagged, lying on the floor in the back. "He had hired a pair of locals who were looking for the Katei document. I found them. They didn't have it. They didn't know who did. But I got something out of them that Philip Doss meant to leave for his son. A piece of dark-red braided cord. Does it mean anything to you?"

Masashi thought a moment. "No," he said.

"Greed turns into stupidity like food turns into shit," Ude said. "Ichimada's stupidity caused him to become vulnerable.

245

Not only to me—that would have been a bad enough loss of face. But to an *iteki*!" He meant a barbarian—a Westerner: Michael Doss. "This *iteki* infiltrated Ichimada's vaunted compound."

"Did it ever occur to you," Masashi said, "that Fat Boy Ichimada wanted to meet Michael Doss? How do you think he knew where to send the Hawaiians to look for the braided cord? Philip Doss must have telephoned him."

"I hadn't thought of that," Ude said.

"Do you know where Michael Doss is now?"

"Yes. He's with Eliane Yamamoto."

"Is he?" Masashi said neutrally. Ude wondered why Masashi didn't seem interested in that incredible bit of news. "I want you to send his sister, Audrey, here to me in Japan."

"That won't be easy," Ude said. "With Michael Doss around and the Feds up in arms over the Ichimada thing, I'm working under a handicap."

"Don't worry. I'll send my private jet. Everything will be prepared for you at the airport. She'll go out in a crate of machine parts. You know the drill, you've done it a dozen times before. But it will be about eight hours before I can get the plane to Maui."

"I'll need the time to prepare."

"Right. I'll make some calls, set you up with some of my people locally. Is there a place where they can reach you?"

Ude gave Masashi the name of the bar he had been in when he was following the Hawaiians. "It's in Wailuku," he said. "They'll know it. It's too early for it to be open, so tell them I'll be in the car across the street." Ude thought a minute. "Tell them I'll also need some hardware."

"They can get whatever you need," Masashi assured him. "Did you find out who killed Philip Doss?"

"It wasn't Ichimada."

"That isn't what I asked," Masashi said.

"I don't have an answer," Ude said. "What do you want me to do with Michael Doss?"

"Michael Doss is only relevant as he pertains to the Katei document," Masashi said. "I want him to get the red cord. To show us its importance. It seems clear that Michael Doss is our only lead to the Katei document."

"I think this is a waste of time," Ude said. "I think the Katei document burned with Philip Doss in the car crash."

"I don't pay you to think," Masashi snapped. "Just do as you're told."

"The Katei document has become everything, hasn't it?" Ude said. "I can hear the urgency in your voice. But it is not your urgency, it is Kozo Shiina's urgency. The Katei document is the *Jiban*'s sacred object, not yours. It seems to me that Kozo Shiina is already the new *oyabun* of the Taki-gumi."

"Silence!" Masashi cried. "You have been eating your mushrooms again. You think that you're eighteen feet tall."

"No," Ude said a bit sadly, for he now saw that he had only one course to take. "But I am seeing more clearly than either you or Kozo Shiina. I can forget the Katei document, I can understand that it is gone forever. I can see that the real threat to you and the Taki-gumi is Michael Doss. He is following in his father's footsteps. Philip Doss succeeded in keeping you out of power while your father was still alive. He would have destroyed you had he lived long enough."

"Or I him."

"Don't you think Michael Doss will try to finish off what his father began?"

"The Tao," Masashi said, "tells us that the wise man places himself behind all others and, in so doing, discovers that he is in the preeminent position."

"What does the Tao have to do with me?" Ude said with undisguised scorn. "The Tao is for old men, blind and deaf to the life around them."

"The Tao is universal law," Masashi reminded him.

"The Tao is dead."

No, Masashi thought. It is your mind that is dead. "You are still a member of my clan," he said angrily. "You will obey your *oyabun*."

The question is, Ude thought as he replaced the receiver, who is my *oyabun*?

Now the way became truly steep. Michael, aware of the vast space at his back, moved with great care. They were surrounded by trees so thick in spots that he could not see more than a foot in any direction. Still, Eliane moved quickly and surely. She had been quite correct: It was a long climb, and Michael began to regret that they had come. His restlessness had evaporated; he was tired and his muscles ached.

At length, Eliane stopped. She turned to him and pointed. Up ahead, he saw a narrow defile, as if a great knife had slashed into the rock face of the mountain. The pass was guarded by a pair of gigantic boulders. They were of the same coruscated igneous rock that had pushed up from the ocean's floor so many centuries ago: twisted and ridged forever by the cataclysm of its birth.

Michael started as the shapes of the boulders registered: Were these really a pair of crouching warriors, as they appeared? He went closer to see if the rock had been carved, but he saw that it had not. The stones' natural formation—abetted by erosion by the elements—had caused them to resemble human figures.

"The passage of the gods," Eliane whispered. But when he moved to enter the defile, she held him back. "Wait," she said, and went through the surrounding trees some distance. When she returned, she was carrying what appeared to be garlands. She draped one about his neck, put the other around hers. "Ti leaves," she said. "The plant is sacred to the Hawaiians because it was much loved by the ancient gods. This is what the *kahunas* wear when they come here. The ti leaves will protect us."

"From what?" Michael asked.

But Eliane was already moving past the strange rock guardians. Into the passage of the gods.

"I believe the most important element in the conversation," Ude said into the phone, "is what was most hidden. What is Eliane Yamamoto doing on Maui, and with Michael Doss?"

Kozo Shiina was silent, thinking. The fact was, Eliane was Michiko's daughter, and he could not imagine what Michiko's daughter was doing at Michael Doss's side. Shiina did not like the idea that something was happening on Maui without his knowledge. "What is your assessment of the situation?" he asked now.

"I don't trust Masashi," Ude said immediately. And Shiina did not know whether to trust the response, wondering how much of it was fueled by emotion rather than reasoning. Shiina did not trust emotion. It colored everything around it, like a filter over a camera lens. "When I told Masashi of Eliane's presence, his response was odd," Ude went on. "It was very offhand, as if he could not wait to get off the subject. As if he already knew she was here."

Masashi, Kozo Shiina thought now, what are you up to?

"Did you find out who killed Philip Doss?" Shiina asked.
"Not yet."

"Keep at it," Shiina said. "As for Michael Doss, do as Masashi tells you. Let Michael Doss have the red cord. I

248

think Masashi is right—the *iteki* will lead us to the Katei document."

So, Ude thought, Shiina does not perceive the threat that Michael Doss presents, either. But then, he reminded himself, neither Shiina nor Masashi has seen Michael Doss in action. To them he is still only the *iteki*, the foreigner.

But Ude knew what to do in this case. Michael Doss was far too dangerous to keep safely on a leash. He was smart and unpredictable. He knew the meaning of *shimpo*, the strategy of deception.

Ude came to a decision. He would obey neither Kozo Shiina nor Masashi. Out here in the field, one had to make one's own decisions. They were life-and-death decisions, and Ude had made his regarding Michael Doss.

He would have to kill him.

They emerged from absolute darkness into the flash of starlight. Everything was stark, two-dimensional, knife-edged, with a supraclarity that was breathtaking.

A night bird clattered in a tree overhead, sweeping away from their presence on powerful wings. Michael caught a glimpse of a horned head, incandescent eyes: an owl?

"Be careful," Eliane said, "not to wander off." She pointed to a bald spot on the cliff face, etched and rutted so that a series of grooves were cut into the rock. "In wet weather, that's a waterfall. In dry times, as now, the spot becomes treacherous because the rock is so smooth."

Michael crouched down, ran his hand over the bare rock. "What happened here?" he asked.

"It depends on what you want to believe," Eliane said. "The Hawaiians say that there was a great battle fought here. At the end of it, the victors threw their enemies over this cliff."

Michael strained his neck, looking as far down as he could. Then he moved back from the dry bed of the waterfall.

"In that time," Eliane said, "the Hawaiians say that the waterfall began, red with the blood of the warriors."

"Is that what you believe?" Michael asked.

"I don't know. This isn't my country. But I feel the power here. Everyone does. It's undeniable."

Starlight threw shadows across her face. They curved like fingers, extending across her cheek and down her neck. That same cool light sparked her black eyes, making them appear

249

startlingly large. The wind caught at her long hair, making of it a raven's wing, never still.

Michael, watching her, seemed not to have really seen her at all until this moment. It was as if he had come upon an image of her, or a painting, and now this night filled with stars, this place of power, was revealing the true Eliane to him.

He touched her and felt her heart beating. It was as if her pulse were his pulse, as if a cascade were linking them, as if they were melting into one another. Michael felt his heart open, felt the shell of bitterness that had surrounded him slough away like a reptile's dead skin.

"Eliane," he said, but she broke their connection, taking her hand from his, moving away from him.

"No," she whispered. "You don't want me. Not really." The shadows of an overhanging rock enveloped her in a darkness so complete it created utter stillness.

"How can you say what I want?"

He sensed rather than saw her ironic smile. "Believe me when I tell you, Michael. You don't want me—or wouldn't very soon afterward. No one would."

"Why not? What is so terrible about you?"

She stirred. "I am ugly."

"No. You're beautiful."

The stillness within which she stood seemed overpowering.

"I remember the day," she said, "when I became aware that my mother and father never spoke kindly to one another. And I remember the night when I discovered that they never made love. It wasn't long after that that I understood that they did not love each other. I wondered if they could love me."

She sighed. "I decided that they could not; that neither of them was capable of feeling love. I realized then that it was all up to me. That whatever my family was going to be would be a function of only me. Remember what I told you before about responsibility? I did whatever I had to do to keep my family together. There was so little regard for one another between my parents, I remember being constantly terrified that one of them would leave, that the family would break up. What would happen to me then? I could not imagine. When I did imagine such a thing, in my nightmares, it was with the most profound feeling of dread.

"So I grew up living my life to control the family, to keep it together. I became a control freak. I had no other choice.

250

I was bulemic for years. Do you know what bulemia is? I was anorectic. It was a kind of madness. But it was a madness I needed in order to stay alive. The ultimate control was mine—and as long as it was, I knew that everything would be all right. My father wouldn't leave us, my mother wouldn't take me away. Everything would be fine." She gave an ironic laugh that chilled Michael. "Was everything fine? Yes and no. I survived; the family remained intact. But I was quite mad."

"And now?" Michael finally found his voice. "Isn't that all over with?"

"Yes," she said. "It's all over with. I'm not mad anymore."

"Nothing you've said has made me change my mind about you," he said.

"I am dead inside."

"I don't understand."

"The things I have done—don't come any closer, Michael—what I have done has created a plague inside me. Whatever was there—is no longer. I am empty, hollow. I look inside myself and see only a gaping hole."

"Whatever you did, you did in order to protect yourself. No one can blame you for that."

"I have killed people!"

Her shout echoed off the rock faces.

"My father killed people," he said. "I've seen what you are capable of when you have to defend yourself."

"I have been sent to kill people. People I never knew, who never hurt me."

"If you feel guilt, if you feel remorse for what you've done, you cannot be dead inside."

"I am a leper," she continued in a more normal tone of voice. Even so, Michael could hear the shiver in her words. "I have become something other than human. A mechanical thing. A terrible sword. A cipher."

"But still you wish," he said softly. "You must dream."

"I am too strong now to do either," she said with infinite sadness in her voice. "Or too hard. I have forgotten how, although sometimes I think that I never knew."

"Eliane." Michael could not see into the dense blackness beneath the overhang, but he knew that he wanted to be there. He moved into the shadows.

"Michael, please don't."

"Stop me, if you want."

He was only a hand's breadth away from her.

"Oh please. I beg of you." She was weeping.

251

"Tell me to stop." Very close to her. He could feel her heat, as well as her trembling. "You have only to push me away."

Instead, her lips opened beneath his. Her tongue twined with his. He felt her moan into his mouth.

"Michael." Her body clung to his as if they were fastened from shoulder to foot. He felt her weight, the sinuous twining, the power of her muscles. He felt more; he felt the force of her *hara*, that inner energy which resides in the lower belly, that defines the spirit. "I'm burning for you."

Eliane's *hara* reached out and encompassed him. And it was as she had said: tough as leather, hard as stone, sere as a desert. But he was also aware of that which she was not: that bright core, encysted beneath the crust she had created, a molten river flowing with need.

She was outside what she was inside. Her mouth possessed him aggressively, her arms held him fast. Then her legs opened and she was drawing them up the outside of his thighs. Her motions were unmistakable; what her body was demanding of him was aggression and more aggression.

But desire and need were at opposite poles. That the human psyche often confused the two led to more misunderstandings between the sexes than anything else.

Michael felt—no, *knew*—that what she desired was not what she needed. Eliane did not herself understand what it was she needed, because there are times when the need is too great to bear and is therefore tucked away in some dark corner of the spirit.

Michael knew that if he responded as she was urging him to—as he himself desired—he would lose her forever.

Gently, he thought. Gently. And unwrapping her arms from around him, he slipped to his knees.

He was acutely aware of the night around him. He felt its breath, heard the nocturnal birds in the trees tending to their sleeping chicks, the hidden predators feasting on their prey. He felt the rustle of the wind against his cheeks, aware of Eliane's long, unbound hair floating across his shoulder.

Then, with her jeans around her hips, he smelled the fragrance of her flesh and plunged his face between her thighs.

Gently, he thought. Gently. Even though the desire she had aroused in him was dangerously high. Even though he longed to possess her in just the manner she craved.

His hands stroked her gently, his tongue laved her gently.

Because in the end, he longed to possess her in every conceivable manner. He wanted *her*.

Having been bathed in starlight, they had returned to absolute darkness. Michael pressed inward toward the core of Eliane's being, while she was bent over him, her hard breasts crushed against the bunched muscles of his shoulders. By the scoring of her nails over the skin of his back she told him how much she loved his ministrations. By the trembling of her thighs she expressed her delight.

She gasped as he licked up and down the length of her. It seemed to her that she was filled with an indescribable heat, as if she were immersed in warm oil. She experienced a tingling all the way to her fingertips. Her hips ground up against his face so that the stubble of his beard scraped the tender flesh on the insides of her thighs. She shivered and bucked upward again and again while the heat opened up inside her, and she lost all coherent thought.

She opened her eyes, felt the scent of his breath on her face, saw his eyes, shining above her.

She imagined the two of them to be a pair of mating wolves, coming upon one another in the wilderness, he in heat, she giving off thick musk.

She was beside herself with passion, reaching down to encompass him, finding that was not enough, and sliding down his naked body, taking him into her mouth, moaning at his taste, feeling herself becoming excited again, touching herself between her thighs in wonder and delight, discovering that she was on the verge of another orgasm.

She felt him expanding inside her mouth and slid upward, placing the tip of him at her entrance. For one long, exquisite moment she did not move. With her hand she held him. They were touching there, but nothing more. For that moment it was enough—more than enough: It was perfect, exciting because of the feeling, exhilarating because of the anticipation of what was to come.

Then she could no longer contain herself and she thrust herself fully onto him, groaning, losing her breath, her forehead lolling against his sweat-slickened chest with the sensation.

Michael, joined with her, felt her pulsing all around him. He did not have to move at all, her fluttering was so pronounced. Her scent surrounded them like a cloud, combined with the peculiar smell of the ti leaves around their necks, and he felt suspended in time as well as in space.

He felt her moving along the full length of his body, as if they were joined in every place instead of just in one. He felt himself coming, tried to hold back, to prolong the moment, but their desire, now a living thing, could no longer be held in abeyance.

He groaned, thrusting, and heard movement into the space outside their shelter of darkness. There was a kind of light and a dim primitive sound, as of drums or chanting or both. He turned his head to see, but Eliane rose up, pressing her breasts against his lips, and he was filled up with her again as the end came, as drawn-out and ecstatic as the prologue had been.

Joji Taki walked into Shozo's room.

Shozo looked up from a twenty-six-inch TV screen dominated by Marlon Brando's prosthetically altered face as the Godfather. The jowls, grayed with makeup, puffed out, making the actor look twenty years older. "Where would Michael Corleone be without the spirit of his father to watch over him?" Shozo said.

He watched as Don Corleone, playing with his grandson in his sun-dappled garden, put a section of orange rind in his mouth. Lumbering after the child, who screamed in mock terror and delight, he made little grunting noises.

"This is where it happens, *oyabun*," Shozo said. "Watch, please."

The gruntings changed in tone as Don Corleone stumbled, then pitched forward. The child, not understanding what had occurred, continued to play the game initiated by his grandfather.

"Poor little one," Shozo said with tears in his eyes. "How can he know that his grandfather has just died?"

"Shozo," Joji said softly.

Shozo hit a button on the remote control. He looked at Joji's face and said, "I'll get my *katana*."

"No," Joji said. "The sword won't be nearly enough."

Shozo nodded. He went to a closet door, slid it open. He put on a black nylon raincoat that reached to the floor. He turned around to face Joji. "How's this?" he said. His right hand emerged holding a shotgun that Shozo had sawed off himself. "Is it enough?"

Joji nodded. "It's enough."

Traffic, as usual, was fierce. It was as if the city could not exist if it was empty. The heat on the road seemed to approach furnace level.

"Where are we going?" Shozo asked.

"To Takashiba Pier."

After two blocks of frustrating stops and starts, Shozo turned off onto a side street, careened around a corner. Then he really took off.

"Why are we going to Takashiba?" Shozo asked.

"Something," Joji said, "important enough to take you away from Don Corleone."

They went through the heart of the city. Sunlight spun off the myriad slow-moving cars, sending dazzling shafts of light along the streets. They were driving north, toward Chiyoda-ku and the Imperial Palace. At Shinbashi, Shozo turned south, paralleling Tokyo Harbor. They were running by the Sho-dome Freight Terminus. The hooting of the barges from the harbor was audible over the traffic noise.

"Takashiba is where your brother Masashi has a business, *neh*?" Shozo said.

"That's right." Joji was looking straight ahead, at the sun dazzle on the hood of the car.

"You should be *oyabun* of the Taki-gumi," Shozo said. "It is your right."

Joji said nothing.

"Perhaps," Shozo said, "after today you will be."

Now they were in Hammatsucho. Shozo swung left onto a side street. They were in the warehouse district that fronted the piers along the harbor.

Joji checked his gun, screwed a silencer on the end of the muzzle. They locked the car, went along the smelly pavement. Shozo kept his hand in the deep pocket of his raincoat as they walked quickly down the street. They ducked into a warehouse door. There was no sign on it, no indication into which company space the entrance led.

In the dimness, they could see that there was no entrance space at all, merely a flight of nearly vertical wooden stairs. The place stank of fish and fuel oil. Joji drew his gun, and they went up the stairs. They walked on the outsides of their soles, so that their weight would not set off the ancient boards' creaking.

A blank wall greeted them at the head of the stairs. There was a hallway to the right. They headed down this cautiously. Ahead, they could make out enough illumination to discern a large open space.

Joji stopped abruptly as a shadow filled the open space. Shozo shrank back against the right-hand wall.

Daizo stood perfectly still. Up close, he was a massive man. Surely that frame would have felt more comfortable in a *sumo*'s costume than in the conservative dark pin-stripe suit that enwrapped its bulging muscles.

"What are you doing here?" Daizo said. "You are no longer Taki-gumi. You have no business here."

"I am meeting my brother here," Joji lied. As he watched, Daizo slowly unbuttoned his jacket. His right hand remained at the level of his ribs.

"I don't believe that is the wisest choice," Joji said, moving the gun just enough for the light to play along its barrel.

"What is that odor?" Daizo asked of no one in particular.

Joji said nothing. But he was thinking, This should be mine. All of this.

Daizo was sniffing the air like a dog. "I believe I recognize the scent."

"Let me pass."

Daizo's eyes locked onto Joji's. "It is the smell of death."

He moved then, very fast. Coming in low, his bull's shoulders hunched, his short, powerful legs propelling him into Joji just as Joji squeezed off the first shot.

Shozo pulled his hands from beneath the raincoat. He leveled the sawed-off shotgun at Daizo. But the man was already at Joji's throat.

Joji grunted heavily as the back of his head struck the rough wood of the hallway floor. Felt an elbow slam into his solar plexus, an immediate shoulder kite, and he lost all feeling in his right hand.

He coughed, desperately fought to force air into his laboring lungs. Out of the corner of his eye saw Daizo reach for the gun he had dropped. The big man had it and, as if in slow motion, Joji saw the thick fingers of the left hand grip the stock, the forefinger insert itself awkwardly through the trigger guard. The gun swung through the air, moving inexorably toward a spot in the middle of his forehead.

Joji centered his concentration, struck Daizo on the side of the neck with the edge of his hand and, at the same time, lunged out. He twisted Daizo's wrist, heard the snap and Daizo's sharply indrawn breath almost at the same instant. The gun dangled from the broken finger, so thick it had to be forced through the trigger guard.

Daizo kicked, began to scramble away from Joji. Joji blocked the strike as best he could. Daizo brought a *tanto*, a long knife, from beneath his jacket. He made a grotesque sight, the useless gun and hand waggling at his side.

Shozo saw the movement behind the two antagonists. Raised the muzzle of the shotgun and squeezed the trigger. Two Yakuza were blown backward into the vast room. Shozo moved along the wall until he was past Joji and Daizo. He ducked as a bullet chipped at the wall just above his head. Then, moving inexorably forward, fired the second barrel. He reloaded and, in a crouch, moved crablike into the open space.

Daizo had already turned and was beginning his attack, a short, vicious overhand stab. Joji took one long step toward Daizo, extending his left leg. At the same time, he jammed the heel of his right hand underneath Daizo's jaw, lifting the head, grasped the right wrist with his left hand. All he had to do now was twist, using Daizo's own momentum against him.

But the heel of his shoe caught on an old nail. His knees locked, his hold broke down, and he collapsed.

Daizo, quick to take advantage, was on top of him, the blade of the *tanto* slashing in toward Joji's jugular. Even a partially deflected cut would end it.

Joji grabbed Daizo's left hand with his right.

A muffled explosion, and Daizo's eyes opened wide.

Joji had worked Daizo's damaged finger, putting pressure on it where it was trapped against the trigger. The gun had discharged, sending a bullet into Daizo's chest.

There was a lot of blood, and Joji called for Shozo.

The other man came running. "What happened?"

"He almost killed me," Joji said. "That's what happened."

"Is he dead?" Shozo asked warily.

"As dead as the last eel you ate," Joji said. He heard a sound, stuck his head around a corner. He saw a door fly open. Another Yakuza peered cautiously out.

"What is it?" Joji could hear another voice calling to the man peering out.

"I don't know," the first man said. "I heard shots. I can't see anything. It's dark down there."

But it wasn't dark in the room the two Yakuza were in. Joji's eyes opened wide and he thought, Sweet Buddha! He remembered the men he could not identify who were with Michiko every time he saw her. He remembered her agitated state. Now he knew the meaning of all of that. For, hidden away in that windowless room at Takashiba, he saw Tori,

Michiko's beloved granddaughter. A Yakuza soldier was holding a gun to her head; he was very nervous, and Joji quickly pulled his head back so that he would not be seen.

Forget about your brother Masashi, Michiko had said. *I beg of you*, Joji had asked her. *Why won't you help me against him?* And she had said, *I cannot intervene. I can do nothing.* And he had been too blind with his own troubles to hear the anguish in her voice.

Joji wanted to race into that room—nothing more than a bleak cell—and take Tori away from them, but he saw the second Yakuza holding the child fast, the muzzle of his gun pressed into her temple. Joji knew that he had no chance to save Tori now. That he must not let them know he had seen the child. Surprise was his only ally in this inimical world of his brother's.

"Quickly," he said. "Leave the shotgun here. Be sure to wipe it down first." He was doing the same with his pistol. The weapons were without serial numbers; they were untraceable.

Outside, they walked at a normal pace, got into the car. "Take off," Joji said.

Shozo did.

Lillian Doss was met at Charles de Gaulle Airport in Paris by a member of the Plaza Athenée staff. *"Bonjour, madame,"* he said as she came through Immigration.

"François."

He smiled, taking her baggage checks. "It is good to see you again, *madame*."

"It's good to be back," she replied in idiomatic French.

She was wearing a summery mauve-and-lilac-print dress. Her hair was swept back from the sides of her face by rhinestone barrettes. Around her neck was a teardrop emerald on a gold chain.

She stood serenely, regarding all the rushing, flushed faces. While she waited for her bags to arrive, she played a game with herself. She tried to categorize each face she saw. Was it American? European? If European, which country? France, England, Italy, Germany? How many Eastern Europeans could she find? Could she discern the Poles from the Yugoslavs, the Rumanians from the Russians?

This last was the really difficult part. It took a sharp eye and more than a little experience. One learned not to be influenced by the face, but rather by the clothes. She turned her attention to those closest to her. By the time François had gathered all her luggage, Lillian was certain she had correctly identified everyone.

"The car is just this way, *madame*," François said.

The day was sunny. Bright, puffy clouds drifted above the skyline like sleeping cherubs. The air was crisp, containing the delicious scents of newly opened buds and blossoms. In the autumn, she knew, the days would be filled with that peculiar acrid scent of burning leaves that Lillian always found heady. In either season, it was as if with every breath she took, she was inhaling a fine aged wine. It was good to know that the modern world had not leached away the sophisticated complexity that time and culture had bestowed upon France.

La Défense and Les Halles struck Lillian not so much as concessions to changing times but rather as singular extensions of the magic that Paris continually exuded, like the rarest of perfumes. To breathe Paris is to preserve one's soul, she thought. Who had written that? Victor Hugo?

Lillian craned her neck this way and that to take it all in. When they merged onto the Périphérique, she felt her first real jolt, as if before this she had not believed she was actually in France. At Porte Maillot, François maneuvered them off the expressway at a speed that made her giddy.

At the hotel, she took a long, steamy bath. She dried her hair and, wrapped in a terry robe, threw open the french doors. She was on the sixth floor, with one of the four rooms blessed with a balcony. By that time, room service had delivered coffee and croissants. It was still too early for the champagne the manager had put in her room; it was waiting for her in its metal cooler.

Lillian sat in the sunlight. She sipped the strong, black coffee and listened to the birds fluttering and cooing all about her. Below, in the garden courtyard, she could hear the waiters setting up for lunch. The tiny, musical sounds wafted up to her. She allowed the sunlight to heat her thighs and back.

She picked up the *International Herald Tribune*, leafed quickly, efficiently through it. She read with some interest a reprint of an article written by Helmut Schmidt, the former chancellor of West Germany, titled "Japan Has No True Friends in the World." There were several sidebars to the reprint. One quoted a United Press Syndicate story citing a recent poll of Korean leaders and intellectuals, a majority of whom felt that Japan was currently a threat to the peace of the region and the world. On the other hand, the story stated, the engines of South Korea's wildly successful new car, the Hyundai, were manufactured by the Japanese.

"Everyone wants Japanese money," a prominent academic in Singapore was quoted as saying. "The feeling is, 'God forbid that tomorrow we'll be left to the tender mercies of the Japanese.' The Americans come and go. When the Japanese come, they're here to stay."

Lillian sipped at her coffee and continued reading. A second sidebar quoted other prominent leaders in Southeast Asia, all of whom seemed terrified of Japan's high-technology progress. All felt that it was only a matter of time before Japan's staggering research capacities were turned to developing twenty-first-century weaponry.

As an example, many mentioned the new Japanese Yamamoto FAX jet fighter currently being designed, which would eventually put the American aircraft manufacturers Boeing and McDonnell Douglas out of business.

Lillian went through the rest of the paper, but there was nothing further of interest. Flowers blooming along the inner walls of the courtyard lent bright bursts of color to the scrolled wrought-iron work. Voices, quickening. She glanced down, saw that the tables were filling up with the first wave of diners.

She recalled a time many years ago when Jonas had taken her to one of his interminable social functions that were nothing more than another vapid layer of the political world in which he thrived. Philip was away, in Bangkok or Bangladesh, God only knew where. Lillian could not remember when she had seen so many ribbons, medals, so much braid sewn, pinned, basted onto the front of so many men's suits.

On Jonas's arm, smiling as perfectly, as purposefully, as a flight attendant, while Jonas worked the room. She had felt trapped. The impossibly beautiful women gliding by looked as if they were store mannequins. Unaffected either by life's trials or by time's travails, they spent their days in sybaritic splendor—hair cut, colored, highlighted; nails (finger and toe) shaped, wrapped and lacquered; faces steamed, cleansed, creamed, massaged; bodies mud-packed, oiled and *shiatsu*ed. In between cosmetic and shopping commitments, they managed to meet with other committee members of the most *au courant* charities. Which was how they deluded themselves into believing that their existence had a modicum of meaning.

How could I ever have imagined that I could fit in here? Lillian had thought. I should have my head examined for accepting Jonas's invitation. She had felt ashamed, as if she were there under false pretenses. At any moment, she fantasized, Mme. Pierre Croix de Guerre-St. Estophe over there will discover that I don't belong here at all. In her clipped, precise English, learned no doubt on the Côte d'Azur, she will call the uniformed guards, and while everyone looks on, they will escort me out.

What? She's got no hyphenated name? What kind of a family does she come from? A field general's daughter. An army brat? Good Lord. Really? However did she manage to sneak in here in the first place? She's obviously not our *kind.*

She had shuddered. Their words—those that she had created for them—left a bitter taste in her mouth. As if the champagne she had been consuming was sour.

At one point Jonas had told a joke—to the Australian ambassador's young and ambitious ADC—to the effect that in America the men crave power, and the women crave the next best thing, an erect penis.

The two men had laughed, making Lillian feel even more out of place. It was a joke at women's expense, and here she was, a woman herself, as anyone with half a brain could plainly see, treated as if she didn't exist. Forget that Jonas should not have thought of telling it in her presence. He had not even turned to her to say, "Present company excepted, of course." She was there merely as an extension of him, the finishing touch to his image.

Lillian remembered the coldness that had formed in her stomach. Looking around the colonial blue-and-white room, with its fifteen-foot windows covered with richly patterned French fabrics. Formally attired, white-gloved waitresses—no waiters here, please!—making the rounds, attending to the needs of the beribboned, medaled, braided men.

The Australian continued to speak directly to Jonas, ignoring her. An American brigadier, a Pentagon attaché, approached her, but it was as if he spoke in an alien tongue. When she did, in panic, open her mouth to respond, what came out seemed to her like an inarticulate squeak.

Her cheeks were flaming. Even before she overheard the Australian ADC say to Jonas, "I say, that quiff's one fine-looking animal, what?" And wanting only to die when the shock wore off enough for her to realize that he was talking about her.

She broke away from the leash of Jonas's arm and made her way to the ladies' room. It seemed grossly unfair that this was the only place where she could find surcease from a world dominated by men.

She had stared at herself in the mirror. Now that she was alone, she recognized that coldness in her stomach as disguised fury. Her anger was not directed at the Australian, who—pig though he was—meant nothing to her. Or even at Jonas—who should have known better, but didn't; you could reasonably expect a dog to fetch, but not to speak.

In the sanctuary of the ladies' room, she had wept with an abandon she could never show even in the privacy of her own bedroom; it was Philip's bedroom, too, after all.

How she had hated Philip at that moment, for abandoning her. For consigning her to this seemingly endless purgatory of being alone. For binding her with love to a life she despised.

Morning found their bodies still entwined. The ti leaves that covered them were turning brown; their scent was gone.

Michael stirred, opening his eyes. A beetle crawled across his forearm, disappearing into the mulch beneath the rock overhang. He touched Eliane, and she started awake. Her wide-open eyes stared into his, and Michael shivered at the absence of emotion there. It was as if a cold wind had passed between them. In a moment it was gone, and Eliane had come back from whatever eerie place she had been inhabiting.

"Good morning," he said, kissing her on the lips.

She put her hand up. A fingertip traced its way down the line of his jaw.

"Did you sleep well?" he asked.

She nodded. "I did not dream. That hasn't happened for many years."

"I dreamed all night," Michael said. "Of battles and warriors armored in circular shields made from the shells of giant sea turtles."

He began to get dressed, and as he did so, he took off the dried ti leaf garland.

"Leave it there." Her hand stayed him. "Until we're home."

He looked at her, and she gave him a small smile. He remembered the sounds from the darkness of the night, the movement he had thought he had seen just outside their sanctuary.

"Eliane," he said, "last night I heard noises. I even thought I saw something moving. What happened out there"—he raised an arm to point—"when we were making love?"

262

"I don't know. Nothing. Or perhaps a night creature. There are wild boar and mongeese all through the wilderness here."

"Boar and mongeese are diurnal," Michael said. "They wouldn't be around at night. Besides, you turned my head away."

She stood up. "Whatever it was doesn't matter." She began to get dressed.

Michael picked up the ti leaf garland that lay around his neck. "You said that we had to wear these to protect us. Protect us from what?"

She shrugged. "It depends on what you believe. The *kahunas* say that the gods still move here—the ancient warriors who fought and bled and, perhaps, died here centuries ago."

"Are you saying that's what I heard?"

She shrugged again. "Why not? Their spirits are all over this island."

"Feeling a power is one thing, seeing spirits is something else again."

"If you don't believe it," she said, "then it didn't happen. But I'll tell you one thing. The gods who fought here were armored in the shells of giant sea turtles."

Michael wasn't sure whether she was making fun of him. She leaned over, kissed him on the lips. "Don't look so quizzical. It's the truth. Look it up in any history of Maui."

Michael thought about this while he finished dressing. "Dreams don't exist," he said. "They take form from what's in your subconscious, not from what's around you."

"The human mind isn't rational, Michael. You should know that already. Yet you're expecting a square peg to fit into a round hole. It just won't go, no matter how hard you try to force it."

He said, "The spirit world is what fascinates you, isn't it? But you know that it's no substitute for real life."

"What are you saying?"

"Just that this obsession might be another flight from reality."

"Like the bulemia and the anorexia?"

He shrugged. "You're the only one who can know that."

"I don't know anything," she said sadly. "Because the only lesson I've ever learned is never to trust anything." She began the long, precipitous descent to the valley floor.

"Not even yourself?" Michael asked, scrambling after her.
"*Especially* not myself," Eliane said.

Michiko was kneeling before the shrine of the fox-goddess when she became aware of someone behind her.

"Michiko?"

Joji's voice.

"Yes, my brother." Her head continued to be bowed in prayer. "How are you?"

"I must speak with you."

"When I finish my prayers," she said, "we can take a walk around the garden."

Joji glanced surreptitiously at the guards, standing uncomfortably close, watching Michiko, watching him, and said, "No. I must speak with you in private." He had turned his head so that the guards could not read his lips.

"If this is about Masashi, my answer is the same as before."

"Michiko, I beg of you. I know who these guards are. I must see you alone."

Hearing the note of desperation in his voice, she said, "All right." She considered the options. "In the hour of my bath," she said at length. "At six o'clock. Do you remember that part of the fence that was in need of repair?"

"The place where the foxes used to come?"

"Yes," she said. "I put morning glories up instead of repairing it. It is important for the foxes to be here. It is a sacred spot for them." She smiled because she did not want the guards to think that they were speaking of anything serious. "The hole is big enough for you to fit through. Come to the kitchen entrance just before six. I'll arrange for the cook to let you in."

At a quarter to six, Joji slipped through the ragged hole the foxes had made in the bamboo, edged his way to the kitchen entrance of his stepsister's house.

As arranged, the cook, an old woman who had been in the Yamamoto employ for years, opened the door, ushering him inside. She took him silently through the house. At length, she knelt in front of a sliding door, knocked very softly. Apparently hearing an affirmation from inside, she beckoned for Joji to enter.

He went across on his knees. The room was all of stone. Steam swirled white, and he immediately began to sweat. He could see Michiko's bare back as she sat upright in the tiled tub.

"I have sent the girls out," Michiko said. "Whatever you have to say, say it quickly, Joji. We have little time."

"I know where Masashi is holding Tori."

For a moment Joji thought she hadn't heard him. Then Michiko gave a stifled cry. "Where?" she whispered. "Oh, where is my granddaughter?"

"At the warehouse in Takashiba. Do you know the place?"

Michiko nodded. "Of course I know it. It is half owned by Nobuo's Yamamoto Heavy Industries." She turned to face him, and he could see how pale she was. "But how did you find this out, Joji-chan?"

He told her, then, how he had tried to enlist the aid of Kai Chosa, how he had finally gone to Kozo Shiina, what Shiina had told him to do, what had transpired at the warehouse in Takashiba when he and Shozo had gone there.

Michiko hung her head. "Oh, you stupid, stupid boy," she said in a sigh.

"None of this would have happened," he pointed out, "if you had agreed to help me against Masashi. But when I saw Tori, I understood everything. I knew why you had to refuse to help me."

"Oh Joji," she said sadly, "you don't understand anything. I had hoped to spare you all this. I had hoped that at least you, of all the family, would not become involved and be imperiled."

Joji stared at her. "What do you mean?"

"Months ago, your brother Masashi made a deal with Shiina."

"What!"

"Keep your voice down, Joji-chan, and listen to me. If Shiina says he is your ally against Masashi and he tells Masashi that he is *his* ally, he must be up to something. But what?" She thought a moment. "Buddha," she said. "It was Shiina's idea for you to invade the warehouse at Takashiba?"

Joji nodded.

"Masashi is going to find out, of course. Perhaps he already knows. Masashi will be after you. That's what Shiina must want. If Masashi kills you, only one Taki brother will remain. Knowing Shiina, he has already devised the method by which he will eliminate Masashi. Then he will have what he's wanted all along: the destruction of the Taki-gumi!"

"Oh no!"

"Quickly," Michiko said, rising. "Get my towel. You must take me to the warehouse. We must rescue Tori. Once I know

265

she's safe, perhaps we can deal with Kozo Shiina in his own perverse manner." She smiled as Joji dried her. "Yes," she said, "that would suit me very well. Kozo Shiina has a great many sins to atone for."

"My time is over here," Michael said. They had made their way back to Eliane's house in silence. Once inside, they had gone their separate ways to shower and change. Now, they met in the kitchen. It was just before eight o'clock in the morning. "I'm off for Tokyo in a couple of hours."

Eliane was fixing fresh-squeezed juice. "You're going to have some trouble at the airport," she said, shoving the morning's *Honolulu Advertiser* at him. The banner headlines told of the "Massacre in the West Maui Mountains," as the newspaper had named the battle at Fat Boy Ichimada's. "The local police are going to be swarming all over Maui, not to mention every available agent of the U.S. Immigration and Naturalization Service. The INS is the federal agency most involved in cracking down on the Yakuza activities on the Islands. You'll never get through Immigration."

"There's no problem there," Michael said. "I spoke to my contact in Washington this morning. He's squared everything with the Feds. We'll be left alone—that, I can guarantee. Anyway, I'll be better off in Tokyo. That's my turf. I can use my contacts there to find Ude. He must be long gone by now."

"Maybe," Eliane said. She split a papaya, scooped out the dark, bitter seeds that looked like caviar. She handed him half a papaya, along with a spoon.

"Thanks."

"And maybe not," she went on. "There's a chance he's still on the island, and if so, I think I know where he would be."

"I don't hold out much hope of that," Michael said, setting aside the fruit. "But if there's any chance at all, let's take it."

In the Jeep, he said, "Why didn't you mention this possibility before?"

Eliane was driving, racing along the narrow road. She overtook a tour bus loaded with Japanese tourists. "The truth is, it just occurred to me. When you told me that your people had fixed it with the Feds so that we wouldn't be involved in the Ichimada investigation, it came to me. Ude couldn't get off Maui the night of the fight at Fat Boy's; it was far too late. And it's a sure bet that yesterday the airport was crawling with INS agents, who would recognize him on sight. The Yakuza here are well connected among the local police, but they're terrified of the INS."

"But even if that's true," Michael said, "how could you know where Ude would hide out?"

"That's not so difficult to work out. Now that Ichimada's dead, the family will be in disarray. Fat Boy refused to groom anyone who might eventually take his place. He believed in *katamichi*, the method the Yakuza bosses used in the old days to weed out the dross: He allowed his underbosses to jockey among themselves for position. "Let the best man win!" Fat Boy was fond of saying. Then he would figuratively cut the legs out from under whoever was left."

They were out of Iao Valley now, swinging around toward Wailuku and the east side of Maui.

"But there is a man named Ome," Eliane continued. "He is centrally located—meaning his turf is in and around the airport. His people took care of that area—import and export—for Ichimada. It's logical to assume that Ude would go to Ome, especially if he's been in contact with Masashi. Ome is Masashi's man."

They had passed through the ramshackle part of town and now were on the road they had come down the day they had met. Eliane slowed, searching for something. Apparently, she found it, for she pulled off the road and came to a stop.

"There." She pointed. "Use the glasses."

Michael could see a paved road winding through the mountains. If one took it heading north, one would come to Kahakuloa. He saw the buildings shimmering in the cool, bluish light, the ancient graveyard he and Eliane had passed on their way down from Kahakuloa when they had first met.

He saw a copse of trees, then, moving the glasses upward, saw the house built into the side of the mountains. In the glasses' heavily magnified viewing field, the house looked as if it were no more than a dozen yards away. A car was parked out front. There was no activity around the house, but it was impossible to see inside.

Michael was about to get out to take a closer look at the house when the front door opened. A pair of Yakuza soldiers came out. They went to work on the car, inspecting it inside and out. Michael kept them in view.

Within minutes, one of the soldiers went back inside. He returned, accompanied by another man. The soldier was loaded down with paraphernalia, which he heaved into the trunk of the car. Michael saw that the second man was Japanese, with a scar running down his right cheek. He described the man to Eliane, who said, "That's Ome. Do you see any sign of Ude?"

"No," Michael said. Then, "Wait. There's someone in the doorway to the house." In a moment, a figure emerged. He was half carrying a woman. She was bound hand and foot. The man turned toward Michael as he bent to untie the woman's ankles. In so doing, his face became visible.

"Is it Ude?" Eliane asked.

"Yes," Michael said. Now his fingers gripped the glasses with a terrible strength. "He's carrying someone. A woman, I think."

"A woman?" Eliane said. "That makes no sense. Ude came here alone."

"Well, he's not alone now," Michael said. "This will make it easier for us. He'll have someone else on his mind when we—" He gave a strangled cry as he saw Ude pull the hair back from the woman's face. His scalp crawled.

"It's Audrey," Michael whispered hoarsely. "That bastard has my sister!"

Without a word, Eliane snatched the glasses from him. She put them to her face. As she watched, Audrey squatted and urinated at the side of the road. Her head lolled on her neck. As soon as she was finished, Ude bound her ankles again. Then, hefting her over his shoulder, he dumped her into the back of the car. Then he got in.

"My dear God!" Eliane said.

"What is it?" Michael asked. "For God's sake, Eliane, what's going on?"

Eliane said nothing. She was staring at Audrey. Her face was white. Michael pulled Eliane out of the driver's seat, got in himself. Before she had time to settle in the passenger's seat, he had pulled out after the fast-disappearing car.

"I want to know what's going on," he said as he drove. "Eliane, what is it?"

"I don't know what's happened," she said. It was as sudden as a dam bursting. It was as if her entire face darkened. "It's all come apart!"

"What has?"

"Michael, I was the one who kidnapped your sister."

"What?"

"I did it to protect her. Masashi had tried to get to her once. I didn't want him to try again."

"But why would he? My father is dead; she can't be used as leverage anymore."

"Philip sent her something, didn't he?"

So I was right, Michael thought. What Dad sent Audrey is vitally important. "It was you I fought in my father's study!"

"I'm sorry that happened," Eliane said. "Your presence was an accident; I had no other choice."

"You could have told me why you were there. We could have worked something out. Faked the kidnapping."

Eliane shook her head. "Would you have believed me? I doubt it. In any case, I couldn't take the chance. Besides, I had to make it authentic. In order to confuse Masashi, I could not dare assemble a fake abduction. And I did not want to implicate you in any way."

"But you took the *katana* my father gave me. Where is it?"

"I don't have it," Eliane said. "Your father stole it years ago from a man named Kozo Shiina. He's the leader of the *Jiban*. The sword, forged for Prince Yamato Takeru hundreds of years ago, is one of the *Jiban*'s sacred symbols, along with the Katei document. It is said that when Shiina next uses the sword, the *Jiban* will have attained its goal. I think Shiina has it again."

"You gave it to him?" Michael asked incredulously.

"No," Eliane said sadly. "It was taken from me by force."

The *katana* was one thing; he could not get Audrey off his mind. "But if you took Audrey for safekeeping," Michael said, "how is it that Ude has her now?"

"I don't know," Eliane confessed. "I brought her here to Maui and stashed her away at Fat Boy Ichimada's hideaway in Hana. I knew he wasn't using it, and it was the last place anyone searching for her would look. Especially Masashi. Or so I thought."

Now for the difficult question, Michael thought. "Does Masashi know about the postcard my father sent to Audrey?"

"He must," Eliane said. "I know he intercepted the letter your father wrote to you."

"But I got the letter," Michael said.

"I'm not surprised," she said. "That means Masashi knows why you're here. He's using you as his ferret. You're going to find the Katei document, but you're going to be doing it for him. You can bet he's got us under surveillance and that he'll be there at the end, to take it from you when you discover where it is your father hid it."

Or, Michael thought, you're Masashi's agent. What better way to keep an eye on me? What better way to be in at the end if and when I do find the Katei document? And how can I divine the truth? You've lied and lied to me in so many layers that I'll never sort the truth out.

"This is my battle now, too," Eliane said. "Michael, I'm responsible for your sister's safety. It's because of me that she's in danger now. Ude's heading for the airport. No doubt arrangements have been made for him to smuggle Audrey out of Hawaii. Masashi will want to know what your father sent her. And when she tells him, which she will, he'll have no more use for her. If we don't stop Ude here, we may never find Audrey alive."

Michael was listening with only one ear. That is, he wondered whether he could trust her and, if so, how far. He remembered what his father had told him, that divining the truth gets harder the older one grows. It was true, peshaps. But Michael possessed *Tendo*, the Way of heaven. *The Way of heaven*, Tsuyo had said, *is truth*.

"Don't worry," he said. "We'll stop Ude here."

Michael knew that when he had accepted Jonas's commission to find out who had killed Philip Doss and why, he had dedicated himself to this path for the rest of his life. And he was not about to give it up now.

There's only one way to find out for certain which side Eliane is on, he thought, gunning the engine. I've got to play this out to the very end.

Ude had parked his car moments before Michael and Eliane pulled into the Kahului airport, some distance away. Now he and the local Yakuza soldier whom Ome had provided were met by airport personnel, who climbed inside the car. Ude started up, drove through the freight entrance. Ten minutes later he and Ome's soldier, dressed in airline-maintenance overalls, emerged onto the tarmac, riding a motorized luggage cart. On the back of it was a large wooden crate, stenciled YAMAMOTO HEAVY INDUSTRIES: AUTOMOTIVE PARTS: FRAGILE.

The private air traffic was directed to land some distance away from the longer landing strip, used by the DC-10's arriving directly from San Francisco and the 707's of the more frequently scheduled interisland airlines.

Masashi's plane, a small DC-9, had already landed. A pax-stand, mobile stairs, was being rolled into position by two uniformed attendants as Ude and the soldier rolled through the freight gate and out onto the tarmac.

In the background Ude could see a much larger commercial DC-10, from which the last straggle of passengers was debarking. No wonder there were so many people here.

As he watched, one of the attendants left the pax-stand to open the DC-9's cargo-bay doors. A uniformed guard sat at a gate in the wire fence that led out to the tarmac. Ude scanned the crowd as he emerged from the freight entrance.

The first uniformed attendant, finished with locking the mobile stairs in place, went to help his companion open the lower-bay doors of the luggage and servicing compartments. Why should they be doing that rather than climbing the stairs to help the plane's crew? Without conscious thought, Ude moved slightly so that he could get a glimpse of the man's face. He saw a swath of bandage across the bridge of the nose.

"Buddha!" he breathed. It was Michael Doss! "Get this crate aboard the plane no matter what happens," he told the Yakuza soldier as he bolted off the luggage carrier.

"Hey!" Ude pointed as he yelled to the guard. He was running at full speed toward the DC-9. "Those people aren't airline personnel!"

The guard left his post, began to run toward Masashi's plane, his hand searching for his holstered sidearm.

Michael sprinted across the tarmac, ignoring Eliane's shout of protest. The jet fumes choked him, turning the air a dirty blue, unbreathable, the atmosphere of an alien planet. His eyes watered and his vision clouded. There was a hot wind pushing him backward, drowning out the guard's shouts. He ducked under the wing of the DC-9, slipped on a patch of iridescent oil, skidded into the base of the mobile stairs.

Shook himself as Ude hurtled into him. Michael went down, his hands raised to keep the blade of a *tanto*, a Japanese knife, from slashing him.

Michael tried a liver kite, finding the steel blade coming at his abdomen. Ude used the haft of the *tanto* to block the strike, then whirled clockwise, picking up energy from the movement of Michael's body, combining it with the momentum of his own.

Michael was aware of how frightened he was. Frightened for Audrey. The thought of her with this beast was intolerable. He bit his lip, fighting back the rage that threatened to overwhelm him.

As long as there is fear, Tsuyo had said, *there will be defeat. Hate, anger, confusion, fright. These are all aspects of one attitude. Fear. The more a warrior can let go, the more he retains. This is difficult for any student to understand, since his labor here is to absorb. If you think only of revenge, your body will be made weak by your obsession. You will cease to have options open to you, until all strategy disappears, leaving only one thing: the thought of revenge.*

But revenge for what Ude had done to Audrey was what filled Michael's mind. Without thinking, he grabbed Ude's right wrist with his left hand, kept his circular motion going so that he took Ude's own motion, using it against him to pull him into another hand strike.

But Ude was prepared and, sidestepping, managed to bypass the brunt of the blow. But in so doing, he crashed against the railing of the cramped mobile-stairs platform.

In that instant, Michael used his legs again, scissoring them at the ankles, trapping Ude's calves between them.

Ude went down. Sirens were wailing, and Michael turned, saw the Yakuza soldier who had been with Ude kneeling in the sharpshooter's position. He dived behind the pax-stand as a bullet slammed into the metal beside his ear.

He was pinned down, and Ude was shaking himself, ready to throw the *tanto* into Michael's chest. Michael wanted to run, but the Yakuza had him pinned down.

Then he saw Eliane emerge from the other side of the DC-9. She hurled a small piece of luggage at the soldier. It hit him squarely on the side of the head and he went down, his gun clattering across the tarmac.

Michael turned and ran. He was thinking of *muto. Muto*, Tsuyo said, *means without sword. If all you can do is encompassed by your skill as a swordsman, then in many, many instances you will be at a distinct disadvantage. The modern warrior must be adept at using everything—and nothing—in order to bring about victory in combat.*

Muto meant this.

Eliane had used *muto*. And this is what it meant to him: It meant life.

Audrey, he thought as he ran, where are you?

Behind him, Ude was lurching dizzily to his feet and heading after him. Saw Eliane emerge from beneath the DC-9's wing, her angle cutting down the distance so that she was at his side.

Across the tarmac, toward the only sanctuary open to them: the DC-10 that had just come in. They raced up the pax-stand. Michael grabbed a flight attendant standing at the top, pushing her heavily backward into the interior of the plane. "Shut the door!" he shouted to the pair of flight attendants, who were staring at him goggle-eyed. Keeping one eye on the captain and copilot, who had come halfway out of their seats.

Michael saw Ude racing up the pax-stand holding a small boy to his chest as a shield. Behind him, the young mother ran, weeping, imploring him to give her back her child.

Michael yelled at the crew, "For Christ's sake, do as I say!"

But they were paralyzed with fear, and only Eliane saved him. She dived at the door, hauling it inward.

Heard the comforting *thump!* as the thick hatch closed and was locked.

Safe!

Jonas was at home, poring through the BITE field reports. At first, he had been dissecting those that went back over the past six years—the time when General Hadley's file had determined that the string of leaks in BITE security had begun. But then something in one of the earliest field reports had jogged Jonas's memory—back to the year before. And from there he had been backtracking.

Now that there was a pattern of sorts, he could see that he had been losing ground to the Soviets for fifteen years at least. Nothing linear; an operative here, an initiative there. And in between, minor advances against the Russians. A game of give-and-take: the norm. Now, with the field reports in front of him, he could see that it was anything but the norm.

A phalanx of paper cups filled with various amounts of cold coffee were lined up beside his papers. He had been at this for so long, he could no longer remember the last time he had eaten, let alone when he had slept. He rubbed his eyes, then rummaged in a drawer, snapped open a bottle of Gelusil tablets, ate several.

Scanned his findings. According to what he had unearthed here, Hadley's file was wrong: The leaks to the Soviets had been going on for far longer than six years. Not only that. The pace of leaking intelligence had escalated during the past year. In much the same way that the Japanese economic aggressiveness had shifted. Odd that both should be happening, Jonas thought wearily.

The red phone on his desk rang, and he snatched it up immediately. It was just past two A.M.—a time when bad news is delivered.

"You had better get over here right away," the duty officer at BITE said. "I've alerted General Hadley's office. There's a Code Blue alert."

Code Blue: highest priority.

It took Jonas just under fourteen minutes to get to the BITE offices, which was a record of sorts. At one point, he had pushed the speedometer up past one hundred.

From the car he had phoned his assistants, and they were on their way. He passed through security and entered the compound. The building was quiet, humming efficiently along. The duty officer was waiting for him in the lobby. Jonas saw security people all over.

"No one in, no one out," the duty officer said, "until you give the all clear."

Jonas gave the names of his assistants to the security people so that they would be let through when they arrived.

Up on the eighth floor, Jonas could hear the murmuring of the all-night monitoring of the Asian and Eastern European stations. BITE was never closed; it was always daytime somewhere in the world.

The duty officer led Jonas down the hall. In Jonas's office, he turned on the computer, accessed the central file. Immediately, lettering came on, surrounded by orange bars. CORE DATA DELETED, the screen flashed over and over.

Jonas sat down at his desk, began punching in codes, getting deeper and deeper into the BITE central memory core.

"Oh Christ," he said in a moment. He passed his hand across his face. His head hurt, and he had trouble breathing. Went back to the keyboard, did the routine all over again. With the same result.

By this time, his assistants had arrived. Jonas looked up. "It's our Russian networks. Someone has accessed all the core data about them: names, dates, contacts, sleepers, everything. And then deleted them from the central file."

"There are no hard copies," one of Jonas's assistants said. "And no backups of any kind. Unless there's an operative with total recall, we've lost all our basic data on every network, field operation and foreign asset pertaining to the Soviet Union."

At that moment, the intercom on Jonas's desk buzzed.

"Yes?" Jonas said, stabbing at a button.

"Someone down here wants to come up." Jonas recognized the voice of one of the security people in the lobby.

"Who is it?"

"General Hadley, sir."

Jonas, his stomach turning to water, said, "Send him up." He sent the duty officer to meet Hadley at the elevator, then cleared his office of personnel. Jesus, Jonas thought, he wasn't supposed to get here for another couple of days.

The duty officer led Hadley into the office, then left, closing the door behind him.

"How are you, Jonas?" Hadley said. "It's been a long time since we saw each other."

Though he was over eighty, Sam Hadley was still a handsome man. His hair was white now, there were deep lines scoring his leathery face and the backs of his hands were darkened by liver spots. But the energy of the frame, the canny intelligence of the eyes remained undimmed.

He sat down in a chair. "How long have we known one another, Jonas?"

"A long time," Jonas said.

"We go back to the beginning, don't we? To Tokyo, to a time before BITE had even been born." Hadley shook his head, let out a sigh. "What's been happening here, Jonas?"

"You mean tonight?"

"It's not just tonight," Hadley said. "Tonight's a disaster that unfortunately has been six years in the making." Jonas thinking, Oh Christ, he's seen the report. "Just how bad is it?"

Jonas told him all he knew.

"Good Christ," Hadley said. "If the Russians have that information, our intelligence has been set back—what?—a decade, maybe more." He shook his head. "Even the sleepers? Oh Lord."

He stood up and began to pace. "Who's the mole, Jonas? Only someone inside BITE had the requisite security codes to access the central file and then delete the data."

"There are only a few people it could be," Jonas said. "Even most of the top-level executives don't have the delete codes."

Hadley frowned. "Why delete the data at all? Why not just

275

steal it? The computer wouldn't have flagged that as it did the deletion of core data. It meant we'd get onto it quicker."

"Maybe," Jonas said, "that's the point. Maybe whoever the mole is wants us to know what he did. Which would mean he's already bolted. I'll get on it right now. Full priority." He was reaching for the phone when Hadley waved him off.

"That won't be necessary."

"What do you mean?"

"We're old compatriots," Hadley said. "More, we're old friends. Maybe it'll be less difficult coming from me." He stopped his pacing, stood in front of Jonas as if he were about to make a last request. "It's the end, Jonas." There was sadness in his eyes. "I'm bringing in new people. Fresh blood. BITE has gotten old, stale; it's been infiltrated. Its time has passed."

Jonas felt dizzy. There was a buzzing in his ears. He felt as if he was having a heart attack. "Sir, you can't—"

"I'm truly sorry," Hadley said, "but the orders have been cut and implemented. The president has been informed, and my men are already sealing the building. My investigators will be here momentarily. So you see, you can relax. There's nothing more for you to do. As of this moment, BITE has ceased to exist."

Jonas, white as chalk, keeled over in his chair.

Ude, keeping the boy against his chest, withdrew the steel *shaken* from an inside pocket of his overalls. He was at the foot of the mobile stairs. The crowd had turned into a screaming, milling mass. Ude could smell the hysteria in the air, like a pungent perfume; it excited him.

The armed guard who had chased after Michael and Eliane was fairly close. Ude flicked his wrist, and the guard's eyes opened wide as the throwing star embedded itself in his chest. He fell to his knees, reached out to support himself, toppled sideways.

Ude ran to where the guard lay, gathered up the fallen pistol. He checked the chambers, filled the two empty ones from the extra bullets on the guard's belt.

There were three more guards—or perhaps policemen—running out through the security gate. Ude aimed and squeezed the trigger and they went down, one, two, three, like ducks in a shooting gallery. He had no time to waste with their meddling, but he was careful to count the bullets used.

He scrambled underneath the carriage of the DC-10. This

was Maui, and it would take some time, he knew, for more police to make their appearance. But even so, he had a finite amount of time. The thing was to get on with it.

On the far side of the jet, he found both the servicing and the luggage compartment doors open. He shoved the boy onto the tarmac. With a grunt, Ude levered himself up into the dark, chill luggage bay.

Stuffing the gun inside his overalls, he reached up, fingertips searching for the seam that would define the inner panel that would give him access into the cabin itself. The bulkhead, as in all such planes, was constructed of aluminum. Every ten or fifteen inches, vertical struts supported the thin sheets that were welded together. Found the panel, and began exploring with his fingertips. Felt the tiny circular ridges that told him there was no way he could open it by conventional means; it was screwed in from the opposite side.

Ude dug into his overalls, found what he had gotten from Ome's people, who had met him outside the bar in Wailuku early this morning. It had been his chosen method of getting into the house in Iao Valley. Ude had discovered through his local contacts where Eliane Yamamoto had rented a house. It was there that Ude had planned to kill Michael. Now that Michael was holed up inside the DC-10, this same method would do quite nicely—for the same purpose.

Working quickly, he extracted a roll of what appeared to be thick tape. It was a quarter-inch wide, a sickly pale-white and had the consistency of plasticene. As he unrolled the Primacord, Ude pressed it just inside the panel's reinforcing structure, which was clearly outlined from inside the bay.

When the Primacord was in place, Ude cut the end with a pocketknife, dropped the roll. Now he searched around. He dragged a crate over to a spot directly beneath the access panel. Wedging two pieces of Samsonite luggage on top did it. Now the Primacord was both braced and covered by the makeshift wall. Explosions, like all such forces of nature, tended to take the path of least resistance. Had Ude not taken the trouble to brace the Primacord, the bulk of what was about to happen would blow through the bay, most likely killing him.

Crouching down behind the crate, Ude lit a match. Put it to the Primacord, which was, in effect, string plastique.
Whoomp!
The DC-10 shuddered, and Ude was up, climbing on the crate. He had no fear of hot metal, since aluminum's thermal

277

coefficient was so high, it lost heat immediately. Dragged himself through the ragged hole where the access panel had been.

Squeezed off two more shots as two of the crew members ran toward him. They crumpled, and he raced past them. He could see them now. They were just turning toward the aft section of the main cabin, where the explosion had taken place.

Michael: the objective.

The Yamamoto Heavy Industries main factory complex took up six square blocks in the outskirts of the port city of Kobe, just south of Tokyo. The conglomerate's offices were so vast that a precise network of shuttle scooters—manufactured by Yamamoto, of course—was needed to ferry personnel from one industry module to another.

When Masashi arrived, his face was checked against a master list by a uniformed security guard. He was directed to park in the main lot. Once there, Masashi found a blue-coded shuttle waiting to take him to the aerospace module.

Yamamoto Aerospace occupied the most southeasterly quadrant of the complex. Its ferroconcrete superstructure rose twelve stories into the smog-laden air. But whereas other sectors of Yamamoto Heavy Industries occupied spirelike towers, the aerospace division—or *kobun*—was housed in a vast series of horizontal buildings.

The shuttle left Masashi at the entrance, where his identity was again checked. A guard was assigned to him, both to guide him to his destination and to keep an eye on him. This was standard company procedure, and Masashi could admire the severity of the conglomerate's internal-security code.

The guard led Masashi inside what at first appeared to be the world's largest—and barest—warehouse. Once Masashi's eyes grew accustomed to the dimness of the light—for there was not even one window—he recognized the space for what it was: an airplane hangar.

Nobuo Yamamoto was standing in the center of the space. Beside and above him loomed a shrouded shape. Immediately, Masashi's pulse began to race. This is it, he thought. This is our agent of destruction. The great winged steed that would bring glory to Japan.

As Masashi began to walk toward Nobuo, he could see that the massive shape was draped in tarpaulins. Nobuo's face was hidden in the shadows cast by the shape.

"Is this it?" Masashi asked. "Is it ready?"

Nobuo nodded curtly. "We are ready for the test run. The first and only. Every component has been exhaustively tested on its own, both before it became part of the whole and afterward."

Masashi's eyes were shining. "I want to see it," he said in the thick tone of voice a man uses when he wants to see his lover's naked body.

Nobuo, watching Masashi's reactions, felt only disgust. For this man, whose greed was seemingly boundless, and for himself for being so weak as to provide Masashi with this instrument of Armageddon. For surely, Nobuo thought, that is what will ensue if Masashi's mad plan reaches fruition.

But what am I to do? He has my granddaughter. Am I to sacrifice her tender life in order to defeat a madman? Will her mother understand that I made the decision that the child must give up her life for her country?

Nobuo was in a frenzy of indecision. Convulsively, his fingers closed around a cord hanging from the near corner of the tarp. He gave a tug.

And the sleek, futuristic shape of the Yamamoto FAX jet fighter was revealed. Its fusilage was stubby, tapered at the nose, blunt and ugly at its rear, where a cluster of cylinders circled its quad tailpipes. Its wings, too, were of a radical shape: wide and impossibly short for a plane, curving down at a steep angle at their tips.

"Is it ready?" Masashi repeated.

"We'll see now," Nobuo said. His heart was encased in ice, his limbs felt numb and it seemed to him that someone else was speaking. As the FAX ground crew began preparations for takeoff, he said, "The cruising speed is Mach-four, but of course, it is capable of bursts upward of Mach-six."

The pilot was being assisted into the cockpit. The canopy slid shut, and as soon as everyone was out of the way, the engines started up.

"But it's not only speed that makes this jet special," Nobuo said. "Not by a long shot."

The far end of the hangar slid open to reveal a concrete runway. The FAX taxied out onto it, came into position and paused. They could hear the whine of its jets cranking up to speed. Blue-black smoke drifted from it, and the heat of the jets made the air ripple behind it.

Nobuo led Masashi to a makeshift command post. They stood in front of a working radar screen that had been set up on the tarmac. "We're ready," Nobuo said. He nodded his head to a man with headphones, who spoke into the mouthpiece.

The FAX leaped forward. It raced down the runway at breakneck speed. One moment it was racing along the tarmac, the next it was airborne.

Upward it streaked, a soaring eagle, its shape strange and ungainly.

Masashi could not tear his gaze away from the jet fighter. "When?" he asked breathlessly.

"The pilot will activate the device in fifteen seconds," Nobuo answered. "As soon as the plane has enough height to be picked up by radar." He eyed the screen, saw the blip come up right on schedule. "There she is." He found that despite his profound fears, the excitement of anticipation ran through him. The FAX was his creation, after all.

". . . four, three, two, one," he said, following the flight path of the FAX on the radar screen.

And in that instant, the plane disappeared from the screen.

"Buddha!" Masashi breathed.

The two men stared into the CRT screen, which was free of blips. The cloaking device works, Nobuo thought. No radar can pick up the FAX. But the plane is there. Now Masashi will use it to drop his nuclear payload on China, and there isn't a thing anyone can do about it until it's too late.

When the explosion came, Eliane was taking a look at Michael's battered nose. It had begun to bleed again during the fight with Ude.

"Michael!" Eliane was saying. "You've had enough. You're no match for—"

Then the ignited Primacord blew open the access panel to the aft luggage bay. White noise, white heat, white smoke, permeated the cabin of the DC-10 at almost the same time.

"What—!" Michael said. His body ached, and his head was spinning. It was taking a great deal of concentration to keep the pain from overwhelming him.

"Ude!" Eliane cried.

Heard the gunshots, saw two of the uniformed crew go down. Eliane turned to the captain, who was emerging from the flight deck with the emergency first-aid kit that she requested he bring for Michael's wounds. "Start up the engines!" she said.

The captain stared at her, dumbfounded. "What was that—"

"Get back into the cockpit and get us rolling!" Eliane ordered.

"But we're low on fuel," the captain protested.

"Is there enough to get us off the ground and circling?"

"Yes, but with the luggage-bay doors open—"

"Then keep us low," she said. "Just do it! Now!" Shoving Michael down, moving quickly away from him.

The captain ducked back, sat down and began flipping switches. The heavy whine of the jets starting.

Michael crouched painfully behind a seat back. He could not see Eliane. The DC-10 began to move. Ude's head popped up. The pistol's muzzle was like a black gaping maw as he leveled it at Michael.

Dived sideways even as he saw the bright flash. The bullet *spannnged!* off the metal frame of the seat top behind which Michael was crouched.

The jet was beginning to taxi now. Fleetingly, Michael wondered how the captain was explaining to the tower about their unscheduled movement. The huge DC-10 in from the mainland was not far away, and the interisland traffic was pretty much constant.

Another shot from Ude, and Michael ducked behind another seat. Again he lurched into the aisle. Again shots ricocheted through the cabin. But Michael was halfway down the cabin, and as he moved again, he heard the click of gun's hammer striking an empty chamber. No shot! Ude's gun was empty.

Michael, already sprinting, closing the gap between them, heard Eliane's warning too late. He saw Ude's hand suddenly filled with the glint of sharp metal. The arm was cocked, the *shaken*, the steel throwing star, already being released.

Desperately, Michael tried to check his forward momentum. He managed to hurl himself out of the way of the whirring *shaken*, but in the process, he slammed into the corner of the bulkhead.

He must have blacked out for a moment, because he was abruptly aware of Ude dragging him down into the rent the explosion had made in the cabin floor.

He summoned up what reserves of energy he possessed. Then the DC-10 lurched left and he was pulled all the way through, down into the aft baggage hold.

He cried out as he hit the edge of a crate. There was little light here. But enough came from the open door out onto the blurred tarmac, speeding by, that he could see Ude crouched down. He was wielding a length of metal chain with a pair of wooden handles.

Michael could see that Ude's lips were pulled back in a combination of smile and reaction to shock and pain. "Now we will see," Ude said, "who is the *sensei*." As he spoke, he whirled the chain in front of him.

Ude, grinning fiercely, held up the dark-red braided cord. "Can't you get up? Here it is, come and get what your father left behind! It will do you little good after I kill you!"

Michael had no strength left. He prepared himself to die.

Then Ude turned away; his expression had changed entirely. Eliane stood before him. She had dropped down through the rent in the floor, and now she confronted the big man.

"You," Ude said. "Well, I don't mind at all. I'll kill you first, then finish off what I started."

Eliane did not respond. She did not speak; she did not move. It was as if she were made of stone. But her mind was alive. It was concentrated on *iro*. Normally, *iro* meant color, but in the martial arts it referred to the intention of the opponent: the color of his mind. Now, as Eliane concentrated, she divined that Ude's intention was for the one killing blow. And knowing that this was Ude's *iro*, she followed it.

All the way to the end.

Ude, intent on strangling Eliane, dropped the braided cord at his feet. It was a gesture of disdain for his opponent. And a distraction. He rushed in, bringing the chain in low and straight on. Eliane did nothing. She had not assumed the attack pose, had not raised her fists. As a result, Ude was already exulting in his victory, already picturing Eliane writhing at his feet, the chain cutting off her breath.

Whirling at the last instant, Eliane slapped at the chain so that its center dipped down, touching the floor. At that instant, she tramped down on it. The chain snapped out of Ude's hands. Eliane took one step forward and began her own killing blow.

The DC-10 was at the limit of its ground space. The forces at play in the jet fluctuated, and the two antagonists lost their balance.

Eliane hit her head on the corner of a crate. Ude recovered, grabbed Eliane by her blouse, whirled her over onto her back, shoved her forward.

Now Eliane's head and shoulders were out of the open

hatch. The DC-10 was lifting off the ground. Half dazed, Eliane felt herself being maneuvered out of the jet. It was a long, lethal way down.

Only her hips and legs were still within the luggage bay. The wind, whipping at her cruelly as the jet picked up speed, made both breathing and seeing extremely difficult. She kicked out, connected with Ude's knee.

Ude turned, picked up the length of chain. With a cry of hatred, he whipped it around Eliane's neck. But at the same time, Eliane was using her hands in the helix, an *atemi*, a percussive strike. Ude, intent in his bloodlust, did not see it coming until it was too late.

His own momentum combined with Eliane's desperate blow. The edge of her hand caught him lengthwise just over his heart. He heard a rib crack, then he was engulfed in a sea of pain.

Immediately, Eliane twisted the chain, wrenching free his grip. She kicked out and, with a cry of total surprise, Ude was catapulted out of the hatch.

Falling like a spent cinder onto the tarmac of the runway.

Because of Colonel Silvers's death—because of the violent nature of that death—General Hadley became directly involved with Central Intelligence Group affairs in the Far East. MacArthur, who made the appointment, saw it as a kind of penance. The CIG was, by and large, Hadley's creation. It was a direct outgrowth of the OSS, the American wartime espionage network that had proved so successful.

But times had changed. It had been President Truman's opinion that such an organization had no place in peacetime. If General Hadley, whom the president held in the highest esteem, had not argued long and vociferously for its inception, it would never have come into existence.

Hadley had pointed out that the CIG—understaffed and underbudgeted as it was in the proposal that President Truman was considering—would be the only organization standing between the United States and a wholesale infiltration of Soviet agents into levels of American government, industry and even intelligence agencies such as the FBI.

The chaos of the world war had made it virtually impossible, Hadley had said, to trace the backgrounds of the thousands of repatriated individuals showing up in hospitals and refugee centers. Further, the Soviet NKVD had become adept at creating convincing legends for their agents that would survive the kind of cursory inspection that was the most the American government could currently provide. He was perfectly serious when he told them of a school for deep-cover agents within the Soviet Union that was known as Little Chicago. There, the NKVD provided its elite with an authentic reproduction of an American city, legendary for the verisimilitude it provided its inhabitants.

Though the president was not inclined to believe that there was, as he put it, "a communist agent under every bed in

America," Hadley had been so eloquent and had presented so much documentation, that Truman had given him the go-ahead to put the CIG together.

It was only right then that, months later, Hadley be the one to clean up the mess the rotten apple inside the CIG's Tokyo station had caused. This Far East outpost of the espionage organization had gained tremendously in stature since Japan was so close to the Soviet border.

Because Silvers had been so high up in the organization, wholesale changes were effected throughout the CIG. Code books were burned, dead-drop and cutout procedures were altered, agents were recalled from their infiltration assignments for fear that their identities were known to the enemy. But that was only the beginning. Entire networks had to be dismantled. The extent of the damage Silvers had caused was, in Hadley's own words, "inestimable."

For the first several months after Silvers's death, Hadley himself took the CIG's Tokyo station helm. But because there was so much cleaning up to be done, he assigned Jonas to handle the day-to-day running of the office, on a temporary basis.

Jonas, with David Turner's steadying assistance, got the organization back on its feet and running so efficiently that Hadley made the appointment permanent. Along with it came a promotion for Jonas to lieutenant colonel.

For his part, David Turner volunteered to continue his irregularly scheduled meetings with Silvers's contact within the *Jiban*. He reasoned that it could only be to their advantage to continue getting intelligence from the *Jiban*. But now, he worked with the knowledge that the cabal of Japanese ministers was providing legends—fictitious backgrounds—on its enemies and passing these individuals off as war criminals beyond the jurisdiction of the war-crimes tribunal.

Jonas and General Hadley pointed out that this was impossible. It was their theory that the *Jiban* had had Silvers murdered because Silvers had got wind that Philip was onto him. He had communicated that fear to the *Jiban*, trusting that they would find a way to extricate him from his predicament. Instead, they killed him.

That being so, the *Jiban* must be aware that the subsequent sweep-out at the CIG was because its infiltration had been blown.

"What if we leaked intelligence that this sweep-out was

caused by another factor," David Turner posed. "A factor totally unrelated to the *Jiban*."

"We have had some serious setbacks recently in a couple of northern networks," Jonas said. He turned to Hadley. "Sir, what do you think? It would be a positive if we could keep the *Jiban* on the line. The more information we can amass on them, the closer we'll come to discovering their identities."

Hadley turned to Philip. "What do you think, son? You're our resident expert on the Japanese way of thinking."

"Jonas is right," Philip said. "The more names we can compile from the *Jiban*'s intelligence, the better chance we have of working backward to discover the makeup of the *Jiban*." Through Wataro Taki, Philip knew the names of some of the *Jiban*. But he was unable—or unwilling—to explain to these men how he had come into possession of those names. "Don't forget that each name the *Jiban* gives us is another enemy of theirs. Through our contacts in Japanese politics, it will be possible to at least narrow the range of ministers who must belong to this secret society."

"Then it's worth the risk," Hadley said. "I can get out some convincing scuttlebutt as to why we're cleaning house here. With their connections, the *Jiban* is sure to pick it up. There's a chance, though, that they won't believe it. Then it'll be Turner here who'll be in jeopardy. His next meeting with the *Jiban*'s contact would surely be his last."

"I'll take that chance, General," Turner said. "Besides, it's in the *Jiban*'s interest to believe the story. They still have enemies they want disposed of."

"That's another thing," Hadley said. "We've got to make the *Jiban* believe we're continuing to terminate the men named in their intelligence."

"Without actually doing it," Philip added.

"Why don't we put these ministers up at our safe house?" Turner suggested. "We've got all the comforts of home, and it'll keep them out of circulation while we disseminate the stories of their 'deaths.' "

"Good idea," Jonas said.

"We're agreed, then?" Hadley looked around the room. They all nodded. "Good. But there can be no foul-ups," he warned them. "We're already on shaky ground with the president. He doesn't want to hear any negative publicity at all."

So it was agreed to allow Turner to continue his rdv's with

the *Jiban* in the hope of eventually amassing enough evidence to incriminate all its members.

"What is it?" Michiko put a hand on his shoulder. "You haven't said a word in hours."

Philip stared at the paper on which he had been doodling. Pencil lines ran around and around in endless circles. Mirroring his thoughts on Silvers's murder. He could not get over the feeling that he was missing something vital. Though it was clear that General Hadley, Jonas and David Turner felt the matter was best left undisturbed, Philip could not let it go.

Who had killed Colonel Harold Morten Silvers? Hadley said that the door was unlocked but closed when he arrived. That was at eleven P.M. Silvers was already dead. But if the door was unlocked, that meant Silvers had to have known his killer, because he had let him in. The colonel would never have opened the door to a stranger at that time of night.

The others suspected that Silvers's contact in the *Jiban* had been responsible for his murder. But that simply did not wash. Philip was certain that no Japanese had used the *katana* to chop up Silvers. It seemed, then, that someone wanted to implicate the *Jiban* in Silvers's murder. Who?

What had happened because of Silvers's death? Philip asked himself. General Hadley had taken over CIG Tokyo station command, at least temporarily. Jonas had been promoted. Turner was still in place. Did any of those changes make a difference? Hadley had been brought directly into the CIG's Far East field. Turner's position was status quo. Jonas, of course, had been elevated faster than anyone would reasonably have predicted before Silvers's death. But the suggestion that Jonas had murdered their CO in order to move up in rank was preposterous.

What, then, am I missing? Philip wondered for the thousandth time. He looked up now into Michiko's concerned face and smiled thinly. "Did you ever feel as if you had an itch you couldn't scratch? I'm sitting here with a bunch of facts concerning Colonel Silvers's murder and I can't seem to make any sense of them."

"You've been at that stone wall for months now," Michiko said. "My father will be returning from Kyushu in a week, and we still have much to do to prepare the way for him."

"I can't get this out of my head," Philip said, staring at the circles he had drawn. They were beginning to make him dizzy.

"What you need," she said, "is to get out of the house." She threw him his overcoat, put on hers.

"Where are we going?"

"Into the country," she smiled at him. "You'll see soon enough."

As they set out, she said, "Hold on," taking the car through a series of evasive maneuvers. It was not something either of them had to be reminded of; it was something they each did automatically.

She took him north, into the foothills of the Japanese alps, which were strung like a spiked belt across the island. It was still cold here, the roads were icy, and here and there, patches of glossy snow lay like wafers along the yellow-brown ground.

As they rose in elevation, the snow became more plentiful, until it lay in connecting swaths around a countryside reluctant to thaw. Open fields, white and reflective in the low afternoon sun, gave way to stands of pines and cedars. Men and women at work beside the road bent to their tasks, oblivious to the cars speeding by.

At length, Michiko turned right onto a dirt path. There had been no sign, but an ancient bamboo-and-wood gate stood open at the entrance to the highway. They rumbled down this track, bumping against ruts, stones and patches of slick ice. Finally, Michiko brought them to a stop.

Out from the dense shadows of the cryptomeria they went. Across the snow field. The sky was white in their eyes, where the sun hung, trying vainly to warm the land. Their breath clouded the air, their shoes crunched and cracked the thin layer of ice that had formed over the snow. There was a hush through the field that Philip found quite extraordinary. It was as if the purple mountains etched in the distance had gathered up all sound, flinging it far away.

They came to a rock shrine. Piles of small stones stood in front of it. Michiko left him and, going toward the shrine, went down on her knees. She took a *joss* stick out of her pocket. Planting it beside one of the piles of stones, she lit it. A thin trail of the incense wafted upward, but the wind took it away from Philip so that he smelled only the country air.

"What is this place?" he asked.

"It is the shrine of Megami Kitsune, the fox-goddess." Michiko was still kneeling. She seemed to be whispering a prayer.

"Who is she?"

288

Michiko raised her arms. "Megami Kitsune is very powerful. She commands all that you see here."

Philip felt a little thrill go through him. Wasn't he the stalker of the red fox? Hadn't he killed a red fox when he was a boy in Pennsylvania? Hadn't it been the red fox that, in fact, had brought him to this very spot? He shook himself like a dog that wishes to rid itself of the cold.

"You mean that she is the goddess of the fields?" he asked.

Michiko rose. Her prayers were done. She came back to him. Her face seemed inordinately pale, as if it were a mirror reflecting the whiteness of the snow all around them.

"You do not understand." She linked her arm with his. "Megami Kitsune controls the actions of men and women; of lovers."

"Like us?"

Michiko lifted her head up to him, kissed him very hard on the lips. He could feel her mouth trembling a little under his, and he reached out to hold her close.

A line of geese, black against the white of the smoky sky, made its way toward the snow field. They appeared to have come from the shadows of the mountain range in the near distance. In a moment, Philip could hear their honking cries.

"One summer a very long time ago," Michiko said softly, "in a small village not far from here, there lived a girl. She was the only child of a stonecutter, whose wife had died in childbirth. She was willful and headstrong. This was not surprising, for the stonecutter treated her as the sole light of his life. Though he often wished to discipline her for her frequent bad behavior, he could not. There was already enough sadness in their lives, he would think, and he would let her have her way.

"One day, an old, blind man arrived at the village. The man was sick with a fever and could not walk. Instead, he was carried on the back of a young, handsome man.

"It happened that the stonecutter was just returning home when the old man on the boy's back came up the street. Being a kind-hearted man, the stonecutter offered his house for the pair to stay for as long as the old man needed to recover his strength.

"The boy thanked the stonecutter profusely. When he brought the old man inside the house, the girl took one look at the boy and fell madly in love with him. Thereafter, though her father sent her to fetch the village physician, though the physician gave her specific instructions on how she must care for the old man, the girl only had eyes for the boy. By day she followed his every move with her mind as well as with her eyes. By night her dreams were filled with his virile presence.

"The stonecutter went to his neighbor and friend the woodcutter and arranged for the boy to work in the village, because he and the old man had no money and the boy was adamant about paying the stonecutter and the physician for the services they had provided. It was true that the girl did many of the things that the physician instructed her to perform on the old, blind man. But it was just as true that she spent hours leaning out of her window to watch the strong back of the boy as, stripped to the waist, he worked at chopping wood for the village's houses.

"This particular summer was the hottest anyone in that village could remember. And perhaps the stifling heat contributed to the old man's eventual death. On the other hand, the girl was certainly not blameless. She neglected to feed the old man some of the potions the physician had prescribed for him. She failed to wipe him down with a cool cloth at regular intervals.

"And yet, even at the funeral, over which the boy and her father presided, along with the village priest, the girl could think of only one thing: the boy. She watched the back of his head when he was turned away from her, the bold silhouette of his face when the priest instructed him in some of the rites.

"The next day, the woodcutter took the boy into the forest. Neither of them returned. A rising storm from the southeast deterred a search party from venturing out into the night. But it did not prevent the girl from hanging out the window. When news that the two were missing flew through the village, her heart had turned to stone. But she thought only of the boy, not the woodcutter, whom she had known from birth, who had brought her presents on each of her birthdays, who had sworn to care for her if ever her own father should meet with an untimely end.

"Long after her father had gone to sleep, the girl, drenched to the bone by the wind-driven rain, still hung from her window in hopes of spotting the boy. She had set a lantern in her room where she was certain it could be seen through her open window.

"In the hour of the rat—sometime between midnight and two in the morning—she started. She had heard a voice.

290

Perhaps it had only been the wind? But no! Now she heard it again. It was the boy's voice, calling to her!

"Without another thought, she raced from the house. The storm beat at her, but she did not care. She heard the boy's voice and she followed it, through the streets of the town and out into the countryside.

"The storm was at its height. The wind howled, the rain poured down in torrents. The ground was a slick morass. More than once, the girl slipped and fell face down in the mud. Always, she picked herself up and, hearing the calling again, pushed on. Deeper and deeper into the woods she flew, until she no longer knew where she was. She no longer cared. The thought of life without the boy was impossible for her to bear.

"At last, the forest gave way to a clearing. She saw a shadowy figure there and, joyously, she shouted the boy's name.

"The figure turned. It was, indeed, the boy. She ran into the clearing and threw her arms around him.

"And then, with a howl of anguish and disbelief, she lurched backward. Only to peer into the boy's face. It was true, she saw, though she pinched herself to make sure that she was not dreaming. The boy's face was as white as a sheet of ice, and as glossy and cold. In fact, as she reached out, her fingers trembling, she discovered that it *was* a sheet of ice.

"As impossible as it seemed, the boy was frozen solid.

"The girl's heart broke. She called out the boy's name one last, desperate time, then she threw herself upon him, clawing at the ice with such ferocity that she tipped him over.

"The two of them crashed to the forest floor, and to her astonishment, the ice shattered, showering her with chill fragments. On her hands and knees, the sobbing girl fought her way through the ice shards in search of the boy. But there was nothing. And soon, the wind-driven rain had melted all the ice away.

"In time, she staggered to her feet. She felt frozen herself. Her heart was encased in ice. She moved with a shambling, uncoordinated gait to the edge of the clearing. There, she threw her arms around the trunk of a tree to steady herself.

"She turned to take one last look at the place where her would-be lover had broken apart. She gasped.

"For on that very spot a kind of gray smoke was coalescing. And as the girl watched, it turned from transparent to translucent to solid. In solid form, it had a shape. And the girl recognized the comely form, the high cheekbones, the long eyes, the flowing hair, stippled by a light that seemed to emanate from all around her.

"A profound fear took possession of her and shook her like the grip of a wild animal. But her utter desperation momentarily overcame her terror. 'The boy!' she called out. 'What have you done with him!'

"The figure turned, and a grin so horrifying emanated from it that the girl cried out and was forced to throw an arm across her eyes. 'The boy,' a voice like a knife cut came to her. 'There is no boy. There never was a boy. Nor an old, blind man.'

"Now the girl could see that the figure was frosted in snow. On her shoulders, her arms and legs glistened a pure snow of a white so luminescent and brilliant that for an instant the girl was blinded.

" 'There was only me, who knows only eternal sadness and despair. I am come to lead you to that which is your reward.'

"Then the painful light was gone. The girl blinked her eyes. The glade was deserted. She returned home, but no one recognized her, not even her father, whom she discovered weeping for his daughter lost in the storm.

"It was not until she looked in a mirror that, horrified, she at last understood. Her white face was filled with the lines and sags only time can produce. In the space of a heartbeat, she had gone from being a girl in the ripeness of youth to an old woman.

"She left the village the next morning, for she could no longer tolerate the presence of anyone she had known and who now did not know her. In time, she came to a mountain pass much traveled by those journeying from Tokyo to Kyoto. There, she settled in a long deserted *anjitsu*, a simple building used by itinerant priests. And there she spent the remainder of her days, dispensing food, aid and comfort to weary travelers using the mountain road.

"But always remaining in her memory was the presence of that ghastly snow-clad figure in the forest glade on that storm-swept night: Megami Kitsune, the fox-goddess."

The geese had landed on the snow-covered field. Their honking filled the air with a melancholy sound. Their waddling gait seemed ungainly and comical compared to their grace in flight.

Philip, with his arm around Michiko said, "Is it this fox-goddess you are afraid of?"

She looked at him with sad eyes and mutely nodded her

head. They walked away from the shrine. The last of her *joss* stick had burned. The geese had quietened, and now only an occasional gust of wind, soughing through nearby branches, brought sound to their ears. A rabbit, frightened by their presence, bolted ahead, its white tail bobbing as it bounded away.

"What I am afraid of—" Michiko stopped, turned her head away as if gathering her courage. "I am afraid that I am like the young girl. I am selfish. I want you. Yet you are married, just as I am married. Sometimes I lie awake at night cold with the dread of my transgression."

"It's mine as well," he pointed out.

She gave him a bleak smile, but she did not respond when he hugged her to him.

As Michiko said, there had been much to do while her father, Wataro Taki, was tending the orange groves in Kyushu. He had already prepared for them files of intelligence on the three most powerful Yakuza families in Tokyo. But this was all background, and useful as it was, he had left it up to Philip and Michiko to ferret out the current activities, inclinations and long-range goals of these three families—or, as they were known in Yakuza society, -gumi.

One of the three families was known as the Taki-gumi, so it was clear to Philip that Wataro wished to take over the operations of this clan. As he had explained to Philip, the overriding power of the *Jiban* in both business and bureaucratic circles had forced Wataro into the only avenue of power he saw open to him: the underworld of the Yakuza. Here, outside the confines of the rigid Japanese caste society, Wataro saw his opportunity to build a power base within Japan.

As the *oyabun*, the boss, of the Taki-gumi, doors into business, the bureaucracy, even the government, would be open to him in the decades to come. For Wataro the visionary understood what few others did: that the Yakuza were still in a stage of infancy. Under his guidance and leadership, he could bring forces to bear against the *Jiban*. The Yakuza, he felt, possessed the enormous potential for good, if taken in the right direction. Already he could see the Communist influence in the worker riots along the docks. If, for instance, he could use the Taki-gumi to help quell these riots, in which dozens of Japanese policemen had been killed, the government would owe him a great debt.

This, too, was part of his strategy. For he also saw the

293

Yakuza as his best base from which to expand into legitimate businesses, the government and, eventually, even the bureaucracy, the *Jiban*'s stronghold. Only then, when he had enough power, would he strike out and defeat the *Jiban*.

But that strategy, he cautioned, would require great patience and discipline. Like the *Jiban*'s scheme, Wataro's plan would need decades to come to fruition. And the first step was to establish his power base by taking over the Taki-gumi. What was less clear was how he meant to handle the remaining two families.

Though there was certainly rivalry among all three, it became increasingly clear that the aftermath of the war and the occupation of the country had in some basic sense united the clans—even if temporarily and a bit shakily. They had begun to close their ranks against what they saw as outside interference: The American Occupation Army had already begun a serious crackdown against Yakuza crime.

Perhaps the intense work of trying to figure out the convolutions of the families' alliances, rivalries and competing territories, both overt and covert, made Philip oblivious to the changes taking place inside his own household. Or perhaps the continuing anxiety he felt over not being able to crack the puzzle of Colonel Silvers's murder caused him to be inordinately distracted. Or again it might have been his mounting obsession with Michiko. When he was with her, Philip felt as if he were sinking deeper and deeper into the continent of Asia, into a mythic realm beyond the pale of mere mortals. He had once read H. Rider Haggard's *She*, and now he was beginning to feel more and more like the hero of that novel, stumbling across a lost civilization ruled by a goddess of extraordinary beauty and power.

In any event, it was not until many years later, when he was on Maui and running from his pursuers, that Philip began to put all the pieces together. Only then did he see the enormity of the puzzle that had haunted him for decades.

As it was, he paid scant attention to Lillian when she told him that she had gotten a job with the American embassy in Tokyo. That David Turner had recommended her. That the ambassador liked her work so much that after six weeks, she had been promoted into his personal staff.

In increasing number, Lillian began reading the books David Turner recommended to her: *The Octopus* by Frank Norris, *U.S.A.* by John Dos Passos, *The Goose-step* and *World's End* by Upton Sinclair. There were also, on occasion, books about

294

the Scottsboro boys and the Haymarket riots. It was a library of philosophical thought heavily weighted toward socialism, but Lillian was too engrossed in the experience of learning to notice.

The world, formerly defined by the iron-bound limits her father had imposed upon it, was opening up to her. Through her dinners with David Turner and through the reading he recommended, she was in a very real sense going back to school. A school run by, to her, the most fascinating professor in the world.

She began to be exposed first to all of the world's economic systems, then to the more complex geopolitical factions. She learned about the history of her own country through its great writers: Norris, Dos Passos and Sinclair. These great minds revealed to her the other side of capitalism—the darker side that General Hadley, her father, had ensured that she would never see.

She read of the French Revolution, the Russian Revolution, as well, and the Spanish Civil War, so that gradually, like the sun rising after a long, arctic night, she became witness to the entire panoply of the imperative of revolution on a worldwide scale.

She became aware of how capitalism exploited the people in her own country—mainly the workers, who were meant to benefit from the system. She saw how a handful of greedy capitalists controlled the lives and fate of tens of millions of people throughout America. She came to understand, at last, how the oppressed were unaware of their terrible oppression—how that knowledge was being systematically kept from them by the same handful of greedy capitalists—just as this knowledge had been kept from her by her father!

And in the end, she could agree with—and sympathize with the cause of—the cadre of right-thinking intellectuals (the moral vanguard, as David Turner referred to them) whose responsibility it was to bring about a revolution to free the masses from this invisible—and insidious—enslavement.

Though Philip was slow to pick up on the changes being wrought in her, realization finally did come.

The argument began mundanely enough. He had come in typically late and, instead of finding Lillian in bed asleep, he saw the light on in their bedroom. Lillian was sitting up in bed, reading a magazine. Turner strictly forbade her to bring home the books he gave her. His explanation—and a perfectly reasonable one it seemed, too—was that he did not want

Philip to question Lillian on who she was seeing and why. "After all," Turner said with a grin, "your husband might think that we're having an affair."

"Where have you been?" she asked, closing the magazine.

He was prepared for this. In fact, he was surprised it had taken her so long to broach the subject. "Working."

"Hardly," Lillian said, staring at him. "I called Jonas."

He was not ready for this. It should have been very simple. Lillian was a simple woman. "You've been checking up on me? Why?"

"Because it seems that you *need* checking up on." She folded her arms across her breasts. "I want to know where you go and what you do so that you're never home."

"Since you're suddenly so chummy with Jonas," Philip said, beginning to undress, "get my itinerary from him."

"Spoken just like my father." Was there an odd note of triumph in her voice? "He was always adept at keeping the real world at arm's distance from me. I was like a prize horse to him, one that he had to put blinders on whenever he took it outside."

Philip looked at her. Was this truly the same woman he had married just over a year ago? he asked himself. What's happened? "I'm not your father," he said, hanging up his jacket and taking off his tie.

"I said you were *like* my father."

"Is this a debate?" He did not think she even knew what a debate was.

"If you want it to be," she said.

Which should have been the first tip-off. This kind of semantic wordplay was far too sophisticated for the woman he had married. The only area in which Lillian had formerly been sophisticated was fashion. In other respects, she had been more like a country girl, simple and straightforward in her personality. At least this was how Philip had seen her. It was part of what had attracted him to her. But now that he was emotionally estranged from her, it was hardly surprising that he should be slow in discerning the changes being wrought in her.

"I don't want it to be anything," he said. He came and sat beside her on the bed, took her hand in his. "Lillian, I've been working very hard these last few months. Silvers's death put us all on edge."

"This has nothing to do with Silvers's death," she said. She searched his face with the intensity of an archaeologist digging

296

for signs of life. "What's happened to you, Phil?" she asked. "It's like we're no longer husband and wife. We never go out. We never make love anymore."

"I know," he said, stroking the back of her hand. "I leave you alone too much."

"It's not that," she said in a peculiar tone of voice. "After all, I have my job at the embassy, and I'm given more responsibility every day. I handle the trafficking of all the sensitive dispatches now, including my father's. And when you're not home for dinner, I fend for myself."

Now Philip recognized the peculiar intonation. Where was that little girl of softness and light he had fallen in love with? Sometime when he hadn't been looking, she had been replaced by a hard, self-sufficient edge. Was that confidence he heard in her voice now? Impossible. That would mean that she had changed more radically than he could imagine.

"What does that mean, fend for yourself?"

"Is that a trick the CIG taught you?" she said. "To turn the questioner's questions around? I asked *you* where you'd been."

"Who are you seeing, Lil?" he asked quietly. "Is it Jonas?"

"You're being idiotic."

But whatever else she had picked up, she had not yet learned to be a competent liar.

"I want the truth," he said, wondering why it was so important. He was having an affair, why shouldn't she? But he knew why. Somehow, he could not consider his relationship with Michiko an affair. It was far from a fling by a discontented husband. What, then, he asked himself, was it? He had no clear answer.

"The truth," Lillian said. "You want the truth? Why? I don't think you'd recognize the truth if you heard it. You're too enmeshed in your secrets, Phil. They've taken you over completely."

"You're exaggerating."

"Am I? Just look at yourself," she said. "You talk to me without saying anything at all. You won't answer my questions—"

"Your prying, you mean."

"You won't answer my question," she persisted. "You won't account for your time, even though much of where you go is not, apparently, related to your work. What am I to think? What would *you* think if the situation were reversed?"

"Do you want to know what the real trouble is, Lil?" Philip

said. "It's that you want me to be someone I'm obviously not."

"It's convenient to lay this all at my feet," she said. "Does that assuage your conscience any? Well, forget it. I won't allow that. You're half of this marriage; the fault is at least half yours."

"The fault for what?"

Lillian closed her eyes. "I love you, Phil," she whispered in a bleak voice. "God help me, but it's the truth." Her eyes snapped open. "If you're cheating on me, I don't think I could forgive you. But I couldn't leave you, either. You're still the man I want, the man I need."

"Maybe you need too much of me," he said. "There's a part of me you'll never understand."

"Is that because I can't?" she said. "Or because you won't let me?"

He said nothing. The truth was that he was afraid to reply.

Lillian shook her head sadly. "That's what's wrong between us, Philip. Don't you see? There's not enough understanding between us. We don't try to know each other. And because we won't try, we'll never know what we're capable of together."

"That isn't altogether true," he protested.

"Of course it is." There it was again, that curious note of confidence. "You'd much prefer to remain unknowable. It appeals to your sense of secrecy. You and Jonas huddle together, plotting your schemes. It seems to me that the two of you *enjoy* hatching those secrets and keeping them between you."

"That's business. I think you're taking this far too personally, Lil."

"No, I'm not," she insisted. "You don't think of it as your business. You *love* it, and I find myself competing with it for your time. But competing with what? The shadows. And I know that given a choice between the shadows and the light, Philip, you'll always choose the shadows."

"Then why can't you accept that?"

"Because it's wrong," she said. "That's no way to live your life. You're like the parts of capitalism—the brutal, power-hungry, war-hungry aspects—we're not meant to look at too closely, that others want to keep hidden."

"What others?"

Lillian shrugged. "People like my father."

He stood up. "That must mean me as well," he said, angry

298

despite himself. "Since you say that I'm like your father."

"How I wish you weren't," she said.

"I'm not, Lil," he said. "I wish I could get you to believe that."

"But don't you see how much alike you two really are? You both crave secrets. You thrive on them. I don't think you'd be able to survive without them. And living in a world built of secrets leaves me out."

"It doesn't."

"By definition, Phil, it does." Her words were measured, controlled. "The first question I asked you when you came in is where you had been."

"Lil—"

She lifted her hand. "It's all right. I didn't expect an answer. I had hoped that you would want to tell me. That you would want to make everything all right between us." She paused, and in the silence he heard her urging him to prove her wrong. In time, she nodded. "But I didn't really expect anything at all."

Philip was preparing the way for Wataro Taki's return from Kyushu. The difficulty lay in the fact that the official American occupation policy of trying to break up the Yakuza had caused the three Yakuza families to form alliances among them. This was not the norm for them.

An enemy with alliances was far more dangerous than an enemy standing alone.

Accordingly, Philip and Michiko had worked on a scheme to break apart the alliance by pitting the three families against one another. Though this would entail considerable loss of life among the three families, it would be a relatively simple thing subsequently, then, to take over the Taki-gumi with a minimum of additional bloodshed.

They presented their complex plan to Wataro Taki upon his return from Kyushu. He was looking fit and strong, but his features were so different that Philip was not certain it was the same man until Wataro Taki spoke.

"Good morning, Doss-san."

Philip continued to scrutinize this man. Had he once been Zen Godo? "What's happened to you?" he asked.

Wataro Taki laughed. "It is good that you did not recognize me. Michiko did not know me either when she met me last night. I warned her not to say anything to you so I could get your honest reaction." His smile faded. "Frankly, I was concerned about my face in my new life. So I did more than pick oranges while I was away. I had myself reborn." He put his fingertips up to his cheekbones. "The doctors cracked the bones to reshape them, cut away flesh here and there, moved pockets of fatty tissue."

His face was coppery, burned by the sun and wind he had encountered during his long hours in the orange groves in the south, so that one had to come very close to him to see the network of tiny scars that were still healing.

"Within a month," he told them, "all trace of the scars will be gone."

But just as impressive as the alteration of his face were the changes in his body. He seemed longer, broader, certainly more muscular. He seemed, in short, in every way a younger, larger person than the man named Zen Godo, who had departed some eight months previous.

"I am concerned, too, about Michiko. She is, still, after all, Zen Godo's daughter, even though she is a Yamamoto by marriage. Therefore, I will hire her. And after I have become *oyabun* of the Taki-gumi, I will adopt her as one of the Taki family. If anyone asks about my close involvement with her, well, she is married to Nobuo Yamamoto, *neh*? A very powerful businessman who can extend my clan's power base into legitimate business."

Wataro Taki listened carefully to their proposal as they sat drinking tea in the new house they had bought for him. Michiko had spent upward of two months laundering the proceeds from the sale of the Godo family house, so that when she bought this one, no one could trace the origins of the money she paid.

In the end, he rejected their scheme. "Too much blood must be spilled," he said gravely. "Not that I harbor any softness in my heart for these bandits who are bleeding their brothers. But it is inefficient to destroy even part of that which one wishes to appropriate.

"I have been thinking long and hard these past several weeks since you sent me your last detailed update on the three families, and I believe that I have found a method of taking over the Taki-gumi without destroying a single life.

"Gen Taki, the current *oyabun*, the boss, of the Taki-gumi has built up a reputation for being a genius in his defensive tactics. It is these well-known—and feared—tactics that keep him as the dominant force in this uneasy triad of Yakuza.

"Now, according to your information, Gen Taki is not the initiator of these strategies as is commonly thought. It is his adviser, Kenji Harigami, who secretly runs the Taki-gumi. Kenji Harigami is Gen Taki's most prized possession. Without him, Gen Taki will turn white with fear, and we will get what we want from him. Therefore, we must find Harigami-san's weak spot."

"I don't think he has one," Philip said. "He is the perfect family man. He is married, has two children. From what we have gathered, his wife is devoted to him."

Wataro Taki grunted. He nodded, and Michiko refilled his cup. "Doss-san," he continued, "you will soon come to realize that family men in Japan—*all* family men—have another life. Sometimes it is secret, sometimes not. But always it is there. We must learn what Kenji Harigami's secret life is."

Philip had come to suspect that they all might have made a terrible mistake. It began with a nightmare that woke him out of a troubled sleep. He was a boy back in Latrobe, Pennsylvania. He carried his father's .22 rifle. It was night, and he was running down his prey. Through fields rimed with frost, into a forest stirring with nocturnal sounds, down into a riverbed turned silver by the light of the full moon. The water burbled, the leaves on the trees rustled. An owl hooted.

He knew that he was gaining on his prey, and he picked up the pace, the rifle at the ready. He forded the shallow stream, feeling the chill biting into his ankles through his boots. He was panting, his breath coming in quick bursts of steam.

Then he had sighted his prey and was stunned to find that it was human, not animal, as he had thought.

Down on one knee, he brought the rifle up to his shoulder and aimed it. Before he had a chance to fire, his prey clawed at his own face. That face came off, and Philip could see another face beneath it. Hauntingly familiar.

Just when he thought he knew whose face it was, it was ripped away and another face appeared. Frightened, Philip squeezed the trigger. The bullet smashed into his prey's face. But, acting unlike a .22 bullet, it shattered the face. Only to reveal another one underneath.

Philip awoke in a sweat. For a moment, he did not know

where he was. Then he turned, saw Lillian lying asleep beside him.

It was then that Philip understood the nature of his dream.

The next morning, he got hold of Ed Porter, the CIG aide who Silvers had assigned to him and Jonas when they had first arrived in Japan.

"I want you to do something for me, Ed," he said.

"Sure." Porter was carrying a sheaf of files from one office to another.

Philip led him into a storage closet, turned on the light. He looked at the sheaf of files Porter was holding. "Got a lot of work?"

"It's crap," Porter said dismissively. "Turner's got me shuttling back and forth as his errand boy. I've got to make sure that all the new ministers that the *Jiban*'s intelligence has accused are put up in our safe house. I've got to make sure that the reports of their 'deaths' are believable and are disseminated to the press. I've got to take care of the grieving families. All so that we can go on gulling the *Jiban* into believing that we're not onto them."

"Not like the old days, huh?"

"Shit, no," Porter said. "Colonel Silvers had me out in the field. I know how to collect intelligence, but since he's gone, nobody here wants to give me a shot."

"That's because of Silvers," Philip said. "Nobody wants to be reminded of the rotten apple."

"And that's another thing," Porter said. "Colonel Silvers was no double."

"He wasn't?" Philip cocked his head. "What makes you say that? The evidence—"

"The evidence was a cock-and-bull story." Porter put down his load, lit a cigarette. "Believe me, Lieutenant, if you gave me half a day, I could make it seem as if you had murdered your mother. I know for a fact that the colonel was legit, because of all the intelligence I passed on to him. I would have known if he was passing my stuff on to the *Jiban* or anybody else. He wasn't. The proper action was always taken on the intelligence I gave him, of that I'm sure."

A shiver of premonition passed through Philip's body, and the fear of his dream of the night before rose up in his mind. "Did you tell this to anybody?" he asked.

"Sure. Turner. He wrote it all down. Said he'd pass it on through channels."

"I see." Why hadn't Porter come to him with this? he wondered. Then he realized that he should have gone to Porter himself. But he had been too ready to accept the evidence. Sure. Why not? It had been spread out for him to find, like a picnic on a table. Angry at himself for being such a fool, he tapped his forefinger against his lips. "Tell me, Porter, how'd you like to get back into the field?"

Porter's eyes lit up. "You wouldn't have to ask twice, Lieutenant. Being Turner's mule is no fun. Besides, I miss it."

"Good," Philip said. "How are you on tails?"

"I could follow Orpheus into hell without him knowing it." Porter grinned. "Besides, I know Tokyo like it was hometown. Every nook and cranny of it." He stubbed out his cigarette. "Just give me the target's name and description, and I'll do the rest."

"All you need is the name," Philip said.

Something in his voice made Porter turn serious. "What do you mean?"

"I mean," Philip said, "that I want you to follow my wife wherever she goes."

It was Philip who found the way into the Taki-gumi. Reading one of the weekly CIG field reports that concerned a U.S. Army raid on a Yakuza gambling syndicate in the northern suburbs of Tokyo, he came across a familiar name: Kenji Harigami, the Taki-gumi's chief counselor.

The CIG's interest in the gambling syndicate extended to one of the owners, who was suspected of illegal importation of small arms. Kenji Harigami was one of the gamblers caught in the raid. However, according to the report, he had bought his way out of the mess and had never been arraigned.

Philip pondered this for a time. The information could mean nothing. Many Yakuza were inveterate gamblers. But he did some digging on Kenji Harigami and found that the man frequented a number of independent gambling-syndicate parlors not under Yakuza control. This seemed more significant, and he reported the information to Wataro Taki.

Taki spent two weeks charting Kenji Harigami's movements. Interestingly, Harigami's favorite gambling spot was an out-of-the-way place so small it was bound to elude the growing presence of the Yakuza for some time, perhaps forever.

"He is gambling a great deal of money," Wataro Taki told

303

Philip and Michiko at one of their regular meetings. "And he's losing all of it."

"How much?" Michiko asked.

And when her father told them, Philip said, "Where is he getting that much cash?"

Wataro Taki smiled. "When we discover that, Doss-san," he said, "we will have found the lever that will get us into the Taki-gumi."

Several days later, Ed Porter found Philip in the hallway of CIG headquarters. "Had lunch yet, Lieutenant?"

Philip looked at him. "How about the park?"

The first blush of cherry blossoms filled the air with a kind of aural radiance that was possible only in Japan. Children ran, laughing, below the white-pink clouds.

"What do you have for me, Porter?"

"Nothing you'll want to hear, Lieutenant."

Philip watched a small boy clutching the string of a kite, a blue-white and red carp. "Tell me anyway."

"Well, okay." Porter seemed inordinately nervous. "David Turner's got a thing going with your wife, Lieutenant. Sorry."

So it wasn't Jonas after all, Philip thought. There was a sense of relief in that, but also a good deal of anger. He had discovered, much to his surprise, that Lillian was still a part of his life. He did not want to give her up. "What kind of thing?" he said.

The carp dipped and shivered in the breeze as the boy moved it expertly along, keeping it away from the cherry trees.

"Well, that's the odd part," Porter said. "The part I can't figure out. They're not shacking up or anything."

Philip looked at him for the first time since they had entered the park. "Are you sure?"

"Sure I'm sure. They always meet in a public place. A restaurant, a nightclub. The Officers' Club is one of their favorite places."

"What about afterward?"

"That's the odd part, Lieutenant. Afterward, Turner takes your wife home. Period."

"She never goes to his apartment?" Philip asked.

"No. Or to a hotel, if that's what you're thinking."

"What about my apartment?"

"Jesus, Lieutenant," Porter said, "he never stays. He just escorts her upstairs, then leaves. He's a perfect gentleman."

The breeze was picking up, and the boy was reeling in the kite to keep better control of it through the swirling gusts.

"Is that it?" Philip asked after a time.

"Just about," Porter said. "Oh yeah, I almost forgot. There's one place that Turner goes twice a week like clockwork after he has lunch with your wife. A *furo*, a public hot bath." He shrugged. "But so what? He's not meeting your wife there."

"Where is the *furo*?"

Porter told him. "But it won't do you any good, Lieutenant. You can't go in there, just like I couldn't. Not without Turner spotting you right away. It's mostly a Japanese place, but there are some foreigners who frequent it, too."

"Foreigners?"

"Yeah," Porter said. "You know. Diplomatic types. You'd know better than me. The kind your father-in-law, General Hadley, sometimes entertains."

"When I am with you," Michiko said, "I am whole."

Philip held her tightly.

"When you look at me," she said, "you do not look through me."

Oddly, with his eyes closed, there was a quality she shared with Lillian. The new Lillian. Many years later, he was able to identify it as strength. Which was odd. Lillian was weak in so many ways; she struggled with herself in so many others. Whereas Michiko did not struggle at all. Outwardly.

Then he knew. Buried deep inside Michiko there was a fundamental insecurity about being a woman. Buried deep inside Lillian was the strength of a *samurai*.

"I know," she said, "that when you enter me you are searching for something. Something I want to give you. Something I never knew I possessed—or *could* possess."

She took his rampant member in her hand, drew him toward her. They were sitting facing one another on the *tatami*. Michiko was wearing a salmon-colored kimono that was open down the front. Tender shadows outlined the delicious curves of her flawless body. The fire-red line of her underkimono covered her nipples, her knees, her feet. Her inner thighs, bared and curved, were painted in darkness. He could smell her special scent. Forever after in his mind it would be inextricably linked with the fresh, haylike odor of the reed mats.

"If I talk like this while we make love," she said, "I can come as many times as I wish. Until all I see is you. Until all I feel is you." She began to rub the head of him over her

305

moist lips until his mouth parted and he was panting. The sight made her want to faint. She was delirious with the desire she was causing in him.

He reached out, slid the fire-red underkimono away from her nipples. He bent his head toward them. When his lips encompassed one, she hunched her hips forward, taking half of him inside her.

She felt the explosion of his breath against her sensitive nipple, and she caressed his shaft. He moved forward and her thighs parted fully, until the two of them were against one another.

"This is what you're looking for," she sighed. "This is my anchor." She shuddered and came. She could feel him swelling, pulsing at the very core of her. If it ended now, she knew that she could not bear it.

"As I explore you," she whispered, "I discover myself. I have found a secret continent to travel, and in so doing, I come upon the hidden cities inside myself." Moving, moving, swaying as if they were dancing to a slow, sensual beat. "You watch me and beneath your gaze I become real. Now that I am real, I am different. I am no longer content to play the roles of my life. The Japanese wife, the Japanese mother, the Japanese lover." She gasped, spasmed again, moaning, "Oh, oh, oh," in his ear.

Clinging wetly to him, accelerating the beat of her loins as she felt the irrevocable tension grip him.

"You have shown me that my strength is in my heart. And you have changed that forever. Ah, ah, ah," as she heard his deep-felt groan, felt his heavy spurting deep inside her. "You love it too. Oh yes!" Joining him in ecstatic release.

"I have negotiated to buy the gambling syndicate that Kenji Harigami frequents," Wataro Taki told Philip and Michiko a week later. He laughed to see the look on their faces. "It was quite easy, actually." His eyes gleamed. "The fact is that Kenji Harigami has already accumulated a great deal of debt with the syndicate. He refuses to pay off what he owes. Instead, he continues to gamble with cash. The syndicate, of course, is terrified to cross him in any way, since his wrath would surely bring them into the sphere of the Taki-gumi, who would take them over in a minute." He laughed again. "They were really quite pleased to accept my generous buyout offer. Now we have our chance. We must make the most of it."

Three days later, when Kenji Harigami walked into the gambling den, he found the same smoke-filled room, the same squinty-eyed, sour-smelling lot he was used to. A beautiful woman was setting out the tiles, and a Caucasian man by her side was assisting. He had never seen either of these two before, but he hardly cared. He was here to assuage his unending passion. He was interested in the tiles and nothing else.

Evening passed into night, night into early morning, with the usual results. The heavy wad of cash Kenji Harigami had brought with him was just about used up. Many of the gamblers had already left. Only the die-hards were still at it.

It was impossible for Kenji Harigami to see the tiles being played and not to take part. He placed the last of his money on the table. The tiles came down, he lost.

It was the last pass. The remaining gamblers rose and, one by one, left the room. Kenji Harigami did not want to leave, but it was late and the tiles were being packed up.

Kenji rose, stretched and turned to leave. All at once the Caucasian man was at his side. "The owner would like to see you," the man said in idiomatic Japanese.

Kenji hid his surprise as best he could. A look of disdain filled his face. These small fish are all alike, he thought. They think they own the world. "If it's about my debts, I've already told the owners," he said brusquely. "My credit is good."

"This is a new owner," the Caucasian man said. "You'll have to tell him yourself."

"Do you know who—" Kenji broke off, feeling the pain. "What are you doing?" he cried, trying to struggle free of the hold the Caucasian man had on him.

"Come along with me," the man said in Kenji's ear.

"You would be wise to do as he asks," a female voice said.

Kenji turned his head. The woman who was putting away the tiles now brandished a *katana*. "Who are you?" he said, looking from one to the other.

"The new owners," the woman said.

Philip and Michiko took Kenji through the back of the building, into a tiny, claustrophobic office. Behind the tiny desk, wedged into a corner, sat Wataro Taki. He was dressed in a Western business suit.

"Good evening, Harigami-san," Wataro Taki said. "I am pleased that you so graciously accepted my humble invitation." His hands moved across the desktop. "Tea?"

"What is this all about?" Kenji said angrily.

Wataro Taki spread out a wad of chits. "It is concerning these, Harigami-san," he said. "Your debts. I am afraid that the sum is such that I must ask you to pay the full amount, plus twenty-five percent interest, immediately. That comes to, let's see—" He presented a figure.

Kenji laughed. "Ridiculous!" he said. "I don't have that kind of money on me. I lost everything tonight."

"Nevertheless," Wataro Taki said, "I must insist on immediate compensation."

Kenji leaned forward so that his fists were on the desk. He grinned fiercely. "You are either naïve or a fool. I am chief counselor to the Taki-gumi. Yakuza." It was clear from his tone that he was used to invoking the name to inspire fear in those he wished to do his bidding. "Right now my clan takes no notice of your flyspeck of a place. But one word from me and the full might of their fury will come down on you. They will level this stinking place, and you with it." He stood up, his threat complete. "I would be careful, if I were you, about whom you push around."

"Sit down, Harigami-san," Wataro Taki said evenly.

"I've said what will happen to you if you—"

"I said sit down, sir."

Philip kicked Kenji's legs out from under him, and he went down hard. The space was so small, he hit his forehead on the corner of the desk. Philip pulled him off the floor, shoved him onto the one chair the office could accommodate.

"Now," Wataro Taki said, "let me tell you where you stand. I am not afraid of Yakuza. I am not afraid of the Taki-gumi. Most of all, Harigami, I am not afraid of you.

"As I see it, you are in a bind. You owe me a great deal of money. I want that money now—or I want some form of compensation," Wataro Taki said. "That raises several possibilities. I could take your life, for example. A great number of my regular customers know how much you owe me. If I let you get away with that, they will all want the same treatment. I cannot allow that. So your death would be of some good use to me."

"You're insane!" Kenji said. But the sweat breaking out along his hair line attested to his fear.

Wataro Taki ignored him. "I want my money, Harigami, and I want it now."

"But I've told you I don't have it. You can't get water out of a dry sponge."

"Then suggest an adequate compensation."

"Like what?"

"Tell me what your *oyabun*'s weaknesses are."

Kenji's eyes fairly bugged out of his head. "Now I know you're crazy. I'd be a dead man in a matter of hours."

"I will protect you," Wataro Taki said softly.

Kenji laughed. "Against Gen Taki? It's an impossibility. Those who have tried are all with their ancestors."

Wataro Taki shrugged. "Then you leave me no choice. If you do not have the money to repay me and you are unwilling to provide the compensation I seek, I will kill you." He nodded toward Michiko, who brought her longsword up over Kenji's head.

Kenji's neck twisted so quickly they all heard it crack. "You're all crazy!" he said, his eyes open wide.

"I assure you," Wataro Taki said, "I mean what I say."

Kenji wiped his forehead with a handkerchief. "I see that," he said. His hand was trembling. "Just give me a moment. I need to think."

Wataro Taki nodded, and Michiko lowered her *katana*.

"All right," Kenji said. "I can get you your money. All of it, including the usurious interest. But I need two days."

"Twelve hours is all you will get," Wataro Taki said.

"One day, then."

"Twelve hours, Harigami, and that is all."

Kenji nodded, admitting defeat. "You'll get your money." He rose to leave.

Wataro Taki waited the requisite time. He wanted the man to believe that he had fooled them. Wataro Taki suspected that Kenji had no intention of getting the money. The moment he left this building, he would go to Gen Taki and carry out his threat to destroy the gambling-syndicate building and its new owners.

"One moment," Wataro Taki said. "It occurs to me that I might be naïve to allow you to leave here on the strength of your word. Not that I believe for an instant that you are not an honorable man, Harigami-san. But after all, I do not know you at all."

"I assure you," Kenji said, "that you will have your money inside of twelve hours."

Wataro Taki was smiling. "Oh, I have no doubts on that score," he said. Moments before, Philip had slipped out. Now he returned with someone. "That is because I have taken the proper precautions."

Kenji whirled. "Hana!"

"Yes," Wataro Taki confirmed. "It is your daughter, Hana. She will stay with us until you return."

"You bastard!" Kenji was shaking with rage.

"Just prudent," Wataro Taki said. "I knew that you would try to destroy us the moment you left here." He smiled. "You see, Harigami-san, I am neither naïve nor a fool."

In the car, while they followed Kenji, Philip told Michiko about the assignment he had given Ed Porter and what Porter had subsequently discovered about David Turner's movements. Philip did it mainly to kill time, and to use Michiko as a sounding board for his own theories.

"I think Turner's been our man all along," he said as he watched Kenji's car through the *click-clack* of the windshield wipers. A soft spring rain was falling, but the sky did not seem threatening. "I think Turner set Silvers up as the rotten apple."

"You may be right," Michiko said. "If so, we must find out as soon as possible. Because it will mean that Turner is passing all your information on to the *Jiban*. It means they already know that the ministers they have targeted for CIG termination have not really been killed."

"The problem is the *furo*, the bathhouse," Philip said. "I can't get in there, and neither can any CIG agent. Turner would spot them for sure. But the *furo*'s the key, I'm certain. He must be using it as an rdv. We've got to get inside to see who he's meeting on a regular basis."

"I can do it," Michiko said.

"But you won't. It's too dangerous."

Up ahead, Kenji's car had pulled over. They watched him get out, hurry into a *pachinko* parlor. It was one of those on the Taki-gumi's protection list, meaning that the Yakuza clan extorted money from the business on a monthly basis.

Philip and Michiko looked at one another. They followed Kenji to another parlor, then a third and a fourth.

"So that's how he gets his gambling money," Philip said. "He's skimming off the top. He's embezzling from his own employer."

Michiko grinned. "Isn't Gen Taki going to be interested in that!"

Philip grunted. "Knowing your father, Gen Taki will never find out. He's going to use this information to bind Kenji Harigami to him body and soul."

He started the car, and they headed back to the gambling-syndicate parlor where Wataro Taki was waiting with Kenji's daughter.

But Philip's thoughts were far away. He was thinking of how to get inside the *furo*. How to find out what David Turner was up to in there.

My darling, Philip read, *I have done what you suggested. There was merit in it, and I saw that if it was to be acted upon, it was up to me to do it. I have gone inside the* furo, *and have found who it is David Turner is meeting there. That is startling enough. But there is more, I believe. Much more. I have taken Ed Porter with me. I believe that by the time you read this, we will have been successful. Please meet me at eleven at the* sumo *stadium.*

Philip glanced at his watch. It was already past ten. The note had been delivered by hand by one of Wataro Taki's men. Philip shot questions at him as soon as he had read the note, but the man knew nothing more than that Michiko had handed him the sealed note at just past five in the afternoon and told him to deliver it to Philip at ten that evening.

Philip drove northeast, into Ryogoku. To the *sumo* stadium.

He sat in the car, tapping his fingers against the wheel. There was nothing about this situation he liked. He felt like a puppet on a string. He got out of the car. A fine mist was falling. Great gingko trees rose up all around him. They looked as if they were weeping.

What, he thought, had Michiko found out about David Turner? And what was she doing at the *sumo* stadium?

There was no one about, no traffic. He felt alone and terribly vulnerable walking across the deserted street. Touched the inside of his left wrist. Into the shadows of the stadium. He made a complete circuit, found one door ajar.

Poked his head in and quickly pulled it back. A light burned in the concrete hallway. Nothing else.

He was aware of the acceleration of his pulse, the terror knotting his insides. And years later this would be the moment he would remember, when, in retrospect, he could appreciate the enormous folly he had committed when he had unthinkingly verbalized his thoughts to Michiko. She had taken him literally. He knew now that she had believed he had given her an order to infiltrate the bathhouse.

Though he would later say *I never asked her to do this*, he would be ashamed of his words. Of course he had asked her.

311

In the Japanese fashion, he had indicated to her the dire circumstances, the probable rewards and how, in this instance, he himself was incapable of acting.

He had quite deliberately revealed to her this slender, gleaming thread. He had needed her to act, because she could get into the *furo* where he could not, and so had contrived a way to pull her along its fragile length, unmindful of the terrible danger that lurked there.

But this would come later. At the moment, all Philip knew was that he was going into the *sumo* stadium. Michiko and Porter were there.

Inside, the place smelled of straw and sweat. Both were stale odors, as if whatever had occurred here had done so many years ago. There were other manifestations of disuse. There is a sense one gets when a place is deserted. It is akin to the odd—and infinitely subtle—change in sound of a phone ringing at the other end of the line when no one is home.

Whatever that was, Philip sensed it now as he went out into the high-ceilinged arena. Rows of benches, tier upon tier, dimly seen in the partial illumination from the bare bulbs screwed into the sockets along the hallway. In the center, the *dohyo*, the traditional *sumo* ring, raised two feet off the floor. He walked toward it. Once, the fifteen-foot-diameter ring had been constructed by placing sixteen rice bales side by side. Now, of course, more modern methods were used.

There was a sound, and Philip looked up. The center of the *dohyo* was struck by a lance of light. Philip started. An enormous *sumo* wrestler crouched there. The light flooding over him revealed the elaborate nature of his hair style. This *ichomage* was the sign of a grand champion, the highest level of achievement in the world of *sumo*.

As Philip watched, the *sumo* took up a large cup of water and drank from it. This was the *misu-sakazuki*, the water ceremony, one of the rites of purification that preceded a match. In ancient days, the water cup was ritually exchanged between warriors who, before entering into battle, would toast one another's courage, knowing that it might be for the last time.

Putting down the cup, the *sumo* squatted. His weight was on his heels; his hands, curled into fists, rested on the mat. This was *shikiri*, the position of readiness.

It was then that the *sumo* stared directly into Philip's eyes. The challenge was unmistakable.

Philip turned toward the door he had used to enter the

arena area. A second shaft of light revealed another figure. He brandished a sword. The sword-bearer, who traditionally accompanied the grand champion. What was so familiar about this figure's stance? About his silhouette? There was no time to think.

Philip took off in the opposite direction. He was aware of movement. The swordsman was racing after him; the *sumo* had begun his climb down into the aisle nearest Philip.

Philip put on speed, jumping tiers, downward toward another exit door. He crashed into it. Locked. He went on, trying door after door. While the two Japanese closed in on him.

At last he came to a door that gave. Threw it open and dashed through.

When he went down, it was with a sense of despair. Hit the concrete and rolled. The back of his neck, where he had been struck, throbbed, and he felt a tingling down one arm.

Shook it, and kicked out at the same time. Heard a grunt, and kicked again. This time, felt his foot caught, twisted painfully. Used his other leg in a sweep, and his assailant came crashing down atop him.

Philip used the combat judo he had been taught, two short, vicious strikes that cracked the other's rib cage. Then Philip extracted the thin blade secreted along the inside of his left wrist. Slid it home.

Heard noises, becoming abruptly louder, and he scrambled to his feet. Continued to shake his seminumb hand as he ran. Some of the bulbs had burned out along this stretch, and it was difficult to see. He stumbled once over a box or an overturned chair, righted himself and pounded on.

At last he turned a corner and spotted the door through which he had entered the stadium. It was like coming home.

So it wasn't until he was quite close that he saw the odd shadow. The movement caught his eye first, brought him up short. It was swaying. Like a pendulum, it rocked back and forth in a short, twisting arc.

Panting, Philip approached it. A horror growing inside him. "Oh my God," he whispered. The breath sawed in and out of him. His tongue felt like cotton batting. "Oh my God."

Stared up into the shadows, a face without features, the tongue extended grotesquely between slack lips. The noose tight around the neck.

Swinging like a pendulum off the floor.

Back and forth. Back and forth.

313

"Michiko!"

It was a scream to disturb the dead.

"Here, Philip-san." The voice, watery, ethereal. "I am here." Echoing through the deserted corridors of the stadium.

With an inarticulate cry, he turned the body into the light. It was a male figure. With a sickening lurch, he recognized the face of Ed Porter, bloated, drained of blood.

He wheeled from the grotesque corpse, saw by the dim light Michiko huddled in a corner. There was wire flex wrapped around her wrists and ankles. Her skin was broken and bleeding where she had tried to free herself. The flesh was already black-and-blue, puffed up in furrows.

"Michiko!" Took her head in his hands. "Thank God you're alive!" He was weeping with relief. He kissed her cheek, felt wetness, and a salty taste on his tongue.

He turned her head fully into the light, and she gave a tiny cry of pain.

"Michiko! What is it!"

She did not, or could not, answer.

Her head was trembling. There was blood on her face.

In a mounting frenzy, Philip began to wipe it away. It continued to seep out.

"Oh my darling, what have they done to you?" But, his heart lurching, he knew, and an icy fear stole through him. He remembered the fable of Megami Kitsune, the fox-goddess, and Michiko's fear of retribution for the sin of loving him.

"Nothing," she whispered. "Nothing." And then, her head bowed against his breast, she broke down at last, sobbing like a child. "Oh Philip-san, they have taken away my sight! I am blind!"

"Acting on the information Michiko gave me," Wataro Taki said, "I have discovered who David Turner really is."

"But Michiko—"

"I do not wish to speak of her." Wataro Taki poured more tea. They were sitting facing one another in a tea shop in Tokyo. It was the day after the incident at the *sumo* stadium. Philip had not seen—or heard from—Michiko since he had delivered her to her father.

"Is she all right?" Philip persisted.

Wataro Taki stared down into the dregs of his tea. "No," he said at last, "she is not all right. Her wounds will heal in

314

time," he said hastily, seeing the alarm on Philip's face. "On that matter you need have no worries."

"But her sight—" He could not bring himself to go on.

"Her sight, Doss-san, is lost to her forever. We must all get used to that now."

"Because of me, she went to the *furo*. And that led her to the *sumo* stadium."

"This is all a matter over and done with," Wataro Taki said. "Don't you agree?" There was a note of warning in his voice.

Miserably, Philip nodded.

"Therefore," Wataro Taki said, "as to the matter of David Turner. Your suspicions of him were quite well founded, I am afraid."

"Who is he?" Philip asked. "Really."

"His name is Yvgeny Karsk," Wataro Taki said. "He is a colonel in the Soviet NKVD. He was meeting the Soviet first attaché at the *furo*. Karsk, it seems, was trained inside Russia to be as American as you are, Doss-san."

"Jesus." He was an explosion of breath. Philip shook his head. "Then I was right—and so was Ed Porter. Turner-Karsk was the link to the *Jiban*. He always was. He laid the false evidence for me to find that implicated Silvers."

"He knew you were becoming suspicious of the intelligence he was bringing to the CIG from the *Jiban*. He knew that you were suspicious of the *Jiban*'s motives," Wataro Taki said. "Turner-Karsk cleverly provided an appropriate quarry."

"Silvers was murdered before he could refute the false evidence," Philip said. He remembered General Hadley telling him that he had told Jonas and Turner of the evidence that Philip had found implicating Silvers. That had been the night before the murder. So Turner knew what was going to happen, and had the time to do something about it.

Wataro Taki nodded. "It seems clear now that Turner—"

"Don't call him that!"

"That Karsk murdered your Colonel Silvers."

"But what I can't understand," Philip said, "is why Kozo Shiina, the leader of the *Jiban*, a radical reactionary clique of high-level Japanese ministers, would hook up with a Russian agent."

"That is simplicity itself," Wataro Taki said. "Kozo Shiina is the heart and soul of the *Jiban*. It is his brainchild. Shiina has built a kind of philosophical cult around himself. He sees capitalism—the American brand of capitalism, with its em-

315

phasis on free enterprise for the individual gain—as particularly pernicious to the Japanese way of life. After all, here in Japan, we strive together as a nation, for the good of the nation—and the Emperor. The individual is nothing.

"For now, at least, the Soviet way of thinking is enough like Shiina's to allow him to enlist Russia's aid. The Russians can be powerful allies."

"And dangerous foes," Philip said, picturing the ascetic profile of David Turner-Yvgeny Karsk in his mind. "Karsk is a murderer. Who knows what else he's capable of?" Then, in a flash, he remembered the silhouette in the *sumo* stadium. "My God, Karsk was there last night!" he said breathlessly, "when they blinded Michiko."

"Now both Karsk and Shiina are your bitter enemies," Wataro said.

"Why?" Philip asked. "Karsk may know me, but Shiina does not."

"Perhaps that was so up until last night," Wataro Taki said. "The fight at the *sumo* stadium changed everything. You see, Philip-san, the young man you killed during the fight at the stadium was Kozo Shiina's son."

"Jesus!" Philip let out a heavy breath.

"It is fortunate that Zen Godo is dead, *neh*? Otherwise, I am convinced that Michiko would be dead now. But as far as Shiina—and everyone else but you and Michiko—is concerned, Zen Godo and Wataro Taki have no relationship to one another.

"Kozo Shiina has been my mortal enemy for years. Now he is yours as well, *neh*, Doss-san? Shiina is enough to think about. Now a new foe has entered the arena. Yvgeny Karsk. It is clear that, together, Karsk and Shiina must have masterminded the entire affair to permanently cripple the CIG. It seems to me, Doss-san, that in Yvgeny Karsk we have made a most powerful and dangerous enemy."

"Only," Philip said, "until I hunt him down, and put a bullet between his eyes."

"If I cannot have him, I will kill myself."

"You are talking nonsense."

"I mean it," Michiko warned. How had her father found out about her affair with Philip? she asked herself. They had been so careful.

Wataro Taki shook his head. "Then you are a foolish, foolish girl."

"It is not foolish to know what I want. What I need."

He stared at her uncomprehendingly. "What *you* want. What *you* need. This is totally unimportant." He wore a Western business suit. His hands were manicured, his hair pomaded. He was a man of the new, prosperous age into which, he was certain, he and Japan would be entering. "What this family needs should be your only concern."

"He would leave his wife for me," Michiko said. "I know it."

"What Philip Doss would or would not do is immaterial," Wataro Taki said sharply. Looking at her sightless face, swathed in bandages, he wished to cry. But that would be a mistake. He must be strong so that she would remain strong. He knew that any sign on his part of how he was feeling, and she would break down utterly. Far better, he thought, for her to learn to cope from the outset. "Have you forgotten your own vows? What about Nobuo? Have you thought of him? Bad enough that you have had to spend so much time away from your husband. Now you wish to dishonor him completely."

"I never loved Nobuo, Father. You knew that when you set the marriage with the Yamamotos."

"It has turned out to be the best decision I ever made," he said. "The Yamamotos have been my staunchest allies through the worst of times. They have shown their loyalty to me time and again. Which is more than I can say for my own daughter's filial piety. What would your mother have thought of this rebellious behavior? I am glad that she is not here to witness it."

"How convenient," Michiko cried, "that you invoke the memory of my mother only when you need it."

Anger and duty rose simultaneously within him. His heart broke to see his only daughter sightless. In his heart, the need to revenge himself upon those who had mutilated her was a living thing, pulsing, crying out for release. But he knew that he was standing on sand, as his father used to say. Dangerous territory, for here the footing seemed falsely secure. At any moment a wave could rise up and suck the sand from beneath your feet.

Wataro Taki knew that if he made a move against Kozo Shiina or any of the *Jiban* now, their suspicions would be aroused. Who was this man who had moved against them? What were his motives for revenge? They would begin to dig and, with the vast resources at their disposal, he would be in danger of being exposed.

He thought of Philip Doss. It was Philip Doss who had suggested that Michiko follow David Turner. It was Philip Doss who, in a sense, must share culpability for this tragedy. Let Philip Doss become Wataro Taki's stalking horse. Let Philip Doss be the sword of his revenge against Kozo Shiina and the *Jiban*.

This decided, he said, "I forbid you to continue this liaison with Philip Doss." It would now be far too dangerous for Michiko to be near Doss. Michiko had already been blinded by his enemies; Wataro Taki did not want her dead.

"You cannot do this," Michiko whispered. "Please, Father. Oh please! I beg you!"

He ignored her. "Arrange it. Say your goodbyes to your lover and then return to your husband."

Michiko bowed her head. "Now I will have nothing. You have condemned me to a life of ashes and dust."

"Then that will be your own doing," Wataro Taki said. "You have your sins to contemplate and your punishment to serve. It is your liaison with Doss-san that led to your blindness. Nevertheless, you are my daughter, and I know that you will obey me. Your first—and only—duty is to your family. I am confident that you will never forget that, Michiko." He straightened his tie, pressed the palms of his hands against his shiny hair. "Nobuo knows nothing. He will continue to know nothing; I will see to it. As for Philip Doss, you will put your personal feelings aside. As of this moment, it is over."

But, of course, he could not know how wrong he was. He would never know that in disobeying him, Michiko would one day save his dreams.

Jonas called. Philip had just gotten home. He could hear Lillian in the bedroom, stirring. She called out to him, and he said, "I've got it."

He could tell immediately that a wheel had come off. "Where the hell've you been? I've been trying to get you for a half hour?" Jonas was in a sweat. "It's happened, buddy," he said in a breathless voice. "The worst nightmare you could imagine."

"What is it?"

The line was secure, so they could talk directly.

"The safe house where we've been keeping the ministers on the *Jiban*'s hit list has been breached."

"Jesus! What happened?"

"They're all dead, Phil," Jonas said. "Every single one of the ministers. Someone got in and detonated a half dozen grenades. There isn't enough left to scrape off the rugs."

"Where's Turner?"

"What?"

"Turner!" Philip was shouting now. "Where is David Turner?"

"In charge of the preliminary investigation. He's at the safe house."

"I'm going down there," Philip said.

"It's security city there," Jonas said. "I'll call and clear it. I'm on my way there anyway."

"No," Philip said. "I want you to get over to Turner's apartment."

"What for?"

"There's no time," Philip said impatiently. "Turner's a Russian spy, Jonas. He killed Silvers, and it's a sure bet he masterminded the safe house break-in as well. Just do as I say. And for Christ's sake be careful!"

Philip checked his service revolver before going up the steps to the safe house. As Jonas had said, the place was alive with soldiers and CIG personnel. Fire trucks were parked half on the sidewalk, and hoses snaked in through the front door.

He used his credentials, but it was still a tough job getting through. Inside the safe house, an iron-jawed sergeant stopped him in the foyer, got one of his men to keep Philip there while he went off to find Turner. An efficient forensic team was at work. The place smelled like a charnel house. Somewhere the remnants of a fire were still burning, and Philip saw several firemen rushing through.

The sergeant came back, a puzzled look on his face. "That's funny," he said. "Lieutenant Turner was here a minute ago. I was here when he took a phone call."

"How long ago?" Philip barked at him.

"Couldn't have been more than five or ten minutes," the startled sergeant said.

"Do you know who he was speaking to?"

The sergeant shrugged. But Philip was already racing outside, back to his car.

He approached Turner's apartment on foot. There was only one entrance and, as was typical of Japanese apartment buildings, there were no fire escapes. One way in, one way out.

It was clear to him that someone had tipped Turner off that

Philip was on his way. That meant two things: that his phone line wasn't secure after all and that Turner had an accomplice at CIG headquarters, because that was where Jonas had phoned him from. Philip filed the knowledge away.

It was Turner-Karsk he was concerned with now. Karsk, who had set him up to point the finger at Silvers. Karsk, who had murdered Silvers. Karsk, who had murdered Ed Porter. Karsk, who had blinded Michiko. Karsk, who had blown away four top-level ministers at the CIG safe house.

Philip went in the front door, his revolver drawn. The small lobby, dim and cool, loomed empty. Turner-Karsk lived on the fourth floor. The elevator was open in the lobby. Philip found a maintenance mop and wedged it against the door to keep it open so no one could use it. Then he took to the stairs.

Sounds echoed up the open space of the stairwell. None of them were recognizable. Philip kept himself against the inner wall as he went up. He came out onto the fourth-floor landing. Crouching, he looked first one way, then the other. The hallway was clear.

He went down toward Turner-Karsk's apartment. The front door was locked. He stepped back and shot out the lock. Immediately, he kicked the door open, rolled out of the way.

But there was no answering fire. Philip picked himself up, scuttled crabwise into the apartment, his revolver held in the standard two-handed grip before him.

The windows were open, curtains blowing in. The bed was unmade. There were papers scattered all over. Some of them whirled like oversized confetti in the draft Philip had made opening the front door.

Heard a noise coming from the tiny bathroom and threw himself lengthwise across the threshold.

Jonas was in there. He was holding his shoulder, which was oozing blood from around his grip. Jonas's face was pasty white.

"You okay?"

Jonas nodded. "The bastard shot me, then went out the window."

Philip made a move to follow Karsk's escape route, but Jonas said, "Forget it. He went across the rooftops like a bat out of hell. You'll never find him."

Philip climbed out the window. The apartment rose above the height of the rest of the roof. Asphalt rooftops stretched away in every direction. Jonas was right. Karsk had disappeared as if into thin air.

"I have something for you."
"What?"
Michiko came silently across the room, knelt on the *tatami*. The bandages had come off, and one needed to be very close indeed to see the scars. She placed an engraved *kyoki* wood box on the low table between them.
"A present."
"Michiko—"
But her voice deflected him. "First," she said, "tea."
He watched her as she slowly, gracefully, seemingly effortlessly, brewed the green tea. She used the whisk to make the pale froth on its top. Turning the cup, turning. Now her fingers guided her, so subtly that unless one was looking, one would not suspect that she was blind.
Finally, she held out the cup for him to take. She used to love to watch him drink the tea she made for him. Now she listened as he took his first sip.
Only when he had finished it all and had given her back the cup did she prepare the second pot. This time it was for them both. "Will we make love today?" she asked when they were drinking.
"We always make love when we are together," he said. "Among many other things." He cocked his head, perhaps sensing something. "Is today different?"
"I am different." Her eyelids were lowered.
Outside, the rumble of traffic came to them like a distant storm: a harbinger of great change, but not yet near enough to affect them.
"The tea is delicious."
"*Domo*." Thank you.
"There is nothing different about you." He put his cup down. She heard, and cocked her head.
"Michiko," he began, "what happened in the *sumo* stadium—"
"I understand," she interrupted. "You lost a good friend and compatriot in Ed Porter."
"That's true," he said. "But I was speaking about you—"
"Ah." She smiled, so sweetly that he was disarmed. "But there is nothing to say. I am the lucky one, *neh*? I am here. I am alive."
"But if I hadn't told you about the *furo*—"

321

"Then we would never have discovered that David Turner is a Russian NKVD agent."

Philip bowed his head in concession. He knew better than to continue this line with her. In any case, whatever guilt he felt was a purely Western emotion; it had no place here.

He took a moment to clear his throat of all his roiling emotion. "The Taki-gumi has accepted your father's arrival," he said. "Not even his most rabid enemy would ever suspect that Wataro Taki and Zen Godo are one and the same."

"My father has taken a woman," Michiko said. "They will be married inside a month."

He looked at her, knowing that there was something on her mind. "Is that strange? Your father has been essentially alone since your mother died some years back. Are you jealous of this new woman?"

"She is pregnant, I think." Michiko kept her eyes lowered. It was the only sign she gave that there was something wrong with her sight.

"Is that why they are getting married?" He wanted to get to the source of her discomfort.

"I don't think so. No." She seemed inordinately still. "Understandably, my father wishes to have sons. His sons will one day control what he has created."

"Rather than you, his daughter?" He was on a fishing expedition.

"I have no desire to follow in his footsteps," she flared. "Whatever gave you that idea?"

"Michiko," he said softly, "what is it?"

"I want you inside me," she said. "Now."

She was wild, almost brutal. It was as if whatever was inside her had sucked all tenderness out of her so that she engulfed him with every fiber of her being.

Utterly spent, they fell asleep in each other's arms. When Philip awoke, she was already preparing tea. He rose, sat down opposite her. She had not put on her kimono or even her underkimono, which was unusual.

"Michiko?"

"Drink now." She held out a cup to him. It was not the one he had used before. It was much lighter, much finer, a celadon green. It had on its side a gold-billed heron. A black fish was struggling between its jaws, and its spread wings were beginning to open. It was the cup he had almost broken the night of Zen Godo's supposed death; the signal they had

322

agreed upon that would alert her, in another room, to his presence in the darkened house.

He saw that the *kyoki* wood box was open. Was this its contents; his present? He stared at her inquiringly.

"Drink," she said. "Half the tea."

He did so.

She waited until he put the cup back into her cupped hands. She finished off the rest of the tea. Then she carefully wiped the cup with a silk cloth, felt for the *kyoki* wood box, placed it inside. He was right. It *was* his present. But why?

She closed the lid, slid the box toward him. "This is to remember me by," she said softly. Her face was pale, a ghostly reflection half seen in a mirror.

"What do you mean?"

"I am going away," she said. "Back to my husband."

"But why? Did your father order this? Does he know about us?"

She shook her head. "This is my doing. Mine alone. We are both married. There are vows—important vows, holy vows, if we are true to our spirits—which must be preserved. For a time we forgot them. But not forever."

"Not forever," he said, his heart sinking. "But for now. Why not now?"

"It is impossible."

"Michiko—"

"Why must you make this more difficult? You must accept—"

"I can't!"

"But you must!" Her voice was trembling; she was close to tears. "If you care anything about me, you will dress and go. Now. Without saying another word. Without looking at me again."

He was stunned. "Am I crazy? Am I waking up from a dream? Was there nothing between us?"

"This must be *because* there was something between us."

"I don't understand."

She was bent over so that her hair cascaded over her face, over the *kyoki* wood box. She was silent.

In a moment, he rose, went into the bathroom. He stared into the mirror and wondered what it was he saw there. Whose face was that? What deeds had that person done while he was somewhere else? He could not say. Or perhaps, more accurate, he did not want to remember. Suddenly, he was so cold that he began to shiver.

323

When he emerged, he was dressed. The shivering, like an ague, had passed. Michiko had not moved. He crossed to the table, picked up the box. It seemed lighter than air.

Then he did as she had asked. He said nothing. And he did not look at her again.

ZERO

THE ABIDING SPIRIT

PARIS
TOKYO
WASHINGTON
SAINT-PAUL DE VENCE

Lillian went into Ungaro. But everything seemed a bit too way-out for her, and she wound up at Dior. She was feeling exceptionally fine. Having made the break from the deadening circle of Washington life, she felt weightless, as if she had managed to escape purgatory. *If only I knew that Audrey was safe,* she thought.

Dior had always been her favorite. The designs were always *très chic*—never *outré*. The elegance of line was timeless, and this was something to which she responded wholeheartedly.

The fashion house was on the Avenue Montaigne, just steps from the Plaza Athénée. As she surveyed the delicious array of clothes, Lillian felt again that shivery thrill of being far, far from a prison of her own making.

She bought a sequined evening gown, which she asked be sent to the hotel after it had been altered, and an elegant but discreet casual dress, which fit her perfectly and which she decided to wear out.

Back on the Avenue Montaigne, she was at first undecided as to which way to go. She could head down the Rue François 1e to the Cours la Reine, which ran along the Seine. That way she would pass closer to the Grand Palais and the Université. Like her children, she loved the water, and the Seine was no exception. But then she remembered that she would also have to pass the *bateaux* station, watching all the gay tourists piling onto the boats for their mediocre meal while traveling up the river. She couldn't bear the thought of that, so she headed up toward the Rond Point.

At the Champs-Élysées, she turned to look toward the Place Charles de Gaulle. The Arc de Triomphe glowed a cool white. Even with the traffic streaming around it—or, perhaps, because of it—it seemed grander now than the first time she had seen it. But then all of Paris had that effect on her, it

327

seemed. It grew more beautiful, more desirable, every time she visited. That was its most endearing quality. Every large city in the world had a facade it paraded before visitors that made it exciting. But the more one returned, the more the seams showed, the more tarnished the facade became. Until image and reality separated, and one could never think of the place in the same way again.

That would never happen here, Lillian thought as she began to walk down the Champs-Élysées. Here the facade only hinted at the pleasures to be entertained. The more one came to Paris, the more one enjoyed it.

She could see the obelisk at the Place de la Concorde, rising in the near distance. Strolling down the wide avenue, beneath the ancient chestnut trees, Lillian felt the air of centuries rolling over her. She breathed in deeply and sighed. There was a sense of history—and, with it, a sense of place—with which everyone was attuned. She could hear the soft hooting of the *bateaux*. For just an instant she was unaccountably swept up in the utter contentment here, as if she had joined a family whose members, though outwardly forbidding, had turned out to be warm and generous.

The Place de la Concorde was blue with the diesel fumes of the tourist buses lined up like tin soldiers while their progeny swarmed outward toward Rue Royale and Sainte-Marie Madeleine.

Lillian went quickly onward, past the Orangerie and into the Tuileries. Men leaning against the trees were ostensibly watching a group of boys playing boules on a large patch of bare earth. In reality, they were eyeing the fashionable Parisian women striding by. Lillian was happy that she was wearing the Dior dress. In Washington, where power was the only citywide obsession, being well dressed in the Parisian sense was a talent that had atrophied. Maybe it was the crassness of the new world that had done it, or perhaps America's national obsession with disposability.

In any case, one needed only to walk the streets here to see how people should be clothed. Even the elderly were *chic*, not only in the manner of their dress but in their hair style and makeup as well. As often as not, one could not tell the difference between a sixty-five-year-old and a forty-year-old. That was another manner in which the city remained timeless. There were no traces of the aging self-consciousness: as in the graying of America. The Parisians would laugh at such an idea.

Lillian sat down on a bench, watched the children at play. They were very involved in the game, and she wondered what significance winning this match would have in their lives.

All of life is a game, Philip had once said to her. It was early on in their relationship, while they were still in Tokyo, and she had not understood what he meant. His refusal to explain it had only made her resent her own ignorance. Now, of course, she understood it perfectly. She remembered how her discovery of the answer had, in some profound way, also been the answer to her own nature.

She had always believed that she was half a person. That falling in love would produce in her mate her missing half. But her marriage to Philip had, rather, the effect of defining her own limitations. Which certainly, before she had met him, she had no idea of. Being married to Philip had described the boundaries of the world in which she lived. And for that, she supposed, she must always be grateful to him.

But when it came to Philip, there was so much else to take into consideration. Such as their first—and only—trip here. It had been on her insistence, of course. His reluctance to encounter any part of the old world was like an anchor weighing them both down. His idea of a trip had probably consisted of two weeks in the hinterlands of Burma or the Hindu Kush.

For their last night in the world's most romantic city they had booked a dinner cruise on a *bateau mouche*, which Philip had mistakenly called a *barquette*, much to the amusement of the waiter.

She already spoke fluent French, and he was chagrined by his lack of expertise. (If they *had* gone to Burma or the Hindu Kush, Lillian was certain that he would have spoken any dialect they could encounter there.) That had made him angry, of course. Or *angrier*, because he was already angry at having been talked into coming to Paris. There was no such thing as civilization anywhere in Europe, he had told her in no uncertain terms. A European—*especially* a Frenchman— had no concept of what true civilization meant. And furthermore, when he was confronted with someone—a Japanese, say—who was truly civilized, he was incapable of comprehending it.

Maybe, Lillian had said in an attempt to appease him and thus salvage what was left of their trip, the Frenchman was just incapable of admitting it.

That had made him see red. The only thing a Frenchman was capable of admitting, Philip had said hotly, was that he was God's gift to the fairer sex. Which was so patently foolish he did not want to discuss it further.

So she had spent much of the dusky-rose twilight sitting alone at their white-linen-covered table, watching the Right Bank or the Left Bank slide by. When she found herself watching the backs of heads while the boat floated slowly past the Notre Dame, she got up and went in search of Philip.

"You look like death warmed over," Eliane said. "Didn't you sleep at all on the plane?"

Michael maneuvered the rented Nissan through the multi-lanes of traffic. "How could I?" he said. "I kept thinking about Audrey." It was late evening in Tokyo. Was there any time of the day or night when the access roads from Narita Airport weren't clogged? "How did that bastard Ude get her into that DC-9? And how did they get off the ground without tower clearance?"

She did not take her eyes off him. "How are you feeling?"

"Not bad." He flexed his torso in the limited amount of room the seat belt afforded him. Caught a glance at his heavily bandaged nose and upper lip. "I've felt better," he admitted. Thinking, too, about Jonas. How depressed he had sounded. As if he were sick. But Michael could not remember Uncle Sammy being sick a day in his life. Which made this all the more frightening.

There had been no answer at Uncle Sammy's home. The BITE station chief had flown in from Honolulu to straighten things out with the INS. What a mess—but that was his problem. Michael and Eliane had needed to get out of Hawaii quickly. Following the DC-9 with Audrey.

The windshield wipers *whick-whicked* back and forth, smearing the lights of the oncoming traffic as they cleared away the drizzle that had begun to fall. Rain that seemed to him to be the sky crying. There was a mood of despair inside Michael that he found difficult to dispel.

"I can sense that you're in pain," Eliane said. "Are you sure you're all right? You haven't said a word since we left Maui."

"Leave me alone," he snapped. "And stop reading into things. Whatever you sense is wrong."

"Why are you angry with me?"

"I'm not angry," he said, knowing that he was. "I'm just tired of your belief in the spirit world. The next time we're on some kind of sacred ground, leave me out of it, okay?"

"That kind of stupid comment makes me sure I'm right," she said.

"What does that mean?" He wondered why he was suddenly so angry with her. Then, with a start, he realized that he had been angry at her all through the flight.

"It was all right when you saved my life in Kahakuloa, because you're the man," Eliane said. "You're supposed to act heroic. But when the situation is reversed—when I save your life, it's hard to take, isn't it?"

"That's ridiculous," he said, but even he recognized the lack of conviction in his voice.

They continued on in silence. The *whick-whick* of the windshield wipers counted off the seconds.

"I'm sorry," Michael said after a long time. "You're right. But only in a way. I think I'm more angry with myself. I looked like a goddamn amateur back there in the plane."

"But, Michael," she said, putting a hand on his leg, "that's exactly what you are. An amateur. There's nothing to be ashamed of in that."

"Tsuyo, my *sensei*, would never be forgiving. If you hadn't been there, I'd be dead now."

"It's foolish to think about what might have been," she said softly, "don't you think?"

He nodded. Inside, he was more confused than ever. Eliane had saved his life by intervening when Ude was about to kill him. Did that mean she was on his side? Maybe. But if she were working for Masashi, she would want him alive, at least until he had uncovered the riddle of where his father had hidden the Katei document. But then, wasn't Ude ostensibly working for Masashi? Why, then, would he want to kill Michael?

The brilliant lights of Tokyo shone through the rain and mist with such intensity that the night gave grudging way before the power of its aura. Michael drove on, his thoughts chasing one another around and around until he was dizzy. And still in the back of his mind was the nagging suspicion that he was missing an essential element that lay right in front of him.

"Where are we going?" Eliane asked. "You made reservations at the Okura. This isn't the way to the hotel."

"We're not going there," Michael said. "Masashi's sure to have his men on the lookout for me. Maybe they'll find my name at the Okura and waste some time staking it out, waiting for me to show up."

331

She watched him, the silver reflections of the rain sliding down the side of his face. "Maybe you're not such an amateur after all."

He grinned at her. "No," he said. "I'm just a quick study."

Lillian found him, after a fashion.

Rather, she saw him. And what he had found. A tall, slim Japanese woman with a narrow, patrician head and eyes with such pronounced epicanthic folds they were barely more than slits.

There was nothing beautiful about this woman that Lillian could see. But then her heart had been locked tight against Orientals for some time. She could recognize, however, in the sinuous movements of the Japanese woman a kind of sexuality she could only define as sinister. Not only because it was directed at her husband, but because it possessed, in its own right, a quality wholly unknown—and therefore unfathomable—to her. It was something beyond the limits of her world, and thus not only alien but, to her way of thinking, dangerous.

Which was, of course, why, she had told herself, her husband courted it. She was fully aware of Philip's professed affinity with the Oriental mind—it could hardly have been otherwise. But that did not necessarily mean that she believed him. Rather, it was far easier—and safer!—to tell herself that his reaction was akin to hers. He liked danger; he had made no secret of that. Craved it, in fact, like an alcoholic needs his booze. That was all right as long as it went no farther than his work. But Lillian suspected that it did not.

Now, as she watched her husband with the Japanese woman, all her suspicions burst open like a wound. They stood close enough so that their bodies were touching. They were not kissing, but they might have been. There was an odd kind of intimacy at work that caused her to shiver, though the evening air was warm enough.

They were not making love, but they might have been. What is it, Lillian had asked herself with a terrifying degree of desperation, that was passing between them? She was certain that she would never know. She was not even sure that she would understand it if it were explained to her. She felt like Philip's Frenchman confronted with a truly civilized man.

The sense of inadequacy that washed over her was so overwhelming that she was dizzied. And with it came a kind of despair. It was as if she were a little girl watching two adults act and react in a world of which she was not a part. Because it was she who was being betrayed, and the sense of inevitability—that of course this was happening; it was a consequence of her own inadequacy—was crushing.

She fought back tears of hurt. Or so she had thought at the time. Years later, when she contemplated the motivation for her own betrayal, it would occur to her that they were also tears of rage.

Masashi and Shiina were on the wooden catwalk that overhung the vast basement of the warehouse at Takashiba.

"I must admit," Masashi was saying, "that I was wrong about Joji. I didn't think he had it in him to challenge me for the clan."

"I was silent at the time," Shiina said, "because you did not seek my advice. And this is your family, after all. Joji is your brother. But I felt then that he would not accept being cut off from the only legacy your father left for you."

They were watching a large crate being wheeled into the chamber below them. The men surrounding the crate wore loose-fitting suits that covered them from their ankles to the tops of their heads. They wore thick-soled boots. The clicking of their hand-held Geiger counters could be heard, amplified by the acoustics of the open space.

"I suppose," Masashi said grudgingly, "that my brother is not quite the whipped dog I had thought him to be."

"Far from it," Shiina said. "You know Daizo's prowess. He would not have been easy to defeat."

"Joji was always good at learning," Masashi said. "And the martial arts were no exception. I just never believed that cut off from Michiko, his chief ally against me, he would have the stomach for a personal war."

"Now you are witness to your mistake," Shiina said. "And a costly error it has proved to be."

"I'll be able to replace Daizo quickly."

"I wasn't thinking of Daizo," Shiina said. "I was thinking of your loss of face among your men." His old face was shiny in the harsh fluorescent lighting. "You must kill Joji."

The men had the crate open now. They were carefully easing the contents onto a heavy-duty lead-topped trolley.

"I already have the death of one brother on my conscience," Masashi said. "I have no desire for another."

"What other choice do you have?" Shiina said. "If you

don't avenge the dishonor done to you, your power as *oyabun* of the Taki-gumi will quickly erode."

Shiina knew which buttons to push, which strings to pull. Being *oyabun* was paramount in Masashi's life. He was a man who had lived his entire life in his father's shadow. That was a burden that Masashi did not want to bear. Shiina understood this. Men too proficient to be moved by a sword, he believed, could often be manipulated by something that the long years had shown him to be far more powerful: the human mind.

That was the fallacy of being so involved with one's own body, Shiina had learned: One always saw force as action. With the gradual erosion of his own body, Shiina had come to rely more and more on his mind. And gradually his definition of force had changed. He had come to see the truth: that force was intent.

"I read the reports on the FAX's test flight," he said. "Very impressive."

"You should have seen it," Masashi said. "It does everything Nobuo promised it would."

"Good. And he has modified the fusilage for this rather unique payload?"

"It is all done."

Now on to the difficult work, Shiina thought. Knowing the answer already, he asked, "Has Ude brought Audrey Doss back yet?"

"Ude is dead," Masashi said. "There was some difficulty at the airport. Apparently, Michael Doss discovered Ude's plan and tried to prevent him from sending Audrey Doss off. The important thing is that Michael Doss is still on the trail of the Katei document his father stole from me. He will not slip our surveillance."

"Did Ude discover who killed Philip Doss?"

"No. There seemed to be no clues. Then he stumbled upon Audrey Doss, and she took precedence."

Shiina, wanting to know what Masashi was doing with Eliane Yamamoto, said, "How will you ensure that Michael Doss leads you to the Katei document?" He was angry over Ude's death. Ude had been useful to him; it was a shame that he was gone.

"I should kill her," Masashi said, his mind still focused on Audrey Doss, "for the trouble her father has put me to."

"Kill her or let her live," Shiina said. "What does it matter? It is only a life. The Katei document is what is important to us both." He repeated his question.

"Michael Doss will not slip the leash I have on him," Masashi said. "And when the Katei document is returned, that same leash will be wrapped around his neck. He will strangle on it."

Shiina considered. The leash Masashi had on Michael Doss must be Eliane Yamamoto. Why else would she be in Maui, and with him? But why would Eliane do Masashi's bidding? She hated him. Then Shiina remembered a conversation he had had with Masashi. *I wouldn't worry about Michiko*, Masashi had said. *I have already put into motion a plan that will effectively neutralize her.* If that plan neutralized Michiko, Shiina wondered, would it also coerce her daughter, Eliane, into working for Masashi? It seemed so.

Shiina saw it all now: Masashi was using Eliane to get close to Michael Doss, become his companion—his coconspirator, even—in his quest to find the Katei document. Eliane would be useful to leak certain information to Doss at the proper times. She would be even more useful when the Katei document was found. She would kill Michael Doss. This, Shiina could not allow. It had been Philip Doss who had murdered Shiina's son so many years ago. It was Shiina's desire to kill Michael Doss himself. That was only fitting: a son for a son.

"Information has come to me," Shiina said, "regarding the death of Ude."

Masashi turned. "You knew about his death?"

At that moment, Shiina almost felt pity for Masashi. He was so young, far too young to manage the enormous power that Wataro Taki had left behind. Masashi had shown his surprise. A true *oyabun* would not have allowed any emotion to be seen by either friend or foe. Emotions were disadvantageous when they were made manifest. It would be many years, Shiina suspected, before Masashi would learn that vital lesson, and by then it would be far too late for him.

"I knew," Shiina said. "I also know that it was not Michael Doss who killed Ude. It was Eliane Yamamoto."

"Eliane? I don't believe it! Where did you get this information?"

"I have a contact high up in the U.S. Immigration and Naturalization Service in Hawaii. He contacted me some hours ago, after he had finished his preliminary investigation."

"But it is impossible! Unthinkable!"

"Why? Because Eliane Yamamoto is working for you?" Shiina laughed. "Your expression betrays you, Masashi. I guessed. Just as I have guessed that you have coerced her and Michiko in some manner. I congratulate you on your cleverness. But I also must caution you to bring Miss Yamamoto in as quickly as possible, to find out what she is up to. Perhaps she is more devious than you expected, eh? Perhaps she wishes the Katei document for herself."

Masashi thought about this for a moment. He was furious with Shiina for having seen parts of his plan that Masashi had no intention of revealing to him. But he was even more furious with Eliane. What was she doing interfering? And if Shiina's information was correct, why had she killed Ude?

Reluctantly, he nodded. "I'll bring her in," he said.

The men in the baggy suits were finished unpacking the contents of the crate. "Look," Shiina said, pointing. "It's finally here. The beginning of our dreams for a finer Japan."

The two of them stared down at the nuclear device.

"How did you get it?" Masashi asked. He was a bit awed, despite himself.

"The *Jiban* has far-ranging connections," Shiina said. "We have many friends who are sympathetic to our cause."

"It's so small," Masashi said as the men in the antiradiation suits wheeled the device into the underground laboratories beyond the gallery.

"That is its beauty," Shiina said. "And its desirability. But don't confuse size with strength. This device will level one third of Beijing on impact. The inhabitants of the rest of the city will die within several days, those in the outlying suburbs perhaps as much as a week later."

"But long before that," Masashi said, "whatever is left of the Chinese government will have capitulated to our demands. Japan will finally have all the room it needs for its people."

He thought of Hiroshima and Nagasaki. He thought of the air shaking itself apart. He thought of the rip in the cosmic fabric that would be made when the missile they would launch detonated over Beijing. From that moment on he was certain that history would remember him, Masashi, not his father, the god Wataro Taki.

The boys were almost through with their game of boules. The men who had been lounging along the periphery of the rough circle had already begun drifting away. All save one. This man waited until the very end. Then he sauntered over to Lillian's bench and sat down. He was good-looking, obviously French. He did not look at her but, rather, opened up a current edition of the *International Herald Tribune* and began to read.

Lillian watched the boys laughing and cuffing one another good-naturedly. Their cheeks were red from the exertion, and they scuffed clouds of dust wherever they walked. Again she was struck by how at home she felt here. And by how far she had come since standing in Dulles Airport waiting to depart.

It was late afternoon now, and the quality of light was striking. It had thickened all around, as if she had become part of a *pointillist* painting. The glow in the deepening sky came from a sun already behind the western quarter. A cool breeze was blowing. One last burst of laughter from the departing boys, a solitary balloon lofted into the encroaching evening.

The man on her bench rustled the paper as he folded it. He lit a cigarette. When he was finished smoking, he got up and left, heading toward the Rue de Rivoli.

Moments later, Lillian herself left. She strolled back along the Champs-Élysées. The vendors were closing down for the night; lovers walked arm in arm. There was a melancholy air, echoed by a young man, with hair to his shoulders, playing a Spanish guitar. Lillian dropped five francs into his upended hat, and he smiled at her, mouthing a silent, *Merci, madame*.

Back at the hotel, she went into the bar and ordered a Lillet on the rocks. She stretched her legs out, for a moment savoring the appreciative glances from the women as well as the men. She slipped off her high-heeled shoes, luxuriating in the comfort of being barefoot.

Her drink came, and she sipped at it. It occurred to her, as if for the first time, that she could get up right now, go to the concierge's desk and have a table booked for her at a recommended restaurant. Then, tomorrow, she could go home. To Washington. Bellehaven. If that was home. Had it ever been? she asked herself. It depended on one's definition of home, she supposed.

For just an instant, she entertained the fantasy of doing that. But there was only a feeling of emptiness. Why, she asked herself, would anyone willingly return to purgatory? She could not think of an answer.

Instead, she picked up the edition of the *International Herald Tribune* that the man had left on the bench. Now there was a sense of impending quickness. As if she were riding a horse which had just begun to gallop. She had no desire to get out of the saddle.

She opened the paper to the correct page and, as she continued to sip at her drink, read the message meant only for her.

"Howdy," Stick Haruma said. He bowed, then stuck out his hand.

Eliane shook it, startled.

"Come on in, it's pouring out there." He was wearing Levi's jeans, L.A. Gear sneakers without socks and an oversize sweatshirt with OHIO STATE BUCKEYES silk-screened across the chest. He had a face that would have been nondescript except for the inner energy he exuded. Eliane found his intense animation infectious. "Hey, Mike." Stick Haruma's grin faded when he saw the bandages, the cuts and the bruises. "Who tried to erase your face?"

"It's a long story," Michael said. He slapped Stick on the back. "We haven't seen each other in more than five years," he said as he introduced the tall, thin Japanese to Eliane. "We met here many years ago. Stick and I were students together at the same martial-arts *dojo*."

"Yeah, we were real cutups in those days," Stick Haruma said. "Come on in. *Mi casa es su casa*, as they say in the U.S."

Stick Haruma's apartment was essentially an ell-shaped living space with a loft that served as his sleeping quarters. Off the living room was a den, a kitchen and bath. All the rooms were tiny by American standards, but more than adequate to the Japanese way of life.

"I sure was glad to hear your voice when you called from the airport," Stick said. "You don't get back here as much as you should." He did not say a word about the sorry state of their clothes or the fact that they had arrived without any luggage. Nothing surprised Stick. "What can I get you guys? Are you hungry? How about something to drink?"

Michael laughed at Eliane's expression. "You'd better get used to the way he talks. Stick spends all his free time hanging out with the Americans in Shinjuku."

"I love everything American," Stick Haruma said. "My fondest dream is to own a 1961 Corvette. Preferably, white with red leather seats. Then I'm gonna drive it along the Ginza while I scarf down a Big Mac, french fries and a Coke."

Eliane laughed in disbelief.

"He works for the U.S. embassy, translating for the diplomats," Michael said.

"It's a dirty job," Stick Haruma said, "but somebody's got to do it. Besides, they like the fact that I've got all the latest idioms down pat."

He ushered them to the sofa. "Now what'll it be? Beer, Coke? Mike, your face is a mess. That's got to smart some. If you ask me, you'd better have a scotch to kill the pain."

"That'd be fine," Michael said. "Do you mind if I make a long-distance call?"

"Use the phone upstairs," Stick Haruma said, pointing to the loft.

Michael climbed up the wooden ladder, sat on the edge of Stick's *futon*. He dialed Jonas's number. He felt gingerly along his cheekbone, wincing slightly.

"Hello?"

"Is Jonas there?"

"Who's speaking?"

"Michael Doss. I'm calling from Tokyo. May I speak with my uncle, please?"

"Michael, this is your grandfather Sam," General Hadley said from Jonas's study. He had come there the moment his investigators had shown up at the BITE offices. By that time, the ambulance had already arrived and the paramedics had done everything they could to revive Jonas. "I'm sorry to be the bearer of bad tidings, Mike, but Jonas is dead. He had a fatal heart attack about an hour ago. I'm at his house now, going through his papers."

Michael closed his eyes, but the tears squeezed through nonetheless. What will I do without Uncle Sammy? he thought. What would the Darlings have done without Nana?

"Mike?"

"Yes."

"Are you all right?" General Hadley said. "You were quiet so long. I know this must be quite a shock."

"I was just thinking."

"About Jonas. I know." He cleared his throat. "Mike, I've got a lot of work ahead of me. Whatever you wanted to tell Jonas, you can tell me."

Michael remembered what Jonas had said about BITE being closed down. But what did that matter now? Jonas was dead.

"Mike, if you've got something specific, now is the time to say it."

Michael told his grandfather everything that had happened

up until a moment ago, including the existence of the Katei document. When he was done, Hadley was silent a long time.

When he spoke, his voice was grave. "What about Audrey? Have you found her yet?"

"No," Michael said. "But I've followed her this far into Japan. I won't stop until I've found her. I'll bring her back, Sam, don't worry."

"I know you'll do your best," Hadley said. "I've already gone through Jonas's notes on your mission." He paused, cleared his throat. "I want to know, Mike—scratch that. I *need* to know if you will go on. I know you're not an agent. I know that as your grandfather I have no right to ask you to continue to put yourself in danger. But your father's dead, and now so is Jonas. You're the only hope we have. If you can get your hands on that Katei document. This is vital. If it is all you say it is, with it in hand, I have no doubt we can swing a deal."

Michael was bewildered. "What do you mean? What kind of deal?"

"Why, with the Japanese, of course," Hadley said. "At last we'll have something that can cause them a tremendous loss of face. It will give us untold leverage. It will bring them back to the bargaining table, it will force them to come to terms with us in this terribly dangerous trade war. It's what Jonas would have done, what I'll do. Look, Mike, there's very little time. I've been going through the BITE field reports. There has been a systematic leakage of high-level intelligence to the Soviets. The evidence now clearly points to a deep-cover Russian agent inside BITE itself. That's one of the reasons I decided to close the shop down.

"But now that I'm at Jonas's house, I can see what he was talking about. The report I commissioned has the incept date of the leak at about six years ago. According to what Jonas uncovered shortly before his death, the leaks go back much farther than that.

"I think perhaps Jonas was beginning to suspect who the mole was. Pity he's dead."

"If Jonas found the clues," Michael said, "so can you. You're not letting the matter drop, are you?"

"I'm not sure it makes sense to pursue it any further," Hadley said. "At least in this way. You see, the mole took one last massive chunk of information—all the data on our Soviet networks, including active agents, local informants and sleepers. The retrieval of that intelligence is of paramount importance. Also, it appears that the mole has bolted with the intelligence. Most likely, he's already on the other side of the Iron Curtain."

"And that's it?" Michael was incredulous.

"What else would you have me do, son, call out the army? Sometimes you have to take your lumps, learn from your mistakes and get on with the business at hand. This appears to be one of those times." General Hadley cleared his throat. "The only ray of hope from this mess is that you have a lead on the Katei document. Now look, Mike, get it for me, will you? I can't begin to tell you what it would mean for us. It may be our salvation."

Takashiba Pier. Brilliant spotlights, into which moths the color of ash hurled themselves in suicidal abandon, illuminated the purling harbor waters. The light bounced off the low waves, turning the water as black and opaque as obsidian. It looked solid enough to walk on.

Pale wisps of mist crept along the ground, softening the oil-stained concrete slabs. Here, as throughout the city, the streets were arumble with trucks and articulated semis, for in Tokyo, business deliveries could only be made at night. Out in the water, scarred tankers and low-lying ships were ablaze with lights as their crews off-loaded oil and produce bound for Tokyo's varied wholesale markets, where they would be traded at first light.

It had not been difficult to fool Masashi's guards. In the bath at her house, Michiko had called the maids back in, had dressed one of them in her robes and sent her out with the other girl attending her.

"Go to my rooms," she had said to the girl. Masashi's guards never went into her rooms but, rather, stood watch outside. "Get into bed as if you are me and stay there until I return." Which, she had said to Joji, had better be before the breakfast hour, when the guards sent one of the girls in to wake her.

It began to pour almost as soon as Joji and Michiko got out of the car. He pulled the collar of his raincoat up over his neck and, keeping a firm hold on her, hurried them along the pavement. He had kept Michiko in the car for nearly fifteen minutes while he observed the nocturnal rhythms of the area. But her anxiety was overpowering, and at last he broke off his vigil.

There was no one on the street. Several trucks lumbered

by, but they neither stopped nor slowed and Joji concentrated on the building where he and Shozo had encountered Daizo. It appeared just as it had then.

He went to the door, opened it slowly. He went in first, gun at the ready. They stood quite still.

Joji breathing in the same fish-and-oil fumes until his eyes adjusted to the gloom. "Do you hear anyone?" he whispered. Michiko might be blind, but her other senses were, he knew, far keener than his. She shook her head.

The tiny vestibule, the nearly vertical flight of stairs, the shabby walls and ceiling, materialized slowly from out of the darkness. He could hear the rain beating against the door like a drunken vagrant.

The door had creaked slightly on opening. But aside from that, they had made no sound since coming in off the street. He could hear a humming, as of an engine, and a slight vibration coming up through the floorboards. But that was all.

Keeping to the extreme inside of the stairs, they ascended slowly. Every three steps or so, they paused, listening still. The humming was so low now that he could barely discern it. The vibration had lessened as well.

Halfway up, he directed all his concentration on the hallway at the top of the stairs. There was a nimbus of pale light there, no doubt one of the streetlights coming in through a window. To the right, he knew, was the large, vacant room into which Shozo had disappeared, blasting away with his sawed-off shotgun. Joji smiled at the thought. Loyal Shozo.

He turned to Michiko. "I want you to stay here," he said in her ear. Did not wait for a reply, but crept upward, a step at a time. Rain, drumming on the flat concrete roof, quickly became an overpowering sound. He took the last five stairs very quickly.

Now he was in the hallway. He turned left, but there was only blackness. To the right, the watery light. He went in that direction.

In the vast room, the sound of the downpour was very loud. Joji could see why. The windows along the far side were open. Rain dribbled onto the floor, making puddles streaked with pale color as they reflected the arc lights from outside.

Joji crept out into the semidarkness. He could see the closed door behind which he had seen Tori held prisoner. He moved cautiously toward it, keeping to the shadows as best he could.

342

When he was three steps away from the door, he prepared himself. Put his face close to the door and said loudly, "Open up! Masashi-san wishes to speak to the little girl!" Rapping on the door with the butt of the pistol.

The door swung open at his touch, and Joji's heart sank. It wasn't locked. He stepped into the room.

It was deserted.

"Hey, buddy, what happened?" Stick Haruma asked. He handed Michael a glass with scotch and ice. "You look like you've just seen something that goes clank in the night."

"Michael?" Eliane reached for him. "Are you all right?"

Michael, at the foot of the ladder to the loft, gulped the liquor in a convulsive gesture. "My uncle's dead," he said tonelessly.

"You mean Uncle Sammy?" Stick Haruma shook his head. "I'm sorry, buddy. I remember that old bird. I liked him."

Eliane was looking from one to the other, careful to keep her emotions under control.

"Yeah," Stick Haruma said. "Old Jonas Sammartin was the last of a breed."

"How did it happen, Michael?" Eliane asked.

"A heart attack. He keeled over in his office."

"Just like that, huh?" Stick Haruma poured Michael another shot of scotch. "Drink up, Mike. Life is fleeting. You never know when it's your time to check into the astral plane." He lifted his glass, clinked it first against Michael's, then Eliane's. "Let's all toast Uncle Sammy. He was a helluva guy."

Michael drank the scotch mechanically, not feeling it at all. "I've got to get out of here for a while," he said to no one in particular.

Eliane took a step toward him, but Stick made a motion to hold her back. "Whatever you say, buddy," Stick said. "Sometimes it's better to be alone."

But as soon as Michael had left, Stick turned to Eliane and said in Japanese, "I'm going to keep an eye on him. Stay here until we get back. I know something serious is going on, otherwise Mike would have brought a present, *neh*?"

Eliane nodded. Japanese custom dictated that presents be brought for a wide variety of everyday events. Coming to a friend's house was only one of many. To fail to do so was a serious breach of etiquette.

"It's very serious," she said.

He nodded absently, repeating, "Stay here," as he went out the door.

How does one find another human being in a city of ten million souls crowded together like lemmings? The sidewalks of Tokyo were choked with people, the streets strangling in traffic so thick it barely moved. In winter the secondhand button stores did a land-office business; the buttons of one's overcoat were continually being ripped off by the crush of people. In summer it was a futile effort to carry one's picnic lunch to the park. Invariably, the food would be smashed flat by the crush of the masses of people long before one arrived.

As if this were not enough, Tokyo was laid out in no discernible pattern. It was a literal maze of great wide avenues and twisting side streets. No building address was ever posted, so that one continually saw even long-time Tokyo residents asking for directions at the local neighborhood police precincts.

As he wandered through the dense throngs, Michael was appalled by the congestion of human beings and mechanical conveyances. Stick had been right, he thought. It had been a long time since he had been here. Of course he remembered Tokyo as being crowded, but memories were often difficult to assess. This reality stunned him. There was so little space for so many people! He had heard about but had never seen the so-called capsule hotels popular with the frugal Japanese businessmen throughout the country. Instead of a room, one climbed into a capsule of approximately six by four feet. It contained a *futon* on which to sleep, a light and a clock radio. Japanese did not complain about such quarters, which would drive an American into a frenzy. Overcrowding was a fact of life in Japan, something with which one grew up.

Michael stopped to look into a department-store window. It was filled with colored lights, winking and glowing. His gaze shifted, and he saw Stick Haruma's reflection.

"You forgot an umbrella," Stick said, holding his opened one over their heads. "How you doing, pal?"

Michael shook his head. "I don't know."

"Come on," Stick said. "Let's grab a bite."

They went into the department store, a veritable city within a city. There were six restaurants in this one. Stick took them up to the roof level. Soon they were seated at a table overlooking the city. The blaze of light was stunning. Enormous spires rose from the Shinjuku section, reaching skyward with a kind of blind arrogance.

344

"I think you'd better tell me about it," Stick said after they had ordered.

I've got to tell someone, Michael thought. He looked at his friend, and for the first time since Uncle Sammy had called him to tell him that his father had been killed, he felt safe. "Here's how it started," he began. He ran through everything, leaving nothing out except his suspicions concerning Eliane. He did not want to prejudice Stick; he wanted to know what his friend thought of her first.

That's how he wound up. "What do you think of Eliane?" he asked.

The food had come by then, and Stick was already digging in. "First you tell me what you're doing running around with Eliane Yamamoto."

Michael almost dropped his chopsticks. "What do you mean? She told me her name was Eliane Shinjo."

"She lied," Stick said. His face registered real concern now. "Mike, this woman's the daughter of Nobuo Yamamoto, the head of Yamamoto Heavy Industries."

It was as if a shotgun had gone off inside Michael's head. Where there had been only enigmatic darkness now there was light. Michael recalled his conversation with Uncle Sammy. Michael had felt that there must be some ulterior motive for Nobuo's odd behavior at the meeting at the Ellipse Club. At the time, Michael had thought it odd that Nobuo should deliberately seek to torpedo the trade talks. Why would he want to do that? Michael had asked Uncle Sammy. Jonas had told him to keep his mind on the task at hand: finding out who within the Japanese Yakuza had murdered Philip Doss and why.

Now, Michael thought, I run—literally!—into Nobuo Yamamoto's daughter on Maui, who tells me she's Yakuza and who, in effect, becomes my partner. Why? What does she want? What the hell is going on?

"If she is Yamamoto's daughter," he said, still a little disbelieving, "how is it she knows the workings of the Taki-gumi Yakuza clan inside and out?"

"Now, that's a good question," Stick Haruma said. "And one that most people hereabouts wouldn't be able to answer. But I'm plugged into the bureaucratic network that makes this country run. You ever hear of Wataro Taki?"

"The godfather of the Yakuza?" Michael said. "Everybody's heard of him."

"Well, Eliane's mother, Michiko, is Wataro Taki's adopted

345

daughter. Ever since old Wataro died, the Taki-gumi has been ripped apart by factionalism. The youngest son, Masashi, is the *oyabun*, but it's said that he had his eldest brother, Hiroshi, murdered. For sure he threw out the third brother, Joji, so that he would have a clear run at succeeding Wataro. As for their stepsister, no one knows where Michiko Yamamoto's allegiance lies. She was totally devoted to Wataro." He shrugged. "Now that the old man's gone, who knows?"

Michael looked at his friend and thought, Jesus Christ, Eliane's in the middle of it all. She could be working for any of the factions. "Stick," he said, "I'm in trouble. I need your help."

"You've only to ask," Stick Haruma said. He pointed with his chopstick. "You going to finish that *sashimi*? It'd be a shame to waste any."

"Take it," Michael said. "I don't have much of an appetite."

"That's a mistake." Stick Haruma reached over, exchanging his empty plate with Michael's half-full one. "It has always been my opinion that strategy is best worked out on a full stomach." He dipped a piece of raw fish into a combination of soy sauce and *wasabi*. "Hunger never did anyone any good."

Michael laughed, his black mood dispelled. "You haven't changed, have you?" He shook his head. "Thank God for that."

"God has nothing to do with it," Stick said, around another piece of fish. "God is a concept I find it deplorable that honest men are expected to accept."

Michael shook his head. "I've missed you, buddy. That's for sure."

"Okay," Stick said, finishing up, "what do you want to do?"

Michael dug into his pocket, took out the length of dark-red braided cord. He placed it on the table between them. "Do you recognize this?"

Stick picked it up, turned it over as he examined it. "Isn't this from the temple?" There was no need to explain further. The two students, having studied under the same *sensei*, knew which temple.

Michael nodded. "It is. My father left this for me on Maui. I was thinking about it on the plane all the way over here. Now I'm sure that it's a clue to where he hid the Katei document."

"At the temple?"

346

"Right."

Stick sat back. "Okay, suppose you're right," he said thoughtfully. "But what are you going to do about Eliane Yamamoto? You don't know where she stands in all this or what she wants. How are you going to find out?"

"That," said Michael, "is where you come in."

"What's happened? What's the matter?"

He could see her face, dead white in the wash of lights from the windows out onto the pier. He thought that he had never seen so much terror concentrated in one face.

"Tori's not here," Joji said. "They must have moved her."

"Why would they do that?"

"Because of my raid, because Daizo is dead, because Masashi knows I'm coming after him. I don't know."

"Joji-chan," Michiko said, "we must find my granddaughter."

"She could be anywhere. She—"

"No. No." She was shaking him. "Don't talk like that. We have these hours of the night to find her." She took his hand. "Now, come on. And put away that gun. We can't afford the noise. Use this." Joji took the *tanto*, the long dagger she handed him.

She led him back down the hallway. Being blind was no impediment to her. She had long ago learned to compensate by using her other senses. In the darkness of the hallway, in fact, it was Joji who was the clumsy one, bumping into her as she stopped abruptly. He felt something, reached out. "Is that a *katana* you're holding?" he whispered.

"Shhh," she cautioned. "Someone's coming."

Joji strained to hear the sounds of approach. He could hear the dim humming of the machinery, but nothing else. Then he smelled food and heard someone whistling.

In a moment, he saw a Yakuza soldier walking through a shaft of light thrown off by a bare bulb somewhere high above their heads. The man was carrying a tray of food. He was coming toward them from the other end of the hallway. Between where Joji and Michiko stood and the oncoming Yakuza was the staircase down to the street.

Now Joji could see the steel blade of the sword that Michiko carried make its way into the shaft of light. It turned in the Yakuza's direction. He saw it, stood stock still.

"Your name," Michiko commanded.

The Yakuza gave it to her.

347

"I want to know where the little girl is being held."

"The little girl?" the man said. "I don't—"

He gave a little yelp as the tip of the blade sliced through his shirt. Blood oozed from the cut in his chest.

"Take us there," Michiko hissed.

The man nodded, and they followed him as he went down the stairs and then in through the entrance behind the stairwell. There was a flight heading down. The sounds of working machinery were stronger now, as was the deep vibration.

The man took them down the stairs, into the lower level. Into a corridor that appeared to have been abandoned for many years. Dust, cobwebs, rotting boxes and timbers dominated.

There was a door at the end of the corridor, where it dead-ended.

"In there," the man said. "But you'll never get her out alive. You'll never get out alive."

His eyes crossed as Michiko hit the back of his head with the pommel of the sword. Joji snatched the tray out of his hands. He looked at Michiko.

"Why are you hesitating, Joji-chan?"

Joji looked from the fallen Yakuza to the closed door. "Maybe he's right. They could kill her."

"Not if you do this right," she said. "The food is our way inside. Use it." She bent down, dragged the Yakuza into the dusty shadows of the dead end, then, taking up her sword again in the two-handed grip, she nodded.

Joji took a deep breath.

"Remember," she said. "Get them to talk."

He knocked on the door. "Food," he said to the mumbled response. "Dinner break."

The door opened, a man looked out, aiming a gun at Joji's midsection.

"Who're you?" the man said suspiciously.

Joji recognized him instantly as one of Tori's captors. He gave the man a name.

"I don't know you," the man said.

"I don't know you either," Joji said. "I just do what I'm told."

"Good little toad, aren't you?" The man laughed. He opened the door wide.

Joji stepped back, and in the same instant, Michiko rushed from the shadows. Her *katana* flashed downward.

"What?"

The look of shock on the Yakuza's face barely had time to turn to disbelief as the blade sliced into him.

Joji dropped the tray of food, knelt and threw the *tanto*. It embedded itself to the hilt in the second man just as he leaped up from a chair.

The sounds woke Tori up. She sat up on the makeshift *futon* that had been laid out for her.

"Granny," she said, rubbing at her eyes. "Is this a dream?"

Michiko scrambled over the prostrate form of the Yakuza she had killed. She gathered her granddaughter into her arms. "It's not a dream, Little One. Here I am." She was weeping silent tears.

"Granny, I knew you'd come," Tori said. "Why are you crying?"

Michiko said to Joji, "Keep her head turned away from it." She meant the blood.

"Are the men sleeping?" Tori asked.

"Yes, darling. They're tired from keeping you safe for so long." Michiko nearly choked on her words. But with her granddaughter in her arms, she felt as if she had been reborn. I'm alive again, she thought. She said a heartfelt prayer to Megami Kitsune, the fox-goddess, who, she was certain, had watched over Tori and kept her safe.

Having determined that both the Yakuza were dead, Joji retrieved the *tanto* from its grisly resting place. He wiped it on the dead man's clothing. Then he led Michiko and Tori from the room.

"How are you, Little One?" Michiko said. The combination of joy and relief was making her light-headed, and she leaned heavily on Joji's arm.

"I missed you, Granny," Tori said. "I missed how good this smells." She buried her face in Michiko's thick hair.

The corridor was choked with dust. It was long, dark, deserted. The sounds of the machinery were very strong.

"Is Mommy here too?" Tori asked, yawning. She was already on the verge of sleep.

"She will be, my brave girl," Michiko said. "Very soon now."

Lillian spent a long time staring at nothing while the aromatic steam from the tea penetrated her sinuses. She lifted the cup to her lips and drank.

This morning, when she awoke, she had seen a brown-and-yellow butterfly skip over the ferns. It touched here, there, never alighting for more than the space of a wingbeat. Below it, crawling over the climbing vines and flowers outside her room, a caterpillar made its slow, deliberate way.

Two such different creatures, Lillian thought, pouring herself more tea. And yet, within the space of a week, there would be two brown-and-yellow butterflies darting over the ferns.

Two such different creatures, she thought, and yet both are one. Like me. Yesterday I was the caterpillar I have been for decades, and today I am the butterfly. I have been transformed. I have been set free of the shackles of my life. And I have my revenge, as well.

She saw him the moment he walked into the restaurant. A tall, slim, handsome man with thick, straight salt-and-pepper hair, searching gray eyes. She was wearing her Dior gown, and felt alive and free. Terribly free.

He was wearing a pearl-gray suit with deep blue pin stripes. Lillian was pleased to see that it was the one she had picked out for him, the cut flatteringly elegant. (Years ago, he wore the old-fashioned wide-lapeled style in inappropriately heavy wool.)

She had seen him right away because she was looking for him in the corner facing the door. (She had often made fun of this habit of sitting in the same place no matter which restaurant they were in. Until he had explained to her why he did it, that it was part of his training. She had understood that immediately, even admired his discipline.)

The maître d' led her to his table, and he rose, smiling, kissed her on each cheek. He ordered a gimlet with a twist for her. He was drinking a Campari-and-soda, having fallen into the current Parisian habit of drinking lightly at mealtimes.

"How are you?"

He never addressed her by name or even by a nickname—unless, of course, they were in bed making love. Then he always did, as if making up for lost time.

"Was your trip eventful?"

Which was just like him. Not, Did you have a safe trip? He always needed to elicit information, she had found, even in their most personal conversations. That, too, was part of his training, she supposed.

"It was pleasant," she said, nodding to the maître d', who had brought her drink himself. They were regulars here.

"Then, here's to it," he said, raising his glass. He clinked it against hers, and they both drank. "I'm glad to see you."

"You say that as if you weren't sure whether you would see me this time." She watched his eyes, something he had taught her, along with the tricks she now used to identify people's nationalities by their facial physiognomy. He was always teaching her something useful.

"To be honest," he said, "I had my doubts."

"Why? I've always come before." She could see some nervousness lurking behind his eyes.

He nodded, acceding the point. "But this is not like before." His deference to the truth always made his comments more forceful. "This is totally different." There was always something to learn in what he said, as well as how he said it. "This is the final time."

"And you thought I might get cold feet?"

"Pardon me?"

She loved to see that perplexed look on his face. It was partly because it happened so infrequently, partly because there was a thrill in knowing that she had caused it. "That I might change my mind at the last minute."

"I was like that," he said meditatively, "just before my marriage." He rarely talked about his wife. Her mother had been a Jew, he had explained. That made her a Jew. He had known that before they had gotten married, had gone on with it even knowing that it would be a liability should her secret come to light. Which it had. A rival had discovered her secret. The rival had tried to bring him down, but instead, he had destroyed the rival. But not before his wife had been imprisoned and tortured. She never emerged from her catatonic state and was now in a sanatorium. He visited her every week. "I got, what did you call it?" He smiled. "Cold feet? Yes. I got cold feet. Not that I did not love her. I loved her. But still." Lillian continued to watch his eyes. "It was a big step. An enormous adjustment. Life is sometimes not so easily disturbed. The mind tends to reject change, don't you think?"

"Sometimes," she said. "It depends."

"On what?" He was genuinely curious, and she liked that.

"On the person. On the circumstances." She sipped at her gimlet. "Change is only difficult when one is either happy or unhappy. As it happens, I am neither. I welcome the change. It makes me feel . . . free."

"And you have no second thoughts." How like him to be so thorough.

"None."

He nodded, serious. "I understand. I think that is very

good." He smiled his quick, charming smile. It made him seem almost boyish. She was reminded of their reunion. It had been many years ago and, of course, she had already been quite friendly with his sister.

It had been his sister who had made the first contact. It had been here in Paris. At a bistro Lillian used to frequent on the Boulevard Saint-German. Lillian loved to sit and sip her Americano while watching the young college students walking by in chattering groups, laughing, singing, perhaps, an old Pete Seeger folk song. She would be swept away by nostalgia and could summon up whole her own college days. Back then, it had been her only escape from Washington. And Philip's excesses of absence and infidelity.

His sister was a nice-looking woman, though in Lillian's opinion quite plain. She was perhaps several years younger than Lillian. But as it turned out, she had the same problems. Her husband continued to cheat on her while keeping the fiction of a happy marriage. She had thought about leaving him, she confided in Lillian one afternoon, but she lacked the confidence.

After that, Lillian spent much of their time together bolstering her confidence and trying to convince her to leave her husband. But that was something his sister just could not do. It was too much of a break, too terrible a schism to contemplate. Her life, she said, was so bleak and stultifying. Imagine, she found herself fantasizing about a clerk in her office. You know, sexual things. Wasn't that weird and a little bit wicked?

Absolutely not, Lillian had said. By now she was fully involved in his sister's life. She found it amazing and just a bit exhilarating to be able to see another person's problems so clearly and to be able to help in solving them. It made her feel wanted. No, *better* than wanted: useful. Fantasies of that nature were quite normal, she said, thinking of her own. And in fact, what was to stop the sister from making those fantasies reality? Oh, she couldn't possibly, his sister had said. Not ever. It would be evil. But why? Lillian had argued. If she could not leave her life behind, what was evil about trying to make it as pleasant as possible?

In the ensuing afternoons she worked on his sister, slowly convincing her of the positive aspects of having an affair. And in the process had convinced herself that it was perfectly all right for *her* to have one.

It had been about that time, hadn't it, that she had been introduced to him. One day his sister had brought him along, a lonely diplomat newly assigned to the Paris embassy, who needed a little orientation. And my vacation's up, his sister had said. I have to go home. She had smiled, almost shyly. Would you be so kind?

Lillian, of course, had. She was ripe to meet him. She was bored, angry, alone. And in the most romantic city in the world.

Had she really been surprised that he had turned out to be David Turner? Or, more accurately, the man she had once known as David Turner. The man to whom, long ago, she had been so attracted. Her teacher, her mentor. The man she had saved so many years ago and who then had vanished without a trace. The man who would now become her control in the world of secrets she so desperately wanted to enter.

He was still handsome, dashing, perhaps even more so. Of course he was in need of a bit of changing here and there. But he was as steady, as stable, as a mountain. His world was so well defined that it, quite naturally, helped her bring hers into perspective. The chaos with which Philip had forced her to deal disappeared when she was with him. And best of all, he never left her. Quite the contrary. It was she who, periodically, was obliged to leave him. What could have been more natural than for the two of them to slip into a delicious affair? On the other hand, who could have foreseen that events would lead her to this point in time?

"How is Mimi?" Lillian asked now.

"She is fine," he said. "She asks about you all the time."

"I miss her."

"Good," he said, putting his hand over hers.

"I've wanted to ask you this." She was suddenly shy. "Why did you use Mimi? Why didn't you come to me yourself?"

"The truth? I didn't know how you would receive me. Back in Tokyo, I left you so abruptly. It was necessary, of course, but I didn't know whether you understood that."

Lillian smiled a little. "I remember when Mimi brought you. I remember thinking that I had been sure I'd never see you again. Of course, that's what I had told myself. But I think, now, that I knew all the time that I would. And then I realized that that was another thing you had taught me: how to be patient."

"I never properly thanked you for what you did for me in Tokyo."

"Yes, you have," she said, squeezing his hand. "Over and over."

Their eyes locked for a moment.

It was time, Lillian knew, to cross the Rubicon. She opened her purse, extracted a tiny packet. "I've brought it," she said. She dropped it into his palm. There, she thought. It's over. And it was easy.

"So," Yvgeny Karsk said, "we have come not to the end"— he lifted his glass again—"but to a new beginning."

When Eliane awoke, Michael was already gone. She turned over on the *futon* in Stick Haruma's tiny guest room and felt the warmth Michael's body had made there. She ran her hand over the depression in the *futon*, stroking it gently. She put her head where his had been, closed her eyes. She dreamed of him without going back to sleep.

When she opened her eyes again, she was ready to get up.

Wrapping one of Stick's spare kimonos around her, she went into the bathroom. They would have to get themselves some clothes today, she thought. When she emerged, she heard someone working in the kitchen. Stick was preparing breakfast.

"Have you seen Michael?" she asked.

"Went out before I got up," Stick said, molding rice balls. He looked up suddenly, said, "You like this stuff for breakfast?"

"Not especially."

He grinned. "Me either. How about we go to a pancake house I know in Shinjuku?"

She laughed. "Let me guess. All the Americans go there, right?"

"Yup. This place makes the best flapjacks this side of the international date line."

"I've never had pancakes," Eliane said.

"Then you haven't really lived."

A half hour later, Eliane looked across the table at Stick Haruma and said, "What is that?"

He held up the glass bottle. "Maple syrup," he said. "It goes over the pancakes."

Eliane looked dubiously at the brown viscous liquid. "You must," Stick insisted. "They're not the same without the syrup."

Eliane gingerly poured some over her pancakes, took a bit. "Hey, this is good," she said.

He had taken her to Pancake Heaven. It was on the second floor of an office tower, built out on a glassed-in balcony overlooking much of the Kabuki-cho, the eastern half of Shinjuku. From this vantage point, they could view streets filled to overflowing with gaily dressed crowds. There did not seem to be one square inch in which to maneuver.

Chrome and pink Formica gave the coffee shop a bright, retro look, and the people who came here to eat the pancakes, eggs and bacon, the meatloaf and mashed potatoes, fit the same description. They were teenagers in black leather jackets or sports jackets out of the 1950s. They laughed and chatted, reaching over one another in a happy tangle to get at the sugar or the salt.

"I like this place," Eliane said. "It's different."

"Yeah," he said, ordering another batch of pancakes, "I don't imagine you'd have much experience with a place like this."

She looked at him. "What do you mean?"

He shrugged. "Your family has so much money, it probably doesn't know what to do with it. What reason would you have to come here? You probably never even had the opportunity."

"I don't understand," Eliane said. But she was terrified that she did.

"Then I'll make sure you understand," Stick said as the waitress replaced his empty plate with a new one filled with steaming pancakes. "Your father is Nobuo Yamamoto. The Yamamotos do not hang around neighborhoods like the Kabuki-cho. He certainly would never have taken his daughter here, now would he?"

"You've made a mistake," Eliane said. "My name is Shinjo. Eliane Shinjo."

"Pardon me, Miss Yamamoto," Stick said, "but there's really no point in going on in this vein. You see, despite the fact that you avoid being photographed, I know who you are. I saw you with your father, Yamamoto-san, at his factory complex in Kobe." He stuck a forkful of pancake into his mouth, continued as he chewed. "Do you remember the day when Yamamoto Heavy Industries announced that it had received government subsidies to develop the FAX jet fighter? I'm sure you do, since you were at your father's side when he made the announcement to the press. There were a lot of foreign dignitaries there. The embassy was in need of my services. I translated your father's speech."

Eliane put down her fork. "All right," she said. "What do you want?"

He shrugged. "That depends."

"On what?" she asked warily.

"On how much of a help I can be to you."

She watched him as a mongoose will watch a snake. "I don't see that you can be of help to me at all."

"Really?" Stick Haruma continued to eat. "Well, that's too bad. Because Mike finally figured out where this Katei document you've been searching for is hidden. Sure, I know all about everything. He told me yesterday. See, Mike trusts me." He swiped up the last of the syrup with the last wedge of pancake. He had this down to a science. "Which is more than I can say for how he feels about you. He's going to take me with him when he makes his final run at the document. You he's going to leave behind, because he doesn't trust you."

"And, I suppose," Eliane said, "that this is where you can help me out."

"Possibly."

"Mike is your friend," she said. "Why would you betray him?"

Stick relaxed back in his chair, contemplating her. "Is that what I would be doing?" he drawled.

"It seems like that to me."

"Everyone's got a price, Miss Yamamoto. At least, all the smart people I know say that. I wonder what your price is?"

"I resent that."

"I wonder who you're working for? Your father? Masashi Taki? Your mother, Michiko? I can't believe that Nobuo Yamamoto is mixed up with the Taki-gumi. Surely you're not Yakuza yourself?"

"No," she said. "I am not Yakuza." She was abruptly exhausted. It seemed to her as if all the layers of deceit beneath which she was operating were like so many sleepless nights laid end to end. The endless lying, the constant fear that she would reveal something that she should not, had worn her down. Having been buried for so long, she now wanted nothing more than to shed all her identities. She wanted to be free.

"Then," Stick said, "who are you?"

Eliane looked away from his intense face, out and down to where the clouds of shoppers and strollers clogged the avenue beneath the riot of outsize neon signs. With all her heart she wanted to be down there, walking carefree in the cool morning air. It had begun to rain again, and she wanted it to rain on her. She wanted to feel the reality of that wetness as it slowly soaked through her clothes. She wanted to know,

356

finally, that she was still alive. But she couldn't. She was trapped here, under the earth, in an identity she did not want, telling lies to people she cared about, perhaps even loved. Without quite knowing how she had gotten there, she had become quite desperate.

"I haven't thought of myself as Eliane Yamamoto in quite some time," she said. "I no longer remember what it is like to be her. And more than anything else, that is what I want to be."

"Well?" Stick said. "What's stopping you?"

"Circumstance," Eliane said. "Obligation." She pulled herself away from the view of outside. It depressed her all the more, seeing what she wanted, what she could not have. Because of *giri*, the burden too great to bear. "Family."

Stick Haruma said nothing. At last she said, "Perhaps I do need your help after all."

"If you can meet my price."

Eliane thought about this for a long time. She seemed to believe that whatever she said next was of the gravest importance. "I want you to help me convince Michael that I am trustworthy." She knew that she was nearing the end of what she was capable of doing. Her anxiety over the fate of Tori colored every word she spoke, every move she made.

"Okay," Stick said. "What's in it for me?"

"I think I made a mistake," Eliane said, starting to rise. "If you were really Michael's friend, you would never ask that. I want only what is best for him. I'm here to protect him, to help him in any way I can. Maybe he doesn't know you as well as he thinks he does."

"Relax, Eliane," Michael said, appearing from out of the throng of teenagers in Pancake Heaven. He was wearing jeans and a leather jacket. With his stubble of beard, he fit right in here. "Stick and I know one another as well as two human beings can. What he did here, I asked him to do."

"What?"

"That's right," Michael said, smiling. "Now that I know whose side you're really on, it's time you and I finally got to know each other."

Tori was dozing in Michiko's arms. There was a great deal of excitement surrounding her, and she was aware of it. But she was also very tired. Fear was an exhausting emotion, and Tori had been frightened for days now. Only the daily calls from her granny had kept her from being hysterical.

Now, riding her grandmother's hip, feeling the slow beat of her heart, she felt warm and protected. It was time to sleep, and to dream. Tori loved to dream: the colors of light filtering through high trees, the sounds of birds flitting from branch to branch, the smells of spring.

Tori was aware of motion as Michiko hurried down dimly lit corridors, Joji at her side. She was aware, too, of sounds. Deep-breathing sounds, like those from a very large animal, perhaps as large as a dinosaur, though Tori was old enough to know that dinosaurs were no longer alive. Then what was making those deep, even sounds?

She opened her eyes, turned her head in order to see if what she had been told was wrong, if indeed there was a dinosaur still alive down here. She saw the shadow moving toward her. It was too small to be a dinosaur, but she recognized it anyway and she said, "Granny . . ."

Michiko and Joji were carefully retracing their steps, alert for any sounds of oncoming men. But the heavy machine thrumming, which Tori, in her childlike way, had attributed to breathing, became more insistent.

"Wait, Joji," Michiko whispered. "Did we just pass a doorway on our left?"

Joji went back. "Yes."

"I want you to take a look in there," Michiko said. "I want to know what Masashi is up to in here."

"Michiko-chan," Joji said nervously, "I do not think this is wise. We have Tori. Let us be off as quickly as we can. The longer we remain here, the greater the danger grows."

"I agree," Michiko said. "But Nobuo has been terrified for weeks. He thinks that he hides his fear from me, but I can sense it, in the way he walks in short, choppy strides; I can hear it in the manner of his speech around the house. What does Masashi want from Nobuo, I have asked myself over and over. I have no answer. But the answer is surely here, Joji-chan. We will never have another chance to find out what is happening here. We must take the risk, no matter how great we perceive it to be." She pushed him. "Now go. And hurry."

Joji ducked through the darkened doorway. Immediately, he felt a rush of cool air. The wind-tunnel effect made it clear that he was in a small room. He groped his way toward the far side, felt along the wall for a door handle. When he found it, he pulled.

He stepped through. Now he felt the full rush of wind, and

358

looked down. He had emerged onto a section of the catwalk that overhung the vast inner space of the warehouse's basement. He was quite near the spot where Masashi and Kozo Shiina had stood watching the unloading of the Soviet nuclear device some time before.

Joji could see men in radiation suits walking swiftly below him. He peered at them. There were markings on their suits. With a start, he recognized the Yamamoto Heavy Industries crest.

The device was visible. The Yamamoto technicians had it out of its lead-lined container and were beginning to lower it gingerly into the nose pocket of what looked to Joji like some kind of missile or bomb casing.

Joji's heart nearly stopped at the sight. He went quickly back through the doorway. His mind was filled with the manner in which he was going to tell Michiko what he had seen. He was halfway across the small, darkened room when he heard voices. They were coming from the corridor where he had left Michiko and Tori, and a vertiginous feeling of terror gripped him.

He moved quickly, clinging like a lizard to a soot-encrusted wall. He moved his head slightly. He saw Michiko. She was clutching Tori tightly to her breast. Beside her was Masashi. He had her *katana*.

Joji strained to hear what was taking place.

"You have already caused me such difficulty," Masashi said. "Your presence here is difficult to understand. I wonder how you found out where I was keeping your granddaughter." Joji could see him shrug. "On the other hand, that does not matter. What is important is that I have seriously underestimated you. I will have to make certain that never happens again. I am operating under a deadline. Interference at this last, critical stage, even from my stepsister, cannot be tolerated. It must be dealt with in the only manner that will have any meaning now."

The sound of the rain was a roar as it bounced off the wood-and-thatch roof of the temple. They were in the northern suburbs, and one could see trees again.

Michael parked near the shrine complex. He looked out at the buildings shrouded in mist and rain and felt as if he had come home. So close to Tsuyo, he felt strength flooding back into him despite his painful cuts and bruises. He kept the engine running, otherwise in this weather the windows would fog.

"Eliane," he said, "you're going to have to tell me everything. Why didn't you want me to know your real name?"

"Do you want the truth?" It was Michael, she suddenly realized. Or, more accurately, her feelings about him that had changed everything. When she was with him, she forgot everything: circumstance, obligation, family. *Giri.* She closed her eyes for a moment and thought, Dear God, I am going mad. I am trapped between my fear for my daughter's life and my love for this man. I don't know what to do. Save me. Please save me.

"I always want the truth," he said. "That's all I've ever wanted from you. But it's been the one thing you've seemed incapable of giving me."

"That's because you seem to want some easy answer," she said, fighting the swirl of emotions that threatened to engulf her. "Something a movie heroine would say to a movie hero, one sentence that will make everything all right and understandable. But real life isn't so cut-and-dried. It's ten thousand subtle shades of gray, one overlapping the other."

She stared out the window. Michael sensed that she was distraught, that whatever she was going to say next had been on her mind for some time. He wanted to make this moment less difficult for her, but he did not know how.

At last she said, "I didn't tell you my real last name because I could not be sure I could trust you."

Michael stared at her. He wanted to grab her and shake her and say, *Trust me? But it was me who couldn't trust you.*

"I was told that I should trust you, that I had to trust you. But I could not know—nor could anybody else, for that matter—who you were loyal to. Was it to Jonas Sammartin? Your father? Someone we did not even know?"

And then Michael saw the maze of uncertainty within which she must have been operating. He saw what he had not been able to even moments before: that he and Eliane were like two blind mice sniffing the air in enemy territory. My God, he thought, how did we come this far without tearing each other apart?

"You said that you were told certain things about me," he said. "You also seem—seemed—to know Uncle Sammy. You'd better explain that."

Eliane sighed. "This is where the layers of gray begin to overlap." She took his hands in hers. "No son wants to hear

360

this, Michael. But now you've asked for the truth, and I see that I have gone as far as I can in withholding that truth."

Her eyes were large. He stared into them, seeming to get lost within their depths. Later, when he replayed this moment in his memory, he would recall the feeling her eyes imparted to him, and the hurt, anguish and disruption would be assuaged somewhat.

"The truth is that your father and my mother were lovers."

Michael did not know what he was expecting, but it certainly wasn't this. "What do you mean?" He said it mechanically, without thinking, filling up a silence too dreadful to allow.

"They met in 1946," Eliane said. "They worked together when your father was in the CIG. Until there came a time when her adopted father, Wataro Taki, forbade her from seeing Philip Doss again."

"And that was the end of it," Michael said, somewhat relieved. "Well, that was a long time ago."

Eliane held his hands tighter, as if he were a child who she knew would be in need of comforting when the pain hit. "No," she said softly. "It wasn't the end for them." It was raining harder now. The windshield wipers slewed the water back and forth. The drumming against the car's top was very loud. "My mother disobeyed Wataro Taki. She had never done such a thing—had never even contemplated doing so—before. But now she felt that she must. She could not let Philip go."

Michael was staring blankly out at the downpour. "You mean all this time, up until his death, your mother and he were . . ."

"Michael," she said, "do you remember I told you about the prayer that was taught to me when I was little? It went, 'Yes is a wish. No is a dream. Having no other means of crossing this life, I must use yes and no. Allow me to keep hidden the wish and the dream so that someday I may be strong enough to do without them both.' "

"I remember."

"It was your father who taught me that prayer." He turned to her. "Yes, your father. But it wasn't until I was much older that I understood the true nature of what he meant. You see, Michael, we are the wish and the dream. Your father sent you to become a warrior. My mother did the same. Was it coincidence? For many years I thought so. Until my mother took me to meet my adopted grandfather.

361

"Surely I had seen him as an infant, even as a young child, but I had no memory of him. Now that I had been through the most arduous martial arts training, he wanted to see me. It seems to me now that what he told me is as important for you now as it was for me then. He said that for many years my mother, Michiko, was his right arm. Philip Doss was his left arm. But times changed, and one must make way for the future. 'You are the future, Eliane,' he told me.

"Then he told me why I was given a Caucasian name instead of a Japanese one. This was my eighteenth birthday, and it was my present from him. He said that he had requested that I be named Eliane. Because I was the future. For the Taki-gumi and Japan. I was to be a living symbol of the internationalization Japan must have in order, not only to prosper in the coming century, but merely to survive. It is difficult for Japanese to move away from such ingrained notions. Therefore, I was to be the reminder."

Eliane took Michael's hands, placed them against her breast. "Now I pass my grandfather's words on to you. Your father should have been the one to do it. But he is not here. I am a poor substitute, but I will have to do. We are the future, Michael. We were trained to answer the call to battle that our families knew was imminent."

"And here we are," Michael said, "immersed in the battle that killed my father, and I don't even know whether I want to be a part of it."

Eliane smiled. "I said the same thing when Wataro Taki recruited me."

"But I thought you said that you weren't Yakuza."

"I'm not," she said. "I never was. Just as my mother never really was. But that didn't stop your father from doing the same thing."

"What did Wataro want you to do?" Michael asked.

"He wanted me to become his new right arm," she said. "He wanted me to keep the peace among the Yakuza families without arousing the attention of the police. But by keeping the peace I knew he meant preserve the Taki-gumi's place of preeminence among the clans.

"I thought it was an impossible task, especially for a female, but Wataro was far more clever than I was. He had already devised his strategy. Together, we created a myth: He provided the history, and I gave that history substance.

"I became Zero."

* * *

362

Lillian took Yvgeny Karsk shopping. This was a great pleasure for her. These days, with the constant terror she felt for the safety of her children, such pleasures were to be cherished.

Karsk was lean and long; he had the body of a swimmer, certainly of an athlete. Time had had a difficult go of making inroads in his form. What he lacked was a sense of style. That wasn't difficult to understand. Russia might be the mother of many things, Lillian thought, but style wasn't one of them.

They blitzed the Rive Droite. She took him to Givenchy for suits, to Pierre Balmain for jackets and slacks, Charvet for dress shirts, Daniel Hechter for sports clothes (of which, shockingly, he had none). For shoes there was Robert Clergerie ("Don't be boring, darling," Lillian told him. "Everyone wears Bally, why should you?"), Missoni for ties, socks, pocket squares and other accessories made of their remarkably patterned fabrics.

They were finished by dinnertime, but Karsk was flagging long before that. "I never knew what hard work was before this," he said, only half jokingly.

"What are you talking about?" Lillian said. "This is a short day. We didn't meet until lunchtime."

"If we had actually gone to lunch," he said, "instead of embarking on this insane shopping spree, I should feel a whole lot better."

"Don't be an idiot," she said. "Now you're the best-dressed spy in all of Europe."

He winced. "I wish you wouldn't do that."

She burst out laughing. "You ought to see yourself. Really." He turned to look at himself in a store window. "No. No," she said. "That expression is gone now."

"I'm sure I won't know where to wear half of what you made me buy."

"I didn't make you buy anything," Lillian said. "You did it all yourself. And quite happily, I might say."

Karsk sighed deeply. He knew she was right about that. He did have some of the most alarming capitalist tendencies. He remembered what his wife said about Europe being his mistress. He knew what she meant by that: He loved being in Europe more than he did being in Russia. But that did not mean that he did not love his country.

"Can we have some dinner now?" he said. "Or at least a drink? That's what I had in mind when I called you this morning."

"Whatever you like. Pick the spot."

They took the *métro*, since the dinner hour coincided with a driver shift change and taxis were almost impossible to get.

Karsk had chosen the best Moroccan restaurant in town for the location. It was out of the way, down a long, dimly lit side street populated only by clusters of students smoking and popping gum. Karsk had had many clandestine meetings at the place and he was comfortable there. He didn't care much for the food; it always gave him indigestion.

The owner was a heavy-set man with a greasy face but an otherwise neat appearance. His one delight in life seemed to be welcoming returning patrons. Therefore, he was solicitous of Karsk's needs and always offered him a table in the darkest corner of the restaurant. As usual, Karsk sat facing the door. He ordered drinks for them both.

"Now," Lillian said, putting her hand lightly over his, "I am content to be with you. In those new clothes you look like a true European. *Tu es très chic, mon coeur.*"

"*Merci, madame.*"

The drinks came, and they both sipped slowly, savoring the quietude.

"I had my people develop what you delivered to me," Karsk said.

"And?" Lillian kept her face neutral. "Is it what you wanted?"

"Well, yes and no."

"Really?" She blinked. "How so?"

"What was developed is right on target. BITE's core data on its covert operations inside the Soviet Union. It is potentially the most damaging information we have ever been able to obtain about America's clandestine Russian networks. As far as it goes, that is. There's less than one tenth of what we were expecting. What you've given us is a tantalizing hint of an enormously exciting breakthrough."

"I know."

Karsk took a long moment to clear his head. He was aware of his pulse pounding and the beginning of a headache behind his right eye, which was a sure sign of excess tension. Very carefully, he said, "What do you mean by that?"

Lillian smiled. "It's simple, really. I gave you exactly what I meant to give you." She raised her eyebrows. "You didn't think I'd just hand over whatever you wanted, did you? There was a great deal of risk involved for me, as well as a major decision to drastically change my life. I can't go back to America. I knew that the moment you asked me to obtain this intelligence for you. So did you. You must have expected a quid pro quo."

Karsk was sitting ramrod straight. His drink and the mood of quiet relaxation were forgotten. "I expected—" His voice was so clotted with suppressed anger that he abruptly broke off, began again. "I thought you were doing this out of a sense of duty."

"Duty?" Lillian almost laughed in his face.

"Yes," he said. "Duty." His manner was becoming stiffer by the moment. "I have a sense of what is ideologically right. I was certain that you did as well. We are fighting a war, not of weapons or battalions, but of thought, of freedom for the common worker from the domination of the elite."

"Stop it," Lillian said so sharply that he was taken aback. "Next you'll be trotting out the ghosts of Marx and Engels. You're mistaken if you thought I was working for you for ideological reasons."

Karsk saw the waiter approaching out of the corner of his eye, impatiently waved him away. "What other reason could you have?"

"My own," Lillian said. "By working clandestinely for you all these years, I had the satisfaction of knowing that I was undermining what those I hated the most—my father, Jonas and Philip—were doing. Why else do you imagine that I never asked Philip for a divorce? Being married to him was part of my cover for you. It was perfect, in fact. Or, I should say, almost perfect. Because there is a price to pay for every joy in this world. And mine was watching my husband being unfaithful to me for decades. He never stopped seeing that Japanese bitch Michiko Yamamoto."

"If you hated him," Karsk said with an edge to his voice, "his dalliances shouldn't have mattered to you."

And Lillian, knowing that she had succeeded in bringing the focus of the conversation to her level—her own turf, as it were, where she was as confident as could be—said, "But it did matter, Yvgeny. I have a great deal of pride. I want to be cared about—to be needed. Everyone does. It was terribly painful to be married to a man who was indifferent to me."

He smiled. The effort almost caused his face to crack. "But you had me. You had our affair to come home to."

"Yes. Exactly." She touched his hand again. "With you, I saw everything that I had been missing for years. Going

365

back to my life with Philip after our times together made the substance of my life seem all the more poor."

He was clearly pleased, and he caressed her hands as he often did when they were in bed together.

"It is wonderful to be needed by a man," she said. "Like coming upon an oasis in the midst of a desert. You have saved my life, Yvgeny, quite literally."

Karsk pressed the back of her hand against his lips. "What would Paris be without you?" He smiled. "Getting back to the intelligence you stole from the BITE computer," he said. "Where is the rest of it?"

"I have it," Lillian said, "in a safe place. But don't worry. I have every intention of letting you have it. That was my promise, after all. And I am a woman of my word." She frowned. "However, there must be the proper recompense. As I have said, this was a long and arduous assignment. The element of risk was—and still is—enormous. But I willingly— one could say almost joyfully—took it on."

"And why?" Karsk said. He was quite dumbfounded. "Are you asking me to believe that you have betrayed your country solely out of a sense of revenge against the men in your life?"

"*Solely?* What can you possibly mean by that? That the ideals of Marxism-Leninism are the only things that make being a traitor a worthwhile calling?"

"Very much so. Yes. One only has to remember the ideals that caused the glorious people's revolutions around the world. Remember the books I gave you."

"Oh, I do remember them," she said. "I spent more solitary, sleepless nights than you would believe thinking about them and what they meant. But what I considered was what those ideals meant *to me*. And my conclusion was that on a certain level there is no difference between the ideology that fuels Washington and the Kremlin. Power corrupts, Yvgeny. There was never a truer statement made in the entire history of mankind. And the pursuit of absolute power corrupts absolutely. It is so in Washington, no less so in Moscow."

"You're wrong," Karsk said. "Terribly wrong."

"Am I? Let's see. We've only to look at you to prove otherwise. You claim that you are an avid Marxist, a paragon of Russian communism. And I believe you. Yet you are addicted to the West. Look at what you're wearing: the cream of Parisian couture."

"Because you took me to those boutiques."

"And I suppose I made you buy all the clothes you tried

on today. I suppose I paid for them." She shook her head. "No, you loved every minute of it. Just as you adore every minute you are here in Paris. You would rather be here than anywhere else in the world."

"I love Russia," he said, angry at the direction the conversation was taking. He did not enjoy being on the defensive, and he could not understand how he had been put in this position. "I love Odessa in the spring. I love—"

"Do you know what Henry James wrote about this city?" Lillian said, ignoring his protestations. " 'Paris is the greatest temple ever built to material joys.' And here is where you kneel and pray. Paris is where you worship, Yvgeny."

"I don't deny that I enjoy it here."

"And what about at home? Do you live in a cramped one-bedroom Moscow apartment, sharing quarters in a building with your fellow workers?" Her eyes were piercing.

"No," he said.

"Of course not. You no doubt live in a building reserved for high party officials. It is in the best neighborhood. You live in an apartment large enough for a family of six. Perhaps you can see the river from your windows. There is light and air and space to breathe. Isn't that so?"

"It's accurate enough."

"The paragon of socialism." Her tone was caustic. "The righteous warrior of Lenin." She reached into her handbag, shoved a sheaf of folded papers across the table at him.

"What are these?" He was looking at the papers as if they were a nest of scorpions he had just uncovered.

"What is owed me," Lillian said. "What your country owes me. What *you* owe me."

"This is nonsense," he said curtly. "You're being willful, childish. Give me the rest of the intelligence."

"I am quite serious," Lillian said. "Do you think that you will get it by the superior force of your masculine will?"

He touched her in a spot he knew she loved.

Her expression was cynical. "Or that I love you so much I will unthinkingly do whatever you ask?"

When he spoke again, his voice had changed. "I don't believe you understand the ultimate seriousness of your actions."

"Don't threaten me, Yvgeny," she said. "I am made of sterner stuff than that. If you even think of harming me, you'll never get your precious intelligence."

His eyes met hers for a moment, then he drew on a pair

of reading glasses, opened up the papers. There were two sets of three copies each. When he had read the first set through, he raised his gaze. He began to realize that he had seriously underestimated her. "This," he said, "has nothing at all to do with revenge."

"Revenge," Lillian said, "is the personal side of what I did. This is strictly business."

"So I see." His eyes flicked over the papers. "You want a bit more than asylum in my country."

"As I said, I can't go back to America. Ever. I have the rest of my life. I want to be happy."

He took off his glasses. "What you want," he said slowly, "is your own department within the KGB. You want, within one year of moving to Moscow, an appointment to the Politburo. This is impossible."

"Nothing," she said, "is impossible. Think of the intelligence you're getting."

"I understand that," Karsk said. "But the Politburo. My God, there are procedures, discussions that must take place, many individuals who must first give their assent. There must be a period of, er, adjustment."

"You're talking about the chance that I might be a Trojan horse sent over by the Americans." She laughed. "After everyone in the Politburo gets to read the intelligence that this operation—*your* operation, Yvgeny—netted, there won't be a doubt left about my authenticity. Think of the sensitivity—the extreme importance—of what I am bringing you. Every hour that you delay gives the Americans that much more time to cover their tracks."

For the first time, Karsk's face registered shock. "What are you saying? Did you bungle the operation? Do the Americans know what you've done? You assured me that you could access information from the computer without anyone knowing for at least a week."

"That's perfectly true," Lillian said. "But I left an electronic calling card. The people at BITE don't yet know who stole the Russian intelligence out of their central files, but they sure as hell know by now that it's gone."

"Oh my God." Karsk ran his fingers through his hair. His headache was becoming worse by the moment.

"Sign the agreement," Lillian said. "You have the authority to do so. I know it."

He looked at her.

She nodded. "Yes. I know that. I know everything about

you, Yvgeny. Even that you don't have a sister named Mimi. You don't have a sister at all. You used a trained KGB agent to gull me. You weren't sure of me after you fled Tokyo years ago. Yes, it was my call that saved you from Philip and Jonas. But still, you had lost touch with me. Who could know what my ideologies were years later? So you recruited Mimi to sound me out, to lead me back to you."

Karsk was glassy-eyed. It seemed that he had been outmaneuvered at every turn. "How long have you known that I was using you?"

"From the time I got back to Washington after my first meeting with Mimi. It was then that I went into the BITE computer and found you."

He was beginning to think that what she was asking of him was not so outlandish after all. She had a brilliant mind. And she had just proved conclusively that she was eminently well suited to clandestine work.

"All right," he said. He took out a pen, signed the three sets of papers.

Lillian held out her hand. "I'll take two."

"What is the third copy for?" he asked as he handed them over.

"It goes to a numbered bank account in Liechtenstein. Not Switzerland. Lately, the Swiss are becoming sticky about absolute privacy in their banks. If you or any of your people should have second thoughts about our arrangement, there are instructions to send copies of these agreements to every major paper in the world."

He laughed. "That will mean nothing."

She nodded. "On its own, no. But coupled with the evidence I have that you murdered Harold Morten Silvers, colonel in the United States Army, head of the Central Intelligence Group's Far East division, it will have a devastating effect." She thought Karsk was going to be sick. "Yes," she said quietly. "I know. No one else even suspected. But I knew you far better than Philip or Jonas could. I knew where you weren't the night Silvers was killed. I also knew where you were. If something happens to me in Moscow, everyone will know. Then your life will be over. All the gentlemen's rules by which you spies play will be thrown out the window. The Americans will not rest until they have hunted you down and exterminated you."

"But why dwell on such melancholy thoughts?" She nodded at the second set of papers. "There's more."

Karsk slipped on his glasses again. What he read here took all the breath out of him. His hands were shaking imperceptibly when his gaze met hers again. "This is monstrous. You can't mean it."

"But I do."

"Why?"

"Do you love her, Yvgeny? Do you love your wife?"

"Of course I do. I am devoted to her."

"That is not the kind of answer I would expect from a bold warrior such as yourself," she said. "It's something I would imagine an accountant or a bank clerk would say."

"It's just the truth, nothing more."

"So," she said, "it means that I have more to mold than merely your sense of style. Sign the document, Yvgeny, and you will have more than just the glory from the largest Soviet espionage coup of the century." She smiled. "You will be divorcing your wife. You will have me."

"But divorce." Karsk had never contemplated such a thing. It seemed unthinkable to uproot his domestic situation so completely. He had thought his lying about his wife would have avoided this kind of crisis. Suddenly, he got a hint of the enormous changes that must be taking place in Lillian's life.

As if reading his mind, she said, "It will be something that we can share. Our affair has been wonderful. Ecstatic, at times. I love Paris as much as you do. In fact, I found that I loved it more being with you. It didn't matter that we were playing a game. At least, not in that way. The sub-rosa context of our meetings gave our rendezvous an added kick. It certainly provided our lovemaking with spice." Now she took his hands in hers. "The truth is I'm tired of being alone, Yvgeny. I want power, and you're going to give that to me. But will it be enough? I can't fool myself. I will have my own department inside the KGB, I will be a member of the Politburo. But I am still a woman, and no man inside Russia is ever likely to let me forget it. Save you. I want you, Yvgeny. You are part of the deal."

"Lillian." Karsk slumped back in his chair. He had spoken her name at last.

"Sign this," she said, "and I'll give you all of the intelligence. Believe me, it's more than worth this price. It's everything you need to utterly destroy the American intelligence community abroad. Sign, and we'll leave Paris as soon as I pick up the rest of the intelligence. We'll disappear for a while. You'll need time to transcribe the material. It's massive, encyclopedic, and I doubt you'll want any clerks to see it at this stage. I know a place where neither your people nor mine will ever find us. In between the work, we'll have time just for ourselves. And then you can take me anywhere you want." She laughed. "Where will it be? Odessa? I have always wanted to see Odessa in the spring."

Michael hurled himself out of the car. He stood in the driving rain, oblivious, staring out at the great cryptomeria that rose above even the roof of the Shinto shrine.

Eliane watched him from inside the Nissan. There was no point in following him right away, she knew. He had forced her to throw too much at him in too short a time.

The dark sky opened up and Michael, seeing the pale oyster-gray rift in the charcoal thunderheads, began to cry. It was as if that contrast in colors, the ephemeral beauty that only nature—even in the most unexpected moments—can create, were the trigger. Inside him, his anger, his desperate love for his father coalesced, swirling, emotions of different colors, light and dark like those he saw displayed before him.

Michael wished with all his heart that his father were by his side now. There were so many questions he wanted to ask. The shock, the anger at what Philip Doss had done to Lillian was passing. And in its place was a sadness, the lost hope that all children born into difficult family situations must feel. That if only they could turn back the clock, they would have the power to make things right between their parents. If only . . . If only . . .

He turned and looked at Eliane. All he could see was an outline behind the beaded glass. The door opened, and she came out. As he watched her walking toward him, Michael felt closer to her than he had to anyone. He felt with a kind of eerie resonance her words, *We are the wish and the dream, Michael. We are the future.*

"Do you want to talk?" she asked.

"Not now," he said. "Not yet." This was his power spot, as hers had been the passage of the gods in Iao Valley. He felt the spirits calling to him.

"Let's get on with it," he said.

There was a set of wide stone steps up which he and Eliane climbed. Above them, a great red-lacquered *torii* rose, a silent sentinel amid the unquiet morning. On either side, groves of huge cryptomeria swayed and whispered in the wind and the rain. It was as if this part of the world—so near the city, yet centuries removed—were alive with their coming. Thinking of the *shintai* in his father's death poem, Michael smiled to himself.

At the top of the steps was a small covered area. He and Eliane were obliged to huddle together in order to make use of the shelter. All about them, the rain plummeted down as if seeking revenge against some unknown sin.

In the center of the shelter was a cord on which were tied several bells. Michael reached up and pulled the cord, sending the shivery sounds out into the countryside.

"Waking up the spirits," Eliane said, "so that they will be sure to hear our prayers."

"This is the Shinto shrine," Michael said, "where Tsuyo, my *sensei*, is buried. It was to Tsuyo that my father sent me many years ago."

He reached into his pocket, held up the braided cord. "Does it look familiar now?"

Eliane stared at it. Then, slowly, she took it out of Michael's hand, held it up against the Shinto bell cord. "They're identical," she said.

Michael nodded. "The priests here make them by hand; this particular braiding is their design."

A bell tolling.

"When I studied with Tsuyo, the priests taught me how to make these. My father knew that; I had given him this as a present one time when he came to visit me here. My father left it for me for a reason. He knew that I would be the only other person to recognize it. Unless you'd seen it before, you'd never know."

The echoes, picking up depth and breadth from the inner spaces of the temple, hung in the air.

"Whatever my father stole is here."

The echoes, spreading now, like ripples in a pond.

"Where Tsuyo is buried."

Until it was clear that it was the sound of the echoes, rather than of the bell being rung, which possessed significance here.

Eliane breathed: "The Katei document."

Yes, the Katei document: the end of one enigma. Michael was thinking, *Where Tsuyo is buried: Ask my son if he remembers the* shintai? The guiding spirit of a shrine. The guiding spirit of this particular shrine was Tsuyo's.

The scent of cedar was very strong; somewhere, incense was burning. They were waiting for the priest to come.

372

"I think that this is the heart of the fight my father sent me to Japan to train for," Michael said, the idea surprising him as he said it. "This was why I was sent to study under Tsuyo." But it was true; it must be true, Michael thought with a shiver of both recognition and anticipation. He was momentarily dazed by this revelation. What was my father involved in, he wondered, that he was preparing for his own death so early on? For the first time, Michael began to consider the scope of the quest he was involved in—his father's quest. What could be so important that a man would devote his entire life—and the life of his child—to it?

Whatever the mystery was, Michael found himself more determined than ever to unravel it.

The sound of footsteps, growing louder, until it took precedence over even the echoes of the tolling bell. Those reverberations were gone when the priest appeared before them.

He was a thin man, with a bald head and the face of an ascetic. Clearly, he was a man used to a life of prayer—and of denial. He was neither young nor old. In the dim light of the temple it was impossible to determine his age.

He peered into Michael's face. "You are the student," he said. "The *sensei*'s last student."

It was a polite way of saying that Michael had been Tsuyo's only Caucasian pupil. And, therefore, an object of intense scrutiny by the priests of this Shinto temple. Tsuyo had worshiped here. But more, he had been one of them.

"*Hai.*" Michael bowed, and the priest returned the gesture. Michael handed him the length of red cord. "I believe this belongs to you."

The priest was not surprised to see the cord. He nodded as he took it. "Will you come with me, please?"

The priest led the way through the main section of the temple. This was a holy place. Shintoism differs from most other religions in that its shrines are built specifically to house *kami*—spirits—and to worship them, rather than to proselytize or to teach the faith.

With every step they took, evidence of the presence of the *kami* could be discerned: in the banners that floated from the walls, in the *shintai*, the sacred spirit of the shrine—in this case, the burled center of one of the hallowed trees near which Tsuyo was buried, in the mirrors—in which was reflected only pure light, in the *gohei* stand of paper offerings and in the *haraigushi*, the wand used by priests to purify an object or an individual.

373

They were led past the inner compartment inhabited by this temple's *kami*. In a side pavilion, the priest left them for a moment. But not before extending his arm to the lead-framed windows. "From here," he said softly, "it is possible to see the place where the *sensei* is buried."

Michael knew the spot well. Within the stand of sacred trees. He could see the one riven so long ago by lightning. From its stump, the *shintai* had been extracted. The *shintai*, the divine body of the *kami*, the spirit, of Tsuyo. He watched the rain slide down the slim white stone block that marked the place where Tsuyo was buried.

He remembered the morning he had been summoned here. For the funeral, and then the burial. The litany of the chanting filled the air so completely it was possible to believe that one was breathing something other than air.

The cancer that had taken Tsuyo's voice box had at last claimed his entire body. He had not rested even one day. He had lived the life he always had—the life that made him happy—until the last night, when he had gone to sleep and had never awoken.

"Is it sad," Eliane asked, "coming back here?"

"Sad?" Michael shook his head. "This is a holy place. I can feel Tsuyo here. Perhaps it is my own imagining, but I believe that he was descended from the *kami* that resides here. There is too much love in this place for me to be sad."

The priest returned. He was carrying an object shrouded in a white cloth. Without a word, he placed it on a scarred wooden table.

Michael and Eliane looked at each other.

"Can it be?" she asked, breathless.

Michael drew the shroud off the object.

"My God!" she gasped.

A box of *kyoki* wood. It was superbly crafted, and very old. But something quite modern had been etched into its top: double phoenixes.

The *kamon*—the crest—of the Taki-gumi.

The priest's eyes bored into Michael's. "Your father stole this. I cannot comment on the justness of his cause. But he sent this here for safekeeping. I have done as he wished."

He left them there alone with the box. For a time they did not move. They were held in thrall by what lay within the *kyoki* wood box. A piece of paper that had caused so many deaths, that might now change the world.

"Open it," Eliane said. She seemed almost desperate. "You must open the box."

This was it, Michael thought. The Katei document would tell him everything. Who was arrayed on what side, what the *Jiban* was all about, why everyone was seeking possession of the document. And last, perhaps most important to Michael, it would reveal what his father's life had been all about. Finally, he thought, I will understand what my father was. He felt his heart beating fast. He wanted so much to know, to understand.

With a convulsive gesture, he opened the box. Inside was a scroll.

"Now," Masashi said slowly and carefully, "I want you to tell me what your father wrote to you just before he died."

Audrey stared at him. "Before he was killed, you mean," she said. "Someone murdered him. Was it you?"

"No, my dear," Masashi said, using all his charm. "I swear to you that I have been searching for the person or persons responsible for your father's death. I want very much to bring them to justice." It was difficult to be clever and charming in English. There were so many words, phrases and idioms he did not know; others he was unsure of, and this was no time to take chances.

Audrey was taking her time in assessing him. She had been in this vast building for some hours now—perhaps even a day, since she was certain that she had slept a little after she had eaten.

She had awoken to find herself in a room with two Japanese women. The *swooshing* of their kimonos was soothing.

"Where am I?" she had asked, fighting down panic. But the women had just giggled and ducked their heads as they helped her out of her filthy, sweaty clothes. She could hardly have still been in Hawaii, she reasoned as she allowed them to disrobe her; it was far too cold.

Wrapping her in a soft cotton robe, the women had escorted her down a hallway that was devoid of all ornamentation. Audrey was aware only of a heavy humming such as massive machinery makes. She knew she could not be in a private home or a hotel. That left a commercial building of some sort, an office or a warehouse.

The women pushed her through a door, and she was enwrapped by steam. She found herself walking on wooden slats slick with warm water. The women took her robe, helped her

375

into a wooden tub of hot water. For the next ten minutes Audrey was scrubbed clean in the most gentle, thorough and pleasurable manner that she had ever experienced.

Then she was led to a second tub, where the water was even hotter. Here she stretched out and relaxed. The women sat by, giggling to themselves. Audrey closed her eyes and breathed deeply. There was a delicious herbal scent to the steam.

She thought of the room in which she had awakened. It was small, almost cramped and, again, devoid of decoration. It had a wooden floor that was in need of polishing, a *futon* on which she had found herself and a lamp, which was on. There was no window.

The women had been kneeling, talking in low tones when she had opened her eyes. They noticed that she was awake, and immediately offered her tea, which she had drunk greedily. Even though she was dehydrated, she was embarrassed by her smell. As if divining her thoughts, they had taken her to the baths.

All in all, Audrey decided, she must be in a warehouse. She thought of the windowless room. There was also a sense of timelessness here, whereas an office building would have a different feel at night than it would when it was fully occupied during the daylight hours.

In time, she was dried, her hair combed, and she was dressed in a silk underkimono of a deep blue, then an exquisitely patterned peacock-blue kimono.

"Where are you taking me?" she asked, forgetting that they did not speak English. More giggles.

Back in the windowless room, she was served food. She ate, ravenous, unmindful of what was put before her. Everything tasted delectable. She was not sure what happened next, but afterward, her sense was that she had fallen asleep because when she opened her eyes, the plates were gone. Her body felt stiff, as if it had been in the same position for some time.

It was at this point that she was taken to Masashi. He sat behind a low lacquered table in a spacious room hung with scrolls covered with calligraphy. *Shoji*, translucent rice-paper screens, allowed light in from a small window. He had introduced himself, had told her where she was and how long she had been there. Audrey knew what a Yakuza was, although this was the first time she had ever met one face to face.

"I know that you are frightened," Masashi said. "And you

must be confused. You will, I know, be reluctant to answer my question. This is understandable. Let me try to explain. You were kidnapped from your home by enemies of your father, possibly the same people who had him killed. By a stroke of fortune, my people discovered you on Hawaii. I had sent them there to find out who had murdered your father." He smiled ruefully. "Unfortunately, in this they were unsuccessful." His smile brightened. "But you see how fortune shines on us both. They discovered you and brought you to me. You are quite safe here, my dear. I have made special arrangements. The people who want you cannot get to you here."

Audrey shivered. "That man in Hawaii," she said. "The one who tied me to a chair—"

"Which man, my dear?" Masashi asked.

Audrey described him. "Did he work for you?"

"No," Masashi lied. "He was the one who kidnapped you. My people were forced to kill him at the airport on Maui. They had to, you see, in order to get you here."

"I must thank you, then," Audrey said. She still felt cold inside. "I owe you a great deal. I wonder if I could use your phone. I'd like to call my family. They must be frantic, worrying what's happened to me."

"You will be pleased to know that my people have already spoken to your mother," Masashi said, improvising. "She was greatly relieved to hear that you are well."

"Thank you so much," Audrey said. "But I'd very much like to talk with her myself."

Masashi nodded. "Of course. But first, if you would indulge me a moment and answer my question as to what it was your father wrote to you. It's very important."

Audrey frowned. "I don't understand. Why would it be important to you?"

"Because it might hold a clue as to who killed him."

"Well, I don't know if it will do you any good," Audrey said. "What he wrote made no sense to me."

Masashi, on the brink of this discovery, held himself back from trembling with anticipation. "Perhaps it will mean something to me," he said.

"All right," she said. "I'll tell you."

"The Katei document!" Eliane said from just behind him.

Michael lifted it out, opened it. It was handwritten in Japanese *kanji*. Michael scanned it quickly. The heart of the *Jiban* was revealed to him. He could feel his blood congealing. This is the manifesto of madmen, he thought as he digested the long-range plan to create a new, more powerful, greatly expanded Japan from the ashes of the old. How could the *Jiban* hope to achieve its goal of expansion into China? It was not only insane—it was impossible.

Michael was reading Kozo Shiina's manifesto against the phoenix of American capitalism, which threatened to destroy the traditions of ancient Japan, traditions that had made Japan great, that were, in essence, the very soul of Japan. And he heard again Eliane's voice, *The* Jiban *wants independence for Japan; freedom from the oil-producing countries, but most of all freedom from American dominance.* The warning bell went off in his head again as he continued to read the Katei document. Wasn't there something he was missing, some link that would push this into the realm of possibility?

But then a paragraph near the end stopped him cold.

"My God!" he murmured.

"Michael," Eliane said, "what is it?"

Michael hurriedly rewrapped the scroll. "The Katei document is much more than the *Jiban*'s manifesto," he said hoarsely. "It's a living diary, updated constantly as circumstance warrants." He looked at her. "According to this, the *Jiban* has made a deal with the Soviet Union whereby the KGB will be providing it with a nuclear device."

"But that's insane," she whispered.

Michael nodded. "That's what they are: Shiina, and the rest of the *Jiban* are madmen."

"Does it say when the delivery is?"

"No," Michael said. "For all we know, the *Jiban* could already have it."

The priest emerged into the shocked silence of the tiny chamber. He looked from Michael to Eliane. "A thousand pardons for this interruption," he said, "but men have come who have not rung the bell." By that he meant that the men were dangerous.

"Do you know who they are?" Michael asked him.

"Their faces are not familiar to me," the priest said. He was obviously agitated. "But I can tell you that there are four of them."

Michael had already put the scroll back in the box. He rewrapped the box in the white cloth. "These men are Yakuza?" Eliane asked the priest.

"Yakuza have no dominion here," he said. "Please hurry. There can be no violence within the sanctuary."

Michael picked up the box and they hastened from the room. Out in the main oratory of the temple the immutable silence of the temple, which allowed the small sounds of nature dominance, had been intruded upon. They could hear the echoes of clipped and urgent voices.

"My brothers will attempt to dissuade the men from entering," the priest said. "We are not in the habit of refusing anyone sanctuary. But these men have hearts of lead."

He led them through the main oratory, past the place where the sacred rope defined the holy places, where only the *kami* could exist. It was hung with the traditional sets of zigzag strips of paper and cloth. Beyond, Michael knew, there was a small pavilion, hidden from here by curtains.

The priest took them down a narrow hallway. He stopped at a door. Pulling it open, he was about to point the way to one of the outbuildings when he caught sight of two men running through the rain. Immediately, he shut the door and said, "That way is already too dangerous. Come with me."

He took them back the way they had come. They had returned to the main oratory. The voices were louder, more insistent. The priest looked anxiously in that direction. They were in front of the sacred rope. The priest glanced behind him, then back to where the querulous voices were coming from.

"That way," he urged, indicating the pavilion beyond the sacred rope.

"But this is where the *kami* dwells," Michael said. "It is sacred."

The priest looked at him, not unkindly. "As is life," he said softly. "Now, go. Hide yourselves while I endeavor to give my brothers aid."

Behind the curtain, it was cool and dark. There was a sense of vast space—even more than in the oratory—although this was, of course, impossible.

"Maybe one of us should try for the car." Eliane whispered. "Your sword is—"

Michael put a finger across her lips, and the silence crept over them again. There was a peculiar quality here, as if they were performers anticipating the rise of the curtain on opening night; a kind of electricity that had nothing to do with the performers themselves but, rather, emanated from the

379

rustling of the unseen audience, and which jumped like a spark to where they stood in the twilight.

"Michael," she said in his ear, "let me go."

He shook his head, but she was already moving. He made a grab for her. Anticipating him, she danced away. Then he had the sense of being alone—or rather, of being without her.

He was not alone.

He felt the presence of the *kami*.

Or of Tsuyo.

Perhaps, after all, there was no difference between the two.

" '. . . tell Michael to think of me when he next has green tea. Tell him to use my porcelain cup. He always treasured it. I'm thinking of the place where you and he almost died. Even in summer, alas, there is not a single heron.' " Audrey finished reciting her father's enigmatic message.

Masashi was concentrating over each word. "This porcelain cup," he said when she had finished. "Do you know it?"

"Sure," Audrey said. "It was one of the mementos my father brought back from Japan."

Masashi, excited, seized on this. "Recently?"

"Oh no," Audrey said. "He brought it back many years ago. It's from a time just after the war, I think."

That can't be it then, Masashi thought. "This place your father mentions," he said, "where you and your brother almost died. Is it here in Japan?"

"No," Audrey said. "I've never been here before. It's in the States."

"Pardon me?"

"In America."

"Why would it be special to him?" Masashi asked.

"Because of what he said, I suppose." Audrey thought a moment. "He was terribly afraid that Michael and I had died. There was a snowstorm, you see, and—"

At that moment the door opened, and Kaeru came hurriedly in. His face was pinched. The fact that he had not bothered to knock was a sign of the greatest agitation.

"What is it?" Masashi snapped.

His *oyabun*'s tone brought Kaeru up short. He remembered his manners. He bowed mechanically, said, "Ten thousand pardons, *oyabun*, but a package is waiting for you."

"Leave me alone," Masashi said. "Can't you see I'm busy?"

"Indeed, *oyabun*," Kaeru said. "If this were not of the

utmost importance, I would never have interrupted you. A messenger is hand-delivering the package. It seems as if it is so valuable that you must sign for it yourself. He refuses to take anyone else's signature in substitute."

"All right," Masashi said. He turned to Audrey and smiled. "I won't be long, my dear," he said. "Rest some now, and when I return, we will conclude this talk."

"But what about a phone?" Audrey said. "I'd like to speak with my mother."

"In time," Masashi said. "For now, I will leave a man just outside this door to make certain no one disturbs you."

"But—" Audrey broke off, for the two men were already gone. Once again, she felt tears welling up behind her eyes. She wanted to get out of here. She wanted to go home, to see her mother and Michael. Oh Michael! she wailed silently. What has happened to you?

Then she thought, Stop feeling sorry for yourself. She got up and went to the door. She turned the knob, but nothing happened. The door was locked. Now that's odd, she thought. She shrugged. Or perhaps it was just another security precaution. Then why hadn't Masashi mentioned it to her?

Well, she told herself as she walked about the room, I certainly feel safer here than I have in many days. She went to the *shoji*, slid them aside. Through the grime-encrusted window she could see docks and water. A river, she decided, since she could see the far shore teeming with buildings and activity. Then she had been right: She was in a warehouse. There was some satisfaction in having worked that out.

She turned away from the window and saw the doorknob moving. That's strange, she thought. If Masashi were coming back, he'd have a key. She moved closer, watching. Something was being slipped between the door and the jamb. She heard a click, then the knob turned and the door opened.

A man rushed in. Behind him, Audrey could see the form of the fallen guard, the man Masashi had left to protect her. And she thought, Dear God, they've found me.

She whirled to run from the man, but she felt him seize her from behind. She tried to scream, but his hand was firmly clamped over her mouth. And fear had her by the throat.

The Taki-gumi soldier who had searched the outbuildings had returned to the main temple. He was soaked and angry. As was the other one. A silent signal passed between them, and they pushed their way past the protesting priests. All

381

carried drawn *katana*. They moved methodically through the oratory. They appeared to have no regard for the sanctity of the place. But then these were young men, with spirits as rough as sandpaper. Just months ago they had been riding their motorcycles, drinking beer, outfitted in stinking leather, shiny with wear. What did they know of Shinto, of shrines, of groves of sacred trees and of *kami*? They cared about neon, about speed, about anomie and the loss of consciousness. They hated because they were too cowardly to face their own fears. Thus their hate made them arrogant, wild and, in the end, infinitely malleable. They only required an object at which to direct their hate—no matter how temporarily. This was what Masashi had understood, and used. It was why they obeyed him without even understanding that that was what they were doing.

The pockmarked one came upon the sacred cord. He saw the curtain beyond. It was obvious that it was a symbol of something of which he was ignorant. With one slash of his sword, he severed the cord. Then, cautiously, he advanced on the curtain and the space beyond.

The one with the bald head saw a flash of movement out of the corner of his eye and ran in that direction. Around a turning he saw the shape of the woman slip out a side door, and he smiled.

He did not follow further but, rather, turned and headed back through the main oratory to the front of the temple. He crashed through the knot of priests and went out into the rain-filled night. Down the path to the small enclosure, where the wind, picking up, plucked at the bells. He went down the wide flight of stone steps three at a time.

He knew where the woman was headed. They had been to the car and knew that the *katana* was there in the back seat. They had disturbed nothing, not knowing where their quarry was or what they would do. Now the bald-headed man knew.

He was there well before her, and he settled himself within the shadows of a creaking pine. He did not have long to wait. Eliane came running through the woods, heading straight for the car. The bald-headed man chuckled.

He was already moving as Eliane reached the car. She had grabbed the handle of the *katana*, but now she saw the reflection of his movement in the slightly curved surface of the window. The rain made it impossible to get more than a fleeting impression. But it was enough.

She swiveled her hips, bent her left knee, lifting her right

382

leg and slamming it into the oncoming assailant. She grunted as she made contact, bringing all her weight to bear on the blow.

The bald-headed man staggered, and Eliane was whirling, leaving her feet, kicking out with the other foot. The toe of her shoe caught the bald-headed man on the point of his chin. His head snapped back and there was a crack as sharp as a rifle shot. He collapsed, his head at an unnatural angle.

Eliane reached down, took up the fallen *katana*. As she raced back toward the lights of the temple, she thought she heard the cough of a car engine, but with the sounds of the wind and the rain she could not be sure.

Inside, the pockmarked Yakuza was approaching the curtain. He was in the first attack position so well known in *kenjutsu*. His right side was held forward, his knees bent, his fists were at the height of his sternum, the blade angled forward.

He was not more than eighteen inches from the curtain. He stood very still, listening. But all he could hear were echoes swirling all about him as his colleagues went about their search.

Very carefully, he extended the tip of his sword until it touched the curtain. He saw that he could easily pull it aside in this manner, and was about to do so when it flashed open. He gave a little scream as the demon leaped out at him.

It was all white, this demon. Its head was horned, and it had a great grinning mouth as red as blood. It was only after the demon struck him with an *atemi* so powerful it broke three ribs that he recognized the face as a mask, the body as wrapped in a white cloth. But by then he had been struck again and there was very little conscious thought left.

Michael threw the mask aside as he scooped the sword out of the dying soldier's hand. He unwrapped the cloth from around his upper torso and leaped over the supine figure.

In a moment, he saw the leader, a slim, suited man with a thin moustache. He was unlike the others. He was older, and he had never been on a motorcycle. There was a flame inside him that the others lacked. He among the Yakuza knew precisely where they were and what the nature of sanctity meant. He just did not care. Or, perhaps somewhat more cruelly, his sense of desecration was deliberate.

Certainly, Michael thought, there was a measure of satisfaction if not outright pleasure in the way he brought the blade of his *tanto* to bear on the bald-headed priest who had given the box to Michael.

He drew a line of blood on the priest's flesh the moment he saw Michael. "Get it," he said curtly. "Don't waste time in denials. Don't waste time at all."

"But I don't—"

He drew another line of blood on the priest. "This will happen," he said, "over and over. Until you bring me the box."

Michael turned and went back down the oratory. In the sanctuary of the *kami* he retrieved the box, brought it back to where the soldier stood imprisoning the priest.

"Ah," the Yakuza said, exhaling deeply. "Put it down." He nodded. "Just there. Close enough so the priest can fetch it for me."

Michael did as he was told.

"All right," he told the priest. "Get it." He lifted the blade to allow the priest to move. As he did so, his own body moved just enough for Michael to see a sliver of another figure behind him. It was dripping water.

"Don't hurt him," Michael said.

He laughed. "Shut up!" He gestured with his head. "And tell the girl creeping up behind me to stay where she is unless she wants this priest's blood all over her."

"I won't move." She took a deep, shuddering breath.

"You've already killed one of my men," the Yakuza said to Michael. "Where is the other one?"

"Out by the car," Eliane said. "I broke his neck."

"I'll take the box now." The Yakuza was very smart, Michael saw. He refused to be provoked into making a blunder.

Michael walked to the box and bent down.

"Not you. The girl."

When he hesitated, the Yakuza said, "I only require a tenth of a second to take this old man's life."

The *tanto* flicked upward, back. "The box."

Eliane brought the box to the edge of the doorway. As she did so, he retreated, keeping the distance between them.

The blade glinted at the priest's throat. "Now. Come here."

Eliane went into the darkness.

Michael saw the Yakuza press the blade to the side of her neck just before they disappeared into the rain.

"Quiet," Joji said in Audrey's ear. "Keep still, or you'll give us both away." He kicked the door shut, moved them into the center of the room. "Don't be scared," he said. "I know who you are. I'm a friend."

Joji, having lost Michiko and Tori in the maze of corridors, had panicked. He had been too cautious, following too far behind for fear of alerting Masashi's men of his presence.

He had wandered down this corridor and that, twice nearly coming upon Masashi's soldiers. Then he had turned a corner and had seen the guard stationed outside the door to this room. His heart had leaped. He had been certain that fate had led him to the very spot where Masashi was holding Michiko and Tori.

He had overpowered the guard and, not finding the key to the door on his person, had picked the lock. Entering the room, he had been all set for a reunion with his stepsister and her granddaughter, only to come face to face with Philip Doss's daughter, Audrey. He had known of her, of course, from Michiko, and had seen the photographs of Audrey and Michael that Michiko kept.

"I'm not here to hurt you," he said now. "I'm going to take my hand away from your mouth." He did so, turning Audrey around. Then he told her who he was and what he was doing here.

Audrey listened. The more he spoke, the more terrified she became. "Masashi is my father's enemy?" she said. "But he told me just the opposite."

"He lied," Joji said. "My brother is quite adept at that."

Audrey backed away. "One thing's for sure. One of you is lying. The problem is, I don't know which one."

Joji thought a moment. "I understand how you feel," he said. "I have an idea. Come with me just long enough to find my stepsister, Michiko. Masashi is keeping her and her granddaughter, Tori, here against their will. He kidnapped Tori, in fact, so that Michiko and her family would do what he wants. Please. I'm sure Michiko will be able to persuade you that what I've said is the truth."

This made sense to Audrey. Joji was offering her the two things that she wanted most now: her freedom and the chance to make up her own mind. She nodded. "I'll trust you that far," she said warily. "But only that far."

Joji bowed. "That's fair enough. Come on."

Masashi signed for the package, and the motorcycle messenger sped off. The package was small, almost fitting into the palm of his hand. There was a purple URGENT: OPEN

385

IMMEDIATELY stamped on the wrapping. Masashi opened it. Inside was a single audio cassette. There was no message, nothing written on either side of the cassette shell.

He and Kaeru went back inside the warehouse, up the stairs to Masashi's third-floor office. Masashi went to his desk, popped the cassette into a tape recorder.

A voice came on. It was speaking Russian, but with a decided accent. The voice sounded familiar, but Masashi could not quite place it. His finger stabbed out, stopped the cassette.

"You know Russian," he said to Kaeru. "Translate."

"It's a long-distance telephone call," Kaeru said. "The man is asking for someone named Yvgeny Karsk. He's a general."

"In the Russian Army?"

"No," Kaeru said. "The KGB."

"The KGB?" What is the purpose of this tape? he wondered.

Kaeru, with his head cocked, listening intently. "According to what's being said, Karsk is one of the chiefs of the KRO, the KGB's Counterintelligence Department."

Kaeru looked at Masashi. "How does the Soviet spy apparatus concern us?"

"Other than that I would like to kill them all, nothing," Masashi said. He set the cassette to playing again. More Russian, this time from the other end of the phone line.

"They're saying that Karsk is at home at that late hour of the night. The call is being transferred."

Switching sounds, electronic beeps and clicks. Then:

"Moshi moshi?" Japanese for hello.

"I called the office." No wonder it had sounded so familiar. It was Kozo Shiina's voice!

Masashi and Kaeru, staring at one another, listening to the conversation between Shiina and Karsk, two friends of long standing, discussing the destruction of the Taki-gumi, the bargain between Shiina and Karsk that would bring about the destruction of the American economy, the enlistment of Joji Taki to get the Taki brothers to kill each other.

"Shiina is working for the KGB?" Masashi's face was white with rage. "That goddamn sonofabitch!" With a snarl, he swept everything off his desk top.

"You mean working *with* the KGB," Kaeru said as calmly as he could.

"Idiot! No one works *with* the Soviets," Masashi said with contempt. He was shaking, unable to sit or even to stand still. "They are masters of manipulation. My father used all

386

the resources of the Taki-gumi to fight the Soviets. The thought of them on the soil of Japan made him ill. It makes me ill." His fist hit the desk, making the wood groan. "Now to find out that I am in league with them. It is too much!"

"This is the man who suggested you murder your brother Hiroshi, the man who has urged you to kill your brother Joji," Kaeru said. "Shiina has used you for his own ends." He was watching Masashi for renewed signs of anger. "The Russians get two birds with one stone. They use us to launch a preemptive strike against their enemies the Communist Chinese, and they get what they have been wanting for decades, a toehold in Japan. After the strike, Shiina will need them to stay on Japan's side. With what they know of his own machinations here, they will very effectively be able to blackmail the *Jiban*. And since the *Jiban* will have become the ruling power in this new Japan . . ."

"The KGB will be the power behind the *Jiban*," Masashi said. "They will run Japan." He strode back and forth like an animal desperate for escape. "I cannot allow that. I will kill Shiina and scuttle the entire project first."

"I hope you're prepared to act on that," Kaeru said. "Because that's just what you'll have to do."

"Kozo Shiina is a dead man. He's here in the warehouse now, fussing over Nobuo's nuclear engineers. I couldn't get him to leave. The meddler wants to be here when I bring Eliane in." Masashi looked down at the result of his rage, strewn across the office floor. His gaze fell upon the cassette recorder and its contents. He bent down, picked it up. "What I'd like to know," he said, calmer than he'd been for some time, "is who sent me this tape?" He looked at Kaeru. "I've got a guardian spirit looking out for me, *neh*?"

There was a single road from the temple, narrow and twisting, cut into a mountainside. Michael drove hard and fast, against the wall of rain and the diminishing glow of the Yakuza's taillights. It was a nightmarish drive, made without benefit of headlights, which would surely reveal his tail to the Yakuza.

Here and there, partial washouts had strewn rubble and muddy earth across the road. Encountering the first of these, Michael's Nissan fishtailed dangerously. A massive tree trunk reared into his vision range as the Nissan continued its skid. He pumped the brakes desperately, found some traction and geared down.

The Yakuza headed southwest when they came down off the mountain road. They went across the bridge spanning the Sumida on Route 122. The Yakuza's car was going very fast. But he had not tried any evasive maneuvers, and Michael was certain that he had not been spotted.

Then the Yakuza turned off 122 at Takinogawa, and Michael almost lost him at a traffic-clogged intersection. Still heading southwest. Into Toshima-ku, into neon-spangled Shinjuku, and southeast to Minato-ku. Then they were into side streets and Michael had to be extremely careful because at this time of the night, areas away from the effervescent new-wave cityscapes were relatively dark and deserted. They slid past Shiba Onshi Park and, abruptly, he could smell the river. They were out onto Takashiba Pier.

The Yakuza had turned a corner and slid to a stop in front of a line of warehouses. Michael cut his lights and let the Nissan drift around the corner. He watched the Yakuza, the box with what should have been the Katei document under his arm, get out of the car. Eliane got out on her own. The Yakuza did not hold a gun on her. Together they went across the street to where a man was waiting for them. He came into the light to greet them. It was Masashi Taki.

Michael sat in the Nissan thinking, Was everything she told me a lie? She's working for Masashi. His hands felt cold; his mind was numb. Was the battle at the Shinto shrine a performance for my benefit? He remembered her saying, *You seem to want some easy answer. One sentence that will make everything all right and understandable. But real life isn't so cut-and-dried. It's ten thousand subtle shades of gray, one overlapping the other.*

He took several deep breaths, calming himself. Then he slid out of the car.

Joji said, "It's useless. This place is a labyrinth, a warren of corridors and rooms. We'll never find Michiko in time."

"In time for what?" Audrey was grateful for any conversation. She had tried to start one several times, but Joji had put his hand over her mouth each time, even though they were catching sight of fewer and fewer Yakuza. They all seemed to be heading downward, to a level below the one she and Joji were on. Conversation, Audrey felt, was her only weapon now against confusion. The more she could get Joji to talk, she figured, the more she would get to know about him. In truth, he seemed far removed from a villainous type. For one thing, he hadn't wanted to keep her under lock and key as Masashi had. For another, she had caught sight of a gun he had tucked into his trousers. He hadn't tried to use it to threaten her. Audrey found herself wondering what he would do if she were to get it away from him. Perhaps that was the true test she was looking for.

"Masashi's people are arming some kind of bomb or missile," Joji said. "Out there"—he pointed to a spot beyond the inner wall of the hallway—"is a catwalk overlooking a cavernous space. Not long ago, I saw men in radiation suits working on the nose cone."

"Radiation suits?" Audrey said. "As in nuclear radiation?"

Joji nodded. "God alone knows what my brother is up to. But it's far more deadly than I had thought. Masashi's power comes from a man named Kozo Shiina—a man your father knew, I believe. Shiina's group, the *Jiban*, has powerful connections both inside Japan and throughout the world. The *Jiban* wants more space for the Japanese, and that means moving into Manchuria and China, just what was planned in the years before the war in the Pacific. It seems clear now that Shiina has provided the nuclear device and my brother has provided the manpower."

"But what do they want to do with the bomb?" Audrey asked.

Joji pressed his fingers against his eyes. "I don't know," he said. "But I have an idea that is straight out of a nightmare." He looked at Audrey. "They are going to drop the bomb on China."

"That's ridiculous," Audrey said. "They'd never get away with it, would they? I mean there's radar, an international-alert network, so that something like that can't happen without other nations' advance knowledge."

"That's true enough," Joji conceded. "Of course they would be stopped. Yet they must have figured out a way. It's the only answer that makes sense."

Audrey saw the gun sticking out from Joji's trousers. The handle was well within reach. Should she make a grab for it? She decided against it, wanting to find out without coercion the truth or falseness of Joji's story. "Come on," she said, pulling at him. "Let's find your Michiko. Maybe she will be able to tell us."

* * *

389

The rattle of the rain was like a million heartbeats. Michael, on the second floor of the warehouse in Takashiba, watched the silence.

There was a lacquer-and-rice-paper screen in gold, black and blue depicting a serene, mist-enshrouded Mount Fuji in moonlight. The surrounding landscape was aglow, as if the great mountain, acting as a mirror, reflected that light, bathing everything in its immediate vicinity. The screen cut the room in two: pale shadow, dim light. In back of it was an old step-cupboard, common in many Japanese farmhouses, and a window overlooking the harbor. In front of the screen was the main part of the room, which contained a large hibachi, a Japanese oven, used to cook and serve food. Quite near was a stone-and-*kyoki*-wood table on which was set a bronze pot from whose spout steam was wafting. On the table were a pair of celadone-green cups, waiting to be filled. Buckwheat-hull pillows lay on the *tatami*.

Michael had come up one flight of stairs from the entryway. Stick Haruma had given him a length of chain, weighted at either end.

Michael crouched, ready. He listened to the silence piling up on his eardrums. The sense of danger was very strong.

He saw the brush of the shadow as it passed behind the moon over Fujiyama, and he sprinted to his right. Behind him, the rice-paper screen was sliced open by the force of the longsword's thrust. Michael turned and, holding the weighted chain in front of him, rushed through the gap in the screen.

Shadow on the wall, oblique and elongated, waiting for him to step through from one life to another, from one reality to another.

"Eliane!" He tightened his grip on the chain.

"I suppose," she said, raising her longsword in an oblique angle, "that this was inevitable." Her voice and her face were so sad.

"You told me that you had been sent to protect me," Michael said. "But all along you were working for Masashi. You lied and lied to me. And then you lied some more. I don't know how I could have believed you for a moment."

"If only I could have told you. I had no other choice," she said, circling him. "Masashi is holding my daughter hostage. So you see that no matter how I feel about you, no matter what I have sworn to do no longer matters. There is nothing I wouldn't do in order to save my daughter's life."

"Including killing me."

"Masashi has the Katei document." She was slowly closing the space between them. "As soon as he delivers it to Kozo Shiina, it will be over. I will have my baby back."

"Do you really believe that?" Michael was desperate. He did not believe that he could defeat Eliane. "Masashi knows how dangerous you are. Do you think he will allow you to live?" His only chance was to avoid the conflict. To convince her . . .

"I have to believe it," Eliane said. "It's the only thing that keeps me going. I cannot allow him to kill my daughter."

"Together we have a chance," Michael said. "All we have to do is go after Masashi together."

"But that is impossible," Masashi said from just behind Michael's left ear. And Michael, already feeling the bright rush of pain in his head, knew that Eliane had been the decoy all along. Holding his attention while Masashi homed in for the kill.

"Get out of here," Masashi said to Eliane. "The men are massing downstairs. We are almost ready to begin. Make yourself useful there." He was watching Michael lying insensate on the floor. "Much of what he said rings true. You're much too dangerous. I should have realized that long before this. My father created you out of myth, and myth is what you became in the end. Whether because of his storytelling expertise or your physical prowess, you have taken on the mantle of the supernatural."

He stole a glance at her, saw that she had not relaxed her attack pose. He flicked his left wrist, and the blade of his *katana* reared upward into the light. "Would you take me on now? Would you see which one of us can spill more blood, which one of us can outlast the other? This would be a battle of attrition. I would see to it. That is a battle you can never win. I have the stamina. I have the superior strength. Besides, there is Tori to consider. Little Tori. I saw her today. She was crying for her mommy."

"Bastard." Eliane gritted her teeth in anger. "How I would like to raise my sword against you."

Masashi flicked the blade point again. "Then come on."

Despising herself, not wanting to look at Michael, at what she had done to him, she turned and went out of the room. But Masashi's laughter followed her down the corridor.

She went blindly down a flight of stairs, then another. She collapsed in a corner, sick at heart. No matter what she did, it was wrong, evil. Where was the warrior's shining, noble path? That was for fairy tales, she saw now. The real world would not tolerate such benevolence. It was a cruel and unforgiving place.

How could she be part of the hope and the dream? she wondered. If she was truly the future, then she wanted no part of it.

She took her sword and turned it hilt outward. She pressed the blade in until the tip touched her lower belly. She was being ripped apart by her guilt and her devotion to *giri*. If she stayed here, silent and acquiescing, the man she loved would be destroyed, and perhaps her country as well. If she screwed up her courage to return to that vile room where Masashi crouched over Michael, if she killed Masashi, she knew that at the same moment she would be murdering her own daughter. Death called to her. It was her only salvation now. *I am release,* it said. *I am relief from all pain, all suffering, all responsibility. In my arms, duty is but a dream. I am calm, peace, eternal sleep.* Freedom beckoned from this last, dark quarter, and she found herself ready to follow its siren call.

So Eliane prepared herself to die.

If you should fall into unfriendly hands, there will be a finite amount you can tell them. Uncle Sammy instructed him from a podium. *Information is deadly, son.* Uncle Sammy looked like an English sheepdog. *That is, in our business.* Just like Nana, guardian of the Darling children in *Peter Pan.*

What business was that? Michael, tucked in bed, safe and sound, wanted to know.

Uncle Sammy lifted his paws above the top of the podium. They were not the paws of an English sheepdog. They were the black, taloned paws of a Doberman pinscher. With a growl, the animal leaped at Michael . . .

Who raised his head, groaned and opened his eyes. Looked directly into Masashi's eyes.

In a room where Mount Fuji, rent through its center, still shone. Michael blinked sweat and blood from his eyes. After a moment, he could see.

Masashi taking the box and placing it on the table. He leaned over it so far that his face was close to Michael's. Michael tried to move, found that he could not. "Once," Masashi said, "there were three brothers. One went to war for his *oyabun* and was killed. The second went to war for his *oyabun*, and he too was slain." Masashi's hate had turned his eyes colorless. "Now it was the third brother's turn to go to war for his *oyabun*. This he did, as willingly as his two brothers before him. But before he did, he swore an oath to avenge the deaths of those who had gone before him."

His were the eyes of the wolf, the predator. "Your job," Masashi said, "was to lead us to this." His fingers were wrapped around the box. "And now that you have, you are going to die."

Michael, looking into Masashi's opaque gaze, had no doubt on that score. He had encountered a fair number of martial-arts *sensei*; he knew the difference between a boast and a threat.

Masashi opened the latch, raised the lid of the box. For a seemingly endless time, nothing registered on his face. Then he reached in, pulled out the scroll. "The Katei document." He recognized the seal on the outside. He looked at Michael, his eyes ablaze. "Now I have it all. At last I have the means by which to turn Kozo Shiina to my will. Shiina enlisted the aid of the Soviet KGB. He meant to sell me out to a Russian named Yvgeny Karsk as soon as he had used the Taki-gumi's manpower. But I have outmaneuvered him. I have the Katei document. Without it, Shiina's power within the *Jiban* will erode. In order to keep that power, he needs me."

"Where is my sister?" Michael said. "Where is Audrey?"

Masashi put the scroll aside. "It seems that I no longer need you." He dragged Michael to the hibachi. He opened up the copper top, exposing the coal-driven fire within. The light, flickering across his face, lent him a spectral cast. "Time to die."

It was Audrey who saw Eliane's crumpled figure first. She stopped them. "Is that her?" she asked Joji. "Is that Michiko?"

Joji started, peering into the gloom of the corridor. "My God," he said, "that's her daughter, Eliane! What is she doing here?" Then he caught sight of the longsword, and he called to her as he ran.

Eliane, her mind lost in the iron resolve required to settle the spirit, to steel the will for the advent of death, was aware only of a man running toward her. Shadows raced along the wall, nearing her.

"Stay away!" she cried. She was terrified that it was Masashi come to stay her hand, to bind her yet again to the torment he defined as life. "I am already dead!"

Audrey caught up with Joji and, from some intuitive sixth sense, pushed him back. She saw Eliane's anguished face, and she knew what she must do.

"Get back!" she said. "Joji, do as I say. If you want to save her, get back around the corner, where she can't see you."

When Audrey was certain that Joji would stay where she had directed him, she turned to Eliane. Her heart hammered painfully against her chest. She knew that she was staring death in the face. Eliane's features were those of a skull, drawn and hard and shining with an odd, lambent light.

Audrey was appalled. She remembered Michael talking to her about the storm in the mountains of Yoshino so long ago. She remembered his voice as he told of seeing Seyoko disappearing into the wind and the rain, whirling down the abyss. Michael had described her face, but Audrey had not understood. Now she did. Dear God, she thought, how has he been able to sleep at night?

"Eliane."

"Who are you?" Eliane said. "Get away from me!"

Audrey, desperately trying to remember everything Michael had ever told her about Japan, knelt on the floor of the corridor. She was perhaps two arm's lengths from the other woman.

"I am Michael Doss's sister," she said slowly and carefully. "Do you know him?"

There was a flicker behind Eliane's eyes. She peered at Audrey for the first time and, recognizing her, said, "Good God, you're still alive. Well, that's something. I thought I had destroyed you, too." Then, in an agonized voice: "Yes, I know him. I destroyed him."

Audrey bit her lip to stop herself from screaming. She fought down panic. "What do you mean?" she said as calmly as she could.

"My mother ordered me to find Michael and stay close to him, to help him. But then Masashi kidnapped my daughter. He made my father and mother do what he wanted. He made me do what he wanted. I brought him the *Jiban*'s sword; I brought him Michael and the Katei document. Now he has them all. He has all the power. And he will kill Michael. I know he will."

Much of this, coming out in a rush, was difficult for Audrey to understand. But enough of it jibed with Joji's story to convince her once and for all that he was telling the truth.

"Do you mean that Michael isn't dead yet?"

"Perhaps." Eliane said. "I don't know." She gave Audrey a despairing look. "Leave me alone to die in peace."

"Then there's still a chance," Audrey said, ignoring her. "Eliane, listen to me. Joji is with me. He found out Masashi was keeping your daughter here at the warehouse. He came here with Michiko to save her. Your mother and Tori are together. Here."

Eliane lifted her head. Those terrible dead eyes seemed to burst with an inner fire, her breast began to rise and fall and color returned to her ashen cheeks. "Can this be true?"

Audrey called for Joji. He came at once, and the effect he had on Eliane was astounding. She dropped her sword, rose to hug him to her. "Oh Joji!" she cried. "Tori is safe?"

He looked over her shoulder at Audrey, who nodded emphatically. "Yes," he said, holding her. "She and your mother are quite safe now."

Then Eliane tore herself from his warmth. She whirled, and her face was stricken. "Dear God," she whispered. "Michael! What have I done?"

This battle was no different than if the two of them had *katana. Find the locus of the battle,* Tsuyo had taught him. *Direct yourself there.*

Michael was full of pain, but he must not concern himself with it. If he allowed his mind to dawdle for just an instant over the pain, he would be defeated.

Which was, of course, Masashi's purpose. This was the supreme battle of endurance. Where defeat was not measured in the cessation of a heartbeat but in the breaking of a will.

The pain seared through Michael's head like a river of fire. Blasting into every corner of his mind, filling it with a light so brilliant it sucked the air from his lungs.

And the fire spoke. It shouted, screamed, bellowed, as it licked at him, burning in agonizing ribbons, until it was impossible for any one coherent thought to manifest itself. Until the mind began to shut down, to turn inward on itself, retreating from the terrible pain. *Find the locus of the battle. Direct yourself there.* A whisper absorbed within the roaring conflagration. The battle? The battle? He was drowning in a sea of fire, his mind shrinking from the crushing agony. That was the battle.

Until he found himself on the brink. Behind him was quiet. Utter peace. A stillness he could hear as well as sense. It would be so easy to just sink back into that stillness. Wouldn't that be fine? A cessation of the noise, the light, the pain? It would be . . .

Stop it! That's just what he wants!

But it's so quiet, so still.

Find the locus of the battle. Direct yourself there.

Just one more step to back up. Then tumbling in blackness, in stillness. In peace. An end to the battle. Forever.

No! *The battle is—*

It was Masashi's strategy to convince Michael that the locus of the battle was inside his mind.

not—

But now Michael saw the falseness of this.

here—

It was, instead, at the point where Masashi was concentrated. And, truly, it was no different than if he had been wielding a longsword. The spot was in his hands. That was where he was directing his energy, and therefore his mind.

Then Michael's mind was free. It moved. And thus became *Kara*. The Void.

Used his head, butting it into Masashi's nose. Blood spurted, and Masashi's hold on him faltered. Michael kicked out, missed.

Masashi had retreated. Now wielded the *katana*. Michael had nothing. Nothing but the Void. His mind did not alight on any one thing. It planned no strategy; it did not seek to operate within the boundaries of any law, even the universal law that all *sensei* obey, no matter the school of discipline they were taught.

Michael did not concentrate on any one thing. He did not see and react. Rather, he moved to the locus of the battle: Masashi's hands. In so doing, he did not consider Masashi's strategy. He did not contemplate the blade of his opponent's *katana* or the nature of the attack.

Instead, he did what he needed to do. What the Void told him he must do. He reached inward, grabbed Masashi's hands and wrested the sword from him.

Astonished at this prowess, Masashi drew his *tanto*, his dagger. He slammed the hilt against the side of Michael's head. Michael dropped to his knees. A thousand bees buzzing inside his head stung him as one.

Masashi, holding tightly on to the Katei document, bent to take the weapon out of Michael's hand. When he straightened up, he directed the blade at Michael's heart. He was about to strike when he heard a sound. He turned, startled, to see Kozo Shiina standing no more than a foot from him. Shiina was holding the *Jiban*'s sacred *katana*.

"What is this?" Masashi said. He laughed to himself, seeing this old man with a *katana* in his hand—the sacred *katana* of the *Jiban* at that—as if he were still a warrior. "I resent this intrusion." He tightened his grip on the Katei document, his power over Shiina. "You have no business here."

"On the contrary," Kozo Shiina said. "Now that you have fulfilled your role and have provided Nobuo Yamamoto's FAX fighter for the *Jiban*'s cause, I have just one last piece of business here." And he lunged forward, his speed stunning. He drove the ancient *katana* through the center of Masashi's chest.

Masashi had no time to complete his defense. He was rammed backward, stumbling, in the grip of the enormous force of the attack, and only the steel he had retrieved from Michael kept him on his feet.

The point of the sword had gone all the way through him, and now it embedded itself in the wall. His breath was like frost, and his lungs seemed to be under water.

"You thought you had it all figured out," Kozo Shiina said. "You were on the top of the world. I heard everything. I don't know how you found out about my deal with General Karsk, but I know that you will agree it hardly matters now." With a grimace, he twisted the blade.

Masashi grunted in pain. He stared into Kozo Shiina's eyes and saw the fool that was himself reflected there. He seemed to see his father laughing at his inadequacies. Or was the old man weeping?

"There is no justice in this," Masashi whispered. He seemed unable to catch his breath. He thought he heard his father's spirit calling to him from across a vast distance, as if they were two suns burning in the heavens. It seemed to Masashi that Wataro Taki told him what to do. And now, with the last of his ebbing strength, he threw the Katei document into the hibachi fire.

Kozo Shiina screamed. He made a lunge for the burning scroll, jerking the sword out of the wall.

Smiling, Masashi watched the scroll turn to cinders in Shiina's burning hands. Then he turned his gaze away, unable to stand the sight of the other man. Saw light in an otherwise dark, dank night.

It was chilling to be watching and falling at the same time. Watching and falling. The blood ribboning like bunting blown in the wind, the room canting over on edge, the floor becoming the wall, hearing his teeth rattle as his jaw snapped shut.

Masashi was falling, but he felt himself to be in midair. He could see the lights of Tokyo below him, the brightly lit harbor, where merchant ships close to the warehouse were busily being loaded and unloaded.

Through the rain he saw the black square of the window on the second floor of the warehouse. Inside there, he knew, something dark and evil was stalking, but it had nothing to do with him. He was aloft, buoyed by the stormy wind, floating, free of pain or fear.

Remembering a story his father had told him when he was little. About a boy who wandered away from home at night. Lost in the forest, surrounded by snuffling shadows he could not identify, wild cries that made him spin and start, the boy began to cry. Until the moon came out from behind scudding clouds. It was a full moon, its color as rich as gold, for it was late summer and near harvest time. A shower of shimmering light rained down upon the boy, who raised his head as the shimmering light arranged itself into a series of steps floating through the forest.

The boy went up the steps. And with each step he took, he found that he was becoming lighter and lighter. Until he was obliged to hold on to the steps in order not to float away.

By then he was up so high that, staring down at the forested countryside from which he had come, he grew frightened and began again to cry. This caused him to lose his hold on the step, and he began to float into the sky.

Just as Masashi was doing now. The sense of elation was so strong that he felt himself to be that boy in the story—or perhaps he was the child he had once been, listening to his father spin magic webs in the air.

"Now," Wataro Taki says, "the boy feels no fear at all."

"Why?" Masashi asks.

"Because," his father says, "the whole world is his now. It curves below him, shining bits and dark patches, and the boy can see it all. He can see the good places and the bad ones, and he knows without anyone telling him that he can go any place he pleases.

"He just looks for the light, and off he goes."

Masashi's body was awash in blood. The rain had ceased, and now the only sound in the room was that of Masashi's blood dripping from the edge of the *Jiban*'s sacred *katana*. The thick clouds had ripped asunder, and it was afire with light, as if it were a moonbeam.

"I only wanted you to be proud of me," he whispered to the spirit of his father. "Couldn't you have been proud of me just a little?" Masashi's mind, on the edge of death, looked for the light. And off it went.

What Eliane saw first was the blood.

There was a river of blood soaking into the *tatami*, and Michael's body was sprayed with it. Blood dripped from the snow-covered crown of Mount Fuji.

Terror filled her, and she raced across the room. So focused was she on Michael's form that she failed to see the shadows moving behind the screen, which she had used not an hour before to hide her presence from Michael.

She collapsed onto her knees, cradled Michael's head in her lap. Behind her, Audrey and Joji appeared.

"Michael!" Audrey cried. "Oh God, no!"

Eliane looked up at her. "He's alive."

Audrey closed her eyes in prayer. Tears slid from beneath her lids. She knelt beside her brother, reaching out to touch him. She needed to feel him breathing, to feel his warmth, perhaps to assure herself that he was indeed alive.

Joji said, "Masashi is dead." His voice had a curious tone, as if he could not believe that his brother was no longer among the living. He crouched next to Masashi's corpse. He stared into the opaque eyes, fixed on some shining path invisible to anyone else in the room.

"Masashi." Joji was testing out his feelings. Relief, sorrow, remorse, mingled inside him. But no satisfaction. There was, oddly, not even a feeling that justice had been served. He wondered, rather, what he could have done to avert this tragedy. *Karma*, he thought, finally. This was meant to be.

Michael opened his eyes and saw Eliane's face. He turned his head away.

"Michael," Eliane said.

"I have nothing to say to you," he said, rolling away. He tried to sit up and, in the process, saw his sister.

"Aydee!"

"Oh Michael!" She threw her arms around him, kissing the side of his face and neck. He winced.

"This is where they brought you?"

She nodded. "Masashi tried to convince me that he was on

399

our side. That he was trying to find out who killed Dad."

"That part was true," Eliane said. "Masashi was desperate to find out who had killed your father. Ude, his personal assassin, was close to tracking Philip down. Philip had stolen the Katei document. It was Ude's job to find Philip and torture him until he revealed where he had hidden the document. Then Ude was to kill him. It almost happened that way."

"I thought you were Masashi's assassin," Michael said. "You are Zero."

"I told you," Eliane said patiently, "that Masashi had my daughter, Tori. He was threatening to kill her unless I did what he wanted."

"I don't believe you," Michael said. "You've told me nothing but lies up until now."

"And what he wanted me to do," Eliane persisted, "was to stay close to you. When your father was killed, Masashi was convinced that you would lead him to the Katei document."

"Liar."

"But she's telling the truth about her daughter," Audrey said. "Masashi had Tori here. Joji found out about it and brought Michiko here to rescue her." She looked up. "Joji?"

"It's true," Joji said. "Every word. Masashi was not only using Tori to make Eliane do what he wanted, but also Michiko and her husband, Nobuo. He and Kozo Shiina have gotten hold of a nuclear device. I've seen it here. Yamamoto Heavy Industries' technicians have already put it into a missile or bomb of some sort. But—"

"Wait a minute," Michael said. Something Joji had said had burst like a flame in his mind. It was the last piece in the puzzle, the piece that had been bothering him for so long. Nobuo was being blackmailed. That was the key: to his involvement in the deliberate scuttling of the trade talks, and in something else as well. "The FAX," Michael said now. "The Yamamoto FAX jet fighter is the vehicle Masashi and Shiina are going to use to deliver the nuclear payload! That's why Masashi needed Nobuo's expertise. And I'll bet you that's the main reason Shiina struck an alliance with Masashi. The Taki-gumi manpower was just gravy. Masashi had the way into the FAX, and the experimental jet was what Shiina needed."

"It makes sense," Joji said. "But you've killed my brother. The threat is over."

"I wish it were," Michael said, struggling to get up. He

400

needed the help of the two women. "I didn't kill Masashi. Kozo Shiina did. Their alliance was an uneasy one at best. It seems clear to me from what I heard that each of them was ready to destroy the other as soon as the nuclear device was detonated. They were using each other. Shiina for Masashi's ability to gain access to the FAX, Masashi for the added power Shiina gave him."

"But what brought them to each other's throats now?" Joji asked.

"I'm not sure," Michael said. "But I know that somehow Masashi found out that Shiina had made a deal with the Soviet KGB. With a general named Yvgeny Karsk. Karsk provided them with the nuclear device."

"Yes," Eliane said, nodding. "That kind of knowledge would send Masashi over the edge. He despised the Russians."

"It seems a tremendously lucky stroke indeed that Masashi found out about the KGB involvement," Joji said. "It was like a lethal bomb self-destructing."

"Not quite," Michael said. "There is still Kozo Shiina to contend with. He's here somewhere."

"And he has the Katei document!" Eliane said.

"No." Michael pointed to the hibachi. The copper oven was glowing red. "Masashi threw the document into the fire. It's gone. Shiina doesn't have it, but neither do I." He thought of General Hadley. What would his grandfather use now to hold over the Japanese? "It's a great pity. Other events are already taking their toll. Without the Katei document, I don't know what will happen."

"If Shiina is here right now, our first concern should be the nuclear device," Eliane said, "don't you think?"

"I know the way to the catwalk," Joji said. "I'll take you there."

Eliane turned to Michael. "How do you feel?"

"Don't worry about me," he said. "I can make it." But he took two steps and collapsed. He grunted, having fallen on the weighted chain Stick Haruma had given him.

"Michael." Audrey knelt down beside him.

"Eliane," Joji said, "let's go. We can't have much time."

"I'll stay here with him," Audrey said. "Go on. I can't be much help to you anyway."

Kozo Shiina's mouth twisted in a semblance of a smile. He had a mental image of the spirit of Wataro Taki. The bastard

401

must be grieving to see how thoroughly Shiina had corrupted all that Taki had spent years building.

Then a bright lance of pain ripped through him, and his grin turned into a grimace. He had stood over the dead Masashi and had wanted with all his soul to take up the sword of Prince Yamato Takeru, the sacred symbol of the *Jiban*'s strength, and plunge it into Michael Doss's heart. He had waited so long, so patiently for this revenge, his spirit was besotted by its proximity. And yet the pain in his hands, blistered and swollen from trying to retrieve the burning remnants of the Katei document, had made that impossible.

Still, who is to say what is impossible for one so desperate. Gritting his teeth against the agony, Shiina had wrapped his ruined hands around the hilt of the *katana*. He almost screamed. But he was ready to exact his revenge. Then he had heard approaching footsteps, and he had retreated behind the slashed screen depicting Mount Fuji. Its bloody peak had seemed altogether appropriate to him.

He had overheard everything and, despairing, wished he had had that extra minute needed to kill Michael Doss. But now the situation had changed. Now the *Jiban* was undone, now his plans for a new and glorious Japanese empire had turned to ashes. This was *karma*. But in a flash he saw that his *karma* had been benevolent as well, for as he peered through the rent in the screen, he saw the hibachi. And not more than a foot away was not only Michael Doss, but his sister, Audrey, as well.

Now only his revenge against Philip Doss, who had murdered his son so long ago, was paramount in Shiina's mind. He was alone in the room with Philip's two children: with Philip's legacy, his future. Shiina grasped the sword and stepped through the rent in the screen.

Michael raised his head. He saw the figure approaching, and though the face was unfamiliar to him, the *katana* of Prince Yamato Takeru was not. This must be Kozo Shiina, he thought.

"Michael Doss." Kozo Shiina's voice was harsh with the weight of his desire. After all these years, he was about to exact his revenge for the murder of his own son. Shiina took the attack stance, swung the sword up over his head. Drove it downward as Michael rolled out of the way.

Shiina swiveled, came at him from another direction. As he did so, he heard a soft sound behind him and turned his head. Saw a shadow moving toward him from the other side

402

of the screen. When it stepped through the torn paper, his heart pounded painfully in his chest.

"Who are you?"

"I am the spirit of Wataro Taki," the voice of the shadow said. "The spirit of Zen Godo."

Shiina started. "Zen Godo," he whispered. "I have not heard that name in decades. Zen Godo is long dead." Shiina's mouth twisted into a snarl of rage. "They're all dead. I have no more enemies." Shiina could hear the crackling of the flames, which had consumed the Katei document, like wind chimes in the air. "Who are you?" he whispered. "Really?"

"I am Zero," the voice said.

"Zero?" Shiina started. "Zero is the absence of Law."

"It is also the creation of Zen Godo. A legend he created. It is, in essence, his spirit. It is Zero who has destroyed you as you sought to destroy Zen Godo."

"Again Zen Godo! Zen Godo is dead, I tell you!" Shiina screamed. "I attended his funeral!"

"Then how is it that you are dying?" the shadow asked. As he spoke, the figure moved into the flickering light and Shiina knew who it was. Impossible! he thought. It's impossible!

With that, he leaped forward, thrusting the *katana* of Prince Yamato Takeru. The point of the sword ripped the gun from the shadow figure's hand. Now, grinning fiercely, Shiina slashed quickly upward and from left to right, aiming to open up the figure's rib cage.

Behind him, Michael threw the weighted chain. It snaked out, wrapping around Shiina's moving wrist. Michael pulled, and the *katana* was jerked away from its target.

Shiina whirled even as he stumbled. Then he did a startling thing: He let go of the sacred sword. Michael relaxed the tension on the chain, and Shiina was able to disentangle himself. At the same time, he snatched up Masashi's fallen sword. He attacked.

Michael, cursing himself, ducked wildly, felt the razor-sharp edge of the *katana* rip open the shirt across his back. He dove for the sacred *katana*, took it up.

But now Shiina was upon him, striking blow after blow. Their bodies were entangled so closely they might have been one monstrous form. It was all Michael could do to defend himself. Once, twice and yet a third time, he felt Shiina's weapon begin to slip through his defenses.

Michael summoned all his remaining strength, but now

Shiina's sword was almost at his throat and he knew that he was on the point of death. *There may come a time,* Tsuyo had said, *when all you have been taught here will be useless, when you will battle as a warrior must, but to no avail. Then, strength will fail you, and it will be the time of zero: where the Way has no power.*

Staring up into the lined, grim face of this implacable enemy, Michael knew that this time had come. He was in *zero* and, like Tsuyo, his *sensei*, before him, he was lost. He was at the ultimate precipice where man and warrior merge and, defeated, are helplessly whirled away on the currents of an uncaring fate. It was the time of the ultimate fear. A place where courage was a concept that was yet to be born.

Shiina could sense that the end was near. His nostrils as flared as a predator's when scenting the blood of its victim. He completed two lightning strikes, then, shifting tactics, employing the air-sea change, he went for the killing blow. He arched his body upward, away from Michael's.

At that moment, a shot resounded in the room. Shiina cried out as the bullet fired from the shadow figure's gun smashed into his shoulder.

Michael reacted instantly, using the distraction to slash upward with the sacred *katana*.

Shiina felt the blade slice through the muscles of his side, and reasserting his formidable powers of concentration, he blocked out the pain, dedicating himself anew to his vengeance. He screamed the *samurai's kai*, the bloodcurdling battle yell, struck at Michael's blade with his own.

But Michael was a changed man. He had dwelled in the land ruled by fear, and he had survived. He had accomplished what even Tsuyo had not: he had triumphed over *zero*. And this time, Michael had prepared himself: He had watched the crucial spot, where Shiina gripped his weapon. He anticipated the angle of the strike and, sweeping it aside, drove the *katana* of Prince Yamato Takeru through his enemy's heart.

Blood fountained. Audrey was screaming. Perhaps, Michael thought, she had been screaming for some time. Shiina's mouth was open wide, his body toppling over, as he grudgingly gave up his life. Michael pulled the sword free. Light shone dully off its dark and wet surface.

Kozo Shiina lay crumpled beside the corpse of Masashi Taki. Tatters of what had been Mount Fuji drifted down upon him, a soft shroud not unlike the pink petals of the quince blossoms outside his study window. His eyes were blindly fixed on the sword, which he had coveted so much and which had been the instrument of his death.

For a long time, there was only silence. The rhythmic undercurrent of the machines made it seem as if they were in the bowels of the earth, some monstrous cavern out of a nightmare or a fantasy epic.

Michael and Audrey stared mutely at the figure kneeling beside the corpse of Kozo Shiina. He was no longer a shadow, though to them he could easily have been a ghost.

"Is it really you?" Michael said at last.

"Daddy?" Audrey whispered.

"Are you two all right?" For the moment, Philip Doss was too overcome to say anything more. He had not been so near his children for some time. And Michael, defying death over and over again. Had it not been for Michael . . . He could still feel the power left in Kozo Shiina's old frame, he could still feel the proximity of his own demise. And then the situation had been reversed, and it had been Michael who had been close to death. In the end, it had taken two generations of the Doss family to end Kozo Shiina's life.

But now, as he looked from his son to his daughter, he began to realize that the truly difficult part lay ahead of him. His new life beckoned: not only to him, but to his children as well. It was such a radically different life that he was terrified that they would not be able to accept it, that they would reject him and what he had done out of hand. Battling Kozo Shiina and the *Jiban* for forty years was nothing compared to this awesome task. After all, this was his family. He did not know what he would be without them. He could not bear to contemplate such a thing.

"Daddy! Oh Daddy!" Audrey hurled herself into his arms with such force that she almost knocked him over. She wrapped her arms around him. "We thought you were dead. It's so good to hold you. I never thought—oh my God! Oh my God!" She would not let him go.

"It was a ploy," Philip said. "Only a ploy." He kissed her hair, her cheek, her closed eyes. He could feel the hot wetness of her tears and was astonished to find how moved he was. His love for her burst through the years of restraint that his job, his secret life, had created in him. He felt as if his entire insides were melting, as if he were seeing his daughter, a tiny, crying infant, for the first time. He remembered that moment in a flash, like fireworks, that made him relive it all over again.

He rocked back and forth with her in his arms, and now his love was mingled with a sense of sadness and regret for those times lost to him forever when he was not there to hold her, to bathe or feed her, to sit her on his knee, to tell her stories or to ease her fears and hurts. All that was gone, washed away on a tide of his own making. But he had this, now, and his sense of gratitude was overwhelming.

At last, he opened his eyes, saw Michael staring at him.

"How could you do it, Dad?" Michael was surprised at what he said. He thought he had gotten over his feelings. But now that his father was alive and in front of him, he saw that he had not. "How could you have cheated on Mom?"

Audrey unwound herself from her father's embrace. She looked from one to the other. "What do you mean?"

Michael told her about his father and Michiko, about how their love affair had continued for years, even after Michiko's father had forbidden it.

"I don't understand," Audrey said. "You cheated on Mom?"

"We cheated on one another," Philip said. "I would say that we never should have married in the first place, but you two are the best argument against that." Philip steeled himself for what was to come. Truth had its own rewards, but in this case he dreaded what he had to tell them. They could hate him for it or they could disbelieve him. Either response, he knew, would have devastating results, not only for himself but for them as well.

"The fact is, your mother has a lover of her own," Philip said. His heart was breaking as he saw the expressions of pain on his children's faces. "A man she has known since our courting days in Tokyo. A man named Yvgeny Karsk."

Michael started. "Karsk?" he said, bewildered. "Masashi spoke of him. Karsk is a general in the Russian KGB. He's the one who provided Shiina with the nuclear device."

Philip nodded. "That's right." He told them of his first encounter with Karsk in Tokyo in 1947. "I have been tracking him ever since. Your mother is working for him now, I'm afraid. She's left Washington with some extremely damaging intelligence."

"I don't believe it," Audrey said. "It can't be true."

"I'm afraid it is, Aydee," Philip said. "I know it must be a terrible shock—"

"How long have you known about Mom?" Michael asked.

"I suspected something of the sort for some time," Philip said. "I knew there was a leak at BITE, but it took me a long time to put all the pieces together. Then I had to devise a way to expose her."

Audrey's face was white with shock. "This can't be happening," she whispered. She reached out. "Michael, I must be having a nightmare. Please, please wake me up."

"Aydee," Philip said, "I'm sorry. Your grandfather has taken over BITE pending an investigation of the theft."

"What about Uncle Sammy?" she cried.

"Uncle Sammy had a heart attack," Michael said, putting his arm around his sister. "He's dead."

"Dear God." Audrey put her head in her hands.

Philip looked at his son. "I don't expect you to forgive me," he said. "I used you, just as Michiko used Eliane. We both did what we felt we had to do. If it was not the right thing, then I'm sorry. We needed you two, but we asked you to pay a terrible price. Your lives were not your own. Michael, I—"

"Time," Michael said, waving him away. "Just give me some time. Right now, I don't know how I feel."

Audrey raised her head, looked at her father through tear-streaked eyes. "I want to see her," she said in a quavery voice. "I want to hear Mom's side of everything."

"If only you could," Philip said. "But the truth is, no one knows where she is. She met Karsk in Paris. We traced her to the Plaza Athenée, but that was easy—she always stays there when she's in Paris. This morning she vanished, Karsk with her. His people seem genuinely puzzled. They don't know where he is, either. It's as if the two of them fell off the face of the earth. It's very serious. What your mother stole is vital to us."

Audrey shrank away from them both. She hugged herself tightly. She began to shiver. Michael's face was drawn and lined. He, too, was in a kind of shock. He could not imagine his mother being a spy. But then, weeks ago he could not have imagined it of his father. He felt cold and frightened. Life had become like a stormy sea. He felt buffeted, out of control, with no respite in sight. He could only imagine what was going through Audrey's mind.

"Right now," Philip said, "we need to get you two to a doctor. You've both been through a terrible time."

"Worse than you know," Audrey said softly. "Oh, I wish Uncle Sammy were here to tell us everything was all right."

Perhaps she did not fully understand the impact of her words. It is true that children have the power to hurt their parents more deeply, more completely than anyone else. And now Audrey had done this to Philip. In the space of a heartbeat, she had made clear to him just how inadequate he had been as a father, how incomplete his relationship with his children had been. It was a bitter truth to hear, but Philip had once been told that even angels make mistakes.

He wanted to tell her again how sorry he was. But he sensed, correctly, that words would be ineffective. *Time*, Michael had said. *Just give me some time.* Perhaps that's what they all needed now.

At that moment, Eliane returned. "We haven't been able to find Shiina," she said. "But Joji is taking charge of the Taki-gumi soldiers. I've called Nobuo and told him the good news. He's sending technicians over to take charge of the nuclear device, which will be turned over to the U.S. government. We—" She saw Shiina. She looked at their stricken faces. "Are you all right?"

Philip nodded. "I found Michiko and Tori on my way here," he said. "I want you to go get them." He gave her directions. "I'm taking my children out of this charnel house."

The rain had left the city with a scrubbed and shiny look. Everything in Tokyo looked new, bright, ultramodern.

Philip took Michael and Audrey to meet Michiko. She met them at the front door. She was wearing a peach-colored kimono with a flame-red underkimono. On her kimono was embroidered a pair of herons in flight. Michael was astounded at how much of the daughter was in the mother. In both women he saw beauty, grace, elegance and a kind of delicacy that was heightened, made poignant by the steely strength underpinning it. He saw quite clearly that Michiko was the formidable person that Eliane aspired to be. He wondered how difficult it must have been for Eliane being brought up by such a powerful woman. Then he asked himself whether he was being fair to Michiko. He still did not know whether he wanted to like her.

Michael could see Eliane standing just behind her mother. She held Tori against her shoulder, stroking her back in a circular motion.

Michiko smiled, bowing to them. "Welcome," she said. "I am so pleased that you have come."

Perhaps it was the way in which she held her head, but Michael had an immediate sense about her. They took off their shoes, putting them in the wooden cabinet in the vestibule. When Michiko turned, Michael understood. She was blind. He looked at his father, who nodded at him.

The massive wooden beams of the ceiling made a comforting mesh over their heads. There were flower arrangements in various places, small but exquisite designs that Philip told them Michiko had created from cuttings from her garden.

She led them down a wide corridor, into a large, twelve-*tatami* room. Pale green walls were broken by deep brown wooden columns. A *tokonoma*, a raised platform, was in one corner. A scroll hung on the wall there. Its ancient calligraphy read, "Sunlight paints, but darkness falls. In all, change is apparent even to the blind man."

Or woman, Michael thought as Michiko bade them sit around a low table of a very dark, highly grained wood.

The *shoji* screens had been pushed back, revealing part of Michiko's garden. Beyond a polished wooden porch, box-leaf and gumpo azalea massed beneath the rustling branches of a lion's-mane dwarf maple tree. There was a large stone beside them that looked to Michael like a ship riding a placid sea. A tile overhang above the porch toned down the sunlight so that all the tones within the room were muted, and therefore richer.

Eliane wore a celadon-green kimono with just a thin line of deep hunter green peeking out from beneath. She turned Tori around so that the guests could see her. She introduced them all. Tori giggled, squirming until Eliane let her go. She went across the reed mats, put her hands on Philip's knees.

"Grandfather," she said in Japanese, "will you pick me up?"

"Tori," Eliane said. "Have you forgotten your manners so quickly?"

Philip grinned, hoisted her over his shoulder so that she squealed in delight.

"This is a dream," Audrey said. "Another time, another world."

"No," Philip said, twirling Tori. "Just another life."

"It's what you wrote me," Audrey said. "The end of whatever your life had been up until now."

"I died," Philip said seriously, "in order to be reborn." He put the child down. "I would like to think that I have left all my mortal sins behind in my other life."

"We will have tea now," Michiko said. She had six porcelain cups, a steaming pot, a reed whisk, in front of her on the wood table. There were green tea leaves in each cup.

409

Slowly, surely, with a kind of grace that caused the onlooker to become first interested, then engrossed and, finally, enraptured, she poured the boiling water into the first cup. Taking up the whisk, she turned the tea to a pale green froth. She served Philip first, then Michael and Audrey. The fourth cup was for Tori, the fifth for Eliane. The last was for herself.

They waited for her, then all drank at once in a kind of solemn quietude. Even Tori, feeling the emotions in the room, was still and watchful.

"I want to know what you have to say about this," Audrey blurted out.

Michiko turned her head in her direction, and Michael saw that Audrey, for the first time, realized that the other woman was blind.

"I don't think that it is for me to give an opinion," Michiko said. "First, you must make your peace with your father. When that is resolved, I will be here. I will answer whatever questions you might have. It is your right to know everything."

"But that's not fair," Audrey said. "How can I know how to react if I don't know what you think?"

Michiko smiled. "What I think is not relevant to the situation. You have a great deal to absorb. Your life has been turned inside out. I do not envy you, but I do think that this will test your strength of character. Eliane has told me how you saved her life, so I already know of the power of your spirit."

"I don't know about that." Audrey had never heard the word *power* used to describe herself.

"But others do," Michiko said. "You were put in dangerous circumstances. You have already shown your resilience and your strength, if not to yourself then to those around you." She smiled again. "It is said that the spirit reveals its true nature grudgingly."

Now that people were talking again, Tori had become bored with sitting still. She went over, sat in Audrey's lap. Without thinking, Audrey put her arms around the little girl.

"Hello," Tori said, putting her face up to Audrey's. "Hello." Then she went on in a string of Japanese.

"She is just learning English," Eliane said.

"We are all just learning, *neh*?" Michiko said.

Michael was watching Michiko with a kind of intense scrutiny. She seemed to sense this, for she smiled at him and said,

"You have brought something with you, Michael. Is it a present?"

"Not a present, no." He glanced down. At his side was the sword he had wrested from Kozo Shiina's death grip in the warehouse the night before. It was the *katana* of Prince Yamato Takeru. Once it had been the soul of the *Jiban*. Now it had become a symbol both of its broken dreams and of the continuity of the history of Japan.

"Yet it must have a purpose, *neh*?" Michiko said. "An inanimate object is just that. It is neutral, free from prejudice or the taint of choice. Its purpose is what we choose to give it. And only when it unites with a human spirit is its ultimate end made manifest. Only then are its mysteries solved." She was facing him, and Michael had the sudden impression that she was seeing him more clearly than anyone else in the room. "Is that why you have brought something with you today?"

He knew that it was. It was as if her spirit were a beam of light, banishing shadows from the deepest recesses inside him. Michael lifted the sword. He knew what he wanted to do, but he could not. He looked at his father. He imagined what he would say to him: *You gave this* katana *to me many years ago. I always thought of it as a present. But now I know that I was merely the caretaker.* He would hand it back to his father, bowing. *I swore to protect it, and I have. It was taken from me, and I have gotten it back.*

In truth, Michael had been unsure why he had brought the sword with him, but Michiko's words had reached down into his core, unlocking what was in his heart. Michael looked at her as if for the first time. It was impossible now not to compare her with his mother. He felt the lack of tension and antagonism, and he thought, It is because of Michiko, because of the serenity of her spirit. Did he resent her for possessing what his mother did not? He could not say. He only knew that every gesture, every word Michiko had uttered here had served to further the spirit of wholeness of the family. This was a concept that was alien to Lillian. She had fought Philip on everything, believing that was the only way to assert herself. Here was an entirely different way.

And Michiko had shown Michael the Way: the path to banish *zero*, the place where the Way of the warrior has no power. Michael knew now that if he did not return the *katana* to his father, the rift between them would never be healed. Philip's graduation gift had served its purpose. Now it was time to give his own gift—the *katana* he no longer needed—

411

to his father. Perhaps Michiko knew all this. Or perhaps she had merely wished to draw Michael into the family circle. He saw that it did not matter. In the end, her sense of the family spirit had prevailed, and he suspected that someday he would be immeasurably grateful to her for that. She had shown him the way to feel forgiveness; it was as if she had given him back his father. But not now. Not yet. The anger, the resentment at what Philip had put them all through was too vivid, too much an open wound, for Michael to absolve his father of all the wrongs he had committed in the name of his beliefs—in the name of revenge.

Audrey, her arms around Tori, had been thinking about what Michiko had said. *We are all just learning,* neh? She turned to Philip. "Dad, everything you told us about Mom is true?"

"Unfortunately, yes."

"She's in France?"

"We don't know," Philip said. "She did fly to Paris. She did stay at the Plaza Athenée. Then yesterday, she checked out. Karsk disappeared. Who knows where both of them have gone."

Audrey's heart was beating fast. She held Tori to her. It was like holding the future in her hands. "I think I know where they went."

Out of the tense silence Philip said, "How could you possibly know, Aydee?"

"First," she said, "I want you to promise me something. If I tell you where she is, if you find her, I don't want anything to happen to her." She raised her head and looked at her father. Her eyes were fierce. "I don't care what she's done. I don't care what anybody thinks she's done. I don't want her hurt."

Philip considered this. "All right. You have my promise."

Audrey nodded. She felt Tori's head against her breast. The warmth was a great comfort to her, somehow gave her a sense of the rightness of what she was about to do. "There was a place she used to talk to me about. It was our secret. A hotel she loved, an old place high up in the mountains of the south of France, just outside of Nice."

"Do you remember the name of it?"

Audrey blinked back tears. Tori, sensing that something was amiss, turned around in her arms and touched her cheeks. "Why is she crying, Mommy?" she asked. "Should I be sad?"

"I think you should kiss your Aunt Audrey," Eliane said softly. "That will make her feel much better."

Tori threw her arms around Audrey, kissed her with that combination of earnestness and selflessness present only in a child.

Audrey, weeping openly now, hugged Tori to her. She looked beyond the child to where her father knelt tense and anxious. "It's called the Monastery," she said. There was an odd kind of finality in the air that Audrey was to remember all her life, a stasis of emotion as rich and as palpable as the colors of the women's kimonos.

Outside their window was a pear tree. Lillian could see that it was an old, venerable thing, gnarled, twisted, ugly. But it had grandeur. And now, in spring, its unlovely shape was softened, made beautiful by the blossoms that had burst in profusion like stars on a suddenly clear night. It was as if the tree's soul were being bared during this one special time of year.

She and Karsk had arrived in the Monastery de Bon Coeur in Saint-Paul de Vence in the dead of night, after having driven ten hours straight from their intermediate lodging in an auberge on the banks of the Rhone. Lillian, who had never come this way, found the Rhone Valley a most depressing place. An industrial pall hung in the air, and the sight of the giant cones of the nuclear power plants was somehow unnerving.

The Monastery was set on a wooded hilltop promontory outside of Saint-Paul de Vence, a small village in the most southerly district of Alpes-de-Haute Provence, part of what was known as the Loup Valley. It was an area filled with fantastic vistas across spectacular natural gorges. It was not more than an hour outside of Nice, which was how Lillian had originally stumbled upon the place. Originally built in the fifteenth century, the Monastery had not been used as such for many hundreds of years. Thirty years ago, an enterprising chef had moved his kitchen and his family north from the clutter of tourist-laden Nice. His new enterprise proved so successful that he expanded the Monastery de Bon Coeur into a hotel within two years.

The place still contained the original chapel, with its white stone crucifix and its scarred wooden carvings of John the Baptist on one side and the Apostle John on the other, a clear linking of the Old and New Testaments.

413

Within the walls of the ancient, fortified structures were fantastic fruit and vegetable gardens said to continue the traditions of the original tenants. Beyond, undulating fields of violets massed, guarded by groves of olive trees so old no one in the vicinity could remember a time when they had not been there.

Lillian found this an enchanting spot, a place so old that it was able to scrub away the veneer of newness she often discovered encrusting her soul. There was no television here, no radio, and if one needed a phone, one sought it out in the proprietor's vast pantry.

This was not to say that the Monastery de Bon Coeur was in any way an austere place. On the contrary, the proprietor had gone out of his way to make it as luxurious as possible. But old-world luxury was counted in the finest quality linens, made exclusively for the hotel, as well as the choicest food in the restaurant. The rooms were large, light, with exceptional views across the foothills of the pre-Alps of Grasse. They were furnished with carefully chosen antiques and fine paintings. The service was extraordinary.

On this morning, the second since their arrival, Lillian was roused by Karsk's stirring in bed beside her.

She turned over. "Where are you going?"

"It's nearly nine," he said, looking over at the table where the BITE intelligence lay, still wrapped in its shroud of secrecy. "I want to begin transcribing the BITE intelligence."

Lillian, hearing the birds chirping, smelling the rich aroma of coffee brewing, embraced him. "Not now," she said, pulling him back down. "Not yet."

"There is work to be done," Karsk said. But he did not stop her from sliding down his body. And then the pleasure began. They were here, safe from everyone. One hour more or less was going to make no difference at all. In fact, while he was extremely excited by the thought of the cornucopia of intelligence Lillian had brought him, he realized that it was the victory that was important to him. He wanted to revel in it as long as he could. Besides, he was not looking forward to transcribing the intelligence. It would be a long, wearying task, and donkey work had never held any interest for him. There was such a plethora of data that it required total transcribing. There was no hope of keeping even a small fraction of the names, dates, places and plans in one's mind just by scanning it.

The pleasure was building, and Karsk closed his eyes. The

414

image of his wife appeared before him, a stable, sensible woman. But unexciting. Certainly, when compared with Lillian Doss, she faded into obscurity. A life with Lillian Karsk could be interesting, he thought. Then he was awash in pleasure, and he turned off his contemplative mind.

Perhaps he dozed a little afterward. He remembered drifting off on a soft breeze, bird sounds filling the room. It was quiet. It was peaceful. And there was Lillian's moist warmth half covering him.

He must have been sleeping, if ever so lightly, because the door to their room had opened without his being aware of it. Even so, his acute sense of danger, which had served him so well over the years, lifted him toward consciousness. The movement within the room brought him fully awake.

Lillian sat up in bed and said, "Dear Christ."

"Hello, Lillian," Philip Doss said. He held the .357 Magnum he had used to shoot Kozo Shiina. His face was sad. He had waited forty years, it seemed, for this moment. He had played and replayed it in his mind, but now that it had come, he wished only that he did not have to face this task. "How does it feel?" he said. "You thought you'd outsmarted everyone. Your father, Jonas, me. All the men. Even Karsk, I imagine, because that's the kind of creature you are. But you've lost. You've lost everything."

Lillian summoned up all the bravado she could. "How did you find us?"

Philip smiled. "Audrey told me about this place. When she said that you had told no one else about it, I knew this was where you'd come."

Karsk had never opened his eyes further than slits. He was fully as stunned as Lillian, but he kept his composure. His right arm, thrown out on the sheets as he dozed, was half-hidden beneath a pillow. It now gripped the revolver that was his constant companion.

"Poor Masashi Taki," Philip was saying. "He was so confused when I died. As he was meant to be. It was a tremendous gamble, but it was all we had at the time."

"We?" Lillian's voice was weak with shock.

"Actually, my 'death' was Eliane's idea. You've heard of Eliane, haven't you? Michiko's daughter? Yes, I thought so. The three of us planned my 'death.' Eliane drove the car that 'chased' me on Maui. We procured a corpse. He was beside me in the car as I was being 'chased.' I got out at the last minute, and when the car crashed and burned, I had 'died.'

415

It was the only way to stop Ude. He was very close to getting me. I made some mistakes." He shrugged. "I guess I'm getting old. We all are, Lillian. Look at you. Naked in bed with a KGB executive." He shook his head. "I hope your deal with them is bound in steel. It's going to have to be in order for you to survive."

Philip kept moving around the room. "When I became suspicious of you, I knew I'd need proof. I knew I needed to do something to make you bolt. But what? I knew I needed to be careful, that you'd spot a setup in a minute. Then your father told me about the investigation into the BITE leaks, and I knew that it would only be a matter of time before you felt they'd come too close to you. I needed you to make the move, but you're a woman. Your ties to your family are very strong. So, one by one, I took them away from you. I arranged my death. I had Audrey taken. I had Jonas enlist Michael."

"You're insane." Lillian had regained some of her composure. "You had your own daughter kidnapped? I don't think so."

"Quite frankly," Philip said, "it no longer matters what you think. But when you take the time to think about it, you'll see the truth of it. Would you have been so eager to bolt if it had meant leaving Audrey and Michael at home?"

Lillian knew he was right. Christ, she thought, where did I go wrong?

"Now you're all alone," Philip said, flicking the muzzle of the gun. "Of course you'll have Karsk, but he doesn't really count."

Karsk used the movement of the .357 to whip his revolver out from under the pillow. He shot quickly once, twice, seeing Philip duck, roll to the side. Then he heard another sharp report and pain filled his chest. Lillian screamed, scrambling over him, smearing herself with his blood.

"Are you still alive, Karsk?" Philip said, bending over him.

"He's dying," Lillian said. She should be feeling something, she knew, but she did not. She was absolutely numb inside. She was also terrified of Philip.

Philip saw this. "Don't worry," he said. "I promised the children that I would see no harm came to you." He looked at Karsk then. "I did not intend to kill him," he said, "but it's a kind of retribution, I guess. For what he did to us in Tokyo. For murdering Silvers." He saw the expression on Lillian's face. "Oh yes, I worked that one out right away. Karsk thought that by using a *katana*, he would implicate a

Japanese as Silvers's murderer. But no Japanese would ever have cut and hacked the way Silvers had been attacked. That meant he had been killed by someone who did not know how to use a *katana*. Then I remembered that it was Karsk who pushed for the Japanese-national-as-murderer explanation. That set me to thinking. Just like Karsk's 'miraculous' escape set me to thinking. Your intervention turned out to be unfortunate for him. It took me a long time to figure it all out, but at last I was fairly sure what was going on. I only needed the means to bring it all out in the open."

Philip reached down, touched his wife for the last time. "Don't worry, Lillian. Perhaps you're not all alone, after all. You'll have Mother Russia." He laughed. "I don't know what kind of reception your new masters will give you, coming to them empty-handed. But whatever it is, it will be a more fitting fate than death."

He backed away from the bed, where the two lovers lay. He took up the intelligence that Lillian had stolen and the preliminary notes Karsk had been working on. "Goodbye, Lillian," he said. "In retrospect, I guess I wasn't much of a husband to you. But then you were never much of a wife to me." His face was more than a little sad, watching the rage suffuse her face. It was such a familiar look. "We betrayed each other over and over again. I suppose we both deserve everything we got."

Philip was at the open doorway now, but the muzzle of the .357 never wavered from her direction. "The only difference between us is that I picked the right side."

"Perhaps," Lillian said. "For now."

Philip smiled. He used the gun to make the sign of the cross. "They were good at blessing people here," he said. "Once."

*Tell Michael to think of me when he next has green tea. Tell
him to use my porcelain cup. He always treasured it. I'm
thinking of the place where you and he almost died. Even in
summer, alas, there is not a single heron . . .*

Michael and Eliane walking into the old stone-and-wood
lodge. Even though it was spring, the memory of that winter's
snowstorm so many years ago shone bright and vivid in his
mind.

The place was the same, yet to Michael, it seemed so much
smaller, so much less imposing than he had remembered it.
He looked over the reception desk. Even the moose head
did not seem nearly as large. He saw that it was also mossy
with dust.

"Is it the same," she asked, "as you remember it?"

"Yes and no," he said. "It's like an old movie that you
loved when you were a kid. You see it again as an adult. It's
the same, of course. But it's not the same at all. It hasn't
changed; you have."

He took her around the waist. "Eliane," he said softly, "I
don't know how you survived it all. The pressures must have
been monstrous."

"I might not have survived," she said, "if not for Audrey.
All my life I had been surrounded by men—or in the case of
my mother, someone who was stronger than most men. I was
trained to survive and be victorious in a man's world. And
all this time I longed for—and never knew it!—another female
personality whom I could talk with. Who would understand
what I was expected to do, who would not berate me for
feeling less than adequate, who would be sympathetic to
whatever my weaknesses were. With the men, I was never
allowed weaknesses. My grandfather, my father, even my
husband, before he died, expected me to act a certain way."

418

She put her head on his shoulder. "When I was about to kill myself, I was three quarters gone. I did not even recognize Joji. But then Audrey came and sat beside me. I felt her . . . femaleness. I felt her sympathy. And slowly she drew me back into myself."

"Thank God she was there. You know, in many ways you and she are very much alike. Kindred spirits. I can see why you responded immediately to each other."

"Michael," she said softly, "I'm so sorry for what I had to do to you—for lying over and over again."

He stroked her cheek. "We've been through that already."

"I know. But I can't forget it."

"Don't try," he said. "Just try to understand it."

She looked up at him and smiled.

He leaned down and kissed her hard on the lips.

There was a thin, young girl behind the desk. She was sorting mail into guest-room boxes. She smiled at them. "Flier," she said, handing Michael one. "We're going to close for the summer for renovations. When you come back next year, all this is going to be different. We're going to have an indoor pool, a sauna, a conference room, a real gourmet restaurant. Even a Bogner boutique. Isn't it exciting?"

Michael didn't think so, but he did not want to dampen her enthusiasm. He wanted this place to remain just the way it was—small, musty, damp, in need of a good cleaning. This was a place of his youth, an important place. It was disquieting that next year at this time, it would exist this way only in his mind.

He leaned his elbows on the stone slab of the counter and looked around. At last, he said, "Do you have a package for me? My name's Michael Doss."

The girl put her stack of fliers down, said, "Let's see." She disappeared into a small cubicle, returning some minutes later with a small parcel. She put it down on the counter, pulled off a yellow tag. "It says here," she said, "that I've got to see some ID. Then you'll have to sign for it."

She peered at Michael's passport, took down its number. Then she tore the yellow slip in two, said, "Sign right here."

Michael took the package outside. He and Eliane walked across the gravel drive to where Philip and Audrey were waiting beside the rental car. He opened the package. "It's your porcelain cup," Michael said.

Philip nodded. "The one Michiko gave me years ago. It has always been special to me."

Tell Michael to think of me when he next has green tea.

Michael was turning it around in his hands.

"I sent it here for you," Philip said. "It was my one safety net. After I sent the audio tape of Shiina and Karsk to Masashi, I couldn't be sure what would happen."

Tell him to use my porcelain cup.

"And now that Masashi has destroyed the Katei document, we need it."

"But it's just a cup," Audrey said. "There's nothing in it, is there?"

"No," Philip said. "As you can see, it's empty."

"Then how—"

Even in summer, alas, there is not a single heron.

"The heron!" Michael cried, staring at the design on the outside of the cup. "It's on the heron!"

"That's right," Philip said, more proud of his children than he had ever been. "A microdot over the heron's eye contains the full text of the Katei document. We need to deliver this to Hadley as soon as possible. He's still got a lot of work left to do. The document is the only way we can identify all the members of the *Jiban*. Kozo Shiina was merely the head. But like the Hydra, the *Jiban* will continue to survive, subverting the economic and political policies of Japan until it is utterly destroyed."

Michael got into the car. "I'd better get to the airport," he said. "The jet grandfather sent should be landing in a couple of minutes."

"I'll go with you," Eliane said. "I'd like to meet Sam Hadley."

Philip went around to the driver's side, bent over. "Michael," he said, "there's a lot I want to tell you, too much for a day or even a week."

Michael looked into his father's lined face. It would take time to adjust his thinking. He had believed that he would never see that face again. But at the same time, forgiveness was a long time in the making. His father had used Michael and Audrey in a scheme to, essentially, trap Lillian. Now she was gone. It was impossible for Michael to imagine her in Russia. He found himself praying for patience, for understanding in a world that seemed to have gone quite mad.

"I want—" Philip had to stop, so overcome with emotion was he. "Someday, I want to see your paintings. I know you're passionate about them." He looked away for a moment. "Michael, I'd understand if you blamed me for what I did to you, how I created your life for you. I'd understand if you didn't want me to be a part of your life now."

"Stop it! You're being so goddamn reasonable. I don't want to hear this!"

"But there's more," Philip went on. "I want you to know there's more. The shape your life has taken had a purpose. Just as Jonas's death had a purpose in the overall scheme of things. It's unfortunate, but both were necessary."

"Yeah, I know. The gospel according to St. Philip," Michael said, tramping on the accelerator.

"He's so angry," Audrey said. "It's as if he hates you."

Philip watched them drive off, then he turned back to his daughter. "We'd better get checked in," he said. "I'll have to fly back to Tokyo in a couple of days."

"You're going so soon?" Audrey said.

"I want to get back." Philip kissed her cheek. "I'm needed there."

"By Michiko?"

"Yes," he said. "Among others. Joji's going to need my help. He's *oyabun* of the Taki-gumi now. Until all the ministers of the *Jiban* are taken into custody, there is still a great deal of damage they can do. And even after, the Taki-gumi must remain as a kind of watchdog to prevent the deep-seated ties that the *Jiban* has made throughout Japan from keeping its philosophy alive. In a way, we've returned to the way it was in Japan just after the war. Michiko and I need to help Joji as we once helped his father."

"But Michiko is married," Audrey said. "What will happen to you two?"

"I don't know," Philip said. "But we've never had any guarantees—who does, when it comes to human beings? She and Nobuo never loved one another. Theirs was a marriage of power, arranged by their fathers to cement a merger between the family businesses. But Nobuo would lose great face if Michiko walked out on him. She could never do that, and I would not ask it of her. We'll do the best we can."

The two of them carried their bags into the lodge. Philip, watching her, did not know what to do. "I'm sorry it's turned out like this," he said. "I wish it could be otherwise. But I am what I am. I wasn't a very good husband. I guess I wasn't much better as a father."

"Don't say that," Audrey said. She had her father back, and nothing would make her give him up. "Don't ever say that."

421

"You know it's true," he said. "And until you accept it, the anger and the pain you're feeling will always cause you to resent me."

"I don't want to be angry with you."

"But, Aydee, you are," Philip said. "You have to be; it's only human. I want you to know that it's all right. You can be angry—the way Michael is angry. I know what's beneath the anger and the hurt. I'll still be here when they're gone."

Audrey stopped then. "Dad, do you think it's possible that Mom will come back?"

Philip shook his head. "Honestly, no."

Audrey was crying. "Oh God. I thought she would come home. That she'd miss us too much, that she'd do anything to be with us again." She looked at him. "And now she's gone—forever. It's just as if she's dead."

"I know, Aydee. I know."

"I can't believe it," she said as if to herself. "Not yet, at least. I have to think she's coming back. Dad, I have to keep her alive in my mind. I can't shut her out like that. She's not dead, not really."

"You have to do what's best for you, Aydee."

"You hate her, don't you, for what she's done?"

Philip took his time answering. He wanted to tell her the truth. In time, he said, "No, I don't hate her. I did, once. I suppose I could not have done what I did unless I hated her. But that's gone now. I feel sorry for her. That's all."

"She loved us," Audrey said, "didn't she?"

"As much as Lillian could love anyone, she loved you and Michael."

"I miss her, Dad."

Looking into his daughter's eyes, Philip somehow found the words. "Well hell, Aydee, you haven't got much to hold you here. How about coming to Tokyo in a couple of days?"

She looked at him. "Are you sure? I mean, you'll be so busy."

"Not too busy to spend time with you." He smiled. "There's so much to see over there, so many places I could take you to." He found the thought exhilarating. "Besides," he added, "you won't have to make the trip alone. Michael and Eliane will be coming over with your grandfather."

"They will?" Audrey said.

Philip nodded. "Hadley's putting up a good front. He's as tough as they come, always was. But this news about your mother has gotten to him. Only someone who knows him as ng as I do could see it. He's devastated. He told me that wants out of the intelligence-gathering game. That doesn't und like your grandfather. He'll take care of the Katei ocument, then he's resigning. The president wants me to ke Jonas's place, to head up an all-new agency. There's a t of damage your mother and Karsk have done. 'We're ippled,' the president said, 'but we're not dead yet.' "

He did not want to tell her—or anyone else—the real rea- on the president needed him: Everyone in the American ntelligence community was terrified of Lillian, of her knowl- dge, of her capabilities. Only he, it was felt, had a chance f blunting the enormous edge she could give the KGB. As- uming, of course, that the Soviets would listen to her or trust er now that Karsk was dead. Philip wondered if perhaps Lillian would gain a measure of the equality she hungered or, after all.

"Are you going to take the assignment?"

Philip looked toward the snow-capped mountains. He felt Audrey give a little shiver. For the first time, he was aware of just how much a decision he would make could affect his family. "Right now, I don't know what I'll do," he said. "For the time being, I've convinced Sam to join us in Japan. 'It's good to know I still have family,' he told me. And you know you were always his favorite, Aydee." He gave her a squeeze. "Besides, Eliane would like to get to know you. And I'll bet inside of a week, you two will be inseparable."

"I hope not, for Michael's sake," Audrey laughed. She smiled inwardly. She was very pleased by the thought. "Any- way, I miss Tori already." She nodded. "I'll come. We have to take care of Grandpa." We have to take care of each other now, she thought. "Of course I'll come." She put her head on her father's shoulder. She sighed, thinking, It's so nice to be like this.

At her side, feeling her warmth against him, Philip was certain that he would soon feel her love as well. Time, he thought. All we really need is time. Isn't that what Michael said? I'll do anything to keep us all together.

He began to dream of Japan, of drinking green tea, of watching the cherry blossoms, of being with his family. His only regret was that Jonas would not be there save in spirit.

He hugged his daughter to him. And he thought, That is the real difference between us, Lillian. It took me a long time, but I have finally learned what life is all about.

ABOUT THE AUTHOR

Eric Van Lustbader was born, raised and educated in Greenwich Village. He was graduated from Columbia College in 1969, having majored in sociology. While there, he founded an independent music production company, a move that led to a fifteen-year involvement in the entertainment industry.

Since 1979, Mr. Lustbader has devoted his full time to writing. He is the author of five previous internationally bestselling novels, *The Miko*, *The Ninja*, *Sirens*, *Black Heart*, and *Jian*.

He lives in New York City and Southhampton, N.Y., with his wife, free-lance editor Victoria Schochet Lustbader.